DEATH: GENESIS

BOOK 1

DEATH: GENESIS

BOOK 1

NICHOLAS SEARCY

Podium

To my family,
thank you for all your support.

All rights reserved. No part of this publication may be reproduced, stored in a retrieval system, or transmitted in any form or by any means electronic, mechanical, photocopying, recording, or otherwise without prior written permission from Podium Publishing.

This is a work of fiction. Names, characters, places, and incidents are either products of the author's imagination or used fictitiously. Any resemblance to actual events, locales, or persons, living, dead, or undead, is entirely coincidental.

Copyright © 2022 by Nicholas Searcy

Cover design by Podium Publishing

ISBN: 978-1-0394-1845-5

Published in 2022 by Podium Publishing, ULC
www.podiumaudio.com

DEATH: GENESIS
BOOK 1

1

AN ORDINARY LIFE

Zeke Blackwood sat in the small room, staring at the floor as he tried to come to terms with what he was about to do. Sure, it seemed like the right thing, and objectively speaking, it definitely was, but that didn't make it any less terrifying. In fact, it probably made it worse because that knowledge made him very much ashamed that all he really wanted was to gather his things and run far, far away. But as attractive as that might be, at least in the short term, he knew he could never bring himself to do it. He didn't dare. After all, his little brother was depending on him to save the day.

With a sigh, he stood up and unbuttoned his shirt, then hung it in the small, wooden locker nearby. Next came his pants. Then his underwear. Everything ended up in a neat pile inside the locker. Before he knew it, he was slipping on the hospital gown and struggling to tie it closed in the back. With his limited range of motion in one arm, it wasn't the easiest thing in the world, but after only a few minutes of struggle, he managed to get the job done. Not long after that, a nurse appeared at the door.

"You ready, sweetie?" asked the matronly woman. She was a bit portly, with a kind face and a comforting smile.

Zeke nodded, saying, "Yeah. As ready as I'll ever be, I guess. How's he doing?"

"He's good," the woman said, leading him to the next room. "He's holding steady."

"Good," Zeke said, following her to their destination, where a hospital bed waited. He climbed onto it, stretching his long legs. It barely fit him. "I wish I could talk to him before I go under."

The nurse frowned apologetically. "I'm sorry, but that's not possible," she said.

"I know" was Zeke's response. He'd already said all the things that needed to be said, anyway. Anything else would just be an effort to delay the inevitable. He still wanted to talk to Tommy, though, if only to reassure him that everything was going to be okay.

Of course, there was no guarantee that Tommy would believe him. The kid was only twelve, but that was old enough that he could see the score. He knew that this transplant was his last hope. Without it, he would die. He still might not make it, even if everything went exactly according to plan. Things were that bad, and Tommy wasn't so sheltered that he didn't know that. He had lived a tough life, in and out of hospitals since he was born. He knew the odds better than anyone.

Zeke shifted on the bed, wishing for all the world that he hadn't been put in this situation. After all, he liked having both of his kidneys. And he was deathly afraid of going under the knife. The last time he had, his life had been ruined. Who was to say this time wouldn't be even worse? But Zeke had no intention of letting his little brother down, so the moment he'd found out that Tommy needed a kidney, he hadn't even considered hesitating before he volunteered. However, just because he wholeheartedly wanted to save his brother's life didn't mean that he wasn't incredibly afraid of doing so.

It made him feel like a coward. All his life, he'd taken his role as a big brother very seriously, and despite the fact that Tommy had always been sick, Zeke had tried to teach him all the things he needed to know about being a man. God knew their father hadn't really made any efforts in that arena—especially with Tommy. For the most part, he'd been there, sure, but the moment the man had discovered that his youngest was defective, he'd lost most of his fatherly instincts. No—aside from their mother, Zeke was all Tommy had. So, every time the idea of just getting up and running away crossed his mind, Zeke forced himself to shove it to the side.

Zeke knew that the fear was rational. Healthy, even. It wasn't like it was a split-second decision; he wasn't saving someone in the heat of the moment. That would've been better. Easier. Rather, it had been brewing for months, while Tommy had been waiting on the transplant list, while he steadily got worse and worse until their mother relented and allowed Zeke to make the sacrifice for which he'd volunteered in the very beginning. Ever since then, the fear had all but enveloped him. What if he died? What if Tommy didn't make it? What if he someday needed the kidney he was giving up? A million different scenarios, each worse than the last, had flashed through his mind. For weeks it had been like that, slowly eroding his confidence. Gradually smothering his courage. And by the time he'd trudged into the hospital to make good on his offer, he felt like a weakling. A coward. A selfish and terrible person. It made him sick just to remember the doubts that had assailed him during that period of weakness.

But he was here, wasn't he? That had to count for something. Even if he wasn't the courageous savior he'd always imagined himself to be, he had at least shown up. Not everyone could say that. Not even their father, who should've been the first in line.

He shook his head, dispelling that line of thought. He didn't want to think about their abusive, deadbeat dad. Not now.

As those thoughts flowed through his mind, the nurse set up an IV, then started a saline drip. Over the next hour or so, various doctors, nurses, and anesthetists stopped by to assure him that everything was going to go perfectly. He nodded. He smiled. He tried to put on a brave face. But he knew they could all see through his useless attempts at courage. He knew they could tell just how terrified he was.

None of them were worse than his mother, Janette, who came by about twenty minutes after the nurse started the IV. She asked, "How are you holding up? Do you need anything?"

Zeke shook his head. "I'm fine, Mom," he replied, glancing at his mother. She was a small woman, thin and a bit ragged around the edges. But that was to be expected, given everything she'd had to deal with in her life. If it wasn't enough that she'd married a loser like Zeke's father, she'd also been forced to deal with a child who'd skated from one illness to another, never once getting better. The fact that she was still standing was a testament to how strong she really was, regardless of her frail appearance. "How's Tommy?"

"He's good," she said. "Scared. He keeps asking about you, too. You know he appreciates what you're doing, right?"

Zeke nodded. "I know," he said. "I had a long talk with him last night. Can you believe he actually asked me not to do this? He still thinks the transplant list will come through."

"It actually could," Janette said.

Zeke snorted in derision. "You know that's not true," he said. They'd actually bumped Tommy down a few tiers because of what they considered genetic defects. As if he had any less of a right to live than anyone else. He knew the administrators were simply doing their jobs and giving replacement organs to the people who had the best chance of living through it, but reason didn't really stand a chance against his love for his brother.

"Yeah, probably," she said. "I just wish . . ."

She left the statement hanging in the air. Zeke knew what she would say. He'd thought the same things. They wished that Tommy had been born healthy. They wished the various treatments he'd received throughout his life had worked. They wished it hadn't come to this. But wishes didn't affect reality. Magic wasn't real.

If it were, Tommy wouldn't be waiting on his big brother's kidney, just for a chance at a few more years of life.

"Any of your friends come by?" she asked.

Zeke shook his head. "No," he said. "I talked to a few of them yesterday. It's fine. They all wished me luck and said they were praying for me."

That wasn't entirely true because the only friends Zeke really kept up with were the ones he played video games with. Most of them had no idea who he really was, much less that he was about to undergo a very dangerous surgical procedure. It hadn't always been like that, but after high school, he'd lost touch with most of his old friends as they went on to college or jobs or whatever other big plans they had.

"Well, that's good," she said, patting his arm.

They talked about small things for a few more minutes until yet another nurse came by and told Janette it was time for her to go back to the waiting room. After a tearful goodbye, she assured him that everything was going to be fine, then left Zeke alone with his own thoughts. Inevitably, and mostly due to his mother's mentioning of his friends, they went back to why he'd put his life on hold.

The simple fact of the matter was that he had no idea what to do going forward. Once upon a time, when everything had seemed so clear, he'd had everything planned out. He'd been a hard worker. He had been dedicated. But after one little accident, his dreams had been shattered, and he'd scarcely had the time to wrap his head around it, much less pick up the pieces of his life plan.

As he lay there, waiting on them to wheel him back to the operating theater, Zeke's mind made a beeline back to the day the course of his life had irrevocably changed. The car had come out of nowhere, sideswiping his truck and pushing him off the road. Later, he would be told that his truck had flipped six times, but all he remembered was a cacophony of noise, metal grinding against metal, shattering glass, and his own screams. After that, he'd blacked out, and when he had finally come to, it had only taken one look at his mangled arm to know that his days as a baseball player had come to an end.

It had taken six surgeries over the course of a year just to give the thing 50 percent range of motion. So, the idea of throwing a baseball ever again was ludicrous. For most people, it would've just been a speed bump. After all, it was just a game, right? But for Zeke, it had always been more than that. Playing baseball had been his entire life. From the time he was five years old, he'd practiced almost every day—usually with his father playing a combination of coach, taskmaster, torturer, and drill sergeant. But one car accident, and all his hard work, all his time and effort, had been flushed down the proverbial toilet. In an instant, his aspirations of playing at a collegiate—or even a professional—level had ended. His dreams had been torn asunder. And without that driving him forward, he had no idea what to do with the rest of his life.

Even more than that, most of his friends had been other baseball players. They probably hadn't made a conscious decision to stop hanging out with him or anything, but most of them were like him in that they lived for the game. And now that he wasn't one of them, they'd moved on. Some had gotten scholarships to play in college. Others had gotten drafted into the major leagues. All except Zeke, who'd been left behind to wallow in his depression. It was disgusting, and he hated himself for the way he felt, but he couldn't help it. He wanted to move on. He'd tried so hard to do just that, but it never worked.

"You ready, kid?" came a gruff voice, drawing him out of his reverie. Zeke looked up to see a bear of a man wearing hospital scrubs.

Zeke nodded. "I guess."

With that, the time had come. Zeke's stomach clenched as the burly orderly wheeled him through the hospital corridors. A dark premonition came over him as he imagined the myriad ways such a surgery could go wrong. But he blocked it out, instead trying to focus on his surroundings. The fluorescent lights. The antiseptic smell. The white tiles on the floor. He noticed a thousand little details he probably never would have before, all in an effort to distract himself from the fact that there was a very real chance he was seeing his last sights. In fact, the feeling of impending death became so strong that he had to constantly remind himself that he couldn't back out, that he couldn't abandon Tommy. If he did, he would never forgive himself.

Eventually, they made their way to the operating room. It wasn't a big place, and it was jam-packed with hospital staff, all wearing scrubs and surgical masks. There must've been ten people there, scurrying around as they went about their various tasks. After a few seconds, he was picked up and transferred to another bed in the center of the room. Bright lights bore down on him as another man—the doctor who would be performing the surgery—said something to try to calm Zeke down. It didn't work. By the time the anesthetist placed a plastic mask over his face, Zeke's heart was beating a thousand miles per hour. Thankfully, that all came to an abrupt end when the anesthesia started to kick in. Darkness closed in around him, and all the while, Zeke comforted himself with the fact that he had made the right decision. Unconsciousness soon overtook him, and not long after that, he died.

2

A NEW LIFE

Zeke wasn't certain of when, exactly, he died. Nor did he know why. But as he floated in nothingness, he knew that he was, in fact, dead. His life was over. And there was no going back.

It was a curious feeling, being dead, a consciousness floating in a sea of oblivion. He knew who he was, but he could scarcely remember any details. He was sure that he should be panicking, that he should want something to happen, to break the chains binding him to the void, but he was comfortable. Content. It felt like he'd come home.

For what could've been an instant or an eternity, Zeke floated in that dark contentedness until, suddenly, a white dot appeared in his mind. He had no eyes. No body. There was nothing corporeal about him. In fact, there was nothing physical about his existence at all. But the light, it defied all logic because it slowly drew closer and closer, growing larger all the while.

Zeke—or the entity that had once been him—grew to resent that light. It had disrupted his contentment. It had ruined his eternity. It had dissolved the nothingness. That alone was enough to make him hate it.

But what was he to do? He couldn't stop it. He could barely string two coherent thoughts together, much less act. So, he merely waited, silently seething as the light drew closer. It might've taken seconds. It could've been eons. Eventually, though, the light was all Zeke could see. It enveloped him, forcing an awareness he could scarcely contemplate.

Then, suddenly, he was alive. No—not quite alive. He remembered that he had died. But he wasn't completely dead, either. So, what had happened?

In the space of an instant, he regained his awareness and physical presence. It was a jarring experience, to suddenly have a body again.

Zeke looked down, flexing his hands. He had fingers. Skin. He was whole. That was enough to send him into a panic all by itself, but as he looked around, that panic turned to existential terror. All he saw was whiteness. There was no floor. No ceiling. No earth or sky. It was just an endless white expanse.

"Takes some getting used to, I know," came a voice from behind him. Zeke wheeled around, only to see an incredibly short, bearded man.

"You look familiar," Zeke muttered, searching his mind for why that would be the case. Then it hit him—a memory of a television show he'd watched before he'd died. "Why do you look like Peter Dinklage?"

The small figure laughed. "That's kind of on you," he said. "Something about the way your mind interacts with this place and interprets the projection of my consciousness. I could explain it to you, but you'd probably fall asleep. Or your mind might explode. Either way, it's probably best if we just skip past that."

"W-what's going on? Did I really die? I feel like I died," Zeke said, his mind scrambling to latch on to something that might explain what was happening. It failed to find purchase.

"Hate to break it to you, but yeah," the small man said. "You're dead. I'm Oberon, by the way. In case you were wondering."

"I . . . I'm . . ."

"You're Ezekiel Blackwood," Oberon said. "You're nineteen years old. Died on an operating table while trying to save your little brother's life. Both your kidneys were ruined during the operation, too. Bad break, that. If it's any consolation, your little brother ended up getting a kidney when the story went national. So, in a way, you did save the kid. He ended up living for thirty more years. So, bravo. Good job and all that."

"Wait . . . what?" Zeke said, running his hand through his hair. "Thirty years? I thought . . . I mean . . ."

"Yeah, I always forget how you must see things right now," said the small man. He waved his hand, and suddenly, a pair of overstuffed leather chairs appeared. He climbed onto one, saying, "Have a seat. This might take a few minutes. Or I guess time is sort of relative here, but you get my drift. Sit down."

Zeke collapsed onto the chair, still trying to make sense of what was going on. He came up completely empty, so he just focused on Oberon, who suddenly had a beer in his hand. He took a swig, saying, "I never get tired of that. Humanity did a lot of things wrong, but they definitely knew how to brew a good beer."

"Can you please just tell me what's going on?" Zeke pleaded, a tremor of panic in his voice.

Oberon sighed. "So impatient," he said. "Fine. The gist of it is that humanity's dead. Gone. The Earth is now a wasteland, and everyone you've ever known or heard about is gone. That's the bad news. The good news is that you're getting something of a second chance here."

"Earth is gone? How?" Zeke asked.

"Combination of nuclear war and environmental collapse," Oberon said. "They actually hung on for a lot longer than most of us expected. You're stubborn bastards. But as soon as the last one died, everyone ended up moving on from the tutorial."

"The what? Tutorial? I don't—"

Oberon gave a dramatic sigh. "Everything's got to be explained," he muttered. "Fine. Okay, throughout history, when a human died, they went into limbo. The In-Between. That was that scary black void you were in. Got me so far? Good. Well, once humanity kicked the collective bucket, everyone moved on to the next phase of existence. This is where the next part of your journey starts. The character creation construct."

"Character creation? Like a video game?" Zeke said, not nearly as stressed out about the fact that humanity had become extinct as he thought he should be. Perhaps it was a function of the construct.

"For you, yes," Oberon said. "The Framework takes the form of something you can understand. In your case, it'll seem like a video game. For people from previous generations, a giant tome. The bottom line is that your perception of the Framework is tailor-made just for you. Convenient, right? Besides, where do you think all those people got the inspiration for those video game systems from? Yep. Us."

"Who are you?" Zeke asked. "Not your name. Like, what are you?"

"Think of me as a combination of a middle-manager, entrepreneur, and recruiter," Oberon said with a note of pride. "And I'm here to make sure you don't muck this up too badly. God knows that didn't go well the last time."

"The last time?"

"Oh, come on—you don't think you're the only civilization out there, do you? This has happened with an infinite number of civilizations,"

Oberon explained. "And between you and me, we've gotten pretty good at it. So, let's jump right into it, shall we?"

"I... I guess," said Zeke, though his mind was reeling with everything the small, bearded man had revealed. "How do we start?"

"Eager! I like it," Oberon exclaimed, clapping his hands together. The motion summoned what looked like a free-floating screen. "So, the first step is to allocate your starting attributes. You should know that these statistics, along with your achievements, skills, and paths will affect your class choices."

Suddenly, a table flashed onto the screen.

Name	Ezekiel Blackwood
Class	N/A
Level	1
Race	Human
Alignment	Isphodel
Achievements	N/A
Strength	6
Agility	7
Dexterity	10
Endurance	6
Vitality	4
Intelligence	5
Wisdom	3
Unassigned Attribute Points	30

Zeke scanned the screen over and over, trying to make sense of it. Certainly, it looked just like something you might find in a role-playing game, right down to the stats. However, his rational mind told him that there was absolutely no way that could be real. In fact, he was beginning to think that this entire experience was a dream. Or a delusion. Maybe he'd gone insane or something.

"I know what you're thinking," said Oberon, suddenly standing behind him. "It's real. More real than your old world, even."

"But . . . but what's the point?" Zeke asked. "You say I'm dead. Okay. Fine. And now you're talking about classes and stats like I'm in a video game? Come on, man. What's going on?"

Oberon took a long, deep breath, almost like he was trying to forcibly calm himself. Then, he said, "Look, kid—I know this is a big shock to you. Believe me, I get it. But whether you want to believe it's real or not doesn't matter. Because it is. And when we get finished here, you're going to be thrust into danger. So, you'd better take this shit seriously. Otherwise, you're going to die again. And this time, there's no white room and friendly dwarf waiting on you, okay?"

"You think you're friendly?" Zeke asked.

Oberon ground his teeth together in frustration. "All that, and that's what you focus on . . ."

"Fine, fine—I get it," Zeke said. "I can steer into it, and if it's real, I survive. If it turns out not to be . . . then, well—I don't really lose anything, I guess."

"Something like that," Oberon stated.

"So, you said something about classes," Zeke said. "And a real world. What kind of world are we talking about?"

"The dangerous kind," Oberon said, circling back around to his chair. He turned to face Zeke, saying, "I can't tell you everything—not yet—but there's a war out there. You could call it a war between good and evil. You're on our side because you died trying to save someone else. That puts you firmly on the good side. But there are truly evil people on that other side. Come to think of it, there are evil people on both sides. You need to remember that, Zeke. Just because someone was good back on Earth doesn't mean they'll continue down that path. Throw power into the mix, and there are a lot of people who will be corrupted. And they're going to amass a lot of power very, very quickly. Your job is to do the same so you can oppose them."

"You want soldiers," Zeke reasoned.

"We want heroes," Oberon said. "That doesn't mean you have to fight. Plenty won't. Once you get out into the world, you can choose whatever path you want. If that means becoming a craftsman or a merchant or a goddamned whoremonger, that's your business. But you can be more. You can be a hero."

Zeke stared at Oberon, thinking about the explanation he'd just been given. Certainly, Zeke had never wanted to go to war, but what boy hadn't dreamed of being a hero? Still, he was skeptical, so he went with his gut instinct, asking, "Does that actually work? The hero speech, I mean."

Oberon let out a loud guffaw. "Ha! I knew you were smarter than you looked."

"Seriously, man—just tell me the truth," Zeke said.

"Fine—yes, we want soldiers," Oberon stated. "Happy? We're fighting a war across millions of clusters, and we need people. And before you ask, yes. It's worth it because if we don't fight those bastards, they'll take over everything. Nobody wants to see that."

"So, this is kind of like a holy war or something? Angels and demons?" Zeke asked.

"Something like that," Oberon grumbled. "They might be demons, but we aren't angels. What I said stands, though—once you're in the world, you can do whatever the hell you want to do. There are no restrictions. Just a world."

"And these stats represent my . . . attributes? How?" asked Zeke.

"Aren't most of them pretty self-explanatory?" asked Oberon. Still, he took the time to explain the statistics. Strength represented physical power. Dexterity was coordination. Agility was speed and quickness. Endurance was the body's durability. Vitality represented the body's ability to recover from physical wounds. After that, Zeke got a bit of a surprise when he found out that wisdom and intelligence both governed the use of and defense against magic.

"Wait—like real magic? Shooting fireballs and stuff?" he asked.

"Yes," Oberon said. "There are millions of different ways to do magic, but shooting fireballs is one of the popular ones. As I was saying, wisdom governs your mana regeneration as well as your defense against mental attacks. Intelligence dictates the size of your mana pool and your defense against the more physical sorts of magic. The ever-popular fireballs and such."

"And . . . and my statistics will determine my class?" was Zeke's next question. "When do I get that?"

Oberon said, "Level twenty-five." Zeke started to say something, but Oberon forestalled him with a raised hand, continuing, "Yes, there are levels. You get them just like you would in your video games. So, don't ask about that. And to answer your first question, your statistics play a large part in which class you get at twenty-five when you move on to the next plane. Other considerations are your skills and proficiencies, paths, your achievements, and general style. After you allocate your statistics, you're going to choose one basic skill, then off you go to start your new life."

"Paths?" Zeke asked with a raised eyebrow.

Oberon let out a long-suffering sigh, saying, "Shouldn't have mentioned those." He looked around, and Zeke followed suit. As always, there was nothing to see, but Oberon seemed satisfied, saying, "I won't fully explain them, but paths represent higher concepts. Once you get a glimpse of one of them, you can use that to empower yourself in an appropriate way. I can't say more than that, or I'll draw the Framework's attention."

Zeke wanted to ask why that would be a problem, but he got the picture that Oberon was explaining more than was normal, and he was limited in what he could and couldn't tell Zeke. So, he let it drop, asking, "Any advice? On the stat allocation, I mean."

"Depends on what you want to do," the small man said. "You want to be a traditional mage? Put your points in wisdom and intelligence. A fighter? Concentrate on strength and endurance. Vitality's never a bad idea. But one piece of advice I can give you—doing the most damage really isn't all that useful if you're dead. That's how glass cannons end up—dead."

Zeke thought about it for a minute. On the one hand, the idea of using magic was an enticing one. It was easy to imagine himself as a supreme wizard throwing waves of fire and ice at his enemies. However, it was almost as enticing to think of himself as a warrior, swinging an axe or a sword and mowing down legions of bad guys that resembled the orcs and goblins he'd seen in video games and movies.

"You've got to pick something, kid," Oberon said after a few minutes. "I know it's a big choice, but you can't just stare at that screen for forever."

"I can't help it," Zeke said. "There're so many choices . . ."

"Okay, I'm not really supposed to do this, but let me give you another tip," Oberon said. "Play to your strengths. Humans have a maximum attribute of ten without any Framework alteration. So, you did something in your old life to warrant maximum dexterity. You've got decent agility and strength, too. Bad wisdom and intelligence, though. So, I'll go ahead and leave you with that. And no, putting all your points into intelligence doesn't actually make you smarter. It just facilitates certain types of magic."

Clearly, Oberon was trying to guide Zeke toward skewing his stats toward physical abilities, and his reasoning made sense—enough that it actually tipped the balance in Zeke's head.

"Alright, here goes," he said before allocating ten points in strength and five points each in dexterity, agility, endurance, and vitality. "Okay, that's done. What now?"

"Now, we get to pick skills," a grinning Oberon said, and with a wave of his hand, the screen changed. "There are a little over forty-seven thousand skills to choose from, and that's just the ones that are categorized as beginner skills by the Framework. There are an infinite number of more powerful skills, though. Some are overt combat skills, while the vast majority are noncombat abilities. Needless to say, I recommend the combat skills. Would you like me to narrow it down?"

"Yeah," Zeke said.

Oberon snapped his fingers, and the number went down to nine thousand available skills. "Attack abilities?" he asked. Again, Zeke nodded, and the available pool was narrowed again. "It seems that you've already got some small mastery with blunt weapons, probably from something you did in your old life. So, I suggest that you focus on what you're already good at."

That made sense to Zeke, and so did his supposed ability with blunt weapons. He'd taken enough swings with a baseball bat that he should have something to show for it. Come to think of it, his history as an athlete probably explained his high dexterity skill, as well.

"Narrow it down to attack skills, then," Zeke said.

That took it down to a few hundred, which Zeke immediately began to peruse. There were plenty of obviously magical abilities, ranging from fireballs to poison clouds. There were even a few lightning skills. "Can we narrow it down to melee types of skills?" he asked.

Oberon complied, and from the fifty or so skills that were left, there were four that stood out to Zeke. They were as follows:

[Lightning Strike] (H)—Imbues a weapon with the power of lightning. Upgradable.
[Flaming Blade] (H)—Creates a sword of flames. Upgradable.
[Cudgel of Superiority] (H)—Imbues a blunt weapon with extreme weight, crushing your foes. Upgradable.
[Leech Strike] (H)—Steals a small amount of vitality from an opponent, transferring it to the caster. Upgradable.

[**Lightning Strike**] and [**Flaming Blade**] both seemed to belong to the same family of elemental attacks, and Zeke could certainly see the draw of burning his enemies alive or electrocuting them to death. Similarly, it was easy to imagine how [**Cudgel of Superiority**] would help, especially when he gained a few more points in strength. But to him, there wasn't really a choice, presuming he understood the way things would work. Not only was [**Leech Strike**] an attack, but it was also a heal? That seemed a little overpowered.

He asked Oberon, "What's with this one? If you could steal someone's vitality like that, why would anyone want to do anything else?"

Oberon answered, "It's a very weak attack. Maybe a tenth as powerful as the others up there. And it can lead to some . . . ah . . . less-than-reputable classes."

"What does that even mean?" Zeke asked. "Less-than-reputable? Why does that matter?"

"Because people are people, and if you start fiddling with people's life forces, you're going to have a difficult reputation," Oberon said. "Is it powerful? Sure. It can be. But it takes a lot of work to get it to the point where its usefulness outweighs its demerits. And even if you put in all that work, there's a good chance of you being ostracized because of your eventual class. I can't say more about that, so don't ask."

"Well, that's just bullshit," Zeke mumbled. How was he supposed to decide when he didn't have all the information? Or was that the point? "Just tell me this—will it help keep me alive?"

"Yes," Oberon said. "Better than almost any other skill."

"Then that's all I need to know," he said, selecting the skill. He felt a slight tingle in the back of his mind, but he ignored it. "What now?"

"You're going to have a tough road, kid," Oberon said. "But if you stick to it, you could make some waves, I think. Just remember—no matter what, there's no substitute for hard work."

"That's what my dad used to tell me," Zeke said. Indeed, the man had been all about telling others to work hard. Meanwhile, he'd never actually taken his own advice to heart. "If there's one thing I'm good at, it's work."

"Well, I hope you're right," Oberon said. "Because you're going to get every chance to prove it. See you in a bit."

Before Zeke could respond, Oberon snapped his fingers, and Zeke's world went black once again.

3

A WHOLE NEW WORLD

Zeke awoke lying in the center of a small cave, though when he sat up, he could feel a healthy breeze emanating from a narrow crack in the nearby wall. His eyes opened wide as he strained to see his surroundings, but only the barest outline was visible. Still, with the scant light, even that much was something of a surprise. It was pitch-black inside the cave, so he could only assume that in this new world, he had better night vision than he ever had before.

Slowly, he rolled over to all fours, then pushed himself to his knees. Once, when he was younger, he and a few of his friends had found a low-voltage electric fence. And because kids are stupid and Lower Alabama could be a boring place to live, they'd each taken a turn trying to grab it. When it was Zeke's turn, he'd hesitantly followed in his friends' footsteps, receiving a shock to his system. Back then, it had been like every muscle in his body had contracted of its own volition, and all at once. But that wasn't the worst of it, especially considering that it had faded almost as soon as he'd let go of the fence. Instead, the worst part was that, for a couple of hours afterward, it had felt like every cell in his body was agitated and vibrating. A similar sensation coursed through his body as he sat in that lonely cave, trying to make sense of what had just happened.

His first thought was that it wasn't real. How could it be? Not only had he cast the role of Oberon with a familiar actor, but the entire setup seemed like the beginning of one of his video games. His rational mind told him that he was probably still asleep on some operating table, and everything was just some anesthesia-induced dream.

But something inside of him said otherwise.

Perhaps it was his soul. Or maybe his instincts were better equipped to make heads or tails of the situation. Or it could've been that he was just adept at pushing denial aside. Whatever the case, he knew in his heart of hearts that everything Oberon had said was absolutely, unavoidably true. And that scared him to death.

For a few minutes, Zeke just knelt on that uneven ground, the sharp rocks digging into his knees as panic threatened to overtake him. His heartbeat quickened. His breathing became ragged and shallow. And he found himself on the verge of simply giving in to the overwhelming terror threatening to splinter his sanity.

He had actually died, and a long, long time ago, too. According to Oberon, it had been eons since he'd died on that operating table. Even in his panicked state, he couldn't help but wonder how everyone had reacted to that. His brother. His mother. His so-called friends. Had they mourned? Surely, his family had. But he suspected that his friends' grief had only lasted as long as it took to make a post on social media.

It was a sobering thought, but he'd long known that his friends were really more like acquaintances than anything else. They were shallow relationships of convenience, and little else. None of them would've shed a tear for him.

Zeke wasn't certain how long he knelt in the center of the cave. Hours? Minutes? A day? It could've been an eternity, for all he knew. He slowly pushed through the panic-tinged melancholy to the point where he found himself taking stock of his situation. He might've died, sure. But that didn't mean he had nothing to live for. According to Oberon, there was a whole world out there. Maybe he could even find his brother. More, he resolved to do things better than he had in his first life.

Short as it was, he'd accomplished very little. No friends. No partner. No impact. It was easy to blame his injury, and it had certainly derailed his plans. But it all came down to one simple fact: he'd let himself down. He wouldn't let that happen again. So, with a renewed sense of vigor and purpose, he pushed himself to his feet, thoughts of triumph and heroism in his mind as well as his stance.

It made him a perfect target.

A ball of sharp, burning agony erupted in his back, sending him flying across the small cave. He collided with the rocky wall, his breath exploding out of his body in a sharp exhale. He let out a breathless scream that echoed off the walls as he felt like his every bone was broken, all at once. But that was nothing compared to the pain in his back. It was unlike anything he'd ever felt before, and the shock nearly sent him cascading into unconsciousness. However, a sixth sense born of a natural survival instinct told him that if he succumbed, he wouldn't survive another minute. And he knew that if that came to pass, he wouldn't be reborn into some white room talking about classes and stats. If he died again, that would be the end. So, he clung to that thin thread of instinct, hoping that it would be enough to keep his wits.

It worked, and a second later, he found himself rolling to the side. The ruined mess of his back screamed at him, but he forcibly shut out the agony. It was just pain, after all. And if his life had taught him anything, it was how to push through something like that. He scrambled to his feet, simultaneously turning so he could see his attacker. And what he saw was shocking in its vicious unfamiliarity.

His night vision didn't provide the best view, but it was clear enough that he immediately knew he wasn't facing an earthly creature. The closest thing Zeke could compare the animal to was a rodent, but instead of fur, it was covered in scales. I seemed like an unholy mixture of crocodile, badger, and rat, with gleaming, bloody claws and a mouthful of what used to be Zeke's unblemished back. All in all, the thing was around three feet long, from snout to the end of its thick, crocodilian tail. And it was frighteningly quick, which Zeke discovered only a moment later, when the low-slung monster launched itself at him.

However, Zeke's next discovery was even more shocking.

He knew the croco-rat was fast. Probably too fast, at least by his old standards. But in a way, it seemed like it was moving in slow motion. It was as if his own perception had been sped up. Immediately, his mind went back to his stats. If his suspicions about what the baseline was were accurate, he was already operating on a borderline superhuman level. Or perhaps peak human, like Captain America.

Just as he was about to dodge away, a spark of inspiration took hold in Zeke's mind. In an instant, a sinister red cloud erupted from his clenched fists. Instinctively, he knew this was his chosen skill, [**Leech Strike**], which was supposed to somehow transfer vitality from his enemy to him. However, he had absolutely zero notion of how to actually use the ability. Nor did he have much time to think it through because, despite his enhanced speed and perception, the snarling croco-rat was bearing down on him. And if it got those jaws around him, no degree of enhanced stats was likely to save him.

So, when the creature was only a scant foot away, Zeke struck. Years of spending every waking moment hitting baseballs had given him impeccable hand-eye coordination, and that had only been enhanced by his new stat allocation. The result was that when Zeke sidestepped, simultaneously swinging his fist at the thing, he struck true, unleashing the sort of power Earth had rarely seen. Even professional fighters would've been hard-pressed to match the force of that simple, frantic punch.

What's more, the moment it connected, it felt like a piece of Zeke's soul shot out, plunging deep into the croco-rat's head, snatching at something Zeke could neither perceive nor see. But when it retracted, the red cloud around his fist flashed a deep green that radiated vitality, which then flowed up his arm only to disappear the moment it reached his torso.

Not that he had the time or inclination to notice it, of course. He was too busy watching the croco-rat sail through the air to collide with the other side of the cave wall. It let out a yelp of pain as rock and gravel, shaken loose by the impact, cascaded down the uneven wall.

Zeke stared in shock, trying to understand what had just happened. For a long moment, the croco-rat lay still, but Zeke knew it wasn't dead. His instincts proved right once again as the monstrous creature slowly rose onto its stubby legs, shook itself, then fixed its gaze on Zeke. He felt the hairs on the back of his neck suddenly stand straight up. This thing intended to kill him. Not in the way a wild animal wants to kill its prey. No—this was something more sinister. This was a creature who wanted to murder for murder's sake. And it had its sights set on Zeke.

"Alright, then," Zeke muttered, adopting a fighting posture. It felt a little silly because he'd only ever been in a few fights in all his life, and even those had been during his adolescent years. But this was kill or be killed, and he'd quickly adapted his mindset for survival.

Zeke had already died once, and he had no intention of repeating the experience.

The croco-rat seemed to have learned its lesson, as well, and instead of mindlessly barreling at him, it was content to repeatedly dart forward, testing his defenses. Zeke dodged as best he could, but even his enhanced perception wouldn't let him escape unscathed. Soon, a multitude of scratches and bloody bites decorated his entire body, ripping his meager clothing to shreds. He'd awoken wearing a thin, white tunic and matching linen pants, but they were clearly not much use at stopping the croco-rat's sharp claws.

However, Zeke had also given almost as good as he'd gotten. Each time the creature drew close, his fists arced out, and more often than not, his blows connected. He'd yet to repeat the power of his first strike, but each of his punches landed with a meaty thump. More than that, though, every time he made forcible contact, he stole a little of the monster's life force.

Or vitality.

Maybe even some of its soul.

Zeke really had no idea what, precisely, he was doing. But one thing he did know was that each surge of energy that flowed up his arm had, bit by bit, eased the pain in his back. No single influx of energy was lifesaving, but it had built up to the point where he was almost certain that the wounds had mostly closed, which was miraculous in and of itself. Add the fact that the croco-rat was weakened by each subsequent strike, and Zeke felt confident that he could outlast the monster, even despite his obvious deficiencies in the realm of combat.

The croco-rat seemed to understand this, as well, because it soon redoubled its offensive. It seemed like it was trying to rip through Zeke with nothing but its unbridled ferocity. And in its haste to dispatch the annoying young man who'd invaded its territory, it started making mistakes. Zeke was there to pounce on each and every one, and soon, his fists thundered into the creature over and over, until he'd finally overwhelmed its defenses.

Sensing weakness, Zeke didn't hesitate. By this point, he was running on sheer survival instinct, and there was no room for doubt in his mind. So, when he saw the croco-rat struggling to rise after a particularly vicious blow sent it shooting to the other side of the cave, he leaped atop it. His fists rose and fell like pistons, hammering into the creature until he felt its very skull crack. But he didn't stop there. He couldn't. So, even after the monster had clearly died, Zeke continued to pound the thing's head into a bloody, messy pulp. He might've gone even longer, but his fury was interrupted by an influx of pure energy.

It entered his body through his pores, but it soon traced a series of pathways through his body. In his mind's eye, Zeke couldn't help but be reminded of a glowing stick figure, the sort a kindergartner might draw.

In an instant, the energy found its way to a point just above his navel, where it accumulated into a dense ball.

"W-what the hell..."

However, before Zeke got an answer, he heard a scuttling sound from across the cave. He looked up to see a gaping crevasse in the wall on the other side of the cave, from which emerged a trio of croco-rats. For a moment, his shoulders slumped in exhaustion, and he found himself wondering how he could possibly go on. A fight with one of the monsters had driven him to his limit. What was he supposed to do against three of them?

But then again, what choice did he have?

Just as he rose wearily to his feet, a screen flashed in front of Zeke's eyes. Instinctively, he knew it wouldn't be visible to anyone else. But more, the text it displayed gave him some hope.

New quest acquired!
Objective: Escape the Caracoan Nest
Reward: Wilderness Survival Kit (H)

Zeke had no idea what might be contained in something called a wilderness survival kit, but he felt certain that it wouldn't be the sort he might've bought at a sporting goods store back home. Nor did he have any notion of what the grading system was. If it was the entire alphabet, *H* might imply something of mediocre quality. However, he had a sneaking suspicion that whatever he gained so soon would be the poorest quality out there. Still, he was in no position to refuse any sort of help. And besides, it wasn't like he wanted to remain within the cave for the rest of his life. Escaping was already on the docket.

Either way, the quest had given him a sense of purpose that in turn gave him a burst of energy. He felt like he'd already taken the first step. This was just the next in what he hoped would be a long road. So, without further hesitation, Zeke mentally dismissed the quest screen and launched himself at the croco-rats. Or caracoa, as the quest implied was the creatures' proper name. Whatever the case, the creatures were standing between him and his very survival.

And, miraculously, his first punch connected. So did his second, and both stubby-legged creatures were sent lurching across the cave. However, the reality of his lacking combat experience soon reasserted itself, and he felt the third monster latch on to his leg with what felt like enough pressure to snap his shin in two.

He howled in pain, and his panicked fists rained down on the beast's head with unrivaled fury. Every blow was like a sledgehammer, and it wasn't long before the croco-rat was dislodged from his shin, taking a significant chunk of Zeke's calf with it. He almost fell, then and there. But with the adrenaline pumping through his veins, he managed to keep his mind clear enough to finish the caracoa off, leaving its brains splattered on the rocky ground.

Zeke didn't get much of a reprieve, though, because in a matter of seconds, the other two croco-rats had recovered and were upon him. The next few minutes were something of a blur for Zeke. He punched. He kicked. He grappled. He even bit. And each time he made contact with one of the creatures, a surge of vitality crashed against his accumulated wounds. Still, he was a mess of blood and viscera by the time he finally managed to kill the last caracoa.

Zeke didn't even have time to take stock of his many, many wounds before darkness started to overtake him. Just before he collapsed, though, a very exciting message flashed before his eyes.

Congratulations! You have reached Level 2!

4

ALLOCATION

Zeke's impending unconsciousness fled as the ball of energy below his navel dispersed, leaving only the tiniest of beads behind. The energy arced out via his stick figure pathways to be greedily absorbed by his cells. With it came a sense of euphoria, a sensation of power unlike anything he'd ever felt before, that banished his weariness altogether. For a brief moment, he felt certain that he could run through a wall or lift a car. But it lasted only an instant before it faded away, leaving only the pain and exhaustion of his previous battle in its wake. After that, it took him a moment to process everything and remember the message that he'd received.

A level. Oberon had mentioned them, of course, but in the hectic confusion of being attacked by the croco-rats, he'd forgotten all about it. And even if he hadn't, the idea of gaining levels, just like in a video game, was so foreign that he didn't really know how he was supposed to react. In addition, with the dispersal of the energy having passed, the fatigue of the fight reasserted itself.

He collapsed in a heap, though he managed to maintain his consciousness—much to his dismay, given the sheer number of wounds he'd acquired. Not only did he sport long gashes up and down his arms, but he felt like his entire back had been reduced to ribbons. His legs hadn't escaped the punishment, either, and he could feel that a large portion of his quadriceps as well as a chunk of his calf had been bitten off. And that wasn't even considering the state of his hands.

As it turned out, repeatedly punching a creature whose skin was comprised of rigid scales with the durability of some metals had repercussions, especially considering the incredible force Zeke had managed to put into each blow. He might've been able to punch with the force of a jackhammer, but his hands were still flesh and bone. He suspected they were more durable than ever before, but even that durability was no match for the ferocity with which he'd attacked the croco-rats.

In the dark, he looked down at the results. There wasn't much light—or any, really; his night vision had obviously improved, just like the rest of his body—but he could clearly see the outline of what was left of his hands. His knuckles were caked in blood, some of it belonging to the caracoa, but mostly his own, the result of split skin and a couple of protruding bones. If that was it, he might not have been so concerned. After all, he suspected that he would heal much more quickly now. But his broken knuckles were only the beginning of the damage; it was like every bone in his hands had been shattered up to the wrist. And as the adrenaline of the fight began to wear off, it was replaced by undiluted agony.

Before Zeke knew it, tears were trailing down his cheeks as he writhed on the uneven ground, cradling his hands to his chest. It wasn't just the pain in his hands, though that was a big part of it. If it was just that, he probably could've born it. However, the myriad wounds covering his body all coalesced into something greater than the sum of their parts. More, though, there was a sense of helplessness. Despair. He hadn't asked for any of this. He didn't deserve this kind of torture.

But that didn't matter, did it? Life wasn't fair, so why should the afterlife be any different?

He had no notion of how long he lay there, wallowing in mingled agony and self-pity, before he remembered to open his status screen. With a thought, the window opened, displaying the set of statistics that were supposed to represent his very existence.

Fifteen unassigned points. He'd had a plan, coming into this, but making plans in that safe, white room when everything was just hypothetical was one thing. But when he'd just had his body filleted by the croco-rats, things had unavoidably changed. While he desperately wanted to follow his plan and put his points into strength, he knew that probably wasn't a great idea.

First of all, there was his most immediate problem. Not only was he in no condition to fight his way out of these caves, but he was also having quite a difficult time thinking straight amid the pain coursing through his body. Certainly, he thought he could heal from his injuries—especially if he managed to master his [**Leech Strike**]. It had already helped immeasurably, and without it stealing the caracoa's life force, he had a feeling he'd have already died. But was he willing to take that chance?

No. No, he wasn't.

So, strength was out. So were agility and dexterity. Similarly, while his instincts told him to balance out his intelligence and wisdom, he knew they wouldn't immediately help him, either. Given that he didn't have any active skills—[**Leech Strike**] seemed to be toggled; once it was activated, it would remain so until he toggled it off, draining a tiny amount of mana for each second it was active—he wasn't even entirely certain that they'd do anything at all for him. So, with those discarded, there were only endurance and vitality left.

Vitality was an easy one. Even if Oberon hadn't said that it would enhance his physical recovery, his [**Leech Strike**] would've given him plenty of hints to know that it would help him heal from his wounds. And that was something he desperately needed.

However, there was also the problem that he was ill-equipped to withstand using his own strength, which he suspected was tied to endurance. If he broke his hands every time he tried to punch something, then his strength was useless. More, he had no illusions about the croco-rats being the strongest creatures he would face. If they could cut him to ribbons, what would something worse do?

So, with that in mind, his decision proved easy, and he decided to divide his free points between vitality and endurance, with nine going into the former and six going into the latter. His reasoning on the split was that he wanted his endurance to exceed his strength. With a thought, Zeke allocated his points, then looked at his new stats:

Name	Ezekiel Blackwood
Class	N/A
Level	2
Race	Human (H)
Alignment	Isphodel
Achievements	First Blood
Strength	18

Agility	14
Dexterity	17
Endurance	19
Vitality	20
Intelligence	7
Wisdom	5
Unassigned Attribute Points	0

While he looked at the screen that only he could see, a wave of warmth rippled throughout his body. He could feel his shallower wounds close in an instant, and he let out a wordless scream as the bones in his hands rearranged themselves. It was even more excruciating than before, but it passed in a moment, leaving only a mild discomfort behind. He knelt on the ground, his breath coming in shallow gasps as he tried to figure out what had happened. Surely, nine points in vitality weren't enough to completely heal him, right?

So, what was it? The level itself? Or was it something else? After a few more seconds, during which a thousand questions rocketed through his mind, Zeke realized that he had absolutely nothing to base any of his conjecture on. In the end, he was almost completely ignorant of his new world. And he knew that, stuck in this cave, no amount of thought would shed any light on it. So, rising to his feet, he took stock of his situation.

Looking around, he saw the indistinct lumps of shadow that were the croco-rat corpses. When they weren't trying to kill him, they didn't look nearly so intimidating. Sure, they were an unholy mixture of reptile and rodent, with wickedly curved claws that resembled a wolverine's, but they weren't nearly as big as he'd thought. No bigger than a midsize dog, discounting the thick, crocodilian tail. Whatever the case, their corpses weren't useful. Perhaps, if he'd had a knife, he might've tried to skin them and fashion some sort of armor from their tough hide. Or harvest their tail meat, like people did with alligators. But given that he had nothing but the tattered linen shirt and pants in which he had awoken, that was out of the question. So, he continued to scan the cave, predictably finding nothing at all of use.

It shouldn't have been surprising, given the nature of the quest he'd been given. If he wanted to survive, he'd have to find his way out of the caves. And what's more, he'd have to dodge more of the hideous croco-rats along the way. However, despite the surge of vitality that had come with the allocation of his free points, Zeke knew he was in no shape to begin what he suspected would be a difficult journey. So, he quickly made his way to the corner of the cave, sat down, and closed his eyes. Hopefully, his recently boosted vitality would continue what it had started.

Zeke sat there for what was probably a few hours. He had no way to tell how much time had passed, but in that span, his body had continued to recover. He didn't experience another boost like he'd gotten after allocating his stats, which made him suspect that it had been tied to gaining the level, but his body still recovered at an astonishing rate. The bones in his broken hands had been mostly healed by the surge, but they'd still been fragile. He knew that if he'd have tried to punch something—even at half strength—they would've once again shattered. But after a few hours? They felt as whole as they'd been when he'd awoken in the accursed cave. In addition, all but the worst gashes had completely closed, and the missing chunk of flesh in his leg had regrown. It was tender and would probably result in a wicked scar, but it still worked just as well as it ever had. Better even, considering his increased stats.

During his recovery, Zeke had taken the time to explore the various menus available to him. There was, of course, his main status screen, which showed his statistics. There were some categories he didn't understand, like alignment and the categorization of his race as **Human (H)**, but as he focused on each individual listing, a series of submenus became available. As he opened them, he found more information.

The first surprise was that, if he wished, he could change his name. What good that would do, he had no idea, but he chose to leave it as it was. Next, he'd focused on his race, which brought up the following description:

Human (H): Humans are the most prevalent sentient race in the multiverse. However, they are afflicted with unrepentant mediocrity. This is both a blessing and a curse because, while they excel at nothing, they are unfettered by natural attunements or blatant weaknesses. Upgradable.

Zeke could easily read between the lines. Few weaknesses. Few strengths. Never mind that the description basically confirmed the existence of aliens. That was a shocker, in and of itself, but he couldn't really concern himself with that right now. Instead, he focused on how his race might affect his own development. He assumed that meant he could guide his own path, rather than be pigeonholed into doing something just because his race demanded it. At least he had freedom, even if he had no idea what that really meant in an unfamiliar world.

He mentally delved more deeply into his race, which brought up a new screen.

Body (H): Determines physical limitations. Upgradable.
Soul (H): Determines spiritual limitations. Upgradable.

Clearly, the grade of his body had something to do with how physically strong he could become. Perhaps there were stat limits, or maybe upgrading it would simply give him a boost. However, the soul part was a little more ephemeral. What would upgrading it do? Increase his intelligence or wisdom, maybe? Or something less quantifiable? He didn't have enough information to make a determination, so he simply moved on to the next category.

Next, he focused on his alignment, but he was disappointed that it only gave a name: Isphodel. He had no clue what that meant, but he wasn't going to focus too much on it, especially with everything else on his plate. Maybe he could figure it out later.

Finally, he came to achievements. When he mentally zoomed in on the line, another window opened. It was almost completely empty, save for a single line:

First Blood: You have slain your first enemy with your bare hands! All stats +1 per level.

Upon seeing that, Zeke backtracked to his status page, then looked at his statistics. He hadn't noticed it before, but in addition to the points he'd allocated into endurance and vitality, he had gained a single point in every category. It didn't seem like much, but over time, he could see how it could add up. Presuming he actually survived long enough, that was. In any case, he'd recovered enough to start on what he assumed would be a long trail out of the cave system.

With a sigh, he rose to his feet and ran a still-bloody hand through his hair. There was no time like the present, he supposed. And with that, he set out, hoping he could avoid any further threats to his life.

5

COMMITMENT

Zeke crept through the gap as stealthily as he could. His eyes were wide, his head cocked to the side as he strained for any indication that he was about to be attacked. While he could barely make out the outlines of the cave's uneven walls, the gloom quickly swallowed any detail, and after a few feet, there was only a wall of impenetrable darkness. So, he trailed his fingers along the wall as he gingerly stepped through the cave, hardly noticing the sharp rocks scraping against his bare feet.

Thankfully, there weren't any branching paths yet. If there had been, he had no idea how he would choose which way to go. Even more fortuitously, he found himself climbing a slight incline. It was hardly noticeable, at first, but with each step, he grew a little more optimistic about escaping the cave. However, when he saw no change even after what he thought was a few hours, he was forced to reassess his optimistic prediction. But he trudged along, mostly because he had no idea what else to do.

One thing he did know, however, was that his enhanced stats definitely helped with fatigue. Before he'd died, he had been an athlete—and not just a casual one, either. Rather, from the time he was five years old until he'd mangled his arm, he'd spent nearly every day either preparing for or playing baseball. It had been his passion, his entire world. He hadn't simply liked the game; it had been everything to him. So, unlike some of his peers, he'd never once considered slacking off or giving anything less than his best effort. And the results had spoken for themselves when he'd become a top-tier catching prospect who, before his injury, was expected to be drafted into the major leagues.

But then disaster had struck in the form of that car accident, and he'd been cast adrift. One memory, in particular, had stuck with him. It had been about six months after the car wreck, and he'd actually been feeling pretty good. He didn't have full range of motion or anything, but he thought he could at least take some batting practice. So, full of the exuberance and ignorance of youth, he'd gone down to the batting cages with one of his teammates.

The first swing hadn't been terrible. He'd even made weak contact. After all, the hand-eye coordination he'd built over more than a decade of manic practice hadn't dissolved during his recovery. With that swing, he'd dared to hope. The next one mercilessly smothered that spark. The moment the bat solidly connected with the ball, a shooting pain had erupted up and down his arm, bringing tears to his eyes.

It wasn't just the physical agony of it. Just like any serious athlete, he knew how to deal with pain. Rather, it was the emotional toll of seeing the very pillar of his identity crumbling before him that had done him in.

Before, when the doctors had told him that he was lucky he hadn't lost the arm altogether, he'd thought of it as just one more bump in his road to the major leagues. He'd been hurt before. He could get through it again. He'd imagined himself triumphantly defying the doctors' predictions and making it to the level where he knew he belonged. It would make for a good story, once everything was said and done. And all it took was willpower to go that extra mile. After all, until that moment, his body had never let him down before.

But with that one swing, his confidence had shattered. After that, he gave only a token effort during his ongoing physical therapy sessions. Finally, he believed his doctors' predictions that he'd never play again, and with that belief, he had lost his drive. Even once he was healthy, he'd stopped working out. He'd stopped watching what he ate. He had stopped taking care of himself altogether. It was only when his brother's condition worsened and he saw a chance to be the hero that his mindset had even marginally improved.

In a lot of ways, Zeke was grateful for his death. Not only had it served a purpose and, according to Oberon, given his little brother a new lease on life, but it had also given him the chance to start over, albeit in a hellish cave where a monster attack was around every corner. His confidence had started to return, though, and he was beginning to see the opportunity before him. After all, he was stronger than he'd ever been in his life, and in better condition, too. And so long as he kept moving forward, he would only grow more powerful.

The evidence of that was staring him in the face as the hours stretched on, and his energy level didn't even begin to lag. He felt better with each passing second, no doubt because of the effect of his investment in vitality. Already, the soreness in his hands had faded into nothing. The various cuts and scrapes and contusions had healed, as well. The only physical reminder of his desperate battle with the croco-rats was the pain in his thigh, but even that was getting better by the minute. Within a day, maybe two, he'd be back to pristine condition—a cause for positivity if he'd ever seen one.

His optimism hit a brick wall when he heard a scraping sound up ahead. He'd been walking in silence for hours, so even the slightest of sounds was like a blaring horn. More, it was easy to recognize it for what it was—a claw scratching against rock. Clearly, he wasn't done with the croco-rats.

Briefly, he considered retracing his steps. Perhaps he'd missed a branch somewhere, and he could avoid conflict with the local wildlife. However, he quickly dismissed that thought based on one simple fact. His quest had implied that he was within a nest of the creatures. Even if he found an alternate route, he'd probably run into more of the same.

And besides, his increased stats had come with a surge of confidence. He'd already killed four of the monsters. What was one more? Maybe he'd even gain another level. Adrenaline and excitement mingled within him, pushing him forward. With a thought, he activated his [**Leech Strike**], which enveloped his hands in a red cloud. Looking down, he marveled at the ability. It was magic, just like in stories. He shook his head in bemusement; his world had certainly changed.

Just before he was about to start forward, he noticed something, though. Beneath the red cloud of energy, he saw an intricate pattern along the backs of his hands. It was barely noticeable, glowing only slightly more than the cloud itself, but to him, it was as clear as day. On the surface, it almost looked like a Celtic circle, but his instincts told him that it went far deeper than any mere pattern. It was three-dimensional and dizzyingly complex, and that was just what he could make out along the surface. Zeke got a headache just looking at one of the runes.

He shook his head, clearing the cobwebs as he looked away. As much as he wanted to study the runes—and he very much did—he knew this was neither the time nor the place. The croco-rat hadn't noticed him yet, as evidenced by the fact that it wasn't currently trying to shred him to pieces, but it wouldn't be long before his presence was discovered. He desperately wanted to dictate the fight, and to do that, he needed to get the jump on the creature. So, as silently as he could, he inched forward. Careful step by careful step, he made his way down the long tunnel until he saw it open into a huge gallery.

Most of it was swallowed by the pervasive darkness, but even with that limitation, Zeke was awestruck. Stalactites, glittering with crystals, jutted from the cave's ceiling while a forest of pillar-like stalagmites grew upward, blocking his view of the rest of the cave. In addition to the slight scratching sound emanating from nearby, there was the telltale sound of running water coming from somewhere within the cavern, reminding him that he hadn't had anything to drink since his rebirth. Between the stalagmites grew moss and mushrooms, though in the dark, Zeke couldn't really tell the colors. But he did see hints of movement here and there. Usually, it was just a brief break in the lines of a stalagmite, but he could tell that the cavern was crawling with caracoa.

He squatted at the entrance, which was about three or four feet above the cavern floor, wondering what he should do. He couldn't just run in, proverbial guns blazing. Judging by what he'd seen so far, there were at least a dozen of the creatures in the cavern. Maybe more. Luckily, none of them seemed to have noticed him yet, which gave him plenty of opportunity to search for an opening. He wasn't certain how long he sat there, watching the cavern's denizens, but eventually, he noticed a few things.

First, they weren't wandering aimlessly. Instead, the creatures were feeding on the mushrooms that sprouted between the stalagmites. However, it wasn't an uncommon sight to see a pair of the caracoa facing off against each other as they fought for what Zeke guessed was a particularly delectable fungus. Usually, there were no deaths resulting from these confrontations, but there were wounds aplenty. The monsters were equipped with sharp teeth and even sharper claws, after all. And though their scales were tough, they didn't prove a match for the croco-rats' natural weapons.

Another strange thing he noticed was that some of the creatures seemed capable of walking on two legs, albeit for only a short time. They reminded Zeke of long-torsoed toddlers learning how to walk, awkward and unbalanced. But the few capable of bipedal ambulation were the biggest and most vicious-looking of the creatures.

Finally, he saw the detail that he fully intended to exploit. Because fights were so common, or maybe because they weren't particularly social creatures, none of the uninvolved croco-rats seemed to care when a battle broke out. They didn't look up. They didn't respond in any way. And Zeke figured that one more fight wasn't going to draw any more notice than any of the others had. So, he settled down to wait for his moment to strike. As he waited, he considered his chosen course of action; it would've been easy to simply turn around and try to find another way. But there were two problems with that, the first being that he hadn't seen any offshoots along the path. Maybe he'd missed one—he hadn't been in the most attentive of mindsets as he grappled with thoughts of his old life as well as the implications of the opportunity before him—but he didn't think so. There was also the question of water; with the sound of the underground stream, his thirst had chosen to assert itself, letting him know just how urgently he needed to see to the bare necessities. And lastly, he wanted to fight. He wanted to win. And he wanted to level up again. Maybe he was just high off his increased stats, but he thought he could do it, too.

It took almost an hour for one of the croco-rats to separate itself enough that Zeke felt confident that his ambush wouldn't be noticed. But as soon as the monster wandered far enough away from its fellows, Zeke slowly crept forward, crouching low while using the stalagmites and deep shadows for cover. The closer he came, the more rapidly his heart began to beat. Outwardly, though, he remained calm. During his baseball career, he'd learned how to deal with pressure, how to focus on the task at hand, and most importantly, how to keep his cool and block unnecessary distractions out. He used that same strategy with his impending fight against the caracoa. If he could deliver a walk-off home run in the bottom of the ninth in the championship game of the state playoffs, he could successfully jump a creature half his size. That established, Zeke continued his approach until he was only a few feet away. Happily munching on some mushrooms—and getting a fair few rocks with each bite—the thing still hadn't noticed him.

Zeke pounced, springing forward like a hunting cat. He raised his fists in a double-handed strike, bringing them down with thunderous force. The croco-rat never had a chance, and in one blow, he could feel the crunch of the thing's skull. However, he wasn't going to make the mistake of letting it wriggle away with only a fractured skull. So, he punched once again, each blow yanking a bit of the thing's life force away. However, because Zeke had already recovered, it quickly dissipated, only adding a bit of damage to his punches. It didn't matter, though—within seconds, the monster's head had been reduced to a scaly, bloody mush.

Zeke panted, not from exertion, but from excitement—especially when he felt the familiar energy rush through his pathways and to that ball in the pit of his stomach. It wasn't enough to gain another level. Not even close, really. But it still felt good, having that energy sitting inside him, evidence of his victory.

He glanced down at his hands, pleased to see that they hadn't broken like before. They didn't feel good, though. In fact, he could feel that they had barely held up. However, they were still whole and intact, so it was a vast improvement over his first battle.

He had spent almost an entire day trekking through the cave system, but it felt like much, much more. And that feeling was only enhanced by the clear differences his body had already undergone, and that was just from one level. What would it feel like in two? Or ten? How strong would he be when he finally reached level twenty-five and obtained a class? A million thoughts rampaged through his mind, distracting him to the point that he was completely caught off guard when one of the bigger, occasionally bipedal croco-rats barreled into him, its jaws clamping down on his shoulder.

Zeke let out a cry of mingled surprise and pain, but though he was certain that the thing had a bite force rivaling that of a real crocodile, its teeth barely pierced his skin. That wasn't to say that there weren't a couple of cracked bones, though. It seemed that his insides hadn't quite caught up to the outside, in terms of sheer durability.

He crashed against a stalagmite with enough force that it sent a cascade of rocks crumbling down its sides. A spiderweb of cracks spread from the point of impact, and the croco-rat's screeches filled the cave, bouncing off the walls with a wholly disturbing echo. Zeke found himself reacting on survival instinct, reaching up to grab the creature stubbornly trying to rip into his shoulder. It was awkward, trying to get a grip on the thing, but eventually, Zeke managed to dig his fingers into the monster's thick, scaly hide. With a wrench, he ripped the croco-rat away and, with a mighty heave, tossed it into the nearby cave wall. It might've been bigger than the other caracoa so far, but it was still little bigger than a child. And with his increased strength, he was able to throw it with truly impressive force—so much that he could audibly hear its bones breaking.

But it wasn't dead. Not even close, so far as Zeke could tell, and it sprang to its feet in an instant. Its right foreleg hung limp, but that didn't seem to slow it down much as it quickly launched itself at Zeke once again. Just as he was wondering if the thing was really stupid enough to try the same thing twice, he felt another set of jaws clamp down on his hamstring. Then another missile-like impact on his back. And another set of claws raking against his ribs. He almost collapsed as a swarm of caracoa—at least a dozen of the things—piled onto him, biting, clawing, and scratching.

He'd planned it out so carefully, but he'd obviously made the mistake of thinking he knew more than he really did. The croco-rats didn't react to infighting, but an intruder was different, wasn't it? Their reaction suggested that it was. He didn't know if it was the smell, if they saw him, or if the alpha croco-rat had warned them with its piercing screech, but every caracoa in the cavern had responded to its call.

For the briefest of moments, at the bottom of that pile of raking claws and biting teeth, Zeke felt a sense of deep dejection, not unlike how he'd felt that day when he realized that his dreams of playing big league baseball were over. He'd already survived one life-and-death encounter, and he'd all but beaten another. But still, he was being overwhelmed by a dozen monsters that all wanted to kill him. So what if he somehow survived this? There'd just be another monster. Another scrape with death. That was the world he'd entered, after all. He almost succumbed, his story cut short before it even started.

But then he remembered the level he'd gotten. That sense of power. The sensation of victory he'd felt upon defeating the first group of croco-rats. Not only did he want to feel that again, but if he kept going, things would get better. He would get stronger. And soon, nothing would be able to stop him.

And if there was one thing Zeke was good at, it was progressing toward a goal. He'd done it his whole life, sacrificing all the things other kids took for granted as he spent hour after hour, day by day, training to reach the pinnacle of what he could achieve. And while that goal had been derailed, it felt like the perfect training for the world in which he'd found himself.

So, sure—the bites hurt. The claws creasing his skin were agonizing. But they couldn't kill him. He wouldn't let them. In fact, they were no different than all the thousands of baseballs he'd hit over the years. Just a training tool. He bent his mind to the task, pushing his doubts aside as he roared his defiance, throwing the monsters in all directions as he sprang to his feet.

His first kill came when he stomped down with all the force he could muster, his foot collapsing the entirety of an unlucky croco-rat's rib cage. The next came when he lashed out with a punch that hit the previously injured croco-rat alpha in the side of its oblong head, completely caving in his skull. This time, his [**Leech Strike**] did its job, seizing a bit of the creature's waning vitality and feeding it to Zeke's injuries. One after another, Zeke felled the monsters, taking almost as many injuries as his enemies. However, the combination of his investment in vitality and the work of the [**Leech Strike**] made all the difference, and soon, there was only one of the monsters left.

The last monster was one of the croco-rat alphas, and it was easily the biggest of the bunch. When it stood on its hind legs, it came all the way to Zeke's chest, its form thicker and more heavily muscled, with slightly longer limbs in proportion to the rest of its body. After having seen the other caracoa fall, it was also enraged to the point that it kept launching itself at Zeke with a reckless abandon that produced ferocious, lightning-quick strikes. More than once, its claws had raked across Zeke's chest, creating long, deep wounds. Not to be outdone, Zeke's fist found the creature each time, as well, mitigating the damage while calling down plenty of his own thunder. But this creature was different. Stronger. Faster. Cleverer. And because of its clear superiority to its brethren, the fight had devolved into a battle of attrition.

Luckily, Zeke was built for just that kind of fight. Training as an elite athlete had conditioned him toward persistence, pushing him to keep going, to ignore pain and fatigue. He'd forgotten that after his injury, but with his rebirth, his willpower had returned in force. The fight with the caracoa had further sharpened it, and soon, he recognized the croco-rat alpha's waning strength for what it was. Its strikes slowed, the power dissipating, and after a few more attempts, its weakened attacks couldn't even break Zeke's skin. His own strength hadn't abated, though, and it wasn't long before he caught the croco-rat's snapping jaws, forcing them apart. Then, with a mighty roar, he tore them apart, nearly ripping the creature in two. It was dead in an instant.

The battle had lasted only a handful of minutes, but to Zeke, it had felt like an eternal war. All around him, the carcasses of his enemies, still warm and fresh, lay. Some, like the last croco-rat alpha, had been ripped apart. Others had had their bodies pummeled into submission. But they were all dead, and for the first time in what felt like an eternity, silence reigned throughout the cavern.

Breathing hard, Zeke could only smile. Not at the slaughter itself. He was curiously ambivalent about that. Rather, he relished the feeling of power. The sensation of victory. But most of all, he couldn't help but grin at the notification that had just flashed before his eyes.

Congratulations! You have reached Level 3!

Given how many croco-rats he'd killed, that wasn't all that surprising. Besides, Zeke had felt the ball of energy within him straining to its limit, so he knew he was close. However, what he hadn't expected was the addition of another message.

You have earned a skill: [Inspection]!

6
GO BIG OR GO HOME

Zeke desperately wanted to familiarize himself with his new skill—primarily because he was sorely lacking in information, and [**Inspection**] seemed like it would provide just that—but he'd also taken quite a few wounds during his battle with the horde of croco-rats.

So, he muttered, "First things first," before bringing up his primary status window and allocating his free points, five each in endurance, strength, and vitality. Once he'd confirmed his choices, the familiar wave of energy arced through his body, healing most of his superficial wounds. However, he'd also collected a handful of more serious lacerations, bites, and even what he suspected was a fractured bone in his foot. Those would take more than a level surge to heal, so he sat down, ignoring the pain as he set about familiarizing himself with [**Inspection**].

He glanced at one of the croco-rat corpses, willing himself to identify it. But to his surprise, nothing happened. Was there some trick to it? Or did it simply not work on corpses? He had no clue, but a spark of intuition told him that he just wasn't doing it right. So, for the better part of an hour, he pondered a method of skill activation.

"God, I'm stupid," he breathed, at last realizing that he already had an example to study. His [**Leech Strike**] was a skill, right? Even if it was more passive, it could at least give him some clue on how to activate [**Inspection**]. With that in mind, he focused on his hands, but to his distress, nothing happened. Did it take a life-and-death struggle? He'd activated it on pure, Framework-driven instinct before, so that made sense. But he couldn't help but think he was simply missing something.

He stared at his hand for almost thirty minutes before something clicked into place. Suddenly, the familiar red cloud bloomed into existence while the subtle runes on the backs of his hands came into being. Again, he marveled at the intricacy of the designs, and even then, he knew he was seeing only a fraction of the complexity. There were layers upon layers of symbols embedded in each rune, and he suspected that they went down to a microscopic level. He could've stared at them for an eternity and grasped only the tiniest bit of what made them tick. Luckily, he didn't need to understand the runes to accomplish his goal.

For the next few minutes, the runes, along with the clouds, flickered in and out of existence as he activated and deactivated the ability. It was all about focus. Without it, a mental command did nothing, but the moment he was properly focused, a thought was all it took. And while it was moderately difficult to maintain that level of focus, he had ample experience doing just that. It really wasn't so different than the mindset he adopted when stepping into the batter's box, something with which he was intimately familiar.

As he toggled the ability on and off, he studied the flows of energy that made it possible. The energy itself emanated from that core inside him, though it was subtly different from what accumulated with each kill. Zeke turned his attention to that ball of power, his focus drilling past the more nebulous cloud that was left over after his level, and soon, he found a minuscule sphere densely packed with energy. All his pathways led to that core, and it was the source of whatever powered his abilities.

For hours, Zeke sat in that cave, accompanied only by the corpses of the croco-rats as he focused inward, trying to get a feel for what he could do. His first discovery was that, now that he'd familiarized himself with the mechanics of the Framework, he found that activation of [**Leech Strike**] was easier than it had ever been before. It didn't require quite as much focus, and the ability asserted itself far more quickly than it had before.

This newfound ease of activation allowed him to study the way the energy flowed through him as he initiated it over and over. Over time, he came to recognize the current of energy as it pushed through his pathways, and he even found that he could influence it to some small degree. It sped up the activation by only an instant, but his brief experiences in fighting the croco-rats told him that such an advantage could mean the difference between life and death.

His study of his pathways gave him one final discovery, as well. The runes never truly went away; in fact, they were embedded deep within the pathways on his hands, invisible and unnoticed until he mentally triggered them. While some instinctive intuition told him that was important on its own, it also gave him an idea for how to activate his other ability. If the runes associated with [**Leech Strike**] were always there, then so too should the ones for [**Inspection**] be there, as well. So, with that in mind, he began to search his pathways for irregularities.

Again, he found himself in something of a trance as he mentally explored his pathways, his focus far exceeding anything he'd ever been capable of in his old life. Perhaps that was a function of his increased stats. Or maybe it was the new world. He sat there, his eyes closed as he continued his search, hardly aware of his surroundings. Time passed, hour after hour, as he explored every inch of his conduits of power embedded within his body. He started with his right hand, making his way up his arm. When that proved unfruitful, he inspected the opposite arm. Then his legs. His torso. And finally, after what was probably more than an entire day, he found what he was looking for.

The runes themselves weren't nearly as intricate as those associated with [**Leech Strike**]. Certainly, they were dizzyingly complex, at least on the surface. However, they weren't as deep; it was a simpler skill, but as he studied the runes, he noticed some similarities in the patterns. He didn't understand what any of it meant, of course, but he felt like, with enough time, he could crack the puzzle. That notion was so powerful that he spent almost as much time studying the runes as he'd spent searching his pathways, and he probably would've gone longer if the rumble in his stomach hadn't dragged him from his meditation.

Zeke's eyes flickered open, and after pushing his hunger aside, he focused on one of the croco-rat corpses and activated [**Inspection**]. It wasn't difficult at all to push the energy into the rune, and instantly, the familiar floating text flashed across his eyes.

Caracoa Troll Larva—Level 1 (Corpse)

He'd focused on one of the smaller creatures, and he was surprised to see that it was only level one. A quick inspection of the other corpses told him that each of the other, smaller creatures were of the same level. However, the bigger, occasionally bipedal ones were a level higher. It was a sobering discovery, finding that the dangerous creatures were so weak. What would happen if he ran into something a few levels higher than him? Certainly, he wouldn't live through such an encounter. No—he needed to get stronger if he wanted any hope of survival. A lot stronger. Luckily—or perhaps unluckily, depending on perspective—the cave system seemed designed to do just that. He had a suspicion that he'd have to kill a lot more of these troll larvae before he managed to satisfy his quest and escape the caves. In fact, he fully expected to be forced into combat with adult trolls, too. And they would be far more dangerous than the juveniles he'd found so far.

Bemused, Zeke shook his head as he contemplated his situation. He was fighting literal troll babies. And while there was a part of him that found his actions repulsive, it took only one look at the vicious creatures to dispel any sense of revulsion. Despite being infants, they were more than capable of ripping him to shreds. His scarred body was living proof of that. So, moral quandary of killing babies aside, it was kill or be killed. And he knew precisely which one he preferred.

On top of that, he needed to get stronger. In the few days since he'd been reborn, Zeke had had a chance to think about what he wanted out of his new life. Certainly, he had every intention of surviving; that was a given. And he would fight for that, tooth and nail. However, he knew it wasn't enough to simply keep living. He needed a goal. He needed something to shoot for.

Oberon had said that this new world needed heroes, implying that there was a battle of good versus evil overlaying everything that happened. He'd even intimated that there were higher planes. Was it possible that Zeke could become one of said heroes? And more, he wondered how strong he could become. In only a few days, his strength had grown by leaps and bounds. What would he look like in a few years? A decade? Imagining that kind of power was addictive in its own right, and knowing that it was within his grasp was very nearly motivation enough to push him forward.

More than any of that, though, was the thrill of battle itself. While he had been terrified every step of the way, Zeke had never felt more alive than when he faced off against the troll larvae. They had pushed him in a way he'd never experienced, and when he'd come out victorious, it had been intense, addictive, and very nearly overpowering. It was a rush unlike anything else, and even now, as he sat in the cave, he found himself wanting more—not because he was some sort of adrenaline junkie, but rather because he'd always loved pushing himself to the limit. And winning, of course. Emerging victorious from a life-and-death battle? It was easy to get caught up in that kind of thing.

In Zeke's junior year of high school, his team had advanced to the state championship. And with the game still scoreless in the final inning, he'd come up to bat against one of the top pitching prospects in the country. Zeke had faced him before and up until then had failed to achieve anything approaching success. But this was a game where if a hitter was successful 30 percent of the time, he went into the Hall of Fame, so when he stepped into that batter's box, he was still confident that he could come out on top. The at bat quickly progressed, with Zeke getting two strikes on him. However, on the third pitch, the pitcher made a mistake and left a ball over the middle of the plate. Zeke jumped on it, and as soon as the bat connected with the ball, he knew he'd done it. He had won not just the at bat, but the game itself. He didn't even need to watch the ball sail over the fence. He just knew.

Winning against the troll larva had felt like that, only magnified a thousand times by the stakes. And he craved more. So, all of that coalesced into a burning desire to forge ahead, to win, to push himself past his limits and into new territory. It was the most powerful feeling he had ever experienced. And, in his mind, it cemented his path.

Zeke knew that everyone wouldn't feel that way. The veil of mediocrity hung heavy over humanity, and he knew that most people would only do just enough to get by. He had experienced it himself when so many of his teammates had only done the bare minimum. Most hadn't even worked outside of practice. He'd never been given that choice, which was the one thing about his relationship with his father for which he was grateful.

With that in mind, he rose from his meditation and looked around the cave. His night vision hadn't gotten any better, so he didn't see much besides the stalagmites and ever-present mushrooms. And the corpses of his enemies, of course. Those hadn't gone anywhere, and they were starting to smell, too.

Zeke ignored it, instead focusing on one of the nearby mushrooms. As he activated his skill, the floating text identified the fungus.

Caracoan Blue-Spotted Mushroom—Consumable. +1 Vitality. Various alchemical uses.

One point to vitality? Was the effect permanent? If so, he'd just hit the jackpot because there were hundreds of the things within the cave. No wonder the fight had lasted so long; the troll larva had been munching on the mushrooms when he'd arrived. No doubt, they had insane vitality. Suddenly, Zeke didn't feel so bad about struggling with the juvenile trolls. However, it did foster a little doubt about what he would face against the adults he suspected were closer to the surface.

He pushed that aside, thinking that if the trolls were empowered by the mushrooms, then he would be, too. That would even the odds a bit. So, without further hesitation, he reached down and plucked one of the hand-sized mushrooms from the rocky terrain. As soon as Zeke touched it, he felt the glow of bundled energy within. He took a bite, and that energy surged through him. A quick check of his status told him that it hadn't affected his stats, though, so he continued to eat the thing. It wasn't until he'd swallowed the last bit, stem and all, that he was rewarded with the statistical bonus. Grinning to himself, he ate another. Then another. He gobbled each of them down, barely chewing. They didn't taste horrible, but they weren't good, either—not that he cared. He only wanted the increased vitality.

However, after he'd scarfed down the eleventh mushroom, he found himself disappointed when it didn't result in the expected stat increase. Was it defective? Perhaps it hadn't accumulated enough energy or something? But it had felt the same. It wasn't until he ate another that he came to the conclusion that he'd reached some sort of cap. Still, he wasn't too disappointed because he'd just increased his vitality by quite a bit.

With his hunger—both for sustenance and power—briefly sated, Zeke began exploring the cavern. It was about the size of a football field, but it felt much smaller because of how enclosed it was. Aside from the crevasse through which he'd entered, there were a handful of other exits, but he wasn't ready to leave. On top of that, the only other prominent feature within the cave was the small stream cutting through the center. It was the source of the sound of running water he'd heard earlier.

Suddenly, he became very aware of just how thirsty he was. It shouldn't have been surprising, given that days had passed since he'd been reborn, and in that time, he'd yet to drink a single drop of water. Clearly, his body's improved constitution had mitigated his need for water or food, at least to some degree, but it hadn't eliminated it altogether. So, it was with renewed eagerness that he quickly knelt beside the stream, cupped his hands, and withdrew a palmful of water.

Out of habit—he'd been using his ability every chance he could, if for no other reason than to practice—he inspected the water. He didn't expect to be able to identify it, but inspecting everything seemed like a good habit to cultivate. So, he was more than a little surprised when it worked.

Mana Water—Consumable. +1 Intelligence, +1 Wisdom. Various alchemical uses.

Zeke couldn't help but grin as he excitedly drank the water he'd collected. However, he was disappointed to see that it didn't have any effect on his stats. Figuring that he needed to drink more—or perhaps it was just how thirsty he was—he scooped another handful. Then another. And another after that. Finally, on the fifth, it seemed that he'd crossed some threshold, and he saw the increased intelligence and wisdom that he'd hoped to see. Still, he kept going until well after he'd gotten ten points in each. But no matter how much he drank after that, he didn't see any more increases. Instead, he reasoned that he'd reached the same cap he had with the mushrooms.

Not that he was complaining, of course. He'd gotten two levels worth of statistics, just for eating and drinking. It almost felt like he'd found some kind of cheat code. But he wasn't satisfied, either. He had no idea what the mechanics of the world really were, so he didn't know if he'd reached a hard cap on how many stats he could get from the mushrooms and mana water or if he simply needed to wait for his body to effectively reset. So, he settled down to wait, using that time to wash some of the gore and viscera from his scarred body. The water was soothing, even when it was applied only to his wounds, but it didn't result in any extra stats.

Once he'd overcome the worst of the filth, he sat down and continued his study of the runes associated with [**Leech Strike**]. He sat there, mentally examining them for hours until he finally decided to try again with the mushrooms. If there was a timer he needed to wait out, surely it would've passed by now. So, he pushed himself back to his feet, marveling at how much better he felt. It hadn't been that long, but even the worst of his wounds had healed by this point. However, most of them had left angry red scars—evidence of his struggle that he wore like badges of honor.

Quickly, he picked a few mushrooms, but he wasn't willing to brave the earthy taste without a little help. So, he crossed back to the stream, hoping to use the mana water to wash them down. When the two mixed in his mouth, though, he experienced a jolt of energy that almost felt like a physical blow. Reflexively, he spit it out, his mouth burning with the concoction.

"W-what the..."

He stared at the bits of mushroom on the rocky, now wet cave floor, the pain in his mouth fading. Something had obviously changed, and initially, he thought that it was his body rejecting the energy it couldn't use anymore. But one bite of a mushroom by itself put the lie to that.

Then it hit him. Alchemical uses.

Had mixing the two created something more than the sum of their parts? That seemed like the most reasonable explanation. But if that was the case, was the resulting mixture helpful or harmful? What would happen if he drank the mushroom-infused water?

His rational mind told him to simply move on. There was no reason to take such a risk. It would have been different if he had some way to mix the two and inspect it, but [Inspection] didn't work when he floated a few pieces of mushroom in a handful of water. No—if he intended to take his rudimentary potion, it would be without a safety net. For all he knew, it was a poison. Certainly, the burning of his mouth suggested as much.

But his every instinct screamed at him that he should do it anyway. It wasn't that he had some sixth sense about it. He had no clue what it even was. However, he felt like he couldn't get ahead without taking chances. Perhaps it was an opportunity to get a head start.

Or maybe he was looking too much into it, and it really was poison. He had no way of knowing.

"Go big or go home," he muttered to himself, his throat scratchy from lack of use. Nobody ever got ahead by playing it safe. So, having decided on his course of action, he didn't hesitate to get started. But that didn't mean he wouldn't be smart about it. Over the next few minutes, Zeke gathered ten more mushrooms, then set about tearing them into mostly equal pieces. Then, he divided the results into twenty mostly equal piles that he estimated would give the mixture of mana water and mushrooms something approaching a one-to-one ratio.

Once everything was prepared, he sat beside the stream, steadying himself before gathering the first pile of mushroom pieces. Holding them carefully, he dipped his cupped hands into the stream, letting the improvised container fill. Then, without another thought, he imbibed the concoction, ignoring the pain as the mushroom-infused liquid burned a path through his mouth and down his throat.

For a moment, disappointment bloomed in his mind as nothing happened. But then, there was an explosion in his core. It was violent and unrestrained, containing more energy than he'd ever felt before. He'd half expected the improvised potion to poison him, and he wasn't terribly far off the mark. A little energy is good, but too much can easily kill a person. Zeke found that out firsthand as the energies raged through his pathways, scorching them down to nothing.

But he had a plan, and he wasn't going to let something so small as unrelenting, agonizing pain stop him. Not when he could feel the power coursing through him. He pushed the pain to the back of his mind, and with trembling hands, he made another mixture, and a second later, a second stream of energy joined the first. The pain became exponentially worse, and he could feel the tears pouring down his cheeks.

He couldn't stop, though. In fact, he could barely think. So, mechanically, he kept going, imbibing one improvised potion after another until he'd taken everything he'd prepared. But it wasn't enough. Maybe it never would be.

Even as the agony scorched his pathways, Zeke's resolve never wavered. He never doubted the instincts that told him to keep going. Instead, he doubled down, crawling to another batch of mushrooms and gathering them as best he could. Once he had, he retreated to the stream and alternated between tossing back mushrooms and handfuls of water, letting them mix in his mouth. Predictably, as the energy rampaged through his body, stronger with each swallow, his mouth felt like it had become a mass of blisters. It was like drinking acid, and amid the pain, Zeke lost the ability to think rationally. Instead, he retreated inside of himself, going into a trance.

Over the next few hours—or it might've been days, for all he knew—Zeke continued to eat the mushrooms and drink the water. He never stopped, even when the inside of his mouth seemed like it had been liquified by the constant corrosion. His tongue withered away. His teeth were worn down to nothing. And his gums were a bloody mess. But he persisted because, inside, he was fighting a completely different battle as he tried to wrangle the energy. He hardly even noticed the ruin his mouth had become, instead focusing entirely on harnessing the tidal wave of energy coursing through his body.

It was wild. Foreign. It did not belong inside of him. And for the longest time, Zeke found himself fighting a losing battle. He knew something was missing, but he was flying blind. He had no idea what it could be. If he didn't figure it out soon, he knew he would die in that cave. Suddenly, the energy brushed against the core at his center, and realization dawned with him.

Imitating the way his [**Leech Strike**] snatched the life force of his enemies, he mentally snatched at the mana in his core. At first, he only brushed against the energy within, but after a few tries, he managed to drag a thread loose. As soon as he released it, it retracted back inside the core. But with that small success, Zeke redoubled his efforts. After a few more attempts, he could reliably drag it loose every time he tried. But with the energy stampeding unchecked through his pathways, he knew it was only a small victory. He needed more.

So, hour after hour, Zeke bent his will toward mastering that energy. And bit by bit, he managed a little more control. Finally, after what felt like an eternity, he managed to open the floodgates and release the mana within. With a deft touch, he guided his mana through his pathways, flooding them with everything he had. The core emptied at an astonishing rate, making Zeke wonder if he even had enough to do what he wanted to do. But the core was more densely packed than he expected, and soon, his pathways were completely infused with his mana. The mana surrounded the rampaging foreign energies, limiting its damage, but Zeke knew it wouldn't hold for long. Thankfully, he didn't need it to.

Exerting every ounce of his willpower, Zeke contracted his mana, strangling the foreign energy. A new level of agony erupted within his mind, but Zeke persisted. Anything else, and he knew he would die right then and there, forgotten and alone. Even if he managed to see his plan through, he knew the chances of death were high. But that was the whole point, wasn't it? Nothing comes for free, and he suspected that was doubly true in his new world. True progress didn't come without a significant risk. And he'd just risked everything for what he hoped would be an increase in his power.

Suddenly, something snapped, and his mana swallowed the energy, merging with it. That's when Zeke lost control. In fact, he lost consciousness altogether. But as the darkness closed in on him, he couldn't help but smile a bloody smile. His lips and the better part of his face were ruined by the acidic concoction, but he'd managed a victory nonetheless.

7

DRASTIC IMPROVEMENT

Zeke's eyes fluttered open, and for a brief moment, he thought he was hallucinating. The familiar yet stark confines of the cavern where he'd fought his most recent life-and-death battle was gone, and in its place was a vibrant ecosystem full of color, light, and life. After a few minutes of adjustment, he noticed landmarks he recognized, though with his heightened senses, they were all but unrecognizable.

The nearby stream was mostly the same, though it gave off a faint, green shimmer, but the mushrooms that had been the other part of the catalyst bore glowing blue spots scattered along their caps. And that wasn't all, either. Moss he hadn't really noticed before gave off a faint white luminescence, as well, bathing the entire cavern in light. But it wasn't just the visual differences that struck him; rather, the totality of his senses seemed on the verge of being overwhelmed. There was the faint rustling of smaller, previously unnoticed vermin that had come to feed on the corpses of the slain troll larvae. A soft circulation of air emanating from one of the nearby exits. A scent of decay that, while not any stronger, felt deeper and more significant than anything Zeke had ever smelled before. He was so overwhelmed that it was a few seconds before he even noticed a slight pinch on his bare ankle.

Zeke looked down to see that a troll larva, smaller than any he'd seen so far, was gnawing on his ankle. Curiously, it couldn't break his skin, though. Instead, it worried the same bit of skin with its sharp teeth, committed to getting at the meat underneath. With a sharp kick, Zeke sent the vermin-like creature sailing across the cavern to collide with a stalagmite with unprecedented force. It was dead the moment it hit, though Zeke didn't feel the familiar influx of energy. When he used his identification skill on it, he saw that it was only level one. He must have crossed some sort of threshold when he'd reached level three, and it was now too low-level to give him experience.

With that realization, any plans of going on a rampage and killing hordes of the creatures in order to farm levels were dashed. Not that it was terribly surprising, of course. Nor was it disappointing. The Framework wanted to challenge its denizens—a sentiment Zeke could certainly get behind. Beating up on weaklings wasn't a notion Zeke relished. So, for once, he and the Framework were on the same page.

Slowly, Zeke took stock of his body. He still remembered the unbelievable pain he'd experienced after mixing the mushrooms and mana water, and he was horrified that he'd pushed forward, regardless of the clear damage he was doing. It was like he'd completely lost control of his own actions, and that control had been given over to a driving hunger for improvement at any cost. It was as if his every cell screamed for him to keep going, and his mind—and subsequently, his body—had followed suit. Looking back, it was absolutely the wrong choice, even if he'd come out the other side stronger.

But at the same time, he felt better than he ever had in his entire afterlife. The pain was completely gone, and in addition to his improved senses, he felt incredibly fit. More than that, though, the evidence of his poor decision to keep going was entirely gone. He distinctly remembered his jaw actually melting off, but a quick inspection told him that it was still whole. Looking for an explanation, Zeke opened his status page.

Name	Ezekiel Blackwood
Class	N/A
Level	3
Race	Human (G)
Alignment	Isphodel
Achievements	First Blood, Hasty Evolution
Strength	42

Agility	33
Dexterity	36
Endurance	46
Vitality	54
Intelligence	36
Wisdom	34
Unassigned Attribute Points	0

Upon seeing his statistics, Zeke had to do a double take. Unless he was seeing things—which, given what he'd just gone through, was a distinct possibility—his power had very nearly doubled since the last time he'd looked at his status. While he'd expected a big jump from a couple of stats—namely, vitality, intelligence, and wisdom, due to the mushrooms and mana water, respectively—he hadn't expected the sharp increase in his other stats. His strength had ballooned, and he hadn't even gained a level. As he delved into his submenus, he soon found out why. First, he had a new achievement:

Hasty Evolution—Endure the agony of evolving your race before Level 10! +10 to all stats, +5% to Endurance per level.

For more than a few seconds, Zeke could only stare at the achievement he'd earned. Not only was it confirmation that he had, indeed, evolved his race, but it also told him where most of the extra stats had come from. Ten extra points to every category was incredibly powerful, and that alone was worth more than two levels worth of stats. On top of that, he'd received a 5 percent bonus to his endurance. Right now, it only accounted for a couple of extra points, but it could prove very meaningful in the future.

But that didn't account for everything because his racial evolution was also the source of a few points on its own.

Human (G): Humans are the most prevalent sentient race in the multiverse. However, they are afflicted with unrepentant mediocrity. This

is both a blessing and a curse because, while they excel at nothing, they are unfettered by natural attunements or blatant weaknesses. Upgradable.

In the submenu below that, his racial characteristics were broken down into two categories.

Body (G): Determines physical limitations. +3 Strength, Agility, Dexterity, Endurance, and Vitality per level. Upgradable.
Soul (G): Determines spiritual limitations. +3 Intelligence and Wisdom per level. Upgradable.

Zeke was floored by how much he'd improved. Even if he hadn't gotten an achievement for improving his race at such an early level, he would've been ecstatic with the benefits of the evolution alone. Not only did it obviously improve his senses, but it also provided raw stats. But was that the limit? It was difficult to tell, even after he tried to test things out. The massive influx of stats skewed his perception, but he suspected that it wasn't solely responsible for how much better he felt. Clearly, the racial evolution was more than just an increase in stats.

However, Zeke didn't have time to rest; despite his obvious strides toward greater power, he was still stranded deep within enemy territory, and he knew that, even with his increased stats, it wouldn't be an easy task to escape the troll-infested caves. After all, if there were larvae here, then it stood to reason that the adults wouldn't be far away. And after seeing how vicious the infants could be, Zeke had little desire to face a full-grown troll, even if he knew that was probably where the Framework was leading him.

So, after limbering up a little, Zeke quickly made his way to one of the cavern's six exits. Though they were far from uniform, the exits shared certain characteristics. First among those was that they all led gradually upward, just like the passage from which he'd come. Even if logic didn't dictate that he was heading toward the surface, that fact would've been hint enough at his eventual goal. In addition to the grade, their sizes weren't terribly dissimilar, with the biggest, measuring at about nine feet from floor to ceiling, only half again the size of the smallest. The other's sizes were scattered within that same range.

It was the differences that Zeke focused on, though—the biggest of which was the airflow. With his increased sensitivity, Zeke could feel a slight current of air emanating from each of the exits, but one was obviously stronger than all the others. And that's the direction he decisively chose. Soon, he was on his way away from the cavern that had given him so very much.

Zeke's newly enhanced senses bombarded him with stimuli. From the subtly glowing mosses to the sounds of insects scurrying away, he was very nearly overwhelmed with too much information. However, it didn't take him long to learn to filter out the things he didn't need, pushing them to the background where they didn't affect the forefront of his mind.

This almost proved deadly when, after almost an entire day's worth of travel, he found himself at an intersection, where he was confronted by a pair of trolls. Both parties were surprised because, at first, none of them reacted. Instead, they just stared at one another in confusion. Zeke used **[Inspection]**.

Caracoa Troll Adolescent—Level 4

It was as he'd suspected the moment he'd laid eyes on the creatures. Both walked on two legs, and though they resembled their younger brethren, they had clearly evolved. Gone were the short, stubby legs, replaced by much longer limbs. They were still small—only about five feet tall, in fact—but their arms were far too long, and they were tipped with lethal claws. Their faces remained much the same, though some small details had changed. Chiefly, the adolescents had tiny, pointed ears on the sides of their heads and a few extra teeth jammed into their mouths.

But most striking was a glimmer of sapience in their eyes. Zeke had no idea how he recognized it, but it was clear in an instant. These creatures weren't the dumb beasts he'd fought before. They were intelligent life, and judging by the crude clubs they carried, they weren't about to let him off without a fight.

Time reasserted itself as Zeke sprang into action only a moment before the adolescent trolls raised their clubs. Zeke was on them before they had a chance to further react, his fist erupting with devastating power.

On the surface, Zeke knew how much his stats had improved. His strength had doubled since the last time he'd fought. Even so, he was surprised when his fist connected with the first troll's jaw. In the space of an instant, the lower half of the monster's face practically disintegrated, sending blood, scaly flesh, and shards of bone rocketing toward the wall. Zeke didn't stop, though, sending another punch into the creature's stomach. To his surprise, instead of simply knocking the wind from the troll's lungs, his hand broke through the thing's belly and into its guts, not stopping until it hit the troll's vertebrae. With a bestial roar, he grabbed ahold of it and yanked as hard as he could, ripping the spine from its body. It was dead in an instant, collapsing into a twitching heap as soon as Zeke let it go.

Barely a second had passed, and already, one of the trolls was down. If the remaining monster had been slightly more intelligent, it would've fled while Zeke overwhelmed its comrade. Instead, it could only stare in surprise and horror as Zeke dismantled its companion. That hesitation proved fatal as Zeke whipped around to face the unlucky troll, a grin creeping across his blood-spattered face.

Only a handful of seconds later, and he'd taken the remaining threat down. This time, he'd simply collapsed the thing's skull with a well-aimed punch. As he stood there looking down on his handiwork, Zeke couldn't help but feel a sense of pleasure. Not that he'd killed intelligent creatures. That part he studiously ignored. Rather, he was more than pleased with the effect of his new stats. Before his racial evolution, his strength had been stuck at twenty-three. It had increased by a fair margin, but it felt like the effect was far greater than the sum of the stats. Perhaps as the stats got higher, they simply meant more. As always, though, he really had no way to know. But what he did know was that his chances of escaping the caves had just greatly improved, which was all he could really ask for.

With the threat tended to, Zeke took stock. He hadn't been hurt at all, so he didn't need to rest and recuperate—which was a first for him. He hadn't even activated his [**Leech Strike**], which was a mistake that would've meant death in any of his previous fights. He'd have to remember it next time because he wasn't so naive that he thought the rest of his journey to the surface would prove so easily conquered.

That in mind, he remembered that the pair of trolls had been armed. After a quick survey of the tunnel, Zeke found a sturdy wooden club. Standing on its end, the tapered club was nearly as long as its previous wielder was tall, and at its widest end, it was probably seven or eight inches across. Judging by its size, it should've been an unwieldy piece of knobby lumber. However, with his vastly increased strength, it almost felt too light. It had a strip of leather from some unidentifiable animal wound around the narrow end to create a grip. It wasn't exactly a baseball bat, but it still felt familiar, nonetheless.

And didn't Oberon say that he had some sort of proficiency with blunt weapons? He was eager to find out what, precisely, that meant. So, armed as he was, he set off down the tunnel, hunting for more trolls on whom he could test his newfound might.

8

PAIN

Zeke's war club crashed against the full-grown troll's ribs, and he was rewarded with the sound of bones cracking. Before he'd upgraded his race, he never would've heard it, but now, he could tell how many had broken and how severely they'd been fractured. Two had snapped in half, while three more were merely cracked. Given the troll's durability, that wasn't such a bad result.

He had been stalking through the caves for more than a week since he'd acquired his club, and in that time, Zeke had come to feel practically invincible. He had killed dozens of adolescent trolls, in addition to twice as many larvae, and none of them had proved even the least bit challenging. Most were felled by a single swing of his club, and none lasted more than two. Despite cutting a path of murder through the caves, he hadn't gotten another level, leaving him stuck at level three.

His trek through the cave system made it clear that it was quite a bit more elaborate than he'd first expected. He'd covered mile after mile of the tunnels, and he still hadn't discovered the exit. More, he was certain that he'd ascended at least a couple of miles, but still, he felt that the surface was far away. In short, he'd resigned himself to being stuck in the caves for the foreseeable future. Perhaps this new world was all underground. He had no way of knowing, so he'd long since decided to push such thoughts from his mind. However, Zeke's intuition told him that, so long as he kept putting one foot in front of the other, he'd find his way to the surface. So, that's precisely what he did, killing one troll after another along the way—which is how he found himself facing off with a trio of full-grown monsters.

For a troll, progressing through adolescence seemed to entail a massive growth spurt, and unlike the younger examples, these fully grown trolls towered over Zeke by six inches or more, and they likely outweighed him by at least half. Their green, sporadically scaled bodies were densely packed with muscle, and their long arms dangled half again farther than they would on a similarly sized human. Their legs were still a bit short compared to their torsos, but all in all, they were extraordinarily imposing from a physical standpoint.

Or they would've been for most people. For Zeke's part, though, he could only feel a sense of excitement because with their growth came a couple of extra levels, and he hoped that would be enough to get him enough experience to progress to level four. Provided he could actually kill the things, that is.

The other major difference between the trolls he'd already killed and the ones he faced now was more annoying than dangerous. For now, at least. More than once, he'd already felled each of the trolls in front of him, but after only a few seconds, they'd managed to heal from whatever wound he managed to inflict, and it wasn't long after that they would rejoin the fight.

Was it the mushrooms they fed on as larvae? They'd given Zeke ten extra vitality, so it wasn't outside the realm of possibility that they'd do the same for the trolls, especially considering it was their primary source of sustenance. However, Zeke had seen the effect of vitality, and he knew that a mere ten points couldn't account for such rapid healing. If he had to guess, he would've put their vitality at double his own fifty-four. At least. Probably closer to triple.

Their rapid healing aside, the trolls were a lot stronger than their younger brethren, as well, which meant that when they attacked Zeke, he felt it, even when he blocked their strikes. If he failed to block, he inevitably picked up wounds, despite his high endurance. Luckily, these three didn't have weapons, fighting instead with their inch-long claws. Dangerous, to be sure, but unless Zeke made a huge mistake and let them get a solid blow in, the claws wouldn't be enough to fatally injure him.

He hoped.

Already, his body sported a dozen long lacerations, and there was a huge chunk of his shoulder missing from when one of the trolls had managed to latch on with its crocodilian teeth. And despite the effects of [**Leech Strike**] combined with his high vitality and endurance, Zeke could feel that the accumulation of so many injuries was beginning to wear him down. Meanwhile, the trolls seemed mostly unaffected by the many times he'd managed to connect with his club. The only benefit seemed to be that they were hesitant to close within range, proving that while they might be able to miraculously heal from the injuries he'd inflicted, they weren't invulnerable to pain. Having your ribs caved in by a club couldn't have felt good, and the trolls were loath to reexperience it. Zeke could certainly sympathize with the monsters, given how often his own body had been broken in the few weeks since he'd been reborn. Their real mistake was letting their fear of pain affect them, which Zeke strove not to do. He wasn't always successful, but at least he recognized it as a weakness, which was the first step toward conquering it.

Zeke withdrew his club from where it had collided with the lead troll's ribs, immediately redirecting it in a horizontal swing toward another. The troll reacted quickly, leaping back to try to avoid the deadly club, but Zeke still clipped it. The swing held enough force to spin the hulking creature around, but not enough to truly harm the thing—the story of the fight, so far. The biggest problem was that, while Zeke had incredible stats for his level and at least some proficiency with the bat-like club, he'd never been trained as a fighter. He could swing with great force, and he usually hit what he was aiming for, but in a fight, that was only part of the equation. Fighting with a club wasn't just about swinging as hard as you could. It was about angles, anticipation, and timing—characteristics Zeke sorely lacked. Until now, he'd been able to simply overpower his foes. But the fully grown trolls were strong enough to make that impossible.

But as much as Zeke felt like he was banging his head against a wall—sometimes, while having his head literally banged against a wall—he persisted. Could he have retreated? Maybe. The trolls were quick in short bursts, but they couldn't run particularly fast, and if he managed to knock them down, his escape would be all but assured. However, Zeke's time in the caves had fostered in him a stoic inability to surrender, even when the results seemed inevitable. He'd fought one battle after another, against the trolls, the concoction that had evolved his race, and against the very situation that seemed intent on killing him, and after a couple of weeks, he'd been reforged into an entirely different person. A nearly feral being who, when pushed, simply couldn't fathom giving up. So, he forged ahead, swinging his club with all his might.

Zeke wasn't a beast, though, and despite giving himself to a more primal nature, he wasn't unthinking—which was why, when he swung, he'd aimed for the one target the troll in front of him couldn't easily regrow. The club connected with the monster's overlarge head just below its sharply tapered ear. Driven forward by Zeke's superhuman strength, it crashed into the side of the troll's head with truly epic force. While the trolls' healing ability was off the charts, their endurance wasn't anything special, so the impact caved its skull in with relative ease, sending chunks of bone and brain matter to splatter against the tunnel's wall. The rest of the troll's body soon followed, driven by the momentum of Zeke's strike to crash against the rocks. A surge of energy told Zeke that he'd killed it, and for the first time in weeks, he actually felt like he'd progressed in his level. It wasn't enough to push him over the top, but the energy was significant, nonetheless.

The possibility of gaining a level sparked a renewed sense of vigor within him, and Zeke soon followed up his fatal strike with another swing aimed at the next troll's head. However, the monster danced backward with an agility that belied its large frame. Creatures that big shouldn't have been capable of moving so quickly, he thought, but he didn't let up. Instead, he followed that swing with another, hitting the troll's upper arm. The troll let out a curiously high-pitched scream of pain as the bone cracked, and the force of the blow broke the skin. The damage was truly negligible, though, and it was soon negated by the troll's insane vitality.

But that didn't mean Zeke let up. Instead, he grabbed ahold of his inhuman endurance and agility, forcing the speed of his attacks to new heights. His giant club wasn't precisely a blur—it was far too big and unwieldy for that—but the difference was noticeable, and before long, the troll was pressed against the cave wall by his furious assault.

The advantage couldn't last, though. If he'd been facing off against a single enemy, he'd have beaten the thing down without much trouble. But even with one of the trolls having his skull crushed in, there was still a third who'd been recuperating on the ground. Until he wasn't.

Zeke's back erupted into agony as the third troll raked its claws down his back, gashing deep and raking against his ribs. Immediately, blood erupted from the wounds, but the troll wasn't finished. Another slash. Then another, slicing him to ribbons, all in the space of a second. In his mind, he'd once compared the troll larvae to wolverines or badgers due to their ferocity, and it seemed that age hadn't robbed their older brothers of their savagery.

He cried out in pain, spinning around, his club leading the way. But by this point, his attacker had already sprung away to safety, and the war club missed by nearly a foot. What's more, as soon as he turned his back, the other troll leaped into the fray, its own claws doing a fair imitation of its companion's. Soon, Zeke's back was a ragged mess of bloody ribbons of flesh. He ignored the agony. After all, anything else would lead to his demise. And he'd long since mastered the art of suffering. Still, the pain did push him to his limits; he was only human, and the human mind can only take so much pain before it begins to shut down completely.

Gritting his teeth, Zeke sidestepped and turned as he tried to reposition himself so that the trolls could only attack from one direction. It took a few seconds, during which he had to dodge another few attacks, but eventually, he found himself facing off against the pair.

Pain was such a strange thing. In some cases, it was crippling, completely overwhelming a person until they could no longer function. In others, it ignited a fire within them, spurring them to feats they otherwise could never have accomplished. But a scant few people were able to simply push that pain into the background. They still felt it, but they didn't let it affect their actions.

History is full of tales of such people. From gladiators of old to the more familiar athletes of the world he'd left behind, stories of men and women who kept going despite grievous injuries abound. A soldier who gets shot a half dozen times but still manages to drag his comrades to safety. A football player who plays a game with multiple broken ribs or a punctured lung. A track star who manages to break a world record despite a broken bone in his foot. Some people are simply built differently, and in the right situations—or the wrong ones, depending on how a person looks at it—they can truly show just how unique they are.

Zeke had always been one of those people. As a child, when his father had taught him how to block errant pitches by repeatedly throwing baseballs at him, he'd been forced to learn the value of endurance. And given that his father hadn't let him wear any equipment, there was also an added lesson in pain tolerance.

People had always called him tough. And maybe that was true, but Zeke didn't really see it that way. He'd just been cursed with a father who'd pushed him to develop the ability to endure far past what a normal person could be expected to withstand so he could accomplish his goals. His time in the caves had only reinforced that lesson, and it had unwittingly become a mainstay of his fighting mentality.

He wouldn't let something as simple as a ruined back stop him. Not so long as he had breath in his body. So, with an audible growl, he resumed his barrage, pelting the trolls with one blow after another. Bones cracked. Chunks of flesh went flying. And the agonized wails of his opponents echoed through the cave. Still, he pressed on, looking for the opening that would let him finish the fight.

Seconds turned into minutes, and minutes turned into more than an hour, eventually sapping even him of his strength. The trolls were no better off, and as sharp as their claws were, they'd grown so exhausted that they couldn't muster enough force to puncture Zeke's tough skin. More than ever, he knew he could flee. He could run away, recuperate, and come back to fight another day. The trolls were in no condition to follow, so his escape was almost assured.

But Zeke didn't have it in him. And besides, he was winning.

No sooner had the thought crossed his mind than the trolls acted. One swung for his face, a blow Zeke instinctively raised his club to block. A searing agony erupted in his stomach an instant later as the other troll took advantage of the opening and slashed its claws across his midsection, disemboweling him. It must've used every ounce of its remaining strength, but it was enough for its claws to puncture his abdominal wall and rip into his intestines.

Zeke screamed in mingled terror and pain, his club arcing out instinctively. It crushed the first attacker's skull, sending it flying into its companion. But by then, the damage had been done. Zeke looked down to see his insides snaking out of his stomach; it almost looked like a bloody sausage casing. Immediately, he clapped his hand over the grievous wound, stuffing his intestines back where they belonged.

The final troll rose to its knees and glared at him. It barked unintelligibly, but Zeke didn't hear it. He wasn't thinking as he stepped forward, his bare feet crunching on the loose, scattered rocks that made up the cave floor. Then, gathering strength he didn't know he still had in him, Zeke hefted the club with one hand before sending it crashing down on the kneeling troll. It blocked with crossed arms, eliciting a sickening crunch as they buckled. Wailing, it hunkered down, covering its head with its ruined arms. Zeke didn't care. Pulling his hand from the gaping wound in his belly, he grasped his club in a two-handed grip, then raised it high over his head. After pausing for only an instant, he roared a bestial roar as the club descended, powered by every ounce of force he could muster.

Then, he did it again.

And again.

Over and over, he bashed his club against the troll until it was little more than a pile of blood, scales, and slimy flesh. Even then, he kept going, tears of pure emotion tracing a path through the blood and gore covering his face as he screamed his frustration away.

Finally, his strength gave out, and he collapsed atop his victim, victorious. A familiar warmth erupted from his core, spreading through his body as he gained a level. It took care of some of the smaller wounds he had collected throughout the battle, but the more serious injuries on his back and, more importantly, the gash across his stomach, only got marginally better. It was enough to keep his innards where they belonged, but little more.

But he had won, and against three monsters twice his level. Despite the agony still coursing unmitigated through his body, he couldn't help but smile an exhausted smile. However, he knew he couldn't remain stationary for long. His battle had surely attracted the attention of other trolls, and it wouldn't be long before reinforcements arrived. So, he slowly rose on unsteady feet and took stock of his slain foes.

They'd been dressed in simple loincloths—thankfully, as he had little interest in seeing whatever hung between their legs. But one of them had a small pouch tied around its waist. So, he bent near the corpse to retrieve it. As he was untying the rope that the creature had been using as a rudimentary belt, Zeke found himself staring at one of the wounds he'd created. He could visibly see the injury healing, like tiny tendrils of flesh wriggling out to connect with other threads. Luckily, it had been confirmed dead by the energy he'd received, so he likened it to death twitches. Still, it was incredibly creepy, so he quickly retrieved the pouch and backed away, careful not to reopen the wound in his belly.

Inside the pouch was a small stone no bigger than a golf ball, and it was inscribed with what looked like a rudimentary rune. He stared at it for a couple of seconds before a spark of inspiration told him to open up his core and push a bit of his mana into the ball. When he did, a spark erupted above the ball. He repeated it a few more times before he realized that it was a fire starter. Immediately, his grin widened. It was quite cool in parts of the cave system, so a fire—should he find enough fuel—would be a welcome thing indeed.

The only other thing inside the pouch was a stone-bladed knife with nothing but a bit of wound twine for a hilt. It was small—no bigger than a handspan long—and brittle, so it wouldn't be very effective in a battle. But it was extremely sharp, so he figured it would still be useful.

He was in the middle of inspecting the small knife when he heard heavy footfalls coming from down the cave. Even after weeks of living with his improved senses, Zeke still wasn't entirely accustomed to them, so he had trouble discerning just how many pairs of feet were stomping their way through the cave ahead of him. Nor did he know precisely how far away they were. However, he knew there were far more than the three he'd just fought, and they were progressively getting closer.

As quickly as he could, he tied the pouch around his waist. However, it was only a couple of seconds before the lumbering form of a troll came barreling around the corner. It locked its eyes on him, and for a brief moment, did nothing. Then, it barked something in what Zeke had come to recognize as some guttural form of communication, receiving a series of other barks in return.

"Shit," he muttered before turning on his heel and sprinting away.

9

DESPERATE ESCAPE

Zeke barreled down the tunnels like a runaway train, his speed and injuries mingling to undermine any sense of control and sending him skidding into various cave walls as he tried to follow the tunnel's twists and turns. Meanwhile, a horde of trolls were in hot pursuit, enraged by the murder of their fellows. He'd barely caught a glimpse of his pursuers, but what he'd seen had told him that this was a fight he simply couldn't win. There was a huge difference between standing against long odds and committing suicide, and he had no illusions which category fighting the rest of those trolls would fall into. So, he ran, his bare feet slapping against the rocky ground as he traversed the maze of tunnels.

When he'd first been reincarnated in the blasted troll caves, the path had been relatively straightforward. However, soon after that first cavern in which he'd experienced his racial evolution, the cave system had spread out into a spiderweb of caverns, tunnels, and crevasses. Until this point, Zeke had simply followed his instincts when choosing a route, which had led him ever upward, his choices reinforced by the fact that the trolls continued to get stronger the farther he went. That strategy had backfired, though, because he'd obviously angered what seemed like an entire village of the monsters, and he knew that if they reached him, he wouldn't survive for long. Certainly, he might take a few with him, but there was no way Zeke could defeat so many—especially considering he'd been disemboweled and pushed to the end of his rope by only three.

Clutching his wounded belly, Zeke fled as fast as his feet could take him, randomly choosing his directions. And soon, he was rewarded with the discovery of a wide stream that crisscrossed a gargantuan cavern. Or perhaps it would've been better to call it a river, considering that it was at least fifty yards across. Stepping up to the edge, he peered down the length of the river, and he discovered that it soon disappeared underground. Just as Zeke was trying to figure out what to do, agony exploded in his shoulder as something slammed into him. The momentum of the blow was so great that it lifted him from his feet and sent him flying twenty feet toward the middle of the river.

Midair, another burst of pain erupted in his lower back before he splashed into the black water, the pain of his myriad wounds reaching an unprecedented level. Zeke fancied himself a fairly tough guy—and his experiences supported that assessment—but there was a limit to human endurance, a threshold he seemed to have finally reached. Unconsciousness threatened to overwhelm him, but it was staved off by the freezing water that enveloped him.

For a moment, panic seized his heart, but with a mental effort, he shoved it aside. After all, he'd been tempered by his weeks-long life-and-death struggle with the various trolls, so one more brush with mortality wasn't enough to send him plummeting into panic. Quickly, Zeke took stock of his situation, noting that he had a pair of long, wrist-thick poles jutting from his body. Spears, his sluggish mind realized. These trolls had graduated from clubs to spears. And they were obviously skilled at using them, too. He'd been running at a breakneck pace, skidding across the tunnels without much rhyme or reason, and they'd still managed to hit him from forty yards away. Zeke would have been impressed if he wasn't on the verge of passing out from blood loss and exhaustion.

The current was incredibly swift, and before Zeke could really take stock, he found himself being pulled beneath the water and below ground. Suddenly, one of the spears in his back snagged against the water-filled tunnel's ceiling, and with an explosion of blood, the weapon was ripped free. Zeke let out a wordless scream, swallowing what felt like gallons of water as he was swept further down the underground river.

Thankfully, with his increased constitution, the necessity of breathing had been mitigated. He still needed oxygen, but it wasn't as necessary as it had been before his rebirth into the new world. So, he didn't run the risk of suffocating anytime soon. But he also had no idea when he'd get the chance to resurface, either. So, it was with mounting trepidation that he stopped wasting his energy on fighting the current; he couldn't swim against it, anyway, so his only option was to ride it out.

At least he'd left the trolls far behind, though. That was the only bright side to his current situation, as far as he could tell.

No sooner had he thought that than he was spit out of the river, only to find himself in free fall. He windmilled his arms, but he was no more capable of flight than before, so he was soon plummeting down a steep, vertical shaft. Zeke fell for a few seconds before he splashed into a wide pool, soon banging his head against the unforgiving bottom of the pond.

Stars floated in front of his eyes, but his survival instinct, coupled with his Framework-enhanced durability, kept him conscious enough to push himself to the edge of the pool, where he soon collapsed upon the smooth rocks. Behind him, the waterfall roared, but otherwise, he was alone. It seemed that the trolls didn't want to kill him badly enough to follow into the river. Though he had a sneaking suspicion that if they had, they wouldn't have fared so well as him.

He lay there on his stomach for some indeterminate time, wallowing in his own pain. The wound in his stomach had broken open again, but at some point, his abdominal wall had reformed, so at least he didn't have to worry about his organs spilling out anymore. Still, the laceration was deep, and it had plenty of company. Wounds from his battle as well as his trip down the underground river crisscrossed his body.

Finally, a creeping numbness in Zeke's shoulder reminded him of the spear still sticking out of his back. The thing had struck him just above his shoulder blade, so it wasn't a life-threatening injury. But it hurt. A lot. And the wound wouldn't heal until he removed the obstruction. So, reaching back with his other arm, he awkwardly grabbed the shaft and yanked the spear loose.

An anguished whimper escaped from between his lips. Without the adrenaline coursing through his veins, he could feel each laceration, every bruise, and the numerous broken bones throughout his body. And he wanted nothing more than to simply give up, then and there. The pain he could mostly deal with. It wasn't pleasant, but he knew it would eventually fade. However, he'd spent months climbing through the caves, and suddenly, he'd fallen back to the very bottom. What's more, he'd found a challenge he couldn't meet head-on.

Until now, Zeke hadn't actually tasted defeat, and he'd grown confident in his strength. But now? He'd run away like a coward. Certainly, it was the right decision. Rationally, he knew he didn't stand a chance against a dozen trolls or more. He had struggled with three, after all. But just because it was logical didn't mean it sat well with him.

Oberon had told him that this new world needed heroes, and he had long since decided to answer that call. But what kind of hero runs away from dangerous monsters? Retreat was a valid tactic. He knew that. It didn't make him feel any better about his obvious weakness, though.

Zeke lay unmoving for hours as his body repaired itself. Long after he normally would've risen, he remained motionless as he wrestled with his own feelings of inadequacy. It was the same as it had ever been; growing up, he'd never met his own expectations. Sure, he had been an elite baseball prospect with a bright future, but with each at bat where he failed to get a hit, he couldn't help but dwell on his shortcomings. He wanted to be perfect. That was the goal. And in a game where seven or eight times out of ten, you were likely to fail, that was not a productive attitude.

Zeke knew where it came from, too. His father had been a harsh taskmaster who demanded perfection at every turn. And what's worse, he wasn't shy about verbally abusing Zeke when he did fail. He'd been yelled at, both in public and in private, called a hundred derogatory names. It had been humiliating, especially in front of his friends, and it had given him something of a complex about failure. He had thought that, with his father's sudden departure from his life, he'd conquered it for good, but lying there in that cave, it resurfaced anew. And it was at least as overwhelming as his other, more physical injuries.

After a while, Zeke realized something, though—he might have lost the battle, but it didn't mean he had to lose the war. Sure, he wasn't strong enough now, but who was to say how strong he could become? In a few levels, he might be able to take out an entire army of the monsters. And as for his father? Well, the man was dead and gone, and it wasn't likely Zeke would ever see him again.

Zeke had died and was reborn. He had left the old world and his old life behind. It didn't even exist anymore, according to Oberon. He'd fought tooth and nail so far, and he'd already overcome great odds. So, it was high time he left his old insecurities behind. With a mental push, he shoved his issues into the back of his mind and focused on what really mattered—survival.

Climbing the rest of the way out of the pool, Zeke examined his body. Every inch of him still ached, and some of the deeper wounds—most notably, the one in his belly—were still far from entirely healed. But he was mostly out of the woods, in terms of survival. Which left him with one more task to do before he resumed his long journey out of the cave system. When he'd killed the three trolls, he'd gained a level, so, with a little anticipation, he opened his status page.

After a few minutes, Zeke decided to split his points between agility, endurance, and vitality, allocating six points in agility, four points in vitality, and the remaining five in endurance.

Name	Ezekiel Blackwood
Class	N/A
Level	4
Race	Human (G)
Alignment	Isphodel
Achievements	First Blood, Hasty Evolution
Strength	45
Agility	42
Dexterity	39
Endurance	57
Vitality	61
Intelligence	39
Wisdom	37
Unassigned Attribute Points	0

Judging by his starting point, Zeke's stats truly were getting monstrous, and he couldn't help but wonder if other people had gotten the same opportunities he had. Surely, he hadn't been singled out, but he found it difficult to believe that others would've chosen to mix the mushrooms and the water; most probably wouldn't have even tried, instead rushing through the caves to reach the top. Perhaps it was a test, of sorts.

Shaking his head, Zeke rose to his feet and stretched. He couldn't help but shiver. Not only had his clothes long since been ripped to shreds, but the caves were damp and clammy, which reminded him of the curious rock he'd looted from the troll. He took it out of the pouch he'd tied around his waist and injected a bit of mana, causing a spark. If he could find something to burn, he could make a fire, but that was a big if, considering that the only wood he'd seen was his club and the spears the trolls had thrown at him.

Next, he looked at the small, stone-bladed knife. After running it across his arm, he found that it was sharp enough, but he knew it would prove too brittle to use in battle. Its original owner had probably thought the same, considering it hadn't tried to stab him with it. Still, it was a good find, and he replaced the items in the pouch.

Finally, he examined the spear, and he was happy to note that it seemed well-balanced. It also had an iron tip, which made it far more suitable for battle than the knife. Though it was crude, it seemed solid, with the head held firmly in place by some sort of rawhide. Zeke suspected that it would prove a worthy addition to his arsenal, but he very much preferred his club, which he'd miraculously held on to during his trip down the waterfall.

With that done, he settled down against the cave wall to recuperate. At some point, he dozed off, and he slept a thankfully dreamless sleep.

10

ONE IN A MILLION

Abby pushed a stray lock of blonde hair out of her eyes as she sat in the guild lobby. Glancing around, she saw plenty of familiar faces. Vladimir sat nearby, decked in furs and cradling his huge axe like it was a long-lost lover. He was an enormous, imposing man, but he didn't intimidate Abby; she knew he was something of a paper tiger. Even though he had an impressively massive physique, Abby knew that her stats far exceeded his. Not that she was an aberration or anything. She was a bit better than average, and many denizens of the guild were far more powerful than she was—especially among the Champions of Light's inner members. However, among the outer members, she was one of the most capable, even if she didn't possess the most raw power.

On the other side of the room, she saw a small group. Julio and his band of interchangeable miscreants. It was all she could do not to draw her bow and start peppering the detestable gathering of criminals with arrows. She could probably take out a couple of them before the guards responded. Perhaps she could even kill Julio himself. Certainly, the women of Beacon, the town surrounding the Temple of the Sun Goddess, would thank her for putting that horrible man down.

As if he could sense her gaze, Julio looked up and cast a knowing grin her way. He certainly didn't look like a murdering rapist. In fact, he was incredibly handsome, well-built, and carried himself with the sort of confidence most women found attractive. More than that, he was also one of the guild's most successful members, which brought with it both power and wealth. If he'd done things the right way, he probably could've gotten just about any woman he wanted. But he wasn't interested in that, instead getting off on the power he held over his chosen victims. Or that was what the rumors said, at least.

She grimaced, then spat on the floor, heedless of the rich carpeting. It wasn't like they couldn't afford to have it cleaned. In fact, the entire room was a testament to the guild's immense wealth. The Champions of Light weren't strictly part of the Temple of the Sun Goddess, but they certainly enjoyed a position in the temple's good graces. In fact, that close association was one of the major reasons Abby had joined in the first place. They were uniquely suited to helping their members progress, which was the name of the game in the Radiant Isles. Either way, they wouldn't fret over a bit of ruined carpet. Besides, sending a message to Julio was more important than maintaining her manners.

Julio's grin only widened, and he broke away from his group of sycophants. Some held a modicum of power, but their chief ability was to support their leader. Without him, few of them would've even qualified for guild membership, so latching on to that detestable miscreant was their only route to power. For someone like Abby, who'd bled and nearly died hundreds of times just so she could climb the ladder, it was particularly offensive. But the expression on Julio's face as he approached her was even more so.

The man quickly crossed the room, the crowd of other guild members parting before him as he made his way to Abby. No one wanted to get in his way, chiefly because people who did had a habit of going missing. It was precisely that ruthlessness that the guild respected; there were many paths to power, and so long as he continued to complete missives and earn money for the Champions of Light, the guild wasn't going to find fault with his.

As Julio drew closer, Abby stood. Even in the guild lobby, she didn't want to be caught unprepared, and it was much easier to respond to an attack when she was standing than if she'd remained seated. Besides, it grated on her nerves when anyone looked down on her, a sentiment that grew exponentially stronger when facing down someone like Julio.

"What do you want?" she growled, glaring at the handsome man. He was swarthy, but that was more an effect of his ethnicity than any penchant for outdoor adventures. Julio ran a hand over his pitch-black hair, which he wore slicked back and held in place by some unknown product. He might've even used mana, for all she knew.

Julio's appearance was a testament to his wealth. He wore a simple blue doublet and black leather trousers, but even without his trademark black leather armor, he cut an impressive figure. Few others could afford to deck themselves in so many magical items. Certainly, Abby envied the plethora of rings on his fingers, the sun-shaped pendant around his neck, and the metallic bracers around his forearms—all of which exuded a subtle aura of power. She had no idea what any of them did, but they were obviously magical treasures. Likely, they were only items of convenience, but Abby couldn't be sure. By comparison, only Abby's bow was in the same league, and even it had only been enchanted with far more durability than a normal weapon. Any weaker, and it would've snapped the first time she pulled its string.

"Do I need a reason to want to speak to a beautiful woman?" he asked, his voice smooth and steady. "Perhaps I simply wanted to bask in your glorious—"

"Oh, shut up, you preening peacock," came an accented voice from the side. Vladimir had also noticed Julio's approach, and he stood only a couple of feet away, the haft of his double-bladed axe on the floor as his hands rested on the top of outstretched blades. It wasn't an overt threat, but anyone who knew Vladimir knew just how quickly he could swing that thing. While he wasn't as powerful as Abby, the huge man was still a stalwart ally. "Abby has made her opinion of you quite clear. So run along, vermin."

Julio ignored Vladimir, keeping his eyes locked on Abby. Clearly, he didn't consider the Russian giant a threat. In the old world, he would never have ignored such a physically powerful person, but in this new world, things worked a little differently. At only level twelve, Vladimir was vastly inferior to Julio, who was level nineteen. But it was more than simple levels, which were only a baseline. Some people like Julio—and even Abby, to a certain extent—wielded power that far exceeded what should be expected of someone their level. Sometimes, it was the result of a lucky achievement. Other times, it was due to a powerful item. Or a particularly potent skill. Julio had all three. So, the gulf between Julio and Vladimir was nearly insurmountable, and that wasn't even considering the man's lesser-known treasures. Still, Abby appreciated Vladimir's efforts. He was a good man and an even better companion.

But Abby knew that she had to handle Julio herself. Anything else, and he'd just keep coming.

"Piss off, asshole," she spat.

"Is this about the Santolin Reach missive?" Julio asked. "I told you, that was just business. I didn't mean to—"

"It's about me not liking you," she growled, though she admitted that her dislike was probably influenced by the man snaking a missive out from under her. She'd been so close to taking the orc chief's head when Julio and his crew swooped in to steal the kill—and the contribution points that went with it. Doubtless, he'd used that reward to grow even stronger. "You're a creep, and I want nothing to do with you. Not now. Not ever. So, just leave me alone, or I'll have to take this to the next level."

"You would risk that?" asked Julio, fingering the hilt of the blade at his side. She knew it was a single-edged, katana-style blade that was at least as powerful as anything else on his person. She had seen it cut through a palisade made of waist-thick timbers like it was nothing. Even with her endurance having reached fifty-five points, she couldn't stand up to that weapon, especially driven by Julio's far superior strength. "The guild surely would punish you for such a thing. The Champions of Light do not stand for infighting."

Abby wanted nothing more than to wipe that smirk off the man's face, but she forcibly restrained her murderous impulses. Instead, she said, "They would understand. Especially with your history."

Julio rolled his eyes dramatically, saying, "Rumors and conjecture. Besides, I come with an offer."

"No," she said.

"You haven't even heard what I—"

"The lady said no," Vladimir growled, his accent thickening with anger. "Which part of that do you not understand?"

For a moment, Julio didn't respond. Instead, he turned toward the hulking warrior and unleashed his aura. It was a combination of pure power, poisonous sound waves, and lecherous intent, all coalescing into a truly vile mixture that immediately forced Vladimir to his knees. Julio reached out, grabbing the man by the hair, saying, "I can respect loyalty, but if you speak out of turn again, I will be forced to assert my dominance. Even the most loyal dog must know when it's time to slink away from its betters."

With that, Julio gave the man a slight push, tipping him over onto his side. The heavy, double-bladed axe fell to the floor, and a hush fell over the room. What Julio had just done was the height of rudeness.

Differences in power were a reality of their world, but to weaponize the disparity in such a way among guildmates? That was a faux pas that few dared to commit. But Julio was different; he simply didn't care about things like that. To him, power was all that mattered, and anyone who wielded less than him was little more than a pest.

Luckily, Abby was mostly unaffected by the man's projected aura. She said, "Just tell me what you want, then leave."

"Getting right to it," Julio said, the ever-present grin returning to spread across his handsome face. "I like that in a woman. You and I could truly make a wonderful team."

"Is that what this is about?" Abby asked, her tone dripping with disdain. "Assaulting and humiliating my friend is a funny way of trying to recruit me."

"An unfortunate necessity" was Julio's response. Dismissively, he waved his hand toward the fallen giant, who still hadn't recovered. "Some dogs need to be reminded of their place. I'm sorry if it displeased you. I want nothing but amity between us."

Amity. Peace. Cooperation. As if she'd ever stoop to that level. As far as she was concerned, Julio was the enemy, and if they somehow met outside the guild hall again, she would be hard-pressed not to throw caution to the wind and attack. He was a rabid animal, and eventually, someone would need to put him down. But inside the guild hall, there were rules, and she was far from strong enough to break them—a fact of which Julio was well aware.

"I'll ask again—what do you want?" she said.

"I want you to work with me," he said. Before she could respond, he went on, "The mission they're about to announce is too dangerous for me or my team to accomplish alone. I need strong, reliable people, and obviously, I thought of you."

"I will never work with you," Abby stated.

"You say that, but you don't know the reward," Julio said. "I have it on good authority that the guild is offering a bonus for this missive. In addition to the normal contribution points, they are putting two Fruits of Nascent Zeal up as a reward."

"W-what?" she asked, surprised. Fruits of Nascent Zeal weren't just incredibly rare, but they were also one of the most potent components of racial evolution available to the guild. Alone, they could completely evolve a person's soul by an entire stage. Doing so could offer up a host of benefits, from improved mana control to mental resistances, but the biggest benefit was that it would allow a person to push through the bottleneck at level fifteen. Without evolving either the body or the soul, progression past that level was impossible. "Are you sure?"

"I am," he said. "If you agree to assist me, one of them is yours."

This information changed everything. Personal animosity paled in comparison to the pursuit of power. Most people would throw all morals to the side for a chance to break through, and Abby was no different. Besides, the wilderness was a dangerous place. After the mission was completed, there was every chance that Julio would run afoul of some monster. Or at least that would be the official story. She and Vlad could personally benefit while ridding Beacon of a monster in human flesh.

"What's the mission?" she asked.

"Have you heard of Nightweb Ravine?" he asked.

"Past the Trollmoor Bog? Close to Bastion?" was her reply. "I heard a hive of drachnids moved in a couple of years ago."

Julio nodded, saying, "Indeed. The drachnids have been assaulting the caravans that skirt the swamp. The guild has been hired to end the threat. It doesn't pay enough to entice the inner members, so it's been relegated to us. I lack a qualified scout among my party, so naturally, I thought of you."

Abby nodded along. According to rumor, the hive wasn't terribly high-level, so the drachnids posed little threat to the inner members, who were mostly at the maximum level of twenty-five. Any one of them could've cleared out the entire ravine without much difficulty. However, getting them to leave the headquarters of the Champions of Light, much less the city of Beacon, was difficult even if the pay was significant; most craved a challenge or a unique opportunity to grow their immense power, rather than simple coins or contribution points. Wealth held little attraction for people who'd already reached the peak.

So, by default, that left most of the missives to the outer members.

"I want Vladimir with me," she said. "And he gets an equal share of the contribution points."

It was a one-in-a-million opportunity that she couldn't afford to pass up, but she wasn't stupid. She needed someone to watch her back. And while Vladimir wasn't strong enough to stand up to Julio, he was more than powerful enough to handle any of the rest of the man's thugs. If it came down to a fight—and she knew it would—she could only hope that she could take Julio herself.

"Very well," Julio said, barely giving the Russian giant a second thought. "Bring your pet barbarian. But if he gets out of line, I will not be as gentle as I was today."

"Fine," Abby said, extending her hand. Julio took it, and they shook. "But if you betray me, I'm taking you and everyone else with me. Just so we're clear."

Julio only laughed, saying, "As it should be, my dear. As it should be."

11
A SINGULAR PURPOSE

Zeke lay on the ground, peeking over the cliff to see an enormous cavern spread out below him. It was at least a few hundred yards across, and twice as deep. He glanced up; even from where he lay, which was around forty feet up from the cavern floor, he could scarcely see the ceiling. However, the cavern's staggering dimensions weren't what truly caught his eye. No—that distinction was held by the village that took up the centermost portion of the space.

Comprised of lean-tos, huts, and a single central building that was the only truly sturdy piece of construction he could see, the village was home to more than a hundred trolls. Some were adolescents. Others were juveniles. Still others were simply labeled **Caracoa Troll Adult**. However, it was the addition of a half dozen **Caracoa Troll Warriors** that gave him pause. All of them were armed with spears, axes, or clubs, and they'd even donned some rudimentary armor. More, they were half again as tall as any of the others and packed with dense muscle. They were powerful creatures, and Zeke couldn't help but wonder how he'd fare in a fight. However, his intuition told him that even though he'd mostly recovered over the course of the past week that he'd spent exploring the cave system, he wouldn't survive a straight-up fight with the troll village. There were simply too many of the monsters.

But that didn't mean Zeke couldn't do anything. Slowly, he lowered himself from the cliff to lightly fall to the ground below. He barely made any noise, and he was far enough from the encampment that he went completely unnoticed. And besides, most of the trolls had retreated into their respective huts, presumably to sleep. Night and day were undiscernible in the caves, but the trolls clearly had some sense of it. Since he'd begun observing them a few days before, Zeke had mapped out their pattern, so he was certain that he had some time until the majority of the trolls arose—which was perfect for what he had planned.

Zeke crept toward the camp, using the surrounding forest of stalagmites for cover until he reached his destination. Around the camp was a crude palisade of sharpened stakes that only opened in two spots on opposite sides of the rudimentary village. On the far side, there were a trio of troll warriors, each coming in at level nine. However, for some reason Zeke couldn't discern, there was only a single warrior guarding the village entrance closest to him. Not one to look a gift horse in the mouth, Zeke gradually inched toward that solitary warrior, intently watching him the entire way.

His target was level ten, which made it the most powerful enemy he'd seen inside the caves, and even without [**Inspection**], Zeke would've immediately marked him as the most dangerous creature in the village. Not only did the monster carry itself with an air of confidence that none of its brethren possessed, but it also seemed the best equipped. In addition to the iron-tipped spears that were so common among the trolls, it also had a long iron dagger strapped to its bulging thigh. But even if it'd been unarmed, its power would have been undeniable because it was almost half a foot taller than any other troll Zeke had seen, and its scaly musculature was peerless among its brethren.

But that didn't mean Zeke was scared. Certainly, his blood was up, and adrenaline had already begun to course through his veins. But he was confident in his abilities. Besides, he would have the jump on the powerful troll—because, for all its clear power, day after uneventful day of guarding the same spot had taken its toll, and the monster had lapsed into inattentive laziness. Even as Zeke crept within a few yards, he went completely unnoticed; in fact, the thing stared ahead with half-closed eyes that suggested that it was only barely able to maintain wakefulness.

And that suited Zeke just fine.

Once he'd gotten close enough, Zeke sprang into motion, using every bit of his impressive strength to launch himself at the unsuspecting troll. He covered the distance in an instant, his club arcing through the air with unmatched menace. The troll never had a chance, and the moment Zeke's weapon collided with the monster's head, the fight was over. It ended even before it had really started.

The club hit the side of the hideous creature's face with an audible crunch, ripping into it with the force of a fallen meteor. The head didn't precisely explode like a watermelon, but that description wasn't really that far off from accuracy. The troll remained upright for a brief instant before its body recognized that without a head, it couldn't keep going. Once it did, the nine-foot-tall monster crumpled into a heap of lifeless scales and muscle.

Zeke landed hard, but he rolled to dissipate his momentum, falling just short of the palisade before leaping back to his feet, ready for anything. However, the first part of his plan had gone off without a hitch; the village remained just as silent as before he'd begun his attack. Zeke let out a small sigh of relief. He didn't relish fighting a hundred trolls at once, and he wasn't at all confident in his ability to escape, should it come to that. Before, he'd been saved by falling into the river, and he knew he couldn't count on such fortune again. If he did, he'd wind up dead sooner rather than later.

He approached the still-twitching troll corpse, ignoring the tendrils of ruined flesh vainly trying to stitch themselves together. The things had insane vitality, so they could recover from almost any wound, most of the time healing at visible speed. However, without a brain, it was all for naught. Kneeling, he first recovered the thing's dagger. It was almost as long as Zeke's forearm, and it was closer to a machete than a knife. It was also jagged and crudely made, but it was a sight better than the stone-bladed knife in his pouch. So, he quickly unstrapped the harness that had held it in place on the troll's thigh and adopted it as his own. The spear he left where it was; while it was a useful weapon that he could use in a pinch, he felt little affinity for it, and he much preferred his club. Besides, a sturdy, thick-headed club was better suited to take advantage of his monstrous strength.

In any case, he didn't have time to stand around and think about his weapon choices. Instead, he quickly darted through the gap in the palisade and into a deep shadow beside one of the huts. Just as he suspected, Zeke heard loud snores coming from inside. No less than three, no more than five. If it was the former, he shouldn't have any issues. The latter, and he'd have to rethink his strategy, at least for now.

Using the crude wooden hut as cover, Zeke crouched low and crept toward the makeshift building's entrance. It was just an opening with the skin of some unrecognizable animal acting as a curtain; the skin itself was mostly hairless, and the curtain was comprised of multiple pieces that had been stitched together with a thick, sinewy thread. Though it had been cured, Zeke still found it disgusting. He shoved his revulsion to the back of his mind as he stepped through the opening to see four huddled forms inside the hut.

Every movement—even the rustling of the leathery curtain—sounded loud in his ears, but as he slowly inched forward, the trolls sleeping inside failed to react. The hut itself was fairly large, so even the hulking forms of the unconscious trolls had plenty of room to stretch out. More importantly, there was enough space between them that Zeke could go forward with his plan. If they'd been piled atop one another, he would've had to adjust on the fly, and that kind of improvisation, especially when he was skating along a razor's edge in the first place, would've likely proven disastrous.

Zeke knelt beside his first target, and for a moment, doubt bloomed in his mind. The trolls were monsters. They had proven that from the moment he'd first been attacked by the larvae. However, the fact that they had villages and worked together told him that they were at least intelligent, thinking beings. And he was about to kill them, not because he'd been attacked, but rather in cold blood. Certainly, if any of them had seen him, he had no doubt that he would've been attacked with extreme prejudice, but did that give him the right to butcher them like animals?

Probably not, but the fact was that he didn't really have much of a choice. After all, he had no intention of living in the caves forever. He probably could survive, given the prevalence of the blue-spotted mushrooms and the abundance of water, but what kind of life would that be? He wanted to get stronger. He needed to push forward. And the trolls were standing in his way.

With that in mind, Zeke unstrapped his new dagger from his thigh, lofted it above his head in a two-handed grip, then plunged it deep into the sleeping troll's brain. The thing gave a soft grunt, but it died without any other sound. Zeke felt the familiar energy flow into him and make its way to his core, accompanied by a feeling of revulsion. Killing a creature in battle was one thing, but what he'd just done would be better categorized as murder. Necessary, sure, but that didn't mean he had to feel good about it, even if the creature he'd just killed was a hulking monster that would've attacked him on sight.

Zeke took a deep, silent breath. He was in the middle of a troll hut, and the smallest mistake would have him surrounded by almost a hundred monsters who wanted to kill him. This was no time to think about the morality of a preemptive strike. Even so, he couldn't wholly eliminate the thoughts as he snuck to the next-closest troll and repeated his actions. Less than five minutes later, all four trolls had been killed, and he still hadn't been discovered. On the surface, it had gone as well as Zeke could've ever hoped. But still, a sense of unease had draped itself over his shoulders like a blanket. And it wasn't difficult to figure out why.

If nothing else, Zeke had always been a straightforward kind of guy. He almost unfailingly said what he meant, and he'd moved through his life without much in the way of guile. His rebirth hadn't changed that, either. He could fight and kill all day long and feel little remorse, but sneaking around and murdering creatures that had no chance of fighting back? That just felt wrong to him on a fundamental level. But right or wrong, it was necessary because he couldn't very well fight a hundred trolls at once. He needed to thin the herd, and to do that, he had to adopt underhanded and distasteful tactics.

After the fourth troll had died just like the other three, Zeke went back to the opening and dragged the disgusting leather curtain an inch or two to the side, giving him a view of the rest of the village. His infiltration had so far gone completely unnoticed, so he quickly snuck out and, sticking to the shadows, crept to the next hut. He repeated his actions without issue, then went on to the next. Then the next. All in all, over the next few of hours, Zeke murdered almost eighty trolls, and with each kill, he felt his sense of unease grow.

Perhaps that was why he made his first mistake. Or maybe it was always going to happen sooner or later; after all, killing a hundred trolls without alerting the rest of the village was always a long shot of a plan. In fact, when he'd begun, Zeke had fully expected that he'd be forced into retreat, and he'd already planned a route and everything. But still, as he'd killed one troll after another, he'd begun to hope he could get by without a pitched battle.

The dagger strike was only a little off target, but it was enough that it didn't immediately kill the troll beneath him. Zeke immediately struck again, but it was no use. Having been mortally wounded, it let out a wordless shriek, waking up the other troll in the hut. The monster sprang to its feet surprisingly quickly, and it only took it an instant to recognize the threat Zeke posed. It rushed him, swinging its wicked claws with lethal intent.

In his old life, Zeke would've fallen all over himself as he tried to get away. After all, he'd never been much of a fighter. However, living so long in the dangerous cave system and fighting one life-and-death battle after another had honed his battle instincts to a razor's edge. So, he didn't hesitate for even an instant before he acted, ducking under the troll's claws and lashing out with the machete-like blade. Driven by Zeke's superhuman strength, it bit deep into the troll's belly, slicing it open in a wound reminiscent of the one Zeke had gotten during his most recent battle. He knew it wouldn't be a mortal wound; after all, if Zeke's vitality was enough to see him through such an injury, then the troll would shrug it off in a matter of hours. However, Zeke knew just how much it would hurt, and no matter how quickly the trolls healed, they could still feel pain. Zeke was banking on just that to distract the monster.

The troll's claws missed by barely an inch, and its momentum sent it lumbering into the hut's flimsy wall. With a crash, it burst through the upright logs, snapping them like twigs and gaining a few more wounds in the process. Zeke skidded to a stop, then pivoted and sprang back toward the monster, his blade at the ready. The troll was tangled in the broken and scattered remnants of the wall, so it took Zeke only a second to deftly end its life by way of decapitation. Even as its head rolled free, though, Zeke knew that the damage had been done.

He glanced around, and he saw the remaining twenty trolls emerging from their huts, and unlike the one he'd just dispatched, most were armed and ready for a fight. Not that long ago, Zeke had run from half as many monsters, but that was after he was wounded and exhausted. This time, though, he was well rested and mostly healed. What's more, fewer than half of the remaining monsters were warriors. So, he felt at least moderately confident that he could emerge victorious.

And besides, after assassinating so many of the village's residents, he was itching for a straight-up fight, even if it was a little lopsided. On top of that, he could sense that he was on the verge of gaining a level, and he was banking on the accompanying surge of vitality to give him a mid-battle reprieve.

Without any further hesitation, Zeke picked up his club from where he'd left it when entering the hut, then launched himself at the nearest trio of trolls. He swung his club with reckless abandon, perfectly willing to sacrifice his own safety if it meant quickly thinning out his attackers. His strategy was rewarded when his first flurry of attacks struck true, exploding one of the troll's heads while sending its hutmates staggering to the ground, where Zeke quickly dispatched the stunned creatures with practiced ease. He also gained a few long, jagged lacerations on his arms and chest, but they were shallow and easily ignored—especially when the alternative was a distraction that would undoubtedly get him killed.

Immediately after crushing the third troll's head, Zeke darted past them, using the ruined hut as cover. If he let himself be surrounded, he wouldn't survive his raid. So, he kept moving, weaving between the huts so he could spring from the shadows and ambush the remainder of the enraged trolls. And one after another, they fell to his club. It was so much easier than he'd expected, primarily because they couldn't seem to pin him down. It didn't hurt that he could fell each of them with a single blow; they were creatures that relied on their insane vitality and impressive strength to win fights, but Zeke was dexterous enough that he could easily hit his intended targets without sacrificing any strength. So, unless they managed to block—which they really weren't conditioned to do, given their style of simply taking whatever their opponents could dish out and relying on their regeneration to see them through—Zeke made quick work of them, nullifying their advantage in regard to vitality. On top of that, he was agile enough that their strength was mostly irrelevant, as he simply dodged most of their blows. The final piece of the puzzle was [**Leech Strike**], which Zeke had taken to activating at the beginning of each fight. With its constantly feeding him a trickle of vitality, only the most serious wounds would slow him down. And even those were well mitigated by the stolen life force.

Still, there were a lot of them, so it took Zeke quite some time to whittle them down to only a pair of remaining warriors. These were a little stronger, a little quicker, and far smarter than any of the rest of them, save for the one he'd first killed—though that hulking warrior had never had a chance to react. Even so, it quickly became clear that they were outmatched—Zeke had indeed gotten a level, and his quick allocation of five points to agility and ten to dexterity had only further stretched the gap between him and his opponents. Still, he picked up more wounds in that final leg of the battle than he'd gotten in the entirety of fights before, and by the time he finally managed to crush the skull of the last troll, who'd fallen after Zeke had destroyed both of its kneecaps with a well-timed sweep of his club, he looked like he'd been thrown into a meat grinder.

Zeke's entire body was a bloody mess of lacerations, stab wounds, and bruises, but it only took a brief mental inventory of his body to figure out that he wasn't seriously injured. Just a couple of broken bones, a few internal injuries, and countless cuts—nothing his vitality couldn't make fairly quick work of.

All in all, the fight had gone far better than he had any right to expect. He'd killed a hundred trolls, and he'd gotten a level, as well. In addition, he'd finally found something he'd wanted since the first night he'd spent in that cold, damp cave system—firewood. Truly, it had been a profitable battle, and the last bit had even washed away some of the bad taste his previous tactics had left in his mouth.

But he knew he wasn't done, and he suspected that he'd have far more blood on his hands before he escaped the caves that had been his home for the past couple of months. So, he mechanically went about taking stock of his gains, and when he did, he couldn't help but smile at how much progress he'd made in such a short time.

12

A NEW SKILL

Standing amid the corpses of his enemy, Zeke inspected his status page, his grin widening as he stared at the numerical evidence of his progress.

Name	Ezekiel Blackwood
Class	N/A
Level	5
Race	Human (G)
Alignment	Isphodel
Achievements	First Blood, Hasty Evolution
Strength	48
Agility	51
Dexterity	51
Endurance	63
Vitality	64
Intelligence	42
Wisdom	40
Unassigned Attribute Points	0

He had allocated his stat points mid-battle so he could enjoy the rush of vitality that came with it, focusing on agility and dexterity. The way he figured it, he currently had plenty of strength, evidenced by the fact that when his club hit a troll, it practically ripped the flesh from its bones. Besides, he knew he was pushing the limits of what his club could take; already, it was starting to crack, and he knew that if he pushed it any further, it ran the risk of shattering entirely. In any case, damage output did not seem to be an issue, so he'd skipped over enhancing that. The same could be said for his endurance and vitality, which were more than sufficient to survive whatever the cave system threw at him. Instead, he'd decided to spend his points on agility and dexterity, thinking that one could never be too quick or have too much coordination.

Zeke quickly went past his status menu to the next message that had come with reaching level five.

Congratulations! You have reached Level 5. A new skill is now available. Please note that after Level 5, the road grows much more dangerous, and you will no longer receive healing boosts upon leveling.

Much more dangerous? Zeke could barely remember how many times he'd brushed against death, so it was difficult to imagine a more perilous road. However, he had little choice but to accept the new limitations even though he'd come to rely on the surges of vitality that had come with reaching a new level. He could only accept it, adapt, and move on. Besides, it was difficult to be too upset when there was a new skill dangling in front of him. To his surprise, though, there were five choices.

[Troll's Blood] (H)—You have been bathed in troll's blood, which gives you the ability to temporarily increase your rate of regeneration. Only works out of combat. The skill's power is based on vitality. Upgradable.

Upon reading the description, Zeke almost chose the skill without any further deliberation. It seemed especially beneficial, considering that he'd just lost the vitality boost he'd so far enjoyed when gaining a level. In fact, it seemed almost overpowered when he read the final addendum, that its effectiveness would be based on his overwhelming vitality.

However, despite his certainty that he'd pick [**Troll's Blood**], he went on to read the next one.

[**Pestilence**] (H)—**You have proven yourself to be a willing murderer. Walk the path of the assassin as you explore the effects of poison. This skill allows you to poison your enemies with a touch, ensuring their eventual deaths. Skill's damage decreases based on enemy's vitality. Upgradable.**

"Okay, so . . . no," he muttered under his breath. For one, he was supremely uncomfortable that the Framework considered him to be walking the path of the assassin. Certainly, he'd murdered around a hundred trolls in cold blood, but that was necessary, wasn't it? If he wanted to escape the caracoa caves, he had to go through the village, didn't he?

But then again, the more he thought about it, the more he realized that wasn't necessarily true. He'd crept through the village undetected as he killed dozens of trolls. It wasn't out of the question that he could've simply crossed to the exit on the other side of the cavern. The thought had never even crossed his mind, though. Death had become a way of life for him, so it wasn't all that surprising that the Framework had looked at his actions and assumed that he was a cold-blooded murderer. Because he kind of was.

Sure, there were plenty of reasons he'd done it the way he had. But the bottom line was that he had never even considered an alternate path. Still—he wouldn't formalize the fact that he was a budding murderer by picking [**Pestilence**] as one of his skills. So, he moved on to the next one.

[**Heart of the Berserker**] (H)—**You have the heart of a berserker, demolishing all in your path. Your rage gives you the ability to temporarily boost your physical statistics by a large amount. This increase comes with negative consequences, so be wary. Upgradable.**

This one sounded extremely useful. Assuming that it was a percentage-based increase, the skill could allow him to effectively punch above his weight. His stats already seemed far better than even higher-level trolls, so the idea of becoming more powerful—even if it was temporary—might prove the difference between winning and losing a fight against superior opponents. The only issue was the negative consequences the skill's description mentioned. Without knowing precisely what that meant, he wasn't certain he could choose it.

[Warrior's Instinct] (H)—You have defeated many superior foes, cementing your status as a promising warrior. This skill cements your path by formalizing the instincts you've begun to cultivate. Upgradable.

Zeke was even less sure about this one than he'd been about [**Heart of the Berserker**]. On the one hand, anything that promised to passively improve his battle prowess was attractive, but he couldn't help but want something a little flashier. So far, his instincts hadn't been a problem, so it was difficult to invest one of his limited skill choices into something he felt he could do himself, given enough time. He'd been fighting for only a comparatively short time now, and he'd already begun to feel his enemies' blows before they came. What would it feel like in a year? Or two? In a lifetime? While the skill might be useful, Zeke couldn't bring himself to pick it.

[Poison Cloud] (H)—You have taken your first steps down the path of the assassin. This skill furthers that pursuit by summoning a cloud of poison, impeding the effects of vitality in strong enemies and killing weaker foes outright. This skill's power is based on your intelligence. Upgradable.

"Okay, so what the hell?" he growled, resenting the fact that the Framework considered him to be a budding assassin. He'd only killed a few trolls. It wasn't like he'd murdered a head of state or something. Immediately, he pushed that ability to the side, as well; there was just something inherently distasteful about fighting with poisons, and he wanted no part of it. Even if it did sound extremely useful.

So, it was down to [**Heart of the Berserker**] or [**Troll's Blood**]. His survival instincts told him that a temporary boost to his regeneration was the right choice. However, he wasn't so naive that he didn't expect there to be much stronger enemies within the caves. He'd already been pushed to his absolute limit on more than one occasion, so it stood to reason that he would need to grow much, much stronger. [**Heart of the Berserker**] would help with that.

And it was usable in combat, which was a claim [**Troll's Blood**] couldn't make. Zeke had a feeling that he would have to be in the middle of a fight for [**Troll's Blood**] to make a real difference in his survivability, which, given its description, wasn't even possible. After all, he'd already had his stomach ripped open, and he'd survived that. With his already high vitality, he suspected that it would need to be a truly grievous injury to put him down for the count.

With all that in mind, it seemed that his decision made itself. So, despite his earlier certainty that he would choose the regeneration ability, he selected [**Heart of the Berserker**] instead. As soon as he confirmed his choice, he felt a rune brand itself into his pathways just below his left shoulder blade.

As much as Zeke wanted to play with his new ability, he reminded himself that he was standing in the center of the village he'd decimated. So, he quickly set about gathering as much wood as he could carry. Using his ridiculous strength along with the machete-like knife he'd taken from the troll, he soon had an armful of wood. Without a backward glance, Zeke picked his way through the troll corpses and into the tunnel on the far side of the cavern.

For a few hours, he trekked silently through the tunnels, letting his senses lead the way. When he came to a crossroads, he simply took the path where the air smelled a little less stale, hoping that it would lead to the cave exit. It had worked so far, and he'd steadily climbed toward the surface. However, he had no idea if it was because he'd chosen the right paths or if all the tunnels led to the same place.

Eventually, Zeke found his way to another cavern, though this one was far smaller and completely unpopulated, save for the ubiquitous mushrooms that had dominated the landscape since Zeke had awakened in the cave system. In addition, there was a small stream of clear water winding through the center of the cavern. Thinking that he'd found a likely spot to make camp, he set about making a fire. Even with the fire starter, it was at first incredibly difficult; the timber didn't want to catch fire, regardless of how much mana he injected into the small, inscribed stone.

Zeke had never really been much of an outdoorsman. Instead, his entire life had been dominated by baseball—a fact with which he'd never really found fault. But now, he found himself envying his friends who'd spent plenty of time hunting, camping, and fishing with their own fathers. Not that his father ever showed any interest in that kind of thing, of course. Instead, he'd always been the kind of obsessed sports fanatic who spent much of his time cursing at the television because his chosen team didn't perform to his expectations. Often, Zeke would wonder why the man watched so religiously when all it did was piss him off.

He pushed thoughts of his father out of his mind. The last thing he wanted to think about was that man. However, being alone for long stretches of time, often without any real distractions, lent itself to introspection. Usually, that meant that Zeke thought about how his father had influenced him, whether he liked it or not. It was infuriating to think that Zeke wouldn't have gotten where he was without a man he unabashedly hated.

Finally, even as he dwelt on how his father had abandoned him the moment his injury had ended his baseball career, Zeke figured out why the fire wasn't starting. It happened by accident when one of the sparks splashed onto some nearby moss, flaring up with a short-lived flame. He already had the fire starter, and he'd gathered some wood in the troll village, so he needed only tinder to get the fire going. So, with renewed vigor, Zeke gathered as much of the moss as he could find, and only a few minutes later, he had the beginnings of a fire.

For a long time, Zeke just sat there tending the fire as he basked in the warmth he hadn't even realized he'd been missing. Finally, after a while, he decided to test out his new ability. Slowly, he opened his core and guided a trickle of mana through his pathways and to the rune embedded in his shoulder. It lit up, drinking the mana until it glowed in his spiritual senses. With a mental command, he activated the rune, and an instant later, he gasped as his heart rate doubled and he felt a sharp influx of power.

He didn't just feel stronger. Or more coordinated. Or even quicker. It was more than a simple increase in stats, though it was that, too. Instead, the full effect of the skill was more than the sum of its parts. The closest thing Zeke could compare it to was when he'd first evolved his race. Not only was he stronger, but his senses had grown sharper, as well. Finally, it was like his entire body had been flooded with adrenaline, and he found himself twitching with the need to act. The longer he sat still, the more uncomfortable it became.

Pushing his discomfort aside, Zeke inspected his status screen, finding that his strength, agility, and dexterity had been increased by approximately 25 percent. It was a huge increase that would only get stronger as he improved his statistics. However, he couldn't ignore the demerits associated with the skill, either. His endurance had taken roughly a 5 percent hit. That wasn't too bad, though. He had plenty to spare, and . . .

Ten percent, now. About thirty seconds later, the decrease jumped to 20 percent. Then forty. Eighty. Just before he felt like it would increase again, Zeke let go of the skill. The sudden decrease in power left him feeling weak and vulnerable. And most distressing of all, his endurance remained incredibly low. He was on the verge of panic until, almost a minute after he'd deactivated the skill, it started its slow climb back to normal. Each step took almost a minute—roughly twice as long as it had taken to decrease—but after a few minutes, he was back to his normal endurance.

Negative consequences, indeed.

However, as impactful as the lack of endurance was, Zeke was confident that he could mitigate some of the effect with the combination of his high vitality and [**Leech Strike**]. And besides, most fights were over quickly, so he probably would never keep it active long enough for it to really hurt him much. In short, he was happy with the skill. More than that, though, he couldn't help but wonder what the future might hold. If [**Heart of the Berserker**] was that effective, what would higher-level skills do?

As he sat beside the fire, Zeke turned his attention to the rune. He'd done the same to the ones in his hands that activated [**Leech Strike**] on enough occasions that he felt like he almost understood them. He didn't, of course. They were far too complicated for his occasional study to yield any level of understanding. However, with the addition of the new rune on his back, he finally had some basis for comparison. And while he recognized some similarities, he knew he had a long way to go before figuring anything out. That didn't stop him from spiritually inspecting the runes, hour after hour until he drifted off to sleep. His every instinct told him that, one day, his study would yield results. And he wouldn't give that up just because they were slow in coming. Zeke was far too stubborn for that.

13

LOCAL FAUNA

Zeke squatted by the stream, washing the dried blood—some of it his, some of it belonging to the trolls he'd killed—from his upper body. Despite his high endurance and vitality, he'd picked up quite a few scars since being reborn into the hellish system of caves, the most prominent of which was the jagged, red scar angling across his stomach. It had healed, but his brush with mortality had certainly left its mark. Similar pale lines crisscrossed the rest of his body, as well, evidence of his struggle since being reborn into the caracoa cave system.

If it wasn't for the slight glint in the running water, Zeke would have gained another scar, but if nothing else, he had become a product of his environment. And given that his environment was a cave system filled with things that wanted to kill him, he had developed a sixth sense for when danger was afoot. Or in this case, a-fin because only a mere instant after he saw the glint, a yard-long creature rocketed out of the water and straight toward him.

Zeke reacted with exceptional speed, rolling to the side as the fish flew past him, snatching up his club along the way. He came to his feet in a fighter's crouch, fully expecting to pounce on a beached fish. So, he was quite alarmed when the fish came at him again, gliding along in the air like gravity was nothing more than a suggestion. Tiny blue motes trailed behind it, but he was far more concerned with the sharklike teeth in the fish's open mouth. Still, Zeke had the presence of mind to use **[Inspection]** on it.

Flying Barracuda—Level 8

Even as he dodged another one of the fish's kamikaze strikes, he couldn't help but groan. It was bad enough that he had to fight the trolls, but now he had to account for flying fish, as well? What else could this cave throw at him?

He swore under his breath for asking such a cursed question because only a moment later, he felt something latch on to his legs. He looked down to see fleshy tendrils, the bottoms of which were studded with what looked like tiny, toothy suction cups. No sooner had he felt the tentacles wrap around his legs than the pain erupted beneath them. It felt like getting stung by a thousand bees, but it didn't end there. Instead, fire crawled through his veins, emanating from where the tentacles had bitten into him.

Poison.

So, not only was he being assaulted by a flying fish, but he also had to deal with a venomous squid, as well? Or was it an octopus? He didn't have time to figure it out because the fish was making another dive toward his face.

Activating [**Leech Strike**], Zeke waited until the last possible second before swinging at the fish. It dodged to the side, taking a chunk out of his shoulder. Zeke gritted his teeth; he'd survived fighting an entire village full of trolls, and he refused to let a fish kill him, flying or not. So, he activated [**Heart of the Berserker**], feeling the increased strength, dexterity, and agility flowing through him. Even so, the barracuda was quick—unnaturally so—and it took him six more passes before he managed to land a solid blow. Luckily, its constitution seemed to be lopsided, and the moment Zeke connected with his club, the creature went flying across the small cavern to collide with the uneven wall. Zeke was rewarded with a small influx of energy, telling him that it had, indeed, died.

Which left him to deal with his other attacker, the octopus he'd ignored until this point. Only about thirty seconds had passed, evidenced by the first decrease in Zeke's endurance, and already, his leg had gone mostly numb. Part of that was because of the poison, but it was also due to the insane pressure the thing could bring to bear with its tentacles. It was like a boa constrictor, only it also poisoned you while squeezing the life out of you.

Zeke activated his inspection skill, and he was rewarded with the thing's name and level:

Wall Creeper—Level 11

More, he also got a slightly better look at his attacker, and he was horrified to see that its tentacles were around two inches thick and capped with barbed talons reminiscent of a bird of prey's. In addition, Zeke got his first glimpse of the thing's body, and he nearly retched as his disgust reached an entirely new level. It looked like a misshapen chimp, if said chimp had been crossed with a jellyfish. Most of its torso was entirely clear, which let Zeke plainly see the thing's organs, veins, and all sorts of things that should've been hidden by skin. Thankfully, its head was the same pitch-black as the tentacles, preventing him from seeing too much in the dark.

Instinctively, Zeke knew that if he left the tentacles where they were, he wouldn't survive. The poison was mostly being counteracted by his high vitality, but eventually, it would wear him down. Once it did, he'd be easy prey for what he suspected was an ambush predator. The only problem was that the thing was entirely boneless, which meant that each time he swung his club, it bent around the weapon.

Even as he swung wildly at the wall creeper, Zeke knew he was in trouble. Like the fish, the thing was far quicker than him, so trying to hit it was mostly an exercise in futility. He was also on a timer because every second that went by brought him closer to the threshold where he'd be forced to deactivate [**Heart of the Berserker**]. So, if he wanted to survive, he knew he needed to change tactics, and in a hurry. He grimaced as a plan took shape in his mind.

This was going to hurt.

Zeke dropped his club, then bent down to grip the wall creeper's tentacles. Banking on his strength overwhelming the thing's endurance, he started to pull. His primary goal wasn't to dislodge the tentacles, but rather, he intended to rip them apart entirely. He hoped that would give him the opening he needed to dispatch the thing.

However, the moment he wrapped his fingers around one of the tentacles, a few problems manifested. First, the wall creeper went insane, lashing its free tentacles toward him like whips. They didn't just sting, but instead ripped into him like serrated daggers, sawing through his flesh and injecting their hateful poison. In addition, the tentacles wrapped around his leg constricted even further, exerting enough force that they would've ground most bones to dust.

But Zeke wasn't a normal person, and even though he'd already ticked past the second endurance decrease associated with his berserker skill, he had more than enough to prevent his bones from snapping under the pressure. It did hurt, though, and if he hadn't already gone through the crucible that occurred when forcibly evolving his race, he might've succumbed to the agony. Luckily, he had endured far worse pain, and the thing's attack felt almost pitiful by comparison.

With a battle cry that shook the cavern, Zeke exerted every ounce of strength he could muster, ripping the tentacle in two. He tossed the loose piece aside, then went to the next, repeating himself three times before his leg was freed.

That's when the wall creeper tried to flee, using its remaining tentacles to drag itself along the cavern floor. It had just reached the wall when a limping Zeke caught up, bearing his club. It took only two overhand strikes to dispatch the thing, and by the time it was dead, it was an entirely unrecognizable mass of transparent flesh, slime, and snakelike black tentacles. Zeke stood over it, his breath coming in ragged gasps as he released [**Heart of the Berserker**]. It slipped away, the mana that had empowered the rune retreating back into the bead at the core of his pathways, and the overwhelming power that had coursed through his veins was replaced by a hollow weakness. He sagged to the ground, bending double as he tried to get ahold of himself.

It seemed that the skill's price was more than just the steplike decreases in his endurance. There was an aftermath he'd have to learn to deal with as well. But he'd learned not to let his guard down, so he quickly took stock of his injuries.

The fish had taken a few chunks out of his upper body, but he'd dealt with worse from fighting the trolls. They would heal pretty quickly. Looking down at his leg, though, showed him a mass of shredded flesh that looked like it had been through a meat grinder. If his endurance had been any lower, and his bones had actually snapped, the thing would've ripped his leg right off. It was a stark reminder of just how dangerous his world had become.

Zeke looked around for more threats, but he saw nothing, even when he studied the small cavern's ceiling. The wall creeper's name wasn't just for show, so he'd have to be extra vigilant from now on. The same could be said for the various rivers, streams, and lakes that ran through the cave system. He wasn't fool enough to think that his attackers had been unique.

He limped back across the cavern toward the stream. His leg burned with the poison, but he hoped that it had already been broken down by the combination of his high vitality and the effects of [**Leech Strike**]. The skill wasn't extraordinarily strong, but the healing was proportional to the strength behind his strikes, so it had often made the difference between victory and defeat. But without that constant influx of life energy, it was only his natural regeneration that stood in the way of the poison. He could only hope that it was up to the task.

Cupping handfuls of water, he rinsed his leg off. It wasn't a pretty sight, but it was mostly functional—so long as he didn't have to fight again for a couple of days, he'd probably be fine. However, that addendum wasn't the most comforting, given that he had yet to go without battle for such a long time.

Once his wounds were cleaned, Zeke ripped the remainder of his linen shirt into strips, then washed them in the stream before wrapping them around his legs in a makeshift bandage. He didn't know if it would help much, but it seemed like the right thing to do—especially given that he could detect traces of mana in the stream. It wasn't nearly as strong as that first stream he'd come across, but it was still there nonetheless. Perhaps it would assist the healing process, and if it couldn't, there would be no harm done.

His injuries taken care of as best he could, Zeke retreated back to where he'd built his fire. It had died down to embers by now, but he had plenty of fuel. So, he piled a few broken timbers and some moss onto it, and his efforts were rewarded with a healthy blaze. That helped, if for no other reason than that the heat provided a bit of rare comfort.

Finally, he crossed the small cavern to the other side, where he found the dead barracuda. Curiously, it didn't look much different from a normal fish from his old world. It was long, fairly slim, and obviously built for speed. More importantly, it had a healthy bit of meat on it—which reminded Zeke that he'd been living off of foraged mushrooms and mosses for longer than he cared to contemplate. A little meat would go a long way, he thought.

So, without further hesitation, Zeke grabbed the fish's tail and carried it back to his fire. After that, he set about cleaning the thing. As he worked, using the stone-bladed knife he'd gotten from the very first armed troll he'd killed, Zeke idly thanked his uncle Mike for taking him fishing a handful of times. He'd been young then, and he barely remembered the lessons he'd learned, but the vague familiarity served him well.

Inevitably, his thoughts drifted back to his father. Most boys were taught such skills by their dads, but that responsibility had fallen to his mother's brother. He'd been only a few times before his father put a stop to it, though. It wasn't baseball, so it wasn't important, according to his old man. At the time, Zeke hadn't thought much of it, but later, he would figure out that his father was living vicariously through him. The man had failed as a ballplayer himself, and so he'd resolved to push his son toward the peak he'd never reached. Zeke would've felt bad for him if the man hadn't been such a terrible human being who had used abuse as a training tool, then abandoned him the very moment his baseball career had ended.

But even as his mind swirled with resentment, something inside Zeke snapped. He'd been fighting trolls for weeks, maybe months—the days had slipped together to such an extent that he had little concept of how much time had really passed. He had just been attacked by a flying fish and an octopus monkey. And he'd been resurrected into an entirely new world filled with magic and incredibly powerful skills. For all he knew, he would never see his father again. So, why was he still letting the man affect him?

Certainly, he'd had a tough go of it back in the old world. But none of that mattered anymore, right? He needed to look to the future, instead of constantly looking backward at things that had faded into irrelevance. So, with that in mind, Zeke pushed the useless thoughts aside and focused on what really mattered—making his way through his new world. And doing so felt like a weight had been lifted off his shoulders.

Zeke finished cleaning the fish, fileting it before using a pair of sticks to suspend the meat over the fire. He wasn't certain how long he should cook it, so he probably left it there for far too long. But in his defense, he had no idea if there was some sort of magical bacteria living inside of it, so from his perspective, it was better safe than sorry.

Without further ado, he took a tentative bite of the still-steaming meat. At first, he tasted only fish, but after a few seconds' worth of chewing, a searing energy erupted in his mouth. It wasn't painful, though. Far from it. The energy seeped into his very cells, nourishing him in a way he'd never experienced. It was like that single bite had been enough to restore him from the aftermath of [**Heart of the Berserker**].

He stared at it for a long moment, amazed at the power in that meat. He took another bite, then turned his vision inward, where he saw tiny, pulsing balls of energy coursing through his pathways. With each pulse, that area of his body grew a bit stronger, and when they got to his legs, he could feel the injection of vitality. It wasn't enough to heal it outright, but it did give him hope that a single night's rest would get him back on his feet.

It was a great discovery, and he soon wolfed down the rest of the fish before settling in to rest and recover.

14

THE EXPEDITION

Abby loosed her silvery conjured arrow, guiding and empowering it with her skill [**Gust of Wind**]. It required a clever touch because the skill itself was intended more for brute force applications than deft manipulation of the wind. When she'd originally selected the skill—her very first—she'd imagined herself conjuring frightful tornadoes, but the first time she'd used it, she had been severely disappointed by the simple wall of wind it had created. Her enemy at the time—a small creature that resembled a porcupine that breathed wisps of fire—had been sent flying, but it had done little to truly injure the thing. She'd been forced to dispatch it with a nearby rock, crushing it to death. Since that time, she'd spent hour after hour learning to use the skill in a more productive way, and by far the most effective method had been to combine it with archery.

The conjured arrow—the result of another skill that she'd selected at level ten—flew with the speed of a bullet and with unnatural accuracy, piercing the thick hide of the minotaur to plunge deep into its chest. It wasn't enough to down the beast, but it certainly made it stumble. In the space of a handful of seconds, Abby sent three conjured arrows flying, each impacting the monster only inches from where the first arrow had hit. She couldn't help but grin at her hard-won proficiency, as evidenced by a single line on her status page:

Martial Path: Archery (Novice—Middle Proficiency)

Without it, she knew her arrows wouldn't have even been able to penetrate the monster's leathery skin, much less hit anything vital. What's more, the upgrade to middle proficiency had extended her range by nearly half as she was able to eke out every bit of power from her midgrade bow.

So, while she wasn't the mage she might've imagined upon setting out in this new world, she couldn't help but feel satisfied with her progress. With three silvery arrows sticking out of its chest, the minotaur's fate finally caught up with it, and it staggered to a halt, confused and in obvious pain. A moment later, it collapsed.

"I knew I chose well," came a silky voice from beside her. She didn't need to look in order to know that Julio had found her. "Such skill. I love a woman who can take care of herself."

"Go to hell," she said, dismissing the conjured arrow in her hand. As she turned, she rested her hand on a small hatchet at her waist. It was probably a futile gesture, considering that, even if she got the jump on him, Julio would probably win in a fight. He was too fast. Too strong. But that was to be expected, considering he was an entire stage ahead of her. That didn't mean she was willing to back down, though. To show weakness to such a man was to invite attack. Or worse, if the rumors were to be believed.

He laughed, the dismissive sound cutting through her like a knife. "So much fire!" he exclaimed. "My mother would've liked you. You remind me of her."

"Okay, so that's just creepy," she said. "I don't know if you know this, but an Oedipus complex is not attractive. At all."

In an instant, Julio's mirth disappeared, replaced by a savage gleam in his brown eyes. "That was not what I meant," he growled, all hints of levity gone. In their place was an overwhelming sense of danger. Despite her power—and it was nothing to sneeze at—Abby felt like nothing so much as prey before a vicious predator, and it was all she could do not to turn on her heel and run.

It was a silly thought. Not only would it be useless, considering the man was possessed of plenty of speed to catch her in short order, but it was also counterproductive. If Julio was a predator—and she knew he was—showing fear would only encourage him. And flight? Well, that would excite him in ways she didn't want to think about.

"Then you shouldn't have said it," she said, her entire body taut. After pulling her hatchet from a loop in her belt, Abby tightened her hand on the weapon's hilt. She might not be able to stand toe to toe with Julio, but she could extract a price should he choose to attack her. Whatever happened, Abby refused to go down without a fight.

"Um . . . boss?" came a voice from nearby. "What do you want us to do with the bodies? Are minotaurs worth anything?"

Neither Abby nor Julio acknowledged the underling's presence as they stared each other down. Potential violence crackled in the air, waiting to be unleashed as neither backed down.

Finally, Julio blinked. Then, the spell was broken, and he let out another peal of laughter. "Just like mi madre," he said, shaking his head with a grin. "Fierce."

After that, Julio turned away like nothing had happened and addressed his men. All seven of them had gathered around, their expressions almost as bloodthirsty as their leader's. Vladimir was there, too, his axe coated in a sheen of crimson blood. Judging by his stance, he had felt the tension, too.

"Take the horns. They're moderately valuable," Julio said, gesturing to the scattered corpses. "Burn the rest."

Abby let out a breath she didn't know she'd been holding. She'd been closer to death than she had been in years, and she'd almost forgotten what it felt like. The adrenaline. The existential terror. The anger. It all coalesced into something wholly unique, and it had sapped her energy far more than the battle with the minotaurs ever could have. Still, she couldn't be too upset because it had all worked out surprisingly well.

She picked her way through the brush toward the minotaur she'd killed; it was at least a couple hundred yards away, but she covered the distance quickly due to her respectable agility of sixty-one. In seconds, she was hacking through the thick horn with her hatchet. The weapon was nothing special, but it made easy work of the valuable horns, which she then stowed away in her enchanted satchel. The pack was a new addition to her equipment, and it bore a series of inscriptions that nearly tripled its carrying capacity, all without increasing its weight. It truly was a marvel.

"We shouldn't have come here," Vladimir said, kneeling beside her. "They're going to turn on us as soon as we've served our purpose."

"I know," she said, glancing around. They were only a few hours outside of Beacon, and they'd already been attacked by minotaurs. That the creatures dared come so close to the city was troubling, but even more distressing was the fact that Julio's men hadn't led them around the small tribe of bull-headed humanoids. Julio's scouts were talented enough, so there was no way the attack had come as the surprise they pretended it was.

"They were testing us," she said, standing over the corpse. "Gauging our abilities."

"I was thinking the same thing," the big man stated. "What do you want to do?"

"We don't have much choice, do we?" she said. "There's a reason we took this mission."

Indeed, the chance to evolve her race and continue advancing past level fifteen would justify just about any risk—even one so blatant as teaming up with Julio and his ilk. At least the mission itself wasn't complicated. Drachnids were dangerous monsters that were far more intelligent than they had any right to be, but they weren't overly difficult to kill. Culling the nest that had been plaguing the caravans that traveled from Beacon to the southern coastal city of Salvation would be a simple enough task, if a frustratingly tedious one—especially for a party of their caliber.

Vladimir, at level twelve, was the lowest level there, and they even had Julio, who'd already pushed past the bottleneck at fifteen. Abby was the second-highest level, but none of Julio's crew were lower than thirteen. There was a reason they were seen as one of the more successful groups within the Champions of Light, which is why they'd gotten the mission to begin with.

Abby sighed, looking around the forest. Unless she missed her mark—and she usually didn't—it was going to be a long, eventful trip.

"We keep going," she said. "You watch my back, and I watch yours, same as always. Can't be any worse than that nest of wyverns we ran into a couple of years ago, right?"

Vladimir chuckled, stroking his beard. "In my defense, I didn't know they breathed fire," he said. "Besides, it all worked out, didn't it?"

"Aside from you losing all your hair? And most of your clothes?" she said, grinning. "I saw way more than I ever wanted to see of you that day."

"You liked it and you know it" was Vladimir's retort.

Abby retched, which only made Vladimir sputter. It almost felt like old times until Julio's honeyed voice cut through their banter.

"Are you two done?" he asked, sauntering toward them, flanked by a pair of his men. Abby hadn't even bothered to learn their names.

Then, to Abby, he continued, "Keep it up, and I'll get jealous. I don't like competition."

"There's no competition," Abby said, and Julio perked up—at least until she added, "Vlad is twice the man you are. In every way possible, from what I hear around the lower tiers."

For a moment, Abby thought he would erupt into violence. Part of her wished the man would; at least then they'd be finished with the cat-and-mouse verbal sparring that he probably misconstrued as flirtation. But she knew how that would end, so she bit off another insult before it spilled out of her mouth.

"Funny," Julio snorted. "Come on. We have a long way to go before nightfall."

Then, the rakish man turned on his heel and marched away. He had seemed indifferent, but Abby had seen his white knuckles as he clutched the hilt of his sword. Julio had been a hairsbreadth from unleashing his power.

"You shouldn't antagonize him," Vladimir said. "From what I hear, he has a short temper."

"I know," Abby said. "Let's go."

And with that, she followed the man through the forest and to the nearby path where they'd been ambushed. Soon, they were on their way, walking along like nothing had happened. It was going to be a dangerous trip, indeed, but she was determined to survive. After all, there was no reward without risk, and the Fruit of Nascent Zeal that would help her evolve her race was plenty of reward to justify any degree of risk. And once they'd satisfied the terms of the missive, she and Vlad could enact the plan they'd discussed before leaving. Julio might be a much higher level than them, but he could die in his sleep as easily as any other man. Abby just had to make it to that point.

15

A CURE FOR MONOTONY

Zeke stood on a midsize boulder, holding aloft a pilfered spear. He had gotten it in the last village he'd destroyed, and it was obviously a higher quality than any he'd held before. The steel spearhead glistened in the faint light, a far cry from the iron tips he'd seen before. The enhancements didn't end there, either. Indeed, the entire weapon—from the spearhead to the straight shaft—had been vastly improved. And as he stood over the stream, watching various fish swim by, the weapon was precisely what he needed. After all, he couldn't just wait for the fish to attack him. Instead, he needed to be proactive.

With a lightning-quick movement, he sent the spear plunging into the depths of the stream, impaling one of the silvery fish. Over the last couple of months, Zeke had gotten used to his increased dexterity, and his aim had developed in kind. That, coupled with a strength that sent the weapon flying with unnatural speed, made spearing fish an exercise in simplicity.

Zeke crouched to pick up the rapidly unspooling rope he'd attached to the end of the spear and began reeling it in, slowly coiling it around his arm, wrapping it from his palm to his elbow. The fish resisted, trying to wriggle free, but by this point, Zeke was an old hand at spearfishing, and the fish's struggles were for naught. Soon, he'd hefted the thing out of the water and onto his perch.

It wasn't a barracuda, like before. Instead, the fish was identified as a **Mana Trout**, and he knew from experience that it tasted far better than its flying cousin. It had been almost nine weeks since his first encounter with the fish, and in that time, he'd captured and eaten a few dozen of the things. Without them, he'd never have made it so far.

As Zeke gutted and cleaned the fish, expertly fileting it, he thought about his recent struggles with the trolls. Their population had grown denser the higher he climbed, and it felt like he found a new village every day. Some he'd cleared out, just like before, but others he left alone, knowing that they were far more trouble than they were worth. The experience just wasn't worth the risk, especially for some of the larger villages. With huts made out of stone instead of loose timber, their population usually numbered more than five hundred, and that was a conservative estimate. Even at his best, Zeke couldn't kill so many—not even if he resorted to his strategy of assassination. One man can only do so much, after all.

That wasn't to say that he hadn't been busy. He had killed hundreds of trolls over the previous months, and he'd reaped the benefits from it, as well. Not only had he gained new equipment like his spear and the rope, but he'd also managed to gain a level, too. However, after he'd gotten to level six, the experience—even when killing creatures twice his level—had slowed to a trickle. Even now, almost two weeks' worth of near constant killing later, he could sense that he was less than a quarter of the way to level seven. His ideas about quickly reaching level twenty-five and gaining a class seemed like child's fantasies in the face of his slow leveling speed. At his current rate, it would be years before he could reach such a lofty goal.

Zeke retreated back to his makeshift camp, where he'd already built a fire. Even as he entered the cave that had been his home for the past couple of days, he studied the walls. The wall creepers weren't that common, but he'd been attacked a dozen times since that first encounter. The strange, octopus-like creatures were mostly harmless if he managed to ambush them, but if they got the jump on him, they were truly dangerous. On one occasion when he'd reacted too slowly, he'd nearly lost an arm to one. So, since that day, he'd grown careful to the point of paranoia, his eyes constantly searching the walls for the wall-crawling predators.

After living in the caves for close to four months, Zeke had changed in more ways than gaining levels. Certainly, if he could somehow go back to the old world, he'd be considered superhuman, and in every way possible. But aside from the effects of the base attributes, Zeke's mind had been sharpened by the constant struggle for survival. Around every turn, there had been one danger after another, and Zeke had been forced to either adapt or succumb. That meant that he was constantly searching for new threats, and even when he slept, there was a part of him that remained aware of his surroundings. The alternative was death via the innumerable threats hosted by the cave system. And though Zeke might lament the necessity for such constant vigilance, he had to admit that he felt more alive than he'd ever felt before—ironic, considering he'd had to die to achieve that feeling.

As Zeke cooked the filets over his meager fire, he studied his status page.

Name	Ezekiel Blackwood
Class	N/A
Level	6
Race	Human (G)
Alignment	Isphodel
Achievements	First Blood, Hasty Evolution
Strength	61
Agility	54
Dexterity	59
Endurance	70
Vitality	67
Intelligence	45
Wisdom	43
Unassigned Attribute Points	0

He had chosen to put his free points in strength and dexterity, with ten in the former and five in the latter, mostly because he'd begun to consider them his primary statistics. Endurance was obviously important, too, and he intended to focus on it in the future, as well. His reasoning was that, with his preferred method of combat, strength was a crucial part of the equation because he couldn't simply slice through enemies. Instead, he had to rely on blunt force, which made strength fundamentally important. Similarly, he couldn't simply hack through body parts, clearing the way toward more vital targets. So, he needed the ability to hit where he aimed, with little margin for error. Dexterity took care of that as it improved his coordination to absurd levels.

That brought him to endurance. The simple fact was that, eventually, he needed to invest something into defense. Zeke was under no delusions. He knew that he wouldn't be able to lean on the effects of [**Leech Strike**] forever. Certainly, it would always help, especially considering its low mana cost of activation as well as its nearly unnoticeable maintenance cost. But it was never intended to do the heavy lifting he was asking it to do. The same could be said for his vitality, which, while it was likely incredibly high for his level, would probably see diminishing returns as he—and his enemies—got stronger. He could easily imagine a situation where a monster wounded him to the point where he simply couldn't heal from it before succumbing to death.

That left only agility and endurance. Agility was an attractive option, if for no other reason than that it would save him a good deal of pain. Dodging seemed preferable to simply taking a hit, didn't it? But what about when he couldn't avoid damage? If he didn't have the necessary endurance, he'd be ripped to pieces. And if his months in the caves had taught him anything, it was that there was no way to completely avoid getting hit. Eventually, regardless of how quick he was, he'd find himself on the wrong end of a claw swipe. Or a bite. A sword, axe, or spear. It was inevitable.

Focusing on endurance, by contrast, had no real weakness. It was equally effective against strong attacks as well as glancing blows. The only problem was that no matter how much endurance he had, everything still hurt. If his strategy was to simply withstand blows that would've otherwise killed him, Zeke knew he was in for quite a lot of pain. But he'd always been good at enduring pain.

Finally, endurance was already his highest statistic, with his biggest modifier due to the percentage boost of his achievement Hasty Evolution. So, while all his other stats were what he considered pretty high for his level, endurance got a 5 percent increase on top of its base value. That meant that each point he allocated into the stat meant that much more. That made his decision an easy one, giving him an idea of how he would progress with future levels.

Once Zeke had finished eating his meal and restoring his physical energy as well as his mana, he found himself leaning against the cave wall and examining the runes on his hands. They weren't visible to the naked eye, so he instead studied them with what he thought of as his inner sense. On the surface, he was well aware that they were vastly complicated and impossible to truly understand, but even so, he felt like he was on the verge of seeing through the complexity into some sort of truth. A system underlying the intricate knot of patterns that would allow him to see past what they seemed to be and into what they actually meant.

After more than two hours, Zeke didn't really achieve much in the way of quantifiable gains, but he did feel like he understood the runes a tiny bit better. Certainly, it could've been his imagination. After all, his lonely existence of constant struggle had taken its toll on his mental state, pushing him into a state of mind that might have influenced him to see things that just weren't there. But his instincts told him he was on the right track, and over the course of the previous four months, he'd learned to trust those.

Once his body had processed the energy from the fish, Zeke stood up, refreshed. One thing he'd recently learned was that, so long as he wasn't injured, his need for sleep had been vastly reduced. Even now, it had been four days since he'd had so much as a nap, but he was wide-awake and full of energy. Of course, if he was hurt, that need for rest skyrocketed—which was something he wholeheartedly wanted to avoid.

Zeke doused the fire, then gathered his meager possessions. Using one of the flaps that served as the doors of the troll dwellings, he'd laboriously created a makeshift satchel, tying it together with the rope he'd managed to steal. It was crude but sturdy, and it served its purpose of carrying his various knives, the rune-covered ball that was his fire starter, and some tinder. After securing everything and throwing the satchel's strap crosswise over his shoulder, Zeke set off to explore the caves, spear in one hand and club in the other.

His steps were soft and silent as he crept through the system. Even the wall creepers barely noticed him until they got a spear in their slimy torsos. He couldn't leave them alive—not unless he wanted to be attacked at the least opportune moment. Besides, he had resigned himself to quantity over quality, in regard to experience, and every little bit counted.

Over the next couple of months, Zeke managed to kill hundreds of wall creepers as well as destroying two small troll villages, both containing around fifty of the monsters. He was like a deadly shadow, creeping through the caverns and leaving only destruction in his wake. Or that's how he imagined himself, at least. In reality, he was well aware that he was more akin to an opportunistic ambush predator. Or a scavenger. Either way, he couldn't concern himself with things like that. It was a simple matter of survival. Still, the veritable executions he carried out left a bad taste in his mouth, necessary though they obviously were.

The days blended together as Zeke monotonously slaughtered anything in his way, and if anyone could ever become bored with a life-and-death struggle, it certainly would've been him. It would have been different if they offered him any sort of challenge. Or if the scenery changed even the slightest bit. But neither was the case, and the only thing that kept him putting one foot in front of the other was the constant trickle of experience that pushed him toward his next level. Even the far-off goal of escaping the cave system paled in comparison to the real, concrete evidence of progress that the push toward level seven represented. The only thing that came even close to that was his ephemeral progress toward understanding the runes on his hands, though that was even less substantial than the promise of finally seeing the sun again.

However, on the eve of his seventh month in the caves, everything changed.

He'd just killed a pair of wall creepers that had tried to ambush him from above when a horrid smell assaulted him. He followed his nose and saw a yawning opening that actually led down. That wasn't too abnormal. Many of the troll villages were situated in what looked like vast craters within even larger caverns. But none of them had smelled like this.

Trolls, in the best of times, didn't exactly smell like petunias, but the stench emanating from that tunnel was truly nausea inducing. Without Zeke's impressive constitution, he knew he would've been doubled over and spewing the contents of his stomach all over the cave floor. Its rancid odor was like a sewage treatment plant and a garbage dump had somehow been combined into something that far exceeded both. Oh, and with a side of rotting bodies, too.

The smell alone very nearly defeated Zeke's sense of curiosity, but the monotony of the past weeks asserted itself, forcing him into exploration. So, leaving the dead wall creepers behind, Zeke set off down the tunnel, and with each step, he came a little closer to vomiting. And by the time he finally reached the terminus of the cavern, tears were flowing freely down his dirty, smeared cheeks to collect in his matted beard.

But the smell did nothing to prepare him for what he saw within the cavern. When he looked upon the scene that spread out before him, the vomit he'd so far managed to curtail was finally let loose.

16

THE BROOD MOTHER

Zeke stepped into the cavern, hugging the wall so that he wouldn't be noticed. The increasingly rancid smell hit him like a wall of putridity, and it was all he could do not to dry heave. Luckily, he'd left the contents of his stomach at the mouth of the cavern, so nothing came up. Still, the disgusting odor remained, exceeded only by the sight before him.

Like many of the troll villages, the cavern itself was primarily circular in shape, and after a twenty-foot lip, it descended into a depression. From end to end, it was roughly the length of a football field and at least three times as high, which made it one of the most open areas he'd found within the cave system. Not that he cared about the cavern's dimensions—not in the face of what stood before him.

Over the previous months, Zeke had encountered quite a few appalling creatures. From the troll larvae that seemed to be a combination of a few disparate creatures to the wall creepers, with their transparent skin and creeping tentacles, he thought he'd been inoculated against disgust. However, as he gazed out at the cavern—or more appropriately, the behemoth that lay at its center—Zeke was forced to reassess his assumption.

Judging by its scaly, ratlike face and large, pointed ears, the thing was clearly a troll, but it was far bigger than any Zeke had encountered. It was difficult to be certain, considering that it was almost seventy-five yards away, but he judged it to be at least thirty feet long. What's more, it was misshapen, its bulk bulging against its mottled green-and-yellow skin to the point where small cracks had appeared in its scales. Once, Zeke had chanced upon one of those television programs where they document the lives of people who'd grown so out-of-proportion that they needed cranes to lift them from their beds, but even they looked positively thin next to the bulbous mound of scaly flesh that was the troll before him. Reluctantly, he cast [**Inspection**] on it.

The Brood Mother—Level 22

In addition to its massive bulk, it was covered in what looked like tumors. Each one of them oozed pus, which Zeke suspected was the source of the stench that had very nearly knocked him out. Or perhaps the culprit was the nearby piles of refuse and bodily discharge. Either way, the Brood Mother was responsible.

On its torso were twenty or so grossly sagging teats, each one tipped with a wrist-thick nipple. And more of the ubiquitous yellow pus, of course. In fact, the monster's entire body seemed coated in a combination of mucus and pus, making its skin glisten in the scant light. And judging by the gravel imbedded in the disgusting concoction, it was obviously sticky, as well.

It took Zeke a few seconds to recognize that the creature wasn't built like an obese slug. Instead, he saw stubby appendages—six on each side—jutting from its body. All in all, the thing's disgusting appearance was exceeded only by the rancid odor that felt more like a mental attack than a smell.

And all around the monster were its progeny. The crater was covered in troll larvae, their levels ranging all the way up to four. In addition, spaced throughout the cavern were waist-high, softly glowing sacks that Zeke quickly surmised were eggs, considering that he could see the shadows of the creatures within. It was obvious that he'd found the source of all the trolls he'd thus far encountered.

Luckily, the Brood Mother's grotesque appearance and smell prevented him from having second thoughts about killing the presumably helpless creature. It was so huge that it probably couldn't get out of its own way, much less put up a fight, and in another situation, Zeke might have hesitated. Sure, he'd killed plenty of sleeping, defenseless trolls, but murdering a new mother was crossing all sorts of lines. Unless that mother happened to be a grotesque abomination that was almost certainly responsible for giving birth to the creatures who'd been trying to kill him since the moment he'd been reborn, of course—which, as far as Zeke was concerned, was definitely the case with the Brood Mother.

The only question was how he'd go about dispatching the monster along with its many children, who covered the entire cavern floor. Would his club even hurt such a massive creature? Even with his enhanced strength, Zeke wasn't certain of his chances. It was more than three times his level, after all, and those levels didn't come without a significant portion of endurance. In fact, Zeke wouldn't have been surprised if the thing possessed greater stats than he did in every category.

And that wasn't even considering the troll larvae that would doubtless go insane the moment he threatened their mother. And while he had few doubts about how easily he could kill them, Zeke knew that if he ignored them, they would threaten to overwhelm him with sheer numbers—the response of the Brood Mother notwithstanding.

Finally, he felt sure that the Brood Mother would have some sort of ability to protect itself and its children. The lack of guards seemed to support that line of thought, too. So, Zeke had no idea what he was up against, save that he was greatly outnumbered, obviously weaker than his enemies, and entirely lacking enough information to make a plan that had any likelihood of succeeding. The result was that Zeke's every instinct told him to leave the Brood Mother alone. Perhaps, once he'd managed to gain a few more levels, he could come back and kill it then. It was the smart thing to do.

But he knew he couldn't do that.

For one, he'd be lucky if he could ever find the place again. The cave system was a veritable maze, and the only reason he'd made any progress at all was because he followed his nose. So, finding his way back would be incredibly difficult if not downright impossible.

For another, he hated leaving an enemy behind him. Certainly, he'd left plenty of intact troll villages in his wake, but they had each been death traps where he stood absolutely zero chance of overcoming the overwhelming odds against him. He had grown into a dangerous warrior, but even he couldn't kill two-hundred-plus trolls by himself.

But most of all, Zeke felt an irresistible urge to scrub the abomination that was the Brood Mother from the face of the Earth. If any of the creatures he'd encountered since his rebirth could be categorized as monsters, the Brood Mother certainly qualified. That alone was nearly enough to spur him into action, so, with his every instinct pushing him forward, he didn't even feel like he had a choice.

The only question was how he could accomplish his goal of killing the thing without being overwhelmed himself. With that in mind, Zeke pushed his disgust to the back of his mind and began to study the scene before him as he tried to come up with a plan. In the end, though, he could only come up with something bare-bones—not because he lacked the ability to think strategically, but rather because he didn't have enough information to make anything more than a basic attack plan.

After almost an hour's worth of observation, Zeke stood. He discarded everything he didn't need, including his satchel and spear, before hefting his club onto his shoulder. He'd had to replace his favored weapon a couple of times already, but luckily, it was a popular weapon among the trolls. Each time he had replaced it, he'd done so with a slightly sturdier and heavier weapon, so the one he carried now weighed at least forty pounds. However, it still felt light in his hands, and he could swing it for hours.

Without further ado, Zeke leapt down into the crater, and as soon as he landed, began to methodically exterminate the troll larvae. Each swing felled a handful of the creatures, but there were hundreds of them, so he knew it would take hours to whittle them down enough that he felt comfortable attacking the Brood Mother at the far end of the crater. Thankfully, they posed little threat to him; with his increased durability, their sharp teeth could barely even draw blood, and it would take them an eternity to do any real damage.

Zeke was in no mood to give them such an opportunity, and he soon became a whirlwind of death as he plunged into their ranks, leveling eggs and troll larvae alike. The eggs exploded with half-formed troll embryos and the combination of pus and mucus that coated the Brood Mother. To call it disgusting would've been a vast understatement, but Zeke paid it no mind as he decimated the cavern's troll population.

Through it all, he kept [**Leech Strike**] active, so even on the rare occasion that a particularly strong creature managed to wound him, the constant stream of life force quickly healed him. In addition, it kept fatigue at bay, so he swung his club with the regularity of a metronome as he cleared out the cavern.

But what sort of mother could sit by and watch its progeny be murdered by some unstoppable monster? Certainly not the Brood Mother, who wailed with every death. More, it shifted its bulk until it found itself on its belly, its grotesque teats mashed against the rocky ground. With a heave, it raised itself into the air and let out a piercing shriek that cut right through Zeke like an aural scythe.

He fell to the ground, his club forgotten as he clutched his hands to his ears. The troll larvae swarmed over him, their sharp claws and even sharper teeth digging futilely into his skin. His endurance won out, but only barely, and it was clear that soon, they'd wear him down completely. Once that happened, he'd become food for their development.

In the innermost parts of Zeke's mind, he knew he needed to get up, to throw the creatures off and continue his path of wanton slaughter. However, the Brood Mother's scream wasn't just an auditory attack. It was mental, as well, scuttling any sense of rational thought. It was as if his entire mind had been shattered into a million jagged shards, then shoved back together in a jumble of mismatched pieces. One second, he thought he was back in the old world, with his father swearing at him for watching a third strike pass him by, and then the next, he was waking up in the cave and fighting for his life.

He was with his brother, well before Tommy's kidney disease progressed to the point of confining him to his bed. He was happy, then. So was Zeke. But it was all an illusion; eventually, their real lives would reassert themselves. Zeke would go back to his father's abusive training, while Tommy would disappear into his books while he tried to forget about the fact that his days were numbered.

Then he was sitting in his old room, listening as his father beat his mother because she'd had the audacity to apply for a job at the local supermarket. He'd called it humiliating that his wife thought she had to work. It didn't matter that they'd just had their electricity cut off due to lack of payment. Or that he clearly couldn't keep up with their bills, largely because he'd had his hours cut back due to his obsession with training Zeke. No—he didn't care about any of that. Instead, he cared only about how it looked, and he'd taken his frustrations out on his wife.

Meanwhile, Zeke had tried to work himself up to confronting the man. He'd been only eleven years old, so he knew he couldn't really make a difference. But that didn't matter—not to his adolescent mind—and when he couldn't work up the courage, he considered himself a coward. He thought he'd failed his mother.

A million different memories flitted through his mind. Some were traumatizing. Others were pleasant. But they were all designed to distract him from the real world, where he was slowly being eaten alive by a horde of troll larvae. Finally, after an interminable span of time, Zeke gained a foothold of sanity amid his jumbled memories when one of the monsters finally managed to take a chunk out of his arm. The pain brought a tiny piece of his consciousness back, and he used that to drag himself from the quagmire of confusion that had been forced upon him. Slowly, Zeke regained his sense of self, bit by bit, until he finally felt something else. Something far more powerful.

Rage coursed through his veins as his muscles bunched. With a snarl, he triggered [**Heart of the Berserker**], and he felt the increased power flow through his body. He exploded to his feet, sending two dozen troll larvae sailing through the air with enough force that when they finally landed a hundred feet away, they burst like watermelons filled with blood, guts, and other assorted viscera.

Zeke hardly noticed as he charged through the sea of infant monsters, swinging his club with terrifying strength. The air whistled with the momentum of each swing, and the force was so great that before the creatures were sent flying into their brethren, the weapon tore huge chunks from their bodies. But Zeke hardly noticed. He had much bigger game in his sights.

The effects of the aural attack hadn't entirely faded, and Zeke's mind was still a ragged mess, but he could think well enough to know that he needed to discard his plan. Originally, he'd intended to slowly exterminate the troll larvae while destroying the eggs, saving the Brood Mother for last. However, he had little confidence in being able to withstand another of the monster's mental assaults, so he had little choice but to take care of it as quickly as possible.

Thanks to his brutal [**Heart of the Berserker**]-empowered swings, the sea of troll larvae easily parted before him, and before long, he found himself looking up at the Brood Mother's disgusting body. His original estimate had been that it was thirty feet long, but upon further inspection, he realized that it was half again bigger than that. In addition, the pus-filled cysts covering its body had lost their yellowish luster, replacing it with an angry red pulse that gave them an orange cast.

Just as Zeke crashed through the last of the troll larvae, his world exploded in pain when hundreds of cysts burst with explosive force, inundating the entire cavern in thick yellow-and-red pus. All around him, the weak troll larvae screamed in agony as the pus latched on to them, melting through their very skin. In mere seconds, they were reduced to puddles of foul-smelling goop.

Zeke was made of tougher stuff than that, though, and he merely acquired third-degree chemical burns wherever the acidic concoction landed on his body. And considering that he was drenched, that meant nearly every inch of his skin was quickly turned into a mass of unbearable suffering.

But Zeke had spent the vast majority of his new life in some degree of pain. He had endured the acidic combination of the mana water and the blue-spotted mushrooms, even going so far as to seek out more. He'd been riddled with various wounds. He'd been disemboweled. His entire leg had been put through a blender of tentacles and teeth. So, how could something so simple as having his skin melted off stop him?

With a defiant roar, Zeke leapt thirty feet into the air, swinging his club with all the considerable might he could muster. The club almost ignited as it tore through the air in an overhand swing. It hit precisely where he'd aimed—the Brood Mother's scaly, ratlike head.

The snout burst into an explosion of blood, teeth, and spit, and the weapon shattered, sending bullet-like shards deep into the creature's head. It wailed in agony, but Zeke wasn't finished. When he landed, he immediately whipped around, half-dissolved flaps of skin dripping from his body, to see the Brood Mother going berserk as it writhed in pain. Ignoring his own agony and disgust, Zeke leapt atop its bulbous form, his feet burning each time they landed in one of the cysts as he ran up the thing's body. When he finally reached its head once again, Zeke gripped what was left of the thing's snout, and with a mighty heave, ripped it asunder.

It died with a pitiful gurgle, its elephantine body collapsing onto the ground with a thunderous crash. Zeke rolled free, ignoring the sting of the additional pus he picked up along the way. Even as he felt his body beginning to break down, Zeke dispelled his [**Heart of the Berserker**]. A wave of exhaustion hit him, but he pushed through, slowly inching his way out of crater and away from the acidic pus.

Eventually, he made his way back to his discarded belongings. Thankfully, his makeshift satchel had been far enough away from the Brood Mother to avoid the pus, so with bleeding fingers, Zeke quickly found some of his stored fish. Despite his nausea, he wolfed it down; without it, he was certain that his wounds would overcome him. Even with the healing associated with eating the fish's flesh, he wasn't sure if it would be enough.

But if he did survive, he had reason to celebrate, because he'd gotten a few notifications that he hadn't expected.

17

ABOVE AND BEYOND

Zeke leaned against the wall, chewing on a piece of fish as he tried to distract himself from the agonizing pain of his healing body. The good news was that most of his wounds were largely superficial; the acid-like pus had done a number on his skin, but the combination of his high durability and incredible vitality, which had been further boosted by [**Leech Strike**], had prevented him from being melted alive. He wasn't even sure if he'd end up with any scars, which was something of a miracle, considering he'd been drenched in the acidic pus.

Even better, he'd finally gained a level from killing the much higher-level Brood Mother, pushing him to level seven. As he ate his energy- and vitality-boosting meal, Zeke allocated his free points into strength and endurance, putting eight points into the former, with the remaining seven in the latter.

Originally, he'd intended to split the points evenly between strength, dexterity, and endurance, but he felt like his dexterity was in a pretty good place, not least because of his history of handling a baseball bat. Spending most of his teenage years trying to hit a three-inch-wide ball that was speeding toward him in excess of ninety miles an hour had given him the sort of coordination that couldn't be quantified with stats. Plainly put, he could usually hit whatever he was aiming for. And while he still intended to focus on the stat in the future so his coordination didn't lag behind, he thought that strength and endurance were far more important for his current prospects of surviving the cave system.

On top of reaching level seven, he'd also acquired a new achievement, the submenu of which he quickly opened.

Above and Beyond—Complete an optional quest before leaving your starting dungeon. +5 to all stats, +5% to all stats

For a long moment, Zeke just stared at the line of information. It was an incredible, unexpected boost to his stats, and it made him wonder just how much more powerful than a typical person he might become. He didn't think that many people would've attacked the Brood Mother at his level, much less survived to get an achievement. The monster had been more than three times his level, and it had taken everything he had to come out on top. It seemed that the Framework rewarded taking such chances.

More than that, the description of the achievement gave him some hints about his current situation. While his first quest, which was to escape the cave system, had all but confirmed that there was an entire world above him, Zeke had begun to doubt that he'd ever see the light of day. After all, by his reckoning, he'd spent over seven months underground, and he'd yet to see even a hint of humanity. So, it was reasonable to question his situation. But now, he'd received further confirmation that escape was more than just possible; it was necessary and expected. In fact, the troll caves could be seen as something of a tutorial—a place designed to introduce him to his new reality. Driving that notion home was the fact that he'd completed an optional quest he didn't even know was there.

And with quests came rewards, which was the biggest reason for Zeke's excitement. With a flick of his eyes, Zeke navigated to the appropriate submenu and read the text associated with the quest he'd just completed.

Quest (Optional): Destroy the Source
Objective: Slay the Brood Mother (Complete)
Choose Reward: Weapon (G), Armor (G), Accessory (G)

Zeke read and reread the quest text, looking for a hint on how he should make his choice. On the one hand, he certainly needed a new weapon, having shattered his club on the Brood Mother's face. But he'd broken plenty of weapons before, and there was no shortage of clubs to go around. He just had to steal another from the next troll village he came across, and until then, he could use his spear. It wasn't optimal, but he'd gotten decent with it. Then again, this weapon would be G-grade, which was probably a good deal better than any of the clubs he'd used. Even the latest, which had been the strongest of the bunch, wasn't even graded.

The armor would be nice, too. After all, he was wearing nothing but strips of cloth that had once been the linen pants with which he'd been reborn. Anything at all would definitely be an improvement on that, considering he was all but naked. However, Zeke wasn't sure if it would just give him a single piece of armor, or if he'd get an entire set, but he suspected the former. And therein lay the issue. He'd be extremely upset if he forewent a new, upgraded weapon for a bracer. Or a single boot. A helmet wouldn't be terrible, but he couldn't help but feel that his ever-increasing endurance was good enough to see him through to the end of the cave system, at the very least—especially if he kept getting levels and powerful achievements.

As far as accessories went, Zeke had absolutely no idea what that even meant. Perhaps it would be some stat-boosting treasure? Or maybe it was something that would give him an ability? He simply had no clue what was even possible with an accessory, so he didn't feel qualified to even consider it. It was possible he was throwing away a golden opportunity to grow immeasurably stronger, but he couldn't in good conscience pick something without knowing the basic parameters of what it might entail. So, he eliminated that option without any further consideration, which left him with the two others.

Weapon or armor. Offense or defense. It truly wasn't that difficult of a decision, based on his previous experiences. Nothing had killed him yet, so the armor seemed somewhat superfluous, especially considering that he would get progressively more durable with every level. But he'd already gone through a handful of clubs, and he suspected that his enemies would just get stronger the higher he climbed through the cave system. A more durable weapon might be just the thing he needed to not only survive but thrive. Because if the quest had taught him one thing, it was that things weren't as straightforward as they seemed. There were other hidden opportunities in the so-called dungeon, and he intended to pick it completely clean. A strong weapon would surely help him in that endeavor. So, without further hesitation, he mentally selected that option, and a white metal box trimmed in gold appeared in front of him.

For a long moment, Zeke just stared at the case. While he wasn't sure what the white metal was, it didn't seem to have been painted. Its color was a property of the material itself. That, in addition to the gold trim, meant that the box alone was probably worth more than anything he'd ever held in his own hands. And that was just the case. Surely, the weapon would be even more valuable. So, he ignored the pain of his healing body as he bent forward and opened the box to reveal . . .

A three-and-a-half-foot-long bone.

No—it wasn't just a bone, as evidenced by the rough leather wrapped around one end, creating a grip. What's more, on the opposite side, amid what might've been the ball of a joint, there were two-inch metal studs whose material looked very similar to what had been used to construct the case. Finally, the entire haft was covered in glyphs that looked like nothing so much as scrimshaw carvings. After staring at the thing for a few seconds, Zeke remembered to cast [**Inspection**], and he was rewarded with a description of the weapon.

Voromir, the Dragon-Bone Mace (G)—An incredibly durable bludgeoning weapon created from the bone of a powerful crimson dragon. Special functions: Adaptability—adapts weight to suit strength.

Zeke's mouth dropped open as he read the description. Despite his initial impression, the weapon was everything he'd hoped it would be. Not only would it grow with his increasing strength, but due to his lone combat skill being a function of his own damage, it would also enhance his [**Leech Strike**]. If it really functioned the way the description said, he couldn't have been happier with his choice of quest reward. So, he reached down, wrapped his fingers around the leather grip, and without fanfare, hefted the weapon.

True to the weapon's description, even when he held it in one hand, it felt like the perfect weight. The same could be said when he clasped it with his other hand and gave it a few exploratory swings. Even though he was still seated, he could feel the weight and balance adjusting as he swung the weapon around.

However, he couldn't hide his disappointment when the box in which it had come dissipated into white motes a couple of minutes after he'd retrieved the mace. It probably shouldn't have been a surprise, but he was still a little disappointed by the loss.

As Zeke sat there recuperating, he couldn't really contain his excitement. When he was younger, Zeke had often gotten baseball paraphernalia as Christmas presents. Mostly, it was because he didn't really have any other interests, but it was also due to his father's single-mindedness concerning the sport. To him, every occasion was an opportunity to get better at baseball—an attitude that had rubbed off on Zeke. So, when he'd gotten a new bat or glove for his birthday or Christmas, he'd carry it around for the rest of the day, all the while dreaming of all the things he would do with the item. The same thing happened with his new mace, Voromir. Even as he opened his status window, he cradled the mace in his arms like a newborn baby.

Name	Ezekiel Blackwood
Class	N/A
Level	7
Race	Human (G)
Alignment	Isphodel
Achievements	First Blood, Hasty Evolution, Above and Beyond
Strength	81
Agility	66
Dexterity	71
Endurance	95
Vitality	79
Intelligence	56
Wisdom	54
Unassigned Attribute Points	0

His gains from the battle with the Brood Mother were astronomical; getting a 5 percent bonus to all his stats made Above and Beyond his best achievement yet. And Zeke suspected that his new weapon was probably even more impactful than his stat gains. However, it hadn't come without a significant cost, and one he was still in the process of paying.

In the end, it took him most of the rest of the day to recover before he felt well enough to move on. But before he did, he needed to inspect the scene of the battle. While he wasn't exactly excited about revisiting the foul-smelling crater, Zeke knew that he'd be kicking himself for the foreseeable future if he didn't make sure there wasn't anything of value being left behind. So, without further hesitation, he strode down the tunnel where he'd been recuperating and quickly retraced his steps back to the cavern in which he'd most recently fought for his life.

And it was just as disgusting as he expected it to be. Everywhere he looked, there were still steaming puddles of goop that had once been troll larvae. Not a single one of the little monsters had survived intact, and even the Brood Mother had begun to dissolve from the inside out. Zeke suspected that if he were to push against its mottled skin with even a normal human's strength, his hand would break right through the flimsy, revolting barrier. Not that he'd do such a thing, of course. He'd had his fill of the giant, obese troll matriarch.

Zeke crept along the outer edge of the cavern as he circled around the morass of melted trolls, his new mace in one hand while his other trailed along the outer wall. Thankfully, it didn't take him long to cross to the other side, where he was confronted with a surprising sight: a door.

It wasn't the flaps of leather that covered most of the troll huts' entrances, but an actual wooden door constructed of planed wood. It even had a latch, which appeared to have been made of wrought iron, making it far and away the most technologically advanced thing he'd seen since his rebirth.

For a moment, Zeke was certain that he'd found the way out. After all, why else would there be an actual door? But then, he started to think it through, and he realized that his conclusion made no real sense. Killing the Brood Mother had been an optional quest, and he suspected that the primary path to the surface never would've come close to her. If it hadn't been for the smell and his curiosity, Zeke would never have found the cavern in the first place. So, it didn't make sense that the path to the surface would lead past her.

But if it wasn't that, then what was it? A treasure trove, maybe? Would he find another optional quest inside? Perhaps an armory? The quest reward had awakened something inside of him, a newfound sense of greed that was nearly overwhelming as he imagined all sorts of power-ups behind that simple, wooden door.

After taking a deep breath, Zeke kicked the door in. In an explosion of splinters, it flew off its hinges to collide with a very surprised pair of trolls seated within. Zeke was moving in an instant, swinging his new mace with a deftness he'd never felt with any of his previous weapons. With a mental command, the twin runes for [**Leech Strike**] sprang into being, immediately transferring to Voromir, integrating with the other runes carved into the mace's haft.

The first troll had no chance to react, and in the space of a second, its head had been caved in. The second monster was a little luckier, but only just, because even though it managed to raise its spear to block Zeke's next swing, the crude, wooden weapon proved no match for the dragon-bone mace. The spear shattered, barely offering a token resistance before Zeke's swing connected with the troll's neck, breaking it just as easily as it had destroyed the spear.

The familiar vitality associated with [**Leech Strike**] flowed through his body, accompanied by the energy from the kills. Zeke couldn't stop a small smile from spreading across his face as he considered how easily he'd taken the trolls out. Both of them had been level thirteen, but he'd dispatched them without breaking a sweat. Certainly, taking them by surprise had contributed to how easily he'd managed to kill them, but the real star had been Voromir and Zeke's ever-increasing strength.

However, the short fight hadn't gone unnoticed because, just across the room, there was another door, through which Zeke could see a third troll warrior staring at him. Behind that monster, a half dozen others were gathered.

Zeke's grin widened as he thought that there had to be something good waiting for him in the next room if it required so many guards.

18

NO GRAY AREAS

In the past few months, Zeke had gotten into the habit of charging his enemies—a strategy that would be entirely counterproductive in this setting. He was no tactical genius—far from it, in fact. But he couldn't discount the advantages of limiting how many of the trolls could come at him at one time. So, he stood his ground, waiting on them to attack. And they didn't disappoint, the lead troll warrior bellowing in rage as it launched itself forward, swinging a rock-bladed axe.

Parrying with his new mace, Zeke knocked the axe aside before shoulder checking the behemoth of a troll. He didn't put all his strength into it, but it still stopped the monster's momentum cold, even pushing it back a few inches. That didn't mean Zeke was safe, however, because the creature lived up to the ferocity Zeke had come to know and loathe, its jaws snapping as it tried to bite him. Zeke wasn't afraid of its teeth, though. The things had powerful jaws, but they weren't nearly enough to break through his durable skin. It did still hurt, though.

With a growl, Zeke headbutted the troll in the chest, the blow hard enough to crack the thing's sternum, eliciting a howl of agony. Then, with every ounce of strength he could muster, Zeke punched the troll in the ribs. He'd intended the blow to further stun the creature; broken ribs often had that effect. However, he was more than a little surprised when his hand crashed through the troll's scaly skin, sinking deep into its torso. Adapting to the new development, Zeke immediately grabbed whatever he could and pulled with considerable might, yanking the thing's innards out of its body. A few feet worth of intestines came out, held fast by a gory hand. Zeke kicked the troll's knee, buckling it with incredible force before raising his club high above his head. It descended with enough force that the troll didn't even have a chance to look surprised before its entire head exploded, ending its life immediately.

If there was one thing Zeke had learned, it was how to kill trolls. No matter how much damage he managed to do, their insane vitality would eventually heal them. He'd found that out the hard way on enough occasions that he knew that the only way to ensure their deaths was to go for the head. It made the fights a little repetitive, and he feared getting into a rut—after all, he wouldn't always be fighting trolls, and he knew he'd have to expand his fighting style when he escaped the caves—but there wasn't much else he could do.

Over the next few minutes, Zeke made quick work of the other six trolls, felling them by various means. Some he treated like the first, quickly smashing their heads in with his new mace, Voromir. But he was also forced to whittle a few of them down before dispatching them with a blow to the head. Soon, he was alone, surrounded only by the corpses of his enemies.

Zeke panted, the head of his mace falling to the ground. His new weapon had performed beautifully—better than he ever could have hoped, in fact—but even so, the trolls had put up an impressive fight. Despite their crude appearance, those axes had proven extremely sharp, cutting into his flesh with relative ease. The wounds didn't go too deep, but outnumbered as he was, they'd started to add up toward the end. The spears were a little easier to deal with, but even so, he'd acquired more than two dozen new wounds by the time he crushed the skull of the last troll warrior.

As he shook the mace to rid it of the accumulated gore, Zeke couldn't help but wonder how powerful he really was. The trolls' levels suggested to him that he was far stronger than he should be, but considering that he had no context aside from the hundreds of trolls he had killed, he couldn't be sure. Certainly, he'd nearly died so often that he couldn't imagine many others doing the same. He wasn't so arrogant that he thought his survival could be chalked up to talent or skill. Not entirely, at least. He knew he'd gotten lucky on more than one occasion; the early days when he'd gotten the vitality boost associated with gaining a level when he desperately needed it came to mind, and that was just the tip of the iceberg. However, he also knew that he was built very differently than most people.

It really wasn't so different from playing sports. Tens of millions of kids dreamed of being the next professional athlete. Whether it was baseball or one of the other major sports, they all thought they could make it. Some were weeded out when they realized they just didn't have the requisite natural ability to succeed, but even more fell by the wayside because they didn't have the work ethic required to reach that lofty goal. Talent can take an athlete a long way, but nobody reaches the top without a significant offering of blood, sweat, and tears—an offering Zeke had paid many times over.

So, while Zeke was sure that there would be others who'd had similar fortuitous encounters, he knew there couldn't be that many like him. Just like there weren't many who had the combination of talent, luck, and stubborn refusal to quit that it took to succeed in athletics.

Pushing those thoughts to the back of his mind, Zeke inspected his fallen enemies' weapons. He suspected that the axes would shatter the moment he used even half his strength, so he left those behind. However, one of the spears appeared to be better quality than the one he carried, so he quickly swapped them out. The trolls carried nothing else of value, so he left their corpses where they'd fallen.

Thus armed, Zeke went through the second door, finding himself in a long hall that appeared to have been carved by the trolls. The walls were far too even to be natural, and the hall itself didn't wind or curve like most of the tunnels he'd seen. But that wasn't so surprising. If they could create the stone huts that had become increasingly prevalent in the villages, carving out a tunnel wasn't out of the question.

He pushed through the hall, keeping his eyes trained ahead at a smooth wall that appeared to be a dead end. As Zeke drew closer, he saw gaps in the stone, and when he saw a huge iron ring hanging halfway down and to the outer edge of the rock slab, he figured out what he was looking at. It was a huge stone door, big enough that the enormous trolls could walk through the resultant entryway without ducking. If it weighed less than a thousand pounds, Zeke would've been incredibly surprised.

But if the trolls could open it, so could he. Despite the disparity in size, he'd long since proven that his strength exceeded theirs, and not by a small amount.

So, he planted his feet, grasped the iron ring, and pulled. For a short moment, the door groaned, protesting its opening, but it soon started to inch open. To get better leverage, Zeke put his foot on the wall and exerted the entirety of his strength. With a loud creak, the door finally swung open on hidden hinges, eventually crashing against the wall. As he turned to inspect what he hoped would be a treasure trove, Zeke couldn't help but feel a sense of overwhelming excitement.

It all came crashing to the ground a second later when he saw the next room's contents.

Human bodies, hanging from hooks in the ceiling. Appendages, piled against a wall. Torsos, thrown aside. Skin, stretched taught and drying. Everywhere he looked, he saw dead human beings. Bile climbed into his throat as he took in the view, and he fell to his knees, vomiting onto the floor.

By this point, Zeke had killed hundreds of trolls, so he thought his heart had hardened to the concept of death. He hadn't even flinched when his mace had crushed that last troll's skull. Or when he'd executed the Brood Mother. He'd been doing what he had to do to survive. And while he'd initially wrestled with the morality of killing the troll larvae, he had rarely revisited the debate since. What he was doing was necessary, wasn't it? He hadn't been given a choice. And besides—they attacked him first. It was practically self-defense at this point.

But what about all those trolls he'd killed in their sleep? What about the ones he'd ambushed? The Brood Mother who'd been minding its own business as it hatched its disgusting children? The moment they knew he was there, they'd attacked. But he had instigated quite a few of those encounters. So, given that they'd proven themselves to be sapient by creating a society, tools, and communal villages, it wasn't out of the question that he'd feel a little guilt over his actions. They were monsters, but wasn't that a matter of perspective? Wouldn't they see him the same way?

What he had just seen put the lie to any sense of ambiguity. Cold air wafted out of the body-filled cavern, giving him a hint at the room's nature. It was a larder, and it was filled with human corpses. It didn't take Zeke long to pull himself together, and when he looked again, he saw the similarities between the room before him and the meat lockers he'd seen in movies. They even had crude meat hooks hanging from the rocky ceiling, upon which were skinned corpses.

Zeke's fingers grazed the satchel at his side, and he nearly vomited again. The leather it was made of looked quite a bit like the skins he saw in a corner. They were being stretched, so they were very misshapen, but Zeke couldn't fail to recognize them for what they were. Unbeknownst to him, he had been carrying a satchel made of human skin.

Beneath the horror of seeing hundreds of human corpses that had been stored like so much meat, Zeke's thoughts churned. Whatever guilt he'd managed to cultivate fled in an instant, replaced by unrepentant rage. Suddenly, he wished there was an army of trolls in front of him so he could take out his anger on them. Sure—he'd probably die in the attempt, but seeing your race being treated as food was enough to push any sense of rationality aside.

Bur more than that, it opened a door in his mind, behind which was the real, unadulterated truth of his new world.

Kill or be killed. Predator and prey. The strong dictated the rules. Perhaps things would change when he escaped the caves, but then again, each and every person who made it to the surface had been through a baptism of blood. The Framework, whatever it really was, wanted to forge them into weapons. Oberon had said as much, so long ago. And it very obviously did so by putting the reborn humans through a trial of life and death.

Never was that more evident than when Zeke stared at a larder full of human corpses that were probably intended to feed the Brood Mother and its horde of children.

Zeke sat there outside that room, leaning against one of the walls and staring ahead without seeing a thing. He had no idea how long he sat there, but with so many corpses looking down on him, it felt like an eternity as he tried to make sense of it all. Idle questions like how the trolls got so many bodies into the larder were left unanswered because, at the end of the day, he just didn't care. How didn't seem very important in the face of the simple fact that they had killed so many human beings and intended to eat them.

Eventually, though, Zeke's mind turned to revenge. There was a small part of him that knew he couldn't really blame the trolls for acting according to their nature. To them, humans were food. But that didn't mean he couldn't hold them accountable.

Hours later, Zeke rose. Gripping the huge stone door, he pushed it shut before turning and walking away. There was nothing else to do. No one to save. In the end, there was only one thing on his mind. Vengeance swirled in his heart, mingling with righteous anger as he set out to make things right.

From here on out, there would be no quarter. If he saw a troll, he would kill it. Not for the experience. Not so he could escape. No—he would murder every last one of the hateful monsters so that they wouldn't kill any more of his people.

Or maybe it was to feed the raging fire within him.

Either way, he'd found his path, and it led straight through the trolls.

19

INEVITABILITY

Clutching her bow, Abby silently stalked through the jungle, sweat beading on her forehead as she flanked the rest of the party. They'd already lost two men to the cursed place, and though they weren't much better than Julio, she took the loss hard. After all, she was the party's highest-level scout, and as such, they'd depended on her to warn them of any dangers. It wasn't that she didn't take the role seriously, but rather, that her skills didn't really fit their expectations. Despite being an archer, none of her abilities really fit the traditional pathfinder role. She could usually make do because of her stat allocation being partially skewed toward agility and dexterity, but she had nothing that would help her avoid or track enemies. And that lack had come due when they were ambushed a few days before by a troop of fire apes.

The party had reacted like one would expect from an elite squad, giving as good as they got, but there was only so much they could do when faced with such a disparity in numbers. At the end of the day, the expedition had only ten members, and they'd been attacked by three times as many of the fire-wielding simians. They eventually won out due to their varied skills, with both Vladimir and Abby herself playing key roles, but when the dust settled, two of Julio's men had fallen. It was a sobering reminder that the wilderness was filled with risks, even for seasoned adventurers such as them.

As she weaved through the thick underbrush, Abby took a look at her skills.

[Gust of Wind] (G)—Summon a bulwark of wind. Evolution: Grants finer control over airflow.

[Conjured Arrow] (H)—Summons an arcane arrow. Durability and speed of conjuration based on Dexterity.

[Makeshift Camp] (G)—Create a temporary camp that increases regeneration of both mana and Vitality, as well as providing basic protection from wildlife.

[Cure Disease] (H)—Flood a body with purifying mana, curing minor diseases.

Not for the first time, Abby lamented her first skill choice. In her defense, she'd been entirely clueless when she chose it, and back then, she had half suspected that the entire thing had been a dream. It wasn't until her first kill that she had come around to the fact that she was in a new world with very different rules from those associated with her old life. If she'd had it all to do over again, she would have chosen something that offered a little more direct offense—something like the arcane arrows that were a staple for most archers she had come across.

When she got her second skill at level five, she had been prepared to do just that. However, the Framework had other plans, and it had offered her only utility skills. Thankfully, she'd acquired a bow soon after leaving her tutorial dungeon, so she at least got something useful. Without [**Conjured Arrow**], she'd have been forced to take up fletching just to walk down her chosen path. And even then, it would've been incredibly inconvenient.

By the time she reached level ten, Abby had learned enough that she had been looking forward to her new skill selection quite a bit. There was a saying that the Framework laughs at the plans of men, and never was that truer than when she'd finally gained her tenth level. She and Vladimir had been pushing hard to accomplish a mission when they'd come upon a pack of wargs—giant wolflike creatures that traveled in groups of up to twenty. They had only barely survived by running, but the few that Abby had managed to kill had pushed her past level ten, granting her the ability to choose a new skill.

Eagerly, she had opened the submenu, and she was rewarded with three incredibly potent archery skills. She'd been so excited that she almost didn't even look at the other options. However, the battle with the warg pack hadn't come without a price, and Vladimir had been mortally wounded. Without a healer, he would surely die. So, she had been forced to eschew the other skills in favor of the one option that could help them in the short term. That was how she'd chosen [**Makeshift Camp**].

Truly, it had exceeded her expectations. The skill itself had a couple of requirements—chiefly that there needed to be a fire wherever she chose to use it—but once she met them and empowered the skill, it had created a twenty-foot circle of regeneration and protection that had allowed Vladimir to live through that night. In addition, it had even rebuffed a few attacks from monsters who'd smelled the blood and rightly assumed they were weakened. Since then, it had evolved to the next tier, which made the barrier stronger and more versatile, as well as increased the radius of the area affected.

Still, regardless of how well it had worked, Abby couldn't help but feel a little cheated by the Framework. She was an archer without any applicable skills. A ranger without the ability to track. A scout who relied on stats alone to sneak through the wilds. If she hadn't already proved her worth a thousand times over, Abby would've felt weak to the point of giving up.

But maybe that was just her old identity asserting itself.

Abby shook her head, forcibly dispelling those thoughts. She hadn't been that person for nearly a decade now. Even before her death, she'd left that identity behind. And she wouldn't give in to that feeling of worthlessness ever again. Not now. Not after she'd sacrificed so much and worked so hard at becoming the powerful version of herself she'd always dreamed of becoming.

She loped through the jungle, her eyes darting around as she tried to see everything all at once. While she might not have any true scouting abilities, she was still more perceptive than most. Otherwise, she wouldn't have survived in this brutal world for so long. The Radiant Isles were littered with the corpses of the careless.

It was that very perception that stopped her in her tracks as the slightest of movements caught her eye. She didn't give in to the natural inclination to whip around to face the creature that was obviously stalking her. Instead, she let out a high-pitched whistle to let her party know of the danger. It had barely left from between her parted lips before something burst forth out of the underbrush, gleaming claws arcing for her face.

However, Abby's investment in dexterity and agility wasn't just for show, and she easily dodged the creature's attack. Still, its claws passed only inches in front of her, so close that she could feel the wind of their passage. And another set was on its way, coming in from the side. Abby sucked her stomach in, barely avoiding the claws she knew would have disemboweled her.

As a primarily ranged combatant, Abby didn't have the endurance to tank such a blow—not many did—so she'd been forced to adapt to that weakness. Most archers would've taken some sort of movement skill, but she hadn't had that opportunity. Many people were overly reliant on skills, and rightly so. They were often incredibly powerful. But Abby, who had, through circumstance or ignorance, been pushed down a different path, didn't have that luxury. Instead, she had spent hour after hour, year after year, training herself in various acrobatics that took advantage of her strengths. The result was that, even without skills to aid her, Abby was better at avoiding damage than the vast majority of her peers.

As the creature—Abby only got a brief glimpse of black fur—charged at her, Abby leaped over it. Using the monster as a step, she launched herself even higher, twisting as she flew through the air. Pushing mana into the rune in her hand, she cast [**Conjured Arrow**], and a silvery arrow suddenly materialized in her grip. In the space of an instant, she had nocked the arrow, then loosed it at her attacker.

The arrow, propelled with unnatural speed by [**Gust of Wind**], struck true, sinking deep into the monster's neck. A fountain of stark-white blood followed, and the thing wheeled around, completely ignorant that it was already dead. As Abby landed, another arrow sailed through densely humid air, hitting the black-furred creature in the eye with enough force that the arrowhead burst through the back of its skull.

It fell with a thud.

That was when Abby got her first look at the thing, and she was surprised to see that she recognized it as a gaborin—a strange, humanoid mixture of man, bat, and panther that made its home in tropical jungles. She'd run into them before, and back then, she'd only survived because her party had skirted the edge of their territory.

The things were semi-sapient, meaning that they were primarily driven by instinct, but they had also formed a mimicry of a tribal society, not dissimilar from the apes of the old world. If apes were possessed of superhuman speed and claws that could rip through high-grade armor without missing a beat, of course. And like so many monsters, they traveled in packs—a nugget of information that proved accurate when Abby heard a bloodcurdling scream coming from the direction of her party.

Immediately, Abby took off, weaving through the trees like a wraith. Luckily, she'd only drawn the attention of one of the gaborin, else she'd have been shredded to pieces. However, that also meant that the bulk of the tribe—or pack, depending on how much intelligence one wanted to attribute to the monsters—would be attacking her party. And while she didn't really care about any of them, save Vladimir, she'd been given a job, and she intended to do it to the best of her abilities.

Eventually, she found the party, who were engaged in a furious battle against fifteen gaborin warriors. The creatures all looked similar to the one she'd killed—bipedal, black-furred, and with bat-like faces—though some of them had opted to use crude weapons instead of their razor-sharp claws. It seemed a waste to Abby, but one for which she was thankful.

The party itself was holding its own, though the sheer numbers were on the verge of tipping the balance. Just as Abby was beginning to wonder why Julio hadn't simply killed the entire group, the arrogant man made his move. It was almost like he was waiting on her to bear witness, a feeling that was supported by the fact that he looked up at her and winked before unsheathing his katana.

In the blink of an eye, Julio had bisected an unlucky gaborin who'd chosen that moment to charge the man. His blade had moved so quickly that Abby had difficulty even following what had happened, and she was only sure when she saw the black-furred creature fall apart.

How much agility did the man possess? Over a hundred?

Abby didn't have much time to contemplate, because just after dispatching the attacking creature, Julio chose to use his first skill—and it was a strange one, too. He slapped the blade of his katana against his metallic bracer with a clang, then sheathed his sword as a wave of aural power spread out around him, attacking both friend and foe alike.

For her part, Abby was far enough away that she was largely unaffected, but when the wave reached her, she still felt a piercing pain interrupting her thoughts. It was easy to shake off, but the men and gaborin in closer proximity weren't so lucky. One and all, they fell to the ground, writhing in pain.

That's when Julio struck.

He'd dispatched another three helpless gaborin before he realized he'd made a huge mistake. While the rest of the human party had finally succumbed to unconsciousness, the gaborin had adapted surprisingly quickly, and were already rising from the ground, white blood flowing from their ears.

Julio scrambled back, narrowly avoiding one claw after another as he swung his sword. Each swing was accompanied by a high-pitched whistle as it cut through the air—another skill, Abby was certain—but whatever it was meant to do, it was rendered ineffective by the fact that the gaborin had been deafened by his first attack.

Briefly, Abby considered letting the creatures kill the man. It would solve so many of her problems, and the world would be a much better place without the likes of Julio stalking its surface. Certainly, the women of Beacon would be much safer. On top of that, she'd already made her plans to double-cross the horrible man. However, doing so now would mean forfeiting the opportunity to evolve her race. She couldn't accomplish the terms of the missive without Julio; she wasn't strong enough. And she needed that fruit if she wanted to continue to advance.

So, it was with some reluctance that she raised her bow and finally loosed her conjured arrow. Then another. And another. Over and over again, each arrow finding its mark.

Predictably, it wasn't long before the gaborin realized that another threat had joined the battle, and a few turned and charged toward her. All but one went down before they made it to her, and the third was wounded badly enough that it took only one swing of her hatchet to finish the job.

Meanwhile, Julio was still hard-pressed, even by one of the gaborin. He was quick, but obviously out of practice. It seemed that he'd long relied on his overpowering skills, and when they'd proven ineffective, he didn't know what to do. Even so, he was level nineteen, and as such, his stats were in an entirely different category. It wasn't that dissimilar from if Vladimir had attacked her; he was a talented warrior, but the power difference would soon assert itself.

So, given that, Abby was more than a little surprised when Julio misplaced a foot and tripped over a root, giving the final gaborin an opening. Like lightning, its claw arced out, aiming for Julio's throat.

It never made it.

As soon as Abby saw Julio trip, she'd made her decision. She fired an arrow that, propelled by the wind, quickly found its mark.

The gaborin's entire paw exploded from the force, and the creature let out a pitiful howl infused with every ounce of its agony. Julio seized the opening, his katana finding the monster's chest and plunging straight through its heart. The gaborin collapsed atop him, the katana piercing all the way through its torso.

Abby wouldn't have felt guilty if Julio had died. In fact, she might've celebrated. But as much as she hated it, the fact remained that he was the key to her advancement. Without him, who knew how long it would be before she had another opportunity to evolve? Until they had killed enough drachnids to satisfy the terms of the missive, she would keep him alive. After, though? Well, she would put an arrow in him herself, if she got a good chance.

With the gaborin dead, Abby quickly closed the distance to her friend, Vladimir, who like the rest of the party had fallen into unconsciousness. She knelt beside the big warrior, checking his vitals.

"He lives," came a familiar voice. "They all do. Though they'll all awaken with splitting headaches."

Abby turned to the leader of the mission. Julio was coated in white blood, but he seemed unharmed. "What did you do?" she asked.

"Well, that's the problem, isn't it?" he said. Before Abby could react, Julio's hand swept across his body, propelling a mote of rainbow-hued energy toward her. She had no idea what it was, but she wasn't so trusting that she would willingly let it hit her. With inhuman reflexes, she leaped into the air, twisting as she conjured an arrow. Her eyes widened when the mote of multicolored energy followed her up and through the air, hitting her square in the forehead.

It didn't hurt. In fact, she didn't feel a thing. However, when she tried to fire her arrow, something stopped her. She tried to push through whatever barrier prevented it, but nothing seemed to work.

She landed lightly and demanded, "What did you do to me?!"

"Just some insurance," the man said, moving toward Vladimir. "I saw you hesitate back there. Let's just say that you and I are going to get very cozy from here on out."

He knelt beside the big warrior, putting a couple of fingers on his head. Abby felt more than saw a surge of energy before Julio stood, rolling his shoulders. "Very cozy, indeed," he said, grinning at her.

20

RAMPAGE

Zeke hid behind the stalk of one of the tree-sized mushrooms, his heart beating out of his chest while his breaths came in ragged, uneven gasps. He could barely hold Voromir in his blood-soaked hands, and it was all he could do to remain upright. But quitting wasn't an option. If he stopped to rest, even for a scant few minutes, he would doubtless fall prey to the dozens of hunting parties scouring the mushroom forest.

Not for the first time, he glanced down at his forearm. Amid the various gashes and lacerations, there was a softly glowing rune. But unlike the runes that activated his skills, this one pulsed with malevolent power, sapping his strength and igniting his nerve endings with every beat. Alone, the single curse would've been a mere inconvenience, easily ignored. But with fifteen others like it attached to various parts of his body, it had become a life-and-death struggle. And one he was steadily losing.

Zeke had long since become accustomed to pain, but weakness was something entirely new to him. And the cursed runes were more than physically draining, as well; they made everything feel more sluggish—even his mana and skills. With their effect steadily sapping both his mental and physical strength, the effects of [**Leech Strike**] were negligible, and even [**Heart of the Berserker**] had become mostly ineffective. It was like something was weighing down on his very soul. The worst part was that he knew that if he just had some time to study the runes, he could break them down.

He glanced around at the fungal forest. If he hadn't been running for his life, he would've been amazed at the size of the mushrooms in the giant cavern. They were at least as tall as most trees, with caps that spanned hundreds of feet. Like was the case with their smaller cousins that had been instrumental in evolving his body, the caps emitted a blue bioluminescence that was reflected by some sort of crystalline structures hundreds of feet above. The result was that the entire forest was bathed in a soft, blue light that felt almost blinding after spending over a year in darkness.

It would have been so easy to just give in. To give up and succumb to the weakness. He knew that the trolls wouldn't prolong his death; they were far too enraged to take the time to do anything but rip him apart. His life since being reborn had been characterized by agonizing pain, so it wasn't like it would be that big of a loss. And he remembered that nothingness that had preceded his rebirth. It hadn't been comforting, precisely, but there hadn't been any pain, either. Given his horrible state, such a fate didn't seem so terrible.

Zeke knew that he'd never just give up, though. Not only was he incredibly stubborn, but he'd already given up once in his old life. He hadn't acknowledged it as such, but when his future as a ballplayer had been snatched away from him, he hadn't just been depressed or rudderless—he was both of those things, but more than anything else, he'd simply given up on life. Perhaps he might've regained himself after a time, but it was entirely possible that he wouldn't have. In a way, he was glad that he had died when he had, managing to go out doing something worthwhile when he'd tried to donate his kidney to his little brother. Because if he hadn't, he would've only gotten worse.

He refused to let himself fall into that pit again. Not even for a second.

So, summoning what strength he could muster, Zeke turned to face the stalk of the mushroom. Resting his hand against it, he was somewhat surprised at its toughness. The almost rubbery texture wasn't quite as hard as tree bark, but it wasn't far off, either. Even if it was, though, it wouldn't have made much difference. Weakened as he was, Zeke was still much stronger than an old-world human. So, he dug his fingers into the rubbery trunk and began to climb.

It was much more difficult than he expected, especially given that he had to somehow hold his mace at the same time, but eventually, he made it to the cap without alerting his pursuers. That was when things got really difficult, but he quickly found that he could treat the gill-like structures on the bottom of the cap like monkey bars. Soon, he was swinging along, his feet dangling almost a hundred feet in the air while he balanced Voromir across his chest, holding it in place with his chin.

Thankfully, despite a couple of hunting parties crossing below him, Zeke remained undetected as he finally heaved himself onto the top of the enormous, blue-spotted mushroom. He barely had the strength to crawl a handful of feet toward the middle of the fungus before he collapsed in exhaustion. As he lay there, breathing like a bellows, Zeke thought about the past handful of months and how he'd gotten himself into such a pickle.

After finding the larder filled with human remains, Zeke had gone on a rampage, killing every troll he could find. He even went so far as to backtrack to troll towns he'd skipped over for being too populated. In his mind, the only good troll was a dead troll, and he'd lived by that mantra for more than a month, slaughtering everything in his path. And he'd reaped the benefits, too, even gaining a level. He didn't even slow down until he ran into the first troll shaman.

They didn't look that different from the warriors he'd killed, save that they were usually a bit shorter and lacking the muscle that characterized their physically intimidating brethren. In addition, while the troll warriors were typically clad in nothing but a loincloth, most of the shamans wore robes of crudely stitched-together human skin. They also, one and all, carried staffs capped with human skulls that had been painted black. The sight only furthered Zeke's anger and disgust.

He'd charged in, just like he always did, but when he was only halfway there, the shaman barked something in a harsh, guttural language, then pointed its staff at Zeke. A glowing green rune shot out at him, and he instinctively tried to dodge. However, it followed him with unerring accuracy, hitting him square in the chest. As soon as it touched his skin, it disappeared from sight. But it was still there. Zeke had felt it, burrowing into his pathways and obstructing everything from the flow of his mana to his life force. A single rune was little more than an annoyance, and he'd continued his charge, effortlessly taking out the shaman and the accompaniment of warriors—leaving him to study the curious rune the shaman had cast upon him.

In a way, Zeke was thankful for that encounter because it snapped him out of his trancelike, vengeful state. He soon found a secluded cave, where he spent the better part of a week studying the rune. It wasn't nearly as complicated as the ones that controlled his two skills, but it was still multilayered and complex enough that it took him days before he could even see what it did. All the while, he suffered from the stabbing pains and weakness that came with the rune. The effects were more frustrating than truly harmful, but they served their purpose of ruining his concentration, which was enough to slow him down considerably.

And that was probably a good thing because there was absolutely no way that he could've kept going without getting himself killed. It wasn't like his anger over what he had seen had simply faded away; he fully intended to follow through with his plan of killing every single troll in the caves. But he had been going about it all wrong. He hadn't had a plan; he'd simply been running wild through the cave system, murdering everything he saw. It wasn't sustainable, and it certainly wasn't a healthy frame of mind, even if it was justified.

However, having the rune to focus on changed everything, and as he began to understand the layered symbols that empowered the thing, he started to compare them with the construction of his skill runes. And the first thing he noticed was that the troll's curse was far more simplistic than the ones associated with his skills. It was like comparing rudimentary cave art to a Renaissance sculpture. Some of the concepts were the same, but there was ultimately such a wide gulf between them that they became different things entirely.

But studying the two in tandem did give Zeke some ideas about the basic construction of runes. Not enough to truly understand it, of course. But he discovered enough that he could at least break them, which was always far easier. More, it was probably something he was better suited for.

So, he'd slowly gone about unraveling that first curse. It took him nearly a week, and it was a lot more complicated than he thought it would be, but in the end, he finally managed to disperse it. Afterward, he'd sat in his little alcove, marveling at the feeling of finally not being in pain or feeling any weakness. By that point, his other wounds had long since healed, and though he'd added a few more scars to his growing collection, he was far stronger than he'd ever been in his life. On top of that, he felt like he'd made real strides in his understanding of the runes that seemed to drive everything about his new world. He left his self-imposed solitary confinement, for once feeling a little optimistic about his future.

If only it could've lasted.

For three more weeks, Zeke continued to climb the cave system, killing trolls wherever he found them. He ran into a few more shamans, and each of them unerringly cursed him, which had forced him to repeat the cleansing routine. The repetition had continued to give him at least some limited insight, but the real value was that he'd managed to cut the process down to a couple of days for each rune. He couldn't help but feel pleased at the progress.

Disaster eventually struck when he found the mushroom forest.

Zeke had to hand it to the trolls, though. Until that moment, he'd considered them possessed of little more than primate-level intelligence. Like hulking, scaly, murderous cavemen. So, he was more than a little surprised when he saw the trap they had laid for him.

He hadn't had time to count, but there had been more than fifty warriors there, each at least twice his level. And accompanying them were around twenty shamans. Even if he'd managed to find them unseen, Zeke would've fled before such odds. He was strong, durable, and incredibly deadly, but numbers still counted for something—especially when he knew precisely how debilitating those curses could be.

But he didn't have that option because they were waiting on him. And on top of that, he could hear the heavy footfalls of even more trolls approaching from behind, cutting off the easiest method of retreat.

So, he'd had little choice but to grit his teeth and push through, hoping he could lose them in the huge mushroom forest stretching out in front of him. It went on for miles, so with his superior strength and agility, he had a good chance of shaking off the lumbering trolls' pursuit. He only had to survive long enough to make that happen.

Even as Zeke sprinted toward the line of trolls, he had heard the familiar grunts coming from the shamans. Then, each of them had pointed their grisly staffs at him, casting their curses. The fluttering runes shot toward him with unerring accuracy, each hitting a different part of his body. The effect wasn't merely cumulative, but rather, it was exponential. Each empowered the other, sapping his strength to the point that, after only a few steps, he began to stumble. It took every ounce of his remaining strength, even empowered by [**Heart of the Berserker**], to crash through the troll lines, shouldering the brutes to the side as he made his way to what he hoped was safety.

The pursuit had continued for hours, the trolls howling in rage all the while, until, at last, Zeke managed to shake them. Even then, he didn't dare stop. Instead, he stumbled along, running on fumes the whole way, until, in a last ditch effort, he'd climbed atop the mushroom where he now lay, panting with the exertion of the last day and a half.

He lay there for hours as he tried to regain his strength, but the curses made that all but impossible. From experience, he knew that they wouldn't simply go away. He needed to unravel them, one by one, before he would get any semblance of rest. Still, even knowing that, he found it difficult to take that first step.

Finally, summoning the last drops of his willpower, Zeke focused his mind on the cursed rune that had latched itself onto his forearm and began the arduous process of unraveling it. It took him almost six hours, which, given the circumstances, was faster than he could've anticipated, but eventually, he managed to force it to dissipate.

One down, fifteen to go. Even as the troll search parties scoured the fungal forest, Zeke got to work.

21

EXPANDING THE REPERTOIRE

Zeke sat cross-legged upon the mushroom's cap, trying desperately to achieve something approaching peace. It was difficult because he was still exhausted, both mentally and physically, from unraveling the cursed runes. Not only did he feel weaker than he'd felt in months, but it was also as if his very soul had been shredded into pieces, and he was only just figuring out how to put them back together.

Until this point, Zeke had thought of his soul as something ephemeral. Intangible. Mystical. But now? After having spent the better part of a week dipping his mind into those turbulent waters, he knew it was far more tangible than he'd once thought. Of course, that didn't mean he understood it, except at the most basic level, but he had gleaned a few facts while unraveling the curses.

First was that his soul was the battery that provided the mana that fueled his skills. But it was more than that, too. It was also the essence of who he was, and each time he activated a skill, he lost a tiny sliver of himself. It was easily replenished, but he suspected that if he overtaxed his soul, extremely bad things would happen. He didn't know if he'd become a simpleton, a vegetable, or just lose his connection to his identity, but he had little interest in investigating it too deeply.

In addition, he suspected that when he used [**Leech Strike**], he didn't just steal his enemies' vitality. He'd have to test it to be sure, but he was almost certain that the skill also took a bit of their souls. It was the main reason it didn't cost much mana to maintain; it got all the energy it needed from his victims.

And then there was the matter of how his stats affected his soul—or rather, his available pool of mana. His constant manipulation of his mana had given him more than a few hints into its nature and how it related to his stats. Intelligence seemed to be related to the volume; each extra point of the stat would give him more mana. Wisdom, on the other hand, was like the vitality of the soul. The higher it was, the more quickly his mana would regenerate. And to a lesser extent, it also determined how easily his mind would recover from being overtaxed.

The grade of his soul was a different matter altogether, and as far as Zeke could tell, it appeared to affect the quality of the mana. He couldn't be sure because he didn't really have any context, but he expected that as he evolved his soul, his mana would become, for lack of a better way to describe it, thicker and more powerful. Or that was his theory, at least—he could only vaguely remember how his mana felt before evolving his soul, so he couldn't confirm any of it yet. But his instincts told him he was right, and one of the first lessons he'd learned upon being reborn was to trust those instincts.

As he'd worked on unraveling the curses, Zeke hadn't just learned about his soul and how it related to his mana. He'd also learned quite a bit about the runes themselves. Zeke's initial assessment that the troll's cursed runes were less complicated than the ones provided by the Framework was accurate, but that didn't mean the curses were simple. They were still made of layer after layer of intricate symbols and glyphs, each comprised of even more complex patterns. In the old world, Zeke would've taken one look at the tangled designs and abandoned them altogether. There was no way he'd have been equipped to understand them back then. But his increased mental statistics hadn't only enhanced his soul and mana pool. They'd also made it easier for him to concentrate, and to a lesser extent, they'd provided some insight into the complicated tangle of patterns and symbols.

He was a long way from true understanding—he hadn't even scratched the surface, really—but he at least thought such comprehension would one day become possible. And he'd also managed to identify some of the basic repeating structures, even if he wasn't entirely sure of their purpose. However, Zeke felt optimistic that, with enough time and study, he could figure it all out, and he couldn't help but feel a sense of excitement about the possibilities that might open up.

Zeke sat there, pondering the nature of runes, as he slowly recuperated. He hadn't realized how close to death he'd really been, and more than once, he'd found himself wondering how he'd managed to find the strength to ascend to the top of the mushroom and find safety. In the end, it took him nearly three more days before he felt well enough to resume his climb to the cave system's exit.

He still intended to continue his rampage. He hadn't forgotten the grotesque larder, after all. But he knew he couldn't just storm through the caves, taking all comers. He needed to be smarter about it, else he'd just end up in the same situation once again. While he didn't fear the troll warriors much, mostly because he felt confident in being able to escape if things got too bad, he didn't want to find himself on the wrong end of a dozen curses. If he did, that would be the end of him, then and there. He'd gotten lucky when he'd escaped before; expecting that to happen again would be the height of foolishness. He wouldn't even escape his tutorial dungeon.

So, toward the end of his recuperation, Zeke started to formulate a plan. Or considering that he was no tactical genius, it would probably be better categorized as a basic strategy. In any case, as he finally stood, stretching his stiff muscles, he felt confident in his chances.

By this point, most of the hunting parties had moved out of the area. Likely, they assumed that he'd slipped past them to continue his ascent. The mere fact that they hadn't even considered looking up was a testament to their lack of intellect, at least as far as Zeke was concerned. But that only made things easier.

Once he'd limbered up, Zeke picked up his mace and took off across the mushroom cap. The surface was surprisingly firm, but its consistency still felt a little like an exercise mat. It gave a little with each step, but it wasn't enough to slow him down. When he reached the edge, he leaped, sailing through the air and covering the ten feet to the next mushroom. He continued like that, pausing every couple of minutes to listen—or in some cases, smell; the trolls had a very distinctive odor that carried easily through the caves—for his enemies. After half an hour, he was finally rewarded when he heard the telltale grunts that comprised their language.

Slowly, Zeke crept forward and soon found himself peeking over the edge of the mushroom. Below him were seven trolls—one shaman and six warriors. He could handle that many, so long as they didn't get reinforcements. And given the size of the fungal forest, Zeke felt certain that the hundred or so trolls that had ambushed him were spread out enough that they wouldn't be able to respond to a battle, even if they heard it.

Zeke rolled his shoulders, then took a deep breath as he toggled [**Leech Strike**] on. Mana rushed out of his soul core just behind his navel, flowing through his pathways and into the rune on his hand. An identical rune lit up on Voromir, extending the skill to his weapon. For a long moment, Zeke marveled at the complexity of the runes, but he quickly jerked himself out of his stupor. He had work to do.

Without further stalling, he stepped off the edge of the mushroom and fell the hundred-plus feet, plummeting straight into an unlucky troll. Predictably, it practically exploded from the impact, its bones breaking and skin rupturing like it had gone skydiving without a parachute. For his part, Zeke only grunted as the shock reached his knees. It hurt, but it wasn't debilitating, and there wasn't any real damage.

Only a second later, his mace whistled through the air and into the troll shaman's ribs, collapsing them in an instant. But this one was more durable than most, and though it was probably a fatal wound, the monster still managed to cast its horrible, cursed rune. Zeke winced as it connected, but its effect wasn't enough to stall him.

From that point, Zeke was a whirlwind of blunt force trauma. Curiously, even though he hit the trolls with enough force to launch them dozens of feet away, they remained rooted to the ground. Perhaps the more powerful someone got, the less they were subject to the natural laws of the universe. Or maybe this new world didn't work the way the old one did. Either way, regardless of whether or not they went flying, his mace still did plenty of damage, and soon, the entire hunting party became a series of scattered corpses.

Zeke quickly inspected the bodies for anything of value, but the monsters didn't carry anything other than a few knives and their weapons—none of which could even hold a candle to Voromir. So, once he'd taken care of that, he scurried back up the mushroom and, using the tops of the mushrooms as his own personal highway, left the scene of the battle. Once he felt he was far enough away, he began the arduous process of unraveling the rune.

He needed to find a better way.

The troll shamans were too quick. And if he was unlucky enough to come across a hunting party that had more than one, he would have to spend hours ridding himself of their curses. He wasn't in a hurry or anything. After all, he'd spent over a year in the caves by this point. But he hated wasting time that he could be using to get stronger.

It was a stark revelation, figuring out that he didn't really flinch at the thought of dying. But wasting time? That irritated him in ways he couldn't really articulate. Some of it was due to the fact that he'd spent most of his young life pursuing a goal to the exclusion of all else. He had lived and breathed baseball. So, if he wasn't trying to improve, even in this new world, he really didn't know what to do with himself. Zeke was used to that, and he'd long since accepted that it was just how he was. However, his attitude was probably just as much due to how addictive improvement in the new world was.

In his old life, progress was incremental. Gradual. He didn't see it, day by day, but rather week by week, or even month after month. That was what he was used to. But now? He could gain a level, and suddenly, he would feel that influx of power. And that was discounting the addictive nature of coming out on top in a life-and-death struggle. Sure, he'd experienced some shadow of it during his athletic career. Getting a hit, throwing a guy out at second, hitting a walk-off home run—those had once been the pinnacles of that feeling for him. But winning against something that was trying to end your life? That was the culmination of victory, an ideal that he felt like he'd been searching for all his life.

It all coalesced to push him forward, and when circumstances conspired to keep him in the same place, even for a moment, Zeke grew impatient.

So, the last thing he wanted to do was spend another few days unraveling runes. He needed to figure out a better way, so as he gradually picked the curse apart, he bent his mind toward doing just that.

The problem was that he didn't really have much of a strategy aside from full-frontal assault. Sure, he'd assassinated plenty of trolls in their sleep, but his go-to was to rely on the power disparity to see him through. But he wanted to be better than that. No—he needed to be. While the trolls weren't necessarily that big of a threat right now, he held no illusions about the rest of his climb to the top of the cave system. Eventually, he'd run into something he couldn't just overpower. So, he needed to expand his repertoire.

Zeke had almost finished unraveling the curse when the idea struck him. He'd been looking at it from the wrong perspective. He didn't have a lot of skills that had carried over from the old world. His years of swinging a baseball bat had given him some prowess with a club—and later, his mace—and he certainly knew how to take a beating. However, there was one skill he'd so far neglected.

And he knew why.

When Zeke had been in that car accident, he'd come very close to losing his right arm. It had healed, but even then, it had only barely been functional. Because of that, he'd forcefully ignored it for nearly two years. So, the idea of throwing something had never even crossed his mind.

But before he'd been injured, he'd possessed a very good throwing arm—to the point where very few base runners ever even tried to steal on him. In scouting reports, it was even listed as his second-best attribute, only behind his power at the plate. So, what could he do with his massively increased strength and dexterity? As soon as the idea came to mind, Zeke became impatient to try it.

He finished picking apart the curse, then dropped down from his perch atop the mushroom and started gathering rocks. Out of necessity, he still carried the human-skin satchel, and he used it to hold his chosen ammunition. The rocks he found were a wide variety of sizes, but it didn't take him long to accumulate a sackful of fist-sized stones.

When he finally started testing things out, he couldn't help but grin. Oh, this was going to change everything.

22

EXTERMINATION

The fist-sized rock shot through the air like a bullet, and after only an instant, crashed into a troll shaman's cranium. The rock itself shattered into a million shards, but the troll didn't fare any better. The blow didn't kill the sturdy creature outright, but Zeke felt certain that it wouldn't be casting curses anytime soon. A second later, another rock was in the air, and it took out the party's other shaman.

Once the two spell casters were out of the fight, Zeke sprang into action. He leaped from the crown of the mushroom, Voromir singing as it arced through the air in an overhead strike. The trolls were caught entirely off guard, which only served to cement the notion that they weren't dealing with much upstairs. It was like shooting fish in a barrel; the monsters never even bothered to look up, much less watch for an ambush.

Not that Zeke was about to start complaining. During his rampage through the fungal forest, he'd killed fourteen hunting parties and more than a hundred trolls. A dozen shamans had already fallen to his hurled rocks, and by his count, there couldn't be very many more. Waging a guerrilla war had brought with it a plethora of benefits, but none were more appreciated than the fact that he'd only picked up a few superficial wounds. It was a drastic change from his usual tactic of charging in and hoping he didn't take an unlucky blow. In addition, he'd also managed to gain quite a bit of experience, and he found himself on the precipice of another level. It was quite a gain, considering that his previous level had only come after more than a month of killing trolls.

His mace crushed the skull of the first troll warrior, but Zeke didn't pause to admire his handiwork. Instead, he was already swinging his weapon in a horizontal arc intended to destroy another troll's rib cage. It wouldn't kill the creature, especially considering its healing capabilities, but it would certainly slow it down. And given that he was facing eight of the monsters, any small advantage he could muster would make all the difference in the world.

The troll warrior tried to dance back, but agility wasn't its strong suit. So, it managed to lessen the blow by only a small fraction. Its ribs were still crushed, but Zeke could tell that it wasn't entirely out of the fight. So, he followed up that strike with another, which was enough to tip the balance and send it to the ground, where it writhed in pain.

Two warriors and two shamans down, Zeke thought, already stamping his foot down on the shaman who hadn't died to his initial volley. Four warriors to go. He definitely liked those odds.

Over the course of his time in the cave system, Zeke hadn't only benefited from his increased stats and evolved race. Those factors had certainly contributed to his survival, but almost as important was the development of his battle instinct. It wasn't anything overwhelming in nature. Just a sense that showed him the flow of a fight, often warning him of a dangerous situation before it coalesced into something life-threatening.

So, he felt more than saw the axe blade swinging at him from behind. He ducked without a second thought, quickly pivoting and swinging his mace in a vicious uppercut that took the ambitious troll warrior on the chin. The blow very nearly disintegrated the creature's jaw, and Zeke could hear its neck crack from the force. After sailing through the air for a handful of feet, it settled onto the moss-covered ground, never to move again.

Power and instinct could only take a man so far, though; eventually, skill would have to play a part. And throughout his many battles, Zeke had begun to cultivate his own style, which incorporated his titanic strength, his battle instinct, and his talent with his chosen weapon. By contrast, the trolls swung their axes and thrust their spears with undeniable strength but little real prowess. The result was predictable, and if Zeke weren't so grossly outnumbered, he'd have found their attacks laughably easy to parry or dodge.

So, armed with his developing prowess, Zeke managed to kill the trolls without taking more than a few flesh wounds that were easily healed by his natural vitality and the life force he'd stolen via [**Leech Strike**]. In the end, he stood over a pile of mangled troll corpses, barely even breathing hard.

Zeke had come a long way from struggling with a couple of crocorats, that was for sure. And he couldn't help but feel a sense of pride at his progress. However, he still had a long way to go, so he quickly searched the bodies for anything useful. When he didn't find anything, he climbed back to the top of the mushroom and set off to look for another hunting party.

So it went for the next couple of days, with Zeke slowly whittling down his adversaries, and when he was finally satisfied that he'd killed them all, he was disappointed to find that he still hadn't reached level nine. He was frustratingly close, but going by the amount of energy he'd gained in the past few days, it would take a hundred or more kills to pass that threshold. Maybe more, considering how little experience he got from each individual monster.

He sighed, sitting on the edge of a mushroom, his legs dangling under him as he took a moment to rest. Idly, he took out a piece of fish from his satchel, desperately trying not to remember what the sack was made of. If he could've afforded to discard it, he would have. But he had to carry his supplies in something, and his clothing had long since been ripped to shreds. Even if he was willing to go naked—which, if he was honest, he really wasn't far from being—the cloth wouldn't be suitable.

Zeke chewed on the fish. Since killing that first flying barracuda what felt like a lifetime ago, fish had become his primary source of sustenance, to the point where he'd grown extremely tired of the taste. In the days since he'd caught and cooked this particular specimen, it had dried out and grown chewy. He suspected that without his increased strength and durability, he wouldn't have even been able to chew it. Certainly, he wouldn't have dared to eat meat that had been sitting in a skin sack for days. That was a great way to end up eating tainted fish. But Zeke was confident in his sturdy constitution, so he didn't think twice about it—especially considering the fish still retained quite a bit of its restorative property. Truthfully, that was the primary reason he even bothered to eat; with his improved vitality and endurance, he felt certain that he could go quite some time without sustenance. But there was no reason to chance it, given the fact that there were plenty of streams—and thus, plenty of fish—in the underground cave system.

After a while, Zeke slipped off the edge of the mushroom and began stalking through the fungal forest. He was confident that there weren't any trolls left in the area, so he didn't really need to sneak, but old habits were difficult to ignore, and he found himself flitting from trunk to trunk, his mace at the ready. It was a good thing, too, because a pair of wall creepers tried to ambush him after only a couple of minutes. However, he was well used to the danger they posed, and he dispatched them without much trouble.

Eventually, he came to his destination. A yawning opening loomed over him, the ground sloping upward on a sharp incline. He'd entered the fungal forest on the other side of the cavern, so it only stood to reason that the exit lay in this direction. The path's grade only served to reinforce that surety, and Zeke set off without much hesitation.

For nearly a day, he climbed until he came to a branching path. On his right was the way up. He was certain of it. But he smelled trolls on the left. Given that he hadn't forgotten the larder filled with human remains, he didn't even consider ignoring what he knew from experience was a troll village. Sure enough, he had to travel for only a couple of hundred yards before a cavern spread out before him, filled with stone huts. In the center was a raging bonfire, and there were plenty of the hated monsters populating the village, even if most were asleep in their stone huts.

Zeke unhesitatingly went to work, unceremoniously exterminating the village's population. Hundreds of trolls fell before him, most entirely unaware of the death that walked among them. Zeke no longer had any qualms about assassinating the monsters in their sleep, so the extermination went off without a hitch. He left only corpses in his wake as he turned back to the path and continued his climb.

Another couple of months passed like that, with Zeke following the same pattern, and he destroyed six more villages along the way. In retrospect, his earlier estimate that he would need only a hundred more kills in order to level seemed laughably erroneous. He had lost count of how many trolls he'd killed since then, but it had to be over a thousand. The problem was that he barely got any experience from assassinating the monsters in their sleep. However, he couldn't really change his tactics because he knew he wouldn't stand a chance in a pitched battle against a hundred warriors, regardless of how powerful he'd become.

The only good news was that he knew he was drawing close to the exit. The air had changed, and it no longer smelled stale. Instead, it had an aura of life about it that he knew wasn't possible within the cave system. Even the fungal forest, despite its abundance of life, had only managed to smell mustier than the rest of the cave system.

As he trekked through the caverns, the entire thing became something of a monotonous blur. The caves themselves were so similar that they were virtually indistinguishable from one another, and the villages he destroyed differed only in their varied sizes. Finally, almost two years after his rebirth, everything changed when he emerged from a tunnel and into an enormous, cylindrical cavern that stretched upward far enough that he couldn't see the ceiling.

A spiraling ramp had been cut into the cavern walls, and Zeke could tell from how smooth its surface had become that it was a well-trodden path. That assumption was further supported by the thousands of openings that dotted the cavern's walls, presumably leading to the trolls' domiciles.

He hadn't just come upon a village. He'd found a veritable nation of trolls. And judging by the smell of the air, they all stood between him and freedom.

About thirty feet up the spiraling ramp, a troll emerged from one of the openings. For a moment, it only stared at him, obviously confused. But then, it barked a harsh, guttural shout that echoed throughout the enormous cavern. Zeke's heart sank as he saw more of the monsters emerge from the walls. Hundreds. No, thousands of trolls gathered on the ramps, and they were all looking at him with murderous intent.

Zeke sighed, then rolled his shoulders. It had been a good run, and he'd almost made it. But he wasn't optimistic about his chances of getting even halfway up the long ramp. Given the size of the cavern, it would take him hours to cover that much ground, and that was if he met no resistance. But now? If he had to wade through thousands of trolls, it would be days before he reached the top. And that was if his endurance could hold out for that long.

But he'd died before, hadn't he? Perhaps this time, he could be reborn into a more hospitable situation. Or not, and he'd have the peace of oblivion to look forward to for all of eternity.

As hopeless as the situation was, though, Zeke didn't really have it in him to simply give up. Nor did he relish the thought of retreat. He hadn't yet acknowledged it, but he was exhausted, mentally, physically, and morally. Being alone and perpetually on guard for almost two years had affected him far more than he wanted to acknowledge, and that wasn't even considering that he'd forced himself to ignore the moral implications of decimating an entire population of thinking creatures. Sure, he didn't think he'd had much of a choice, especially given the contents of that larder he'd found. But its being necessary and his being okay with it were two very different things. He'd only shoved his objections to the side in favor of survival.

No—he would either go through the trolls, or he'd die. Those were the only real choices. And if he was going to go down, he'd do so fighting.

So, Zeke began his ascent with slow, steady steps that soon took him to the first group of trolls. The first troll swung a wicked-looking iron axe, its jagged, uneven blade aiming to end the conflict before it even began. Zeke easily ducked under it, swinging Voromir with practiced ease. It connected with the troll's kneecap, shattering it to the point where it almost ripped the entire leg in two. The troll instantly collapsed, clutching its ruined leg as it screamed in pain. As Zeke marched past it, he spared only a single stomp to the thing's howling face, crushing its skull without a second thought. By the time he reached the next, he'd already forgotten the dead troll.

Zeke continued in that manner for hours, slaying innumerable trolls. The only solace of his climb lay in the relatively narrow ramp. It was only wide enough to accommodate three trolls standing abreast, so it severely limited their numerical advantage. And three to one was far from enough to overwhelm Zeke, who'd been killing much larger parties for months now.

Every now and then, a curse would sail out of the darkness to latch on to his body. Each time, Zeke felt the accompanying weakness, but over the course of the past months, he'd grown quite adept at unraveling the harmful collections of runes. Thankfully, he didn't have to spare much mental power to continue his steady ascent because he needed everything he could spare to dismantle the curses. It wasn't easy, but the alternative was to let them build up to the point where he eventually succumbed to overwhelming weakness. And while he'd resigned himself to death, he wouldn't stop fighting so long as there was breath in his body.

Zeke lost track of time. There was only one more step. One more dead troll. One more curse to unravel. Over and over until it all became a blur of blood, death, and pain. His wounds began to accumulate, but with

[**Leech Strike**] providing a surge of vitality with each swing, he managed to stay just ahead of his mounting injuries.

The minutes turned to hours, and the hours stretched into more than a day. But still, Zeke managed to keep going. Frightening amounts of experience flowed into his body, and on that ramp, he killed more trolls than he could count. But it never seemed to be enough. For every one that fell, another took its place. It felt like Zeke had fallen into some macabre version of hell that forced him into an endless battle with the hulking, scaly humanoids.

But just when he thought he couldn't take one more step, Zeke reached the top. He looked around, his eyes wild, but there was nothing left to kill. He glanced back and saw the mountain of troll carcasses he'd left in his wake. He shuddered at the sheer volume of death he'd left behind.

A roar broke through his reverie, and he jerked his head back around to see a hulking form looming in the near distance. His fingers tightened on his mace, and he rolled his shoulders before stepping forward, ready to meet the latest, and hopefully last, challenge.

23

UNTENABLE

As the party trudged along the edges of the Trollmoor Bog, Abby glared at Julio's back. Even as her feet sank into the ankle-deep and putrid mud, a searing fury enveloped her entire mind. Inevitably, she turned her sight inward, finding the curse Julio had branded upon her soul. It was an intricate thing, and because it was so complicated, it would dissipate slowly over time. After all, Julio was no rune-master who could keep the thing empowered indefinitely. Instead, the curse was a skill he had either found during his adventures or one he'd purchased via contribution points. Given the nature of the curse, she leaned toward the former. The Champions of Light weren't the bunch of pious saints their name implied, but there were lines the guild simply would not cross.

Julio obviously didn't bear the weight of such scruples, but that was no revelation. Stories of the man's lascivious nature were common enough among the citizens of Beacon, so it shouldn't have been a surprise when he'd branded her soul with such a despicable curse. If she'd had any fewer points in wisdom, she might have succumbed to its full effect. Even with the protection afforded by her high mental stats, she was in no small degree of danger, should she push against the boundaries of the curse.

As it was, the effect was fairly simple. When Julio gave an order, every cell in her body wanted to obey. It was only because of her high wisdom and well-developed willpower that she was able to resist. However, with resistance came pain—and, of course, the man's gleeful laughter. Julio hadn't pushed it too far—not with her, at least; Vladimir hadn't been so lucky, and he already bore a series of self-inflicted wounds, all ordered by

Julio—but it was coming soon. She knew it, and judging by the leers of Julio's men, they did, too. Doubtless, they'd seen many men and women succumb to their leader's curse.

Abby could probably break free, and if it came down to it, she would certainly try. Hopefully, she could take a few of the detestable group with her when she did. However, doing so would create a significant backlash. The longer she could wait it out, the weaker the curse—and the resultant backlash—would become. That was reason enough by itself to wait until the last possible moment, but there was also Vladimir's fate to consider.

The Russian giant was only a few levels behind Abby, but his power level was even lower than that might suggest—especially when it came to the mental stats. Despite looking the part, she suspected that he didn't even have any achievements to bolster his power. The result was that even if she helped him break the curse, it would rip him apart along the way. And she wasn't willing to sacrifice her friend and companion.

As they made their way through the swamp, Abby paid only cursory attention to her surroundings. They were only at the edge of the swamp, so it was unlikely they'd run into the powerful creatures that had given the bog its name. Instead, she watched her captors, looking for anything that might facilitate her eventual escape. She didn't see much, save that they were, overall, even weaker than she had first thought. Even Julio had proved himself to be shockingly inept when the gaborin had resisted his skills.

Not that the knowledge did her any good. She wasn't immune to the strange auditory abilities he'd chosen, so it wouldn't come down to martial ability or stats, where she thought she might have had an edge.

Finally, as the sun was beginning to set, the party found a rare island of dry land. It was only about forty feet across, so it would only barely accommodate all of them, but it was the best refuge from the ubiquitous bog they could find.

Julio ordered them to stop, then turned to Abby and said, "Make your camp, my love."

Abby's fingernails dug into her palms as she resisted the curse's compulsion. She could have ignored it, but to what end? The pain wouldn't be worth it—not for something so small. So, she retrieved some tinder from her enchanted pack and set about following the order. Once the fire had been lit by one of her fire starters, she activated her ability [**Makeshift**

Camp]. Immediately, she felt her vitality surge and her mana regeneration increase.

The skill provided a twenty-point boost to both vitality and wisdom, which was a huge increase for just about anyone. But that wasn't its most desirable effect. Instead, that title belonged to the shimmering wall that sprang up around the small island, extending a few feet past its borders. It would stop most wildlife, and whatever it didn't outright stop, it would slow down. Abby suspected that [**Makeshift Camp**] was one of the primary reasons Julio had asked her to join the expedition, much less kept her around.

But there were other reasons, too. Every time the lecherous man looked at her, Abby felt like she was covered in a disgusting muck that far outstripped anything in the surrounding swamp. The man was a disgusting lech, and she wanted nothing more than to put a couple of arrows through his eyes.

"Don't do anything rash," Vladimir rumbled, putting his hand on her shoulder. "He's not worth it."

"Kind of feels like it'd be worth it," she muttered, but she knew he was right. Even if she somehow managed to kill him, that wouldn't be the end of her difficulties. Best-case scenario, she'd kill Julio, but one of his lackeys would escape, head back to Beacon, and report her "treachery." Worst case? She would fail, and Vladmir would join her in paying the price.

"Our time will come," the man said. "Be patient."

She shook her head, but she didn't respond. What was there to say? Vladimir was right, and she had little choice but to wait and see what happened. That didn't make things any easier, though. She quickly claimed a spot by the fire and pulled a piece of dried meat from her pack. She didn't like travel rations, but it was all that was available. The disgusting swamp was teeming with life, but it was either inedible or far too dangerous to hunt.

Abby had been sitting there for half an hour, staring into the flames, when she felt someone approach from behind. She didn't need to turn around to identify her visitor as Julio; even restrained, his aura was unmistakable—like clashing cymbals and lascivious intent, all jumbled together. He didn't bother asking for permission before he sat beside her.

"I've been wondering something," he said, resting his forearms on his knees. His black leather armor glistened in the dancing firelight, and he cut a handsome, rakish figure. It was a lie, though. All of it. He'd shown himself a coward, and even without everything else, that would've been reason enough to hate him. "Perhaps you'll be so kind as to shed some light on it for me."

Abby felt a mild compulsion, but she pushed it down. A sharp pain erupted in her side, but it was easily ignored. "What?" she asked.

"You and the barbarian—is there something there?" he asked.

"We are friends and battle companions," she answered truthfully. There was no reason to lie. Even though he was the weaker of the two, Vladimir was like an overprotective big brother to her, and had been since they'd met four years before. Back then, he'd been far more powerful than her, but as the years passed, she'd passed him by. Abby was grateful that his attitude hadn't changed one bit in the interim. He would lay down his life for her in an instant, and she would do the same.

"Nothing romantic, then?" Julio asked.

Abby didn't answer, but her silence was enough of a response to satisfy the man. Since Abby had been reborn into the new world, romance had been the last thing on her mind. She hadn't had good luck in that department in her old life, and it had left a bad taste in her mouth. Instead, she'd chosen to focus on growing stronger and more powerful—a sentiment that had led her to the Champions of Light.

"Can you go elsewhere?" she asked, finally glancing in Julio's direction. "You make my skin crawl."

"In a good way or a bad way?" the man asked with a blindingly white grin. "I've been told I have quite an effect on—"

"She said to leave," Vladimir interrupted, suddenly looming over the seated Julio. The giant Russian was good at a lot of things, but looming was something of a specialty. With his hulking frame, massive axe, and bearlike appearance, he was the very epitome of a barbarian warrior. "I suggest you do as she says."

Julio didn't bother responding, and for a long moment, it seemed that he would simply ignore Vladimir's interruption. But then, with a sigh, he snapped his fingers. The next instant, Vladimir exploded, sending a cascade of bone, blood, and viscera sailing through the air. It was so sudden that it took Abby a few seconds to even process what had just happened. But when her brain finally caught up to reality, she could only stare at Julio in horror and disgust.

By contrast, Julio seemed entirely unperturbed by the fact that he was suddenly covered in gore. He smiled again, saying, "I hate it when people interrupt. You can't say I didn't warn him."

Abby's mouth gaped in disgust as she scrambled away in an awkward crab walk. She wasn't trying to escape, but rather, she had succumbed to a primal need to distance herself from the monster who'd just killed her companion.

Julio had obviously detonated the curse. That was the only explanation that made any sense. Even at level nineteen, there was no way that Julio had the means to so easily murder a warrior like Vladimir. Certainly, killing the big man wouldn't have been difficult for Julio, regardless of the method. But to explode him? That was something altogether different, and it was beyond anything Abby had ever seen.

"W-why?" she managed to mutter. Steadying her voice, she continued, "Why would you do that? You could have just ordered him to silence, and he would have been compelled to obey."

Julio shrugged, saying, "But where's the fun in that?"

Abby stared at the man in disbelief. Idly, she noticed that a few of his cohorts were laughing at their boss's statement. She'd just lost the only person she could rightly call a friend, and they were giggling like schoolchildren. It was enough to ignite Abby's anger, and before that flame, all her fears were swept aside like so much detritus.

Her mana surged, targeting the foreign rune that had branded itself upon her soul. She couldn't force it out. Nor could she take it apart, a skill that some rune-masters were rumored to be capable of. She didn't have that deft of a touch, and even if she did, understanding those complicated whorls and symbols was all but impossible. She was far more likely to make things worse than to unravel the thing. But there was another way to deal with unwanted curses.

Abby gritted her teeth as she flooded the curse rune with as much mana as she could force into the small space. It resisted, but ultimately, it had no will of its own. She easily overcame its meager defenses. She felt a creak in her soul as she filled the rune to capacity, but she kept pushing. Bit by bit, she forced more mana into it until, at last, it cracked.

Pain erupted in her side as the rune exploded, taking quite a bit of her flesh and a good measure of her soul with it. But the damage wasn't fatal. She would heal. The rune would remain until she could get the curse cleansed, but it wouldn't be enough to appreciably affect her combat ability. That was a worry for another day, though. For now, she had to escape. For now, she needed to survive.

Julio had already begun his response, whipping his katana out of his scabbard. Before he could activate his skill by banging the blade against his bracer, Abby already had her bow in hand. She conjured an arrow even as she drew the string back, letting it loose. It flew true, guided and empowered by the wind to hit precisely where she intended. But she hadn't aimed for a kill shot. She had no confidence in taking him down like that; his endurance was likely far too high. Instead, the silvery arrow slammed into his right wrist, the impact sending the sword flying from his hand. So, disarming him was the next best thing.

Grimacing from the wound in her side, Abby sprang to her feet as she conjured another arrow. She fired it at one of Julio's henchmen, downing him with a single shot. Then she repeated her actions as she retreated from the camp. The moment she crossed the threshold of her skill [**Makeshift Camp**], she pushed the bulk of her remaining energy into it. A second later, another of Julio's curses slammed into the mostly transparent barrier, sending ripples of energy arcing out along the boundaries of the camp.

It was something she'd discovered soon after acquiring the skill. Not only could it keep monsters and other wildlife out, but with some effort and quite a bit of mana, she could reverse its polarity to keep enemies inside the camp, as well. It was effectively a prison, so long as her mana held out. Sadly, that wouldn't be long, considering that she'd been forced to expend quite a bit of energy to forcibly explode the curse rune.

She had no choice but to flee. In the dark. Through a monster- and troll-infested swamp. But as horrible and terrifying as the creatures in the bog might be, they were nothing compared to what she was leaving behind. Julio and his ilk were exactly as detestable as she'd first thought, and even as she fled through the swamp, clutching the bloody wound in her side, Abby silently cursed herself for ever putting herself and her friend in such an obviously terrible situation. She was smarter than that. She should have known better.

However, she knew exactly why she had taken the chance. If she hadn't been determined to grow more powerful before, she certainly was now. Julio had shown her the price of weakness, and it was a lesson she intended to take to heart.

Still, as Abby distanced herself from the scene of Vladimir's murder, she vowed that before everything was done, she would avenge her friend's sudden death. Vladimir had been a good man and a stalwart friend, her constant companion through countless adventures.

And now she was all alone.

24

WARLORD

Zeke groaned as he stared at the creature that barred his escape. From its basic shape and characteristics, it was obviously a troll, but the monster's physique was so exaggerated that it almost looked like a caricature of the creatures he'd been fighting for almost two years. At over ten feet tall, it towered over him. Its muscles bulged unnaturally beneath its scaly green-and-yellow-mottled skin, and its long fingers were tipped with vicious claws. Even its head was enormous, and its long, pointed ears and jutting snout made it appear even bigger than it was. All in all, it was at least as physically impressive as the Brood Mother had been grotesque.

That wasn't to say the thing was aesthetically pleasing in any way; it wasn't. Just like all the other trolls, its features seemed misshapen, out of line, and of varying sizes. However, its power was undeniable, and it carried the same frightening presence as a hunting crocodile—a presence it had focused wholly on Zeke.

It clanged a pair of gleaming axes together. For a human, they'd have been two-handed battle-axes, but in the hands of the enormous troll, they looked the size of hatchets. In addition to the weaponry, the troll was decked out in rusty-looking chain mail armor that covered its entire torso. Otherwise, it was attired much like its smaller brethren.

Zeke used his skill [**Inspection**].

Makazith, Warlord of the Caracoa Trolls—Level 22

So, it had a name. And it was a warlord, whatever that was supposed to mean. Zeke didn't know if it was a title, or if it was just a new class of troll, but he suspected the former—chiefly because he could feel fresh air coming from the tunnel directly behind Makazith, telling him that the exit was close.

"I don't know if you can understand me," Zeke said, his voice scratchy from lack of use. When he had first appeared in the cave system, he'd talked to himself quite a bit, but that habit had faded as his time in the caves had stretched on. As it stood, he wasn't certain when he'd last spoken aloud. "But I need to get past you. I don't want to kill you, but I will if I have to."

Zeke truly wasn't in any condition to fight, but that wasn't the source of his reticence. Nor was he truly afraid of the warlord. Certainly, the creature was intimidating, and there was every chance it would be his end. However, on his long trek through the caracoa caves, and to a lesser extent, his steady push up the spiraling ramp, Zeke had come to terms with his mortality. Around every corner, death had awaited, and it would've been incredibly easy to simply curl up and wait in the relative safety offered by some of the caves where he'd made camp. In some ways, that would've been the logical thing to do. Self-preservation was a powerful motivator, and some of those caves had been blessed with plentiful food and water. He could've lived there for years, surviving just fine.

But Zeke didn't want to merely survive. He wanted to thrive. Not only had he grown addicted to the slow, upward trajectory of his power, but he'd also come to realize that he wasn't built for a life huddling in the shadows. He was a fighter. So, as much as he might've accepted his own mortality, even coming to peace with it, he had no intentions of going down without a strenuous fight.

Thankfully, the troll didn't seem too keen on charging him, so he took a moment to reach into his pack and retrieve a bit of fish. He ate it quickly, and all the while, the troll stared at him with murderous intent. The trolls had all been vicious creatures—that had made it a lot easier to come to terms with the genocide he'd perpetrated—but the warlord was on an entirely different level. He looked rabid, with flecks of foam coating his snout.

"Monster..."

The rumbled word cut through Zeke like a knife, and not just because he'd never heard a troll speak in a language he could understand. They communicated among one another with what sounded like grunts and growls, but hearing a word—and in English—was more than a little shocking.

And then the implications of what Makazith had said washed over him.

Monster it had called him. And while Zeke desperately wanted to dispute the claim, he could understand the troll warlord's perspective. The evidence lay piled on the ramp behind Zeke, and that was just what was visible. By this point, Zeke had killed many thousands of the creatures. Some he'd fought, but others he'd killed in the dead of night while they slept. *Monster* seemed like an apt description.

"Baby . . . k-killer . . ."

That was true, too. In another world, Zeke might've felt guilty. In a bout of introspection, he might have lamented his actions. But the fact was that the trolls had attacked him first, and if he hadn't fought back, he would've ended up dead before he'd taken one step through the caves.

And then there was the larder, that massive, meat-locker-like room that had been filled to the brim with butchered human corpses. Even the bag at his hip, which had been fashioned from human skin, was evidence that Zeke hadn't struck the first blow.

But at the end of the day, none of that truly mattered. If Oberon and the hints he'd gained throughout his time in the caracoa caves were to be believed, there was an entire world waiting for him behind the warlord. He'd spent two years fighting and clawing and scraping for this opportunity. So, being called a couple of names by a literal ten-foot-tall monster wasn't going to dissuade him. Not now. Not after he'd been through so much.

"Yeah," Zeke said, reactivating his skill [**Leech Strike**]. He tightened his grip on his mace. "Well, you're in my way."

With that, their brief conversation was over, and Zeke shot forward, already swinging Voromir with all his might. For his part, Makazith didn't even try to avoid the blow. Instead, it simply stood there, axes at the ready. Zeke's mace hit the warlord directly in the ribs, and the strike had enough momentum behind it that they cracked in an instant. Every instinct in Zeke's body told him that such a blow should've ruptured every organ in the thing's torso. And while it wouldn't be enough for an instant fatality, it would certainly preclude any response.

So, when Makazith's axe bit deep into his left shoulder, very nearly severing his arm entirely, Zeke was more than a little shocked. He was even more surprised when, after dancing back, the monster showed no signs of his injury at all. No—that wasn't entirely true. Upon closer inspection, Zeke saw that he'd managed to rupture quite a few links of chain mail, and through that, he could see the bloody mess he'd caused. However, he could also see that it was visibly healing.

His mouth gaped open as he realized what was happening. All the trolls were blessed with extremely high vitality. Zeke suspected that it was partially due to the troll larvae's diet of blue-spotted mushrooms, but some of it was probably natural. Makazith's self-healing capability eclipsed anything Zeke had ever seen, so it stood to reason that its vitality was extraordinarily high.

But would that be enough? Zeke's own vitality wasn't anything to sneer at, and it still took him days, even with the help of the fish that gave him a surge of vitality, to heal from serious wounds like what he'd just given the warlord. Given the creature's high level, it stood to reason that its vitality exceeded Zeke's, but he'd had ample time and opportunity to track his own healing ability. And as his stats increased, it grew more powerful at a pretty consistent pace. So, unless things changed after crossing some threshold Zeke hadn't yet reached, the only explanation for the troll's rapid regeneration was that it had used a skill.

Upon realizing that, Zeke just shook his head, saying, "That's just not even fair."

The only good news was that the wound in his shoulder wasn't nearly as severe as he had first thought. It went deep, but his collarbone had deflected much of the force. So, while it was agonizing to move his left arm, Zeke was still in fighting condition—which was good because the warlord had had enough of waiting on Zeke to make the first move. It had decided to bring the fight to him, and was charging at him, its twin axes at the ready.

Zeke ducked under a horizontal cut, then swayed to the side as he narrowly avoided an overhand slash. His own mace swept out, hitting the warlord's unprotected knee; it almost buckled under the blow, but Makazith had impressive endurance to go along with its ridiculous regenerative capability. Still, it gave **[Leech Strike]** an opportunity to work its magic, and the resultant surge of vitality eased the pain in Zeke's shoulder.

On and on it went, with Zeke dodging most of the troll's strikes. It wasn't easy, especially because he wasn't used to fighting a foe that utilized two weapons, but he somehow managed to stay just ahead of the hulking creature. One of the problems was that, with the troll's strength, even a glancing blow was enough to send Zeke reeling. By itself, that wasn't that big of a deal, but it could easily open him up for a more devastating strike. The only saving grace was that the warlord, for all its strength, endurance, and vitality, was still just another troll. And as such, it had many of the same weaknesses—not least of which was that they were a heavy-footed, slow race of creatures that lacked coordination. Succinctly put, Zeke was outmanned by the troll's main stats, but in terms of agility and dexterity, he far outstripped the lumbering creature.

But Zeke knew it was only a matter of time before he made a fatal mistake. His stamina wasn't infinite, and even though [**Leech Strike**] helped to heal his wounds, they were rapidly accumulating and would soon surpass his means of regeneration. No—he had to do something desperate if he wanted to end the battle, and he needed to do it soon because it wouldn't be long before he ended up bisected by one of the troll's axes.

Just as the thought crossed his mind, Zeke saw an opening when he narrowly avoided a vicious, two-handed, diagonal attack that incorporated both axes. The warlord had put everything it had into the strike, so when the dully gleaming blades of his twin axes met only air, he was overbalanced.

Zeke pounced, bringing his mace down on the creature's exposed left foot. It practically exploded, not dissimilar from the way a particularly large bug might burst under a well-aimed boot. Only instead of unidentifiable goo, it instead erupted in blood, bone, and scales. More, most of the troll's weight was on that foot, so when it suddenly became a mass of gore, the creature tumbled to the ground and very nearly went careening to the cavern's floor, hundreds of feet below them.

However, the troll's title wasn't for show. It was a warrior, through and through, and it was the best the caracoa had to offer. So, its battle instincts were second to none. It turned the tumble into a controlled roll that displayed far more agility and dexterity than Zeke thought possible. It came back to its feet a second later.

Or foot, to be more accurate. Still, even propelled by a single leg, the warlord managed to turn the tables on the surprised Zeke and, with a shoulder tackle, send him flying toward the edge of the cliff. He hit only a few feet before, but his momentum was enormous, and he could do little to arrest his flight. Still, with reactions born from years of pitched battle—and with inhuman strength—he dug his fingers into the very rock itself, gouging deep grooves in the stone.

It wasn't enough to stop him from going over the edge, though, and in an instant, he found himself dangling over the side of the cliff. He knew he was far more durable than any human being had ever been in the old world, but just as surely, he knew that such a fall would doubtless kill him.

The troll hopped toward him, its foot already visibly healing, and a manic gleam of bloodlust in its beady eyes. Zeke was out of options. He didn't know what to do, and though he thought he was ready to die, a primal sense of self-preservation bloomed in his chest. But what was he supposed to do against such odds?

2 5

COMPLETION

The axe screamed as it split the air, aimed directly at Zeke's head, and for a fraction of a second, it felt like time ceased to exist. He saw everything—the blood-flecked spittle flying from the troll's mouth; the jagged, uneven teeth; the bulbous snout; the pointed and notched ears. He saw the troll's bunched muscles, its strangely shimmering scales, and its low-quality chain mail. It was a horrifying instrument of death—a huge, scaled grim reaper—and it was coming for him. Finally.

After two years' worth of close calls within the cave system, his time had at last come. But in those two years of constant struggle, Zeke had cultivated an unrivaled survival sense. He hadn't just been living on the edge. He had been dangling from that metaphorical cliff ever since he'd been reborn and promptly attacked by the troll larvae he'd referred to as croco-rats.

And he hadn't fallen yet.

Zeke let go, and for a moment, as a feeling of weightlessness enveloped him, panic wrapped itself around his heart. Even as he fell, the troll's axe skipped off the rocky lip of the cliff, sending out sparks. Then, the monster's second weapon did the same. But by that point, gravity had asserted its will, and Zeke had begun his plummet to the cavern floor.

An instant later, he'd jabbed his hand into the sheer cliff face, his fingers dragging long grooves in the rock as he tried to arrest his fall. It took longer than he expected, and as he failed to gain purchase, the panic that had snaked its way around his heart squeezed. But Zeke wouldn't let it throw him off course. He was made of stronger stuff than that. He'd long since learned to control his fears. So, he thrust his other hand forward, and after only a second, he managed to arrest his momentum.

He looked up. The troll stared down at him with unbridled fury. But there was something else buried beneath the anger. It bellowed, "Up! Fight!"

Zeke didn't really know how to react. Nor did he know what to do. There was every chance that if he climbed back up, the troll would attack him as he climbed over the lip. That's what Zeke would've done. But the warlord also seemed eager to continue their fight, as well. Did it have a sense of fair play? None of the other trolls seemed afflicted with that poisonous notion. Or was it pride? It had been winning the fight, after all.

In any case, Zeke was at a crossroads. As he saw it, he had two choices ahead of him. He could trust that the troll wanted to kill him the right way, which meant slicing him to ribbons with its vicious axes, as opposed to kicking him while he was down. If he chose that direction, the thing would probably let him climb up so they could resume their fight. However, Zeke was in no way sure that he was even reading the warlord's intentions correctly. And if he wasn't, he'd probably end up splattered on the cavern floor hundreds of feet below.

The alternative was to steadily climb his way down to the bottom of the cavern, then mount the ramp to rejoin the fight. That was probably safer, but Makazith would likely grow impatient and meet him at the bottom. And that was assuming his endurance would hold out long enough for him to make that descent in the first place.

Whichever direction Zeke chose, he knew there would be significant risks. Or given that a bloodthirsty and vengeful troll warlord was bearing down on him, perhaps *risk* was too weak of a descriptor. Either way, Zeke needed to make a choice. He couldn't just cling to the cliff face for all of eternity.

He glanced down. The cavern floor was distant enough that it was mired in darkness that rendered it largely invisible. But it had taken him hours to climb that ramp, so he knew just how deep the cavern went. He didn't relish the thought of climbing it again. Besides, even if everything went perfectly, he'd expend quite a bit of energy along the way. Fighting the troll warlord while exhausted was a recipe for disaster. It was better to simply take his chances and climb up now.

As he hung on with one hand, Zeke reached into his satchel, retrieving a slab of the life-boosting fish. He wolfed it down as quickly as possible, hoping that the surge of vitality would make some difference during the upcoming fight. As he chewed, the troll warlord roared its displeasure, but Zeke tuned it out—or he tried to, at least. Ignoring a bellowing, ten-foot troll was easier said than done, regardless of the strength of your willpower. Still, Zeke managed to do just that for a handful of minutes while he let the surge of vitality wash over him. During that time, he constructed a plan—or at least the framework of one, given how few advantages he had with which to work.

So, when he finally made his move, he was just about as prepared as he thought he could be—which is to say that he had the barest hint of a shot at winning the battle. But it was the best he could do.

Zeke shot up the cliff face, his fingers finding purchase on even the shallowest handholds as he propelled himself with inhuman strength and agility. In only a second, he crested the lip of the cliff and dove toward his mace. As soon as he wrapped his hands around its worn leather grip, he rolled away—just in time to avoid the troll's descending axe, which cut a long groove in the tough stone. He came to his feet, crouched in a fighter's stance as he reactivated [**Leech Strike**].

For a long moment, Makazith and Zeke faced off, staring each other down. Most of the troll's wounds had already healed, but it was still hobbled by its crippled foot. In addition, the warlord still favored the side that had been caved in by Zeke's opening salvo, which Zeke had tried to target as often as possible during their battle. However, injured though the troll was, its combat ability hadn't been significantly diminished. But those persistent wounds gave Zeke hope. The thing wasn't invincible. He could hurt it. And if that were true, he could win.

But that was easier said than done.

Even as the battle commenced, Zeke realized that the problem was threefold. The first, and most obvious, issue was that Zeke couldn't afford to take too many hits from the massive troll. He could recover from glancing blows, but the thing was simply too big and too strong for Zeke to tank its attacks. So, he'd been forced to rely on his ability to avoid taking damage, which was a far cry from his usual strategy of simply wading into the fray and taking whatever the enemy could dish out. His stats were high enough to make the new strategy viable, but even he had to admit that he wasn't comfortable with it.

Which brought him to the next problem—the troll, for all its barbarism, was simply a more skillful warrior than Zeke. It swung its axes with obvious and clear intent, and each strike went precisely where it meant for it to go. By contrast, Zeke looked like a flailing novice. It was only because of his battle instincts and quick reactions that he'd developed during his long trek through the cave system that he managed to hold his own.

Finally, the troll's vitality, which was boosted to monstrous levels by whatever skill it was using, largely voided the effects of [**Leech Strike**], which for all its utility just wasn't strong enough to make much of a difference. The surge of vitality it brought with each strike was helpful, but given that Zeke didn't dare let the troll's blows connect, it was mostly wasted. For the first time since waking up in the caves, Zeke regretted choosing the skill. It had helped him survive so far, but one of the more impressive offense-oriented skills would've served him much better in the battle with the troll.

However, Zeke had no other choice but to forge ahead. So, he pushed himself past his limits as he tried to keep up with the superior fighter. He made little headway, but as the fight went on, Zeke began to see something buried deep within the flow of the battle. An opening here. An obvious tell there. A slightly more optimal trajectory for his weapon. He sank into a battle trance, and the hints of something bigger grew even larger in his mind.

Soon, he began to incorporate it all into his fighting style. It almost felt like the troll slowed down, but in the back of his mind, Zeke knew that it was rather his perception that had sped up. Though he didn't swing Voromir with any additional force, his blows seemed to carry more weight. More momentum. It was as if his mace carried three times its normal mass.

It wasn't the weapon's curious ability to adjust its weight to his strength. Voromir hadn't actually gotten any heavier. Instead, it was something connected to the deeper truths of battle that he'd only barely begun to glimpse. It wasn't magic—not like [**Leech Strike**]. It was something mystical and far more profound. Something that Zeke couldn't even begin to understand. However, he could certainly use it.

The clang of clashing weapons echoed throughout the cavern as the battle raged on. But every now and then, a heavy thud, punctuated by a guttural growl, interrupted the cacophony. As the length of the fight stretched on, Zeke's blows began to connect more and more, strengthened by that mystical force that he didn't understand. Slowly, the warlord's wounds mounted, and its reactions dulled, if by only a fraction. It wasn't much, but it was the beginning of the end.

However, in an echo of Zeke's own refusal to give in, the troll's fighting spirit never waned or wavered. It continued right up to the end, when Zeke finally spotted an opening he could exploit, and he swung his club with all his considerable might. Makazith's skull didn't explode. Not like so many that had come before him. But it did crack, its brain instantly turned to mush. And insane vitality or not, nothing could survive that.

It fell with a heavy crash, and the battle was won.

Zeke followed soon after, collapsing in a heap as his breath came in ragged gasps. Even with the mystical advantage he'd gained in the middle of the fight, it had been a close call. Although he had dodged the vast majority of the troll warlord's blows, Zeke still sported numerous wounds. He'd gained the worst of his injuries when he'd been an instant too slow, and the troll's axe had shaved a good bit of his quadriceps clean off. Despite his earlier doubts about the efficacy of [**Leech Strike**], it had been the only thing that kept him from collapsing from blood loss.

Or perhaps it had been that curious battle trance; when it had enveloped him, his wounds had faded into the background, and even the worst of them had felt incredibly distant. In fact, once it had taken hold of him, the entire battle had become something of a blur. He could remember bits and pieces, but it felt like he'd watched it all from afar.

Zeke lay there for a while as he caught his breath. He didn't need to open up his notifications menu to know he'd finally reached the end of his beginning dungeon. If anything had ever felt like a boss fight, then the battle with troll warlord was certainly it. In addition, he could feel the densely packed energy in his core. Not only had he gained a level, but he'd also progressed most of the way to the next. It wouldn't take much for him to finally reach level ten.

Finally, he sat up and pulled a piece of fish from his satchel. He felt the familiar surge of vitality as he slowly chewed on the meat, but he barely paid attention to it. Instead, he opened up the notifications submenu, and he couldn't keep a wide but exhausted grin from spreading across his face.

26

GAINS

Zeke sat next to his slain foe, and even a few minutes after he'd ended the battle, his breathing was still labored. Or perhaps it was just excitement due to his massive gains. It had been a while since he'd really looked at his status, and he couldn't help but stare at the screen in disbelief. However, before he could talk himself out of it, Zeke quickly allocated his free points into strength. With his battle with the troll warlord—and his struggles with doing enough damage against it—he knew that was his best bet. He had been head and shoulders above the troll in agility and dexterity, but he hadn't been strong enough to do much lasting damage.

Name	Ezekiel Blackwood
Class	N/A
Level	9
Race	Human (G)
Alignment	Isphodel
Achievements	First Blood, Hasty Evolution, Above and Beyond, Genocide, Overachiever, Completionist
Martial Path	Blunt Weapons (Novice—Early)

Strength	181
Agility	104
Dexterity	115
Endurance	135
Vitality	107
Intelligence	89
Wisdom	108
Unassigned Attribute Points	0

His stat gains had been monstrous. In strength alone, he had gained over ninety points, almost doubling the stat. And while that was his biggest gain, the others weren't too far behind. Agility and dexterity had increased by nearly forty points each, endurance and vitality by almost thirty each, and intelligence and wisdom by only slightly less. And Zeke was quick to see why. Most of the stats came from three new achievements:

Genocide—You are a bloodthirsty one, aren't you? You have driven a unique species to near extinction. So, good job. +25 Strength, 5% Strength.

Overachiever—You have managed to kill an evolved being before Level 10! Continue to shoot for the stars! +10 Strength, Agility, and Dexterity. +5 Intelligence and Wisdom. +5% to all stats.

Completionist—You have searched high and low, slaughtering everything within your beginning dungeon and completing all optional quests. Don't bite off more than you can chew. You might just choke on it. +15 to all stats. Upgrade of beginner quest reward.

Zeke could only stare at the achievement submenu in disbelief. The flat stat gains were phenomenal, but by this point, he had also gained a few percentage increases that would hopefully continue to pull their weight even as he gained more levels and power. But as pleased as he was with the achievements, he was more concerned with the new line on his status page, which was simply labeled "Martial Path." He navigated to its submenu.

Martial Path: Blunt Weapons (Novice—Early): You have begun to glimpse a tiny fraction of the vast tapestry that is true Martial Insight, concentrating on blunt weaponry. +5 Strength and Dexterity.

Zeke read and reread the notification a dozen times over, but he still wasn't certain what it meant. It didn't take him long to figure out that discovering this martial path was what he'd felt toward the end of his battle with the troll warlord, and he certainly liked the extra stats. But his instincts told him that the stats were merely icing on the cake, so to speak. The real reward for discovering this path was the qualitative increase in his combat prowess that he'd experienced toward the end of the fight with Makazith. He had only a vague idea of what the martial path really meant, but he was more than a little eager to experiment.

Until this point, Zeke had felt like his only real talent was his ability to take a beating, to endure pain, and to persist. Sure, some of his skills with a baseball bat had transferred over to this new world, making the transition a little easier for him. However, he'd never felt like a real warrior. In fact, he had long seen himself as something akin to a caveman swinging his club around, an image supported by the crude appearance of his mace. But now? He'd achieved something not via superior stats, but rather through the development of his fighting ability. And it felt good, especially when it was acknowledged by the Framework.

It was only the first step, though. He was no genius, but Zeke could easily infer the meaning behind words like *novice* and *early*. He didn't know what the stages were, but judging by how long it had taken him to take just that first step told him that he had a long, difficult road ahead if he wanted to achieve something resembling true mastery.

But he was very happy with his progress.

And he had to admit that having reached the top of the cave system had brought with it mixed emotions. He'd lived in the caracoa caves for close to two years, and aside from the brief exchange with the troll warlord in which he'd been called a monster, Zeke hadn't spoken to another being in all that time. So, the prospect of being thrust into an entirely new world where he'd be forced into social interaction was a little intimidating.

He'd never been a social outcast or anything. Zeke had had plenty of friends and teammates. He'd even dated a few girls, even though they'd been what his father considered distractions. Even so, he found that he was a little frightened of what lay outside the caves, which was why he sat there, chewing on an old piece of fish, long after he'd recharged his batteries.

It wasn't something new. Throughout his tenure in the caves, Zeke had often fallen into the habit of deep introspection. There was just something about being alone for such an extended period that brought everything into sharp focus. His old life. His new path. The knowledge that the entire history of humanity had already come and gone and begun its rebirth. But as existentially terrifying as that was, it was a far-off issue, and he could only barely wrap his head around the philosophical implications. However, what he chose to hold on to were the events that had led him to the moment when he'd awoken in that cave. And with the absence of any other real stimuli, Zeke had dwelled on them far more than was probably healthy.

He remembered Tommy, his little brother, and his struggle with his health. Even through all the pain and struggle, he'd been a happy kid, and he was probably the only person in all the world whom Zeke had ever felt truly close to. Zeke missed him more than he really wanted to admit.

When he thought about his mother, bitterness washed over him. She hadn't been an active participant in his father's abuse, but she'd never tried to stop it, either. Zeke knew that it was a complicated situation, and that his father probably hadn't always been the man he'd known, but he couldn't help but resent his mother for ever being with the horrible man. Zeke loved her, and he knew she was probably just as much the man's victim as Zeke himself, but there was also a part of him that hated her, as well.

Mostly, though, he'd thought about his father. He owed a lot to the man. Without him, Zeke would've never survived the caves. It wasn't the skills he'd forced Zeke to develop, though. Rather, it was the pain the man had put him through. The mental strength that had come from enduring his father's many expletive-filled tirades. The bruises from spending one day after another squatting behind home plate as his father skipped baseballs at him. The knowledge that, regardless of what he achieved, he'd never be good enough for his father, and the epiphany that he'd experienced early on that he didn't have to live up to the hateful man's standards. Instead, he had to live up to his own. That had led him down a road that eventually ended with his enjoying improving just for the sake of the improvement, and not some outside approval. It had been invaluable during his trek through the cave system, and Zeke knew it would be instrumental in his survival moving forward.

But he was tired. More so than he'd ever been in his entire life, and not just from the physical exertion of his battle with the warlord. It was something deep in his bones, and it had taken root in his mind, as well. Until now, he hadn't let himself even acknowledge it, but the constant battle and stress had certainly taken its toll. But he couldn't rest. Not now. Not yet. So, he heaved himself to his feet, and after taking a deep breath, he continued on his path.

Zeke didn't have far to go—just an hour or so—before he came to the cave's exit. It was night outside, but even then, it seemed unnaturally bright. Zeke shielded his eyes as he stepped outside, but he didn't have much of a chance to take in his surroundings before he felt something shift behind him. He wheeled around, expecting an attack, but he was surprised to see that, where the yawning opening that led to the cave system had been, there was only a huge slab of solid granite.

Panic gripped Zeke's heart as he reached out to touch it, half expecting some sort of illusion. But when his hand connected with the rock, he knew it was absolutely real. He didn't have much time to ponder, though, because a moment later, he received a new notification.

Congratulations! You have completed the quest Escape from the Caracoa Cave with a grade of [10]. Reward(s) have been upgraded and expanded. Awarded [Stewardship of the Crimson Tower]. Choose: Knowledge, Skill, or Power.

Zeke suppressed a scream as he felt something burning into his chest, but it passed quickly. When he looked down, he saw that on the upper part of his left pectoral, he had a tattoo that consisted of what looked like a silhouette of a chess rook surrounded by a Celtic circle. It took only a glance for him to understand that it was far more than simple body art. Instead, beneath it, etched onto his soul was the most complicated rune he had ever perceived. When he brushed against it with his mind, another notification sprang before his eyes.

Do you accept [Stewardship of the Crimson Tower]? This role is irreversible. [Y/N]

There was a part of Zeke that wasn't entirely prepared to make a decision when he didn't have any information on what that choice would entail. However, the Framework wasn't likely to give out detrimental quest rewards. So, he clicked yes. Immediately, a new notification spread across his vision.

You have accepted [Stewardship of the Crimson Tower]. It is a unique treasure that will grow with you. However, this growth comes at the cost of a small portion of your experience. The cost is minuscule next to the benefits.

Zeke frowned at the notification. The last thing he wanted was to give up some of his own experience. Leveling was slow and difficult enough as it stood, so losing even a small bit might turn out to be a huge deal. But as he turned his vision inward, concentrating on the rune, Zeke completely forgot about the cost of stewardship. Instead, he saw only the benefits.

In his mind's eye, he saw a square room. Right now, it was completely empty, but his new role as the tower's steward came with an innate understanding of how it worked. He took a piece of fish out of his satchel, then concentrated on moving it into the room. An instant later, the piece of fish appeared in the square room. It was a storage space that only he could access, and judging by how little room the fish took up, it was about a thousand square feet.

But as miraculous as that was, Zeke knew that the Crimson Tower was far more than a simple storage space. With a thought, Zeke accessed another of the tower's functions, and a small hut sprang into being. It was barely more than a stone hovel with a thatched roof, but Zeke knew that it would eventually grow into a commanding tower. In fact, he suspected that the tower already existed on some level, and he could even picture it in his mind—a huge, oppressive thing made of white stone streaked with red that made it look like the very walls bled.

However, as happy as he was with the tower's abilities, Zeke was incredibly thankful for one very simple reason—he could finally discard his disgusting satchel.

As he quickly transferred his meager belongings into his new storage space, Zeke dismissed the hut. Once that was done, he threw the human-skin sack as far as he could, and given his much-increased strength, it ended up sailing a good distance away.

Finally, Zeke turned his attention to his other reward. It seemed that he had a choice before him. Knowledge, skill, or power.

"Couldn't be any more cryptic, could you?" Zeke mused.

The only one that seemed straightforward was the final option. Power was fairly self-explanatory, and while he had no idea what form that power would take, Zeke was pretty sure that it would increase his combat capability. It was a strong draw—especially considering that he was about to set out into an entirely new world. While he hadn't been comfortable in the caracoa caves, Zeke had known what he was dealing with. But now? He was entirely in the dark, so any extra power would be greatly beneficial.

But skill seemed enticing, as well. Would it be an actual skill? Or did it refer to something else? He had no idea. And that, ultimately, was the problem. He hardly knew anything, and what knowledge he possessed was mostly inferred from the various menus. Which brought him to the last choice: knowledge.

If he knew what he was up against, would he really need a boost to his power? Zeke couldn't be sure, but he suspected that he was pretty strong already. After all, he'd just defeated a level twenty-two monster, and it wasn't his first, either. He'd been killing creatures with higher levels for two years. But things would've been much easier if he'd just had a little more information. He'd been stumbling along, entirely ignorant. And he was desperate to change that.

So, Zeke made his choice, and as his reward spread out in his mind, he realized that it wasn't anything like what he had imagined.

27

KNOWLEDGE IS POWER

Zeke read the notification a few times over before he began to internalize what it really meant. But even then, he wasn't entire sure.

Artisan Path: Runes (Novice—Early): You have taken the first steps toward mastering one of the most versatile professions in the world. Runes are the gateway to true understanding. +15 Wisdom. 5% Wisdom.

The upgraded statistics were nice, even if some of the efficacy was wasted on him due to his low mana usage. Wisdom, and the mana regeneration it provided, wasn't really one of his top priorities, but perhaps that would change in the future. After all, his martial path had given him statistics very relevant to swinging his mace; it only stood to reason that the artisan path would do the same for its usage.

Still, he hadn't experienced a mid-battle epiphany like he had with the mace, so it was difficult to understand just what the discovery of the artisan path truly did. However, it took only one look at the runes on his hands for him to understand just how powerful the new path really was.

Zeke shook his head in wonder as he studied the swirling glyphs and symbols that made up the rune's many layers. How could he have ever thought he was close to understanding even the tiniest bit of the runes before? They were more complex than he could truly perceive, but now, he had a hint at just how much he didn't know. More, he could instinctually understand what some of the symbols meant and how they interacted with their fellows. It wasn't even close to the point where he would be comfortable reading them, but that wasn't surprising. If rune mastery was akin to writing a book, his new artisan path was like he'd just memorized the first few letters of the alphabet. It was a minuscule but very necessary step, like getting his foot in the door.

For the next few days, Zeke acclimated himself to being out of the cave system. There wasn't a lot of sunlight that made it through the marsh's thick canopy, but even that left his eyes stinging. So, not wanting to wander off before he felt comfortable, he spent quite a bit of time sitting in the hut provided by his new tattoo while he studied his runes. Slowly, even as he began to grow more comfortable without a rocky ceiling over his head, Zeke felt like he was starting to understand the runes a little better.

During this time, he also thought about his next steps. While he was in the caracoa caves, it had felt pointless to make too many plans. He didn't know if he'd survive the next day, much less long enough to escape. So, he'd focused wholly on survival, eschewing any thoughts of what might come next. But now that he was out of the cave system, he needed to decide what to do.

Oberon had explicitly told him that there would be other people, so it stood to reason that there might be some primitive form of civilization by now. After all, he'd spent almost two years in the caves. Surely others had escaped their beginning dungeons more quickly. And those people would've probably begun to rebuild some sort of society. At the very least, they'd have a camp somewhere.

But how would he find them?

That was a valid question, and Zeke had no real answers. More, he wasn't so naive that he didn't expect that the challenges would end just because he'd escaped the dungeon. In fact, he fully anticipated things getting much more difficult. He had been strong within the caves, but the open world would likely prove much different. But he'd survived so far, hadn't he?

Eventually, after another few days, Zeke decided that he was only stalling. And besides, his stock of fish was running dry, and if he wanted to maintain his strength, he knew he'd have to find food and clean water. Regardless, it was still with some trepidation that he dismissed his hut, hefted his club, and started walking.

The plan was simple. He'd pick a direction and go that way. It didn't matter which way he went because he had no idea where he was going. He only knew that he had to move, if for no other reason than to find a better location to make his base camp. Somewhere with water. Somewhere close to a source of food. And hopefully, other people.

Zeke had never really considered himself the most social of people. He had plenty of friends, but most of them were friendships of convenience. Teammates. Guys he worked out with. Classmates. A few neighbors. He didn't have any real connections, other than what he'd shared with his brother and mother. But after two years alone, he desperately wanted to see another face. He wanted to hear someone else's voice. Even monsters like the trolls needed some sort of social interaction, and Zeke was no different in that respect.

For the next few days, Zeke slowly picked his way through the swamp. It was more difficult than he thought it would be, mostly because there was very little dry land. And what there was usually ended up being comprised of soft, smelly mud. In addition, the water seemed to vary between ankle and hip deep, which made traversal slow and frustrating.

And then there was the wildlife to worry about.

He saw a couple of troll villages in the distance, but the denizens were smaller and less aggressive than the ones in the cave, so Zeke left them alone. If they attacked him, he had no qualms about murdering every single one of them—such was his hatred of trolls—but these lower-level creatures just weren't worth the time or effort. Some of them caught sight of him, but they quickly scurried away, instinctively knowing that he was far more powerful than they were. It wasn't just a function of levels, either. Most were at least level ten, so they had an advantage over him there. But after escaping the dungeon, Zeke had begun to emit something like an aura that told the swamp natives that he was far more dangerous than his level might indicate.

However, that didn't stop him from being attacked once or twice an hour. As he crossed the swamp, Zeke was forced to defend himself from rats the size of German shepherds, enormous alligators, and even a nest of spiders whose webs spanned hundreds of yards in every direction. The arachnids themselves were the size of car tires, and judging by how much it burned when they bit him, they were incredibly venomous. Thankfully, his high vitality proved equal to the task, and he managed to kill the creatures before they could overwhelm him.

Through it all, his martial path had proven increasingly valuable, adding weight and speed to his every attack. It was like a passive enhancement that made him that much more dangerous. Because of that, he spent a portion of each day pondering how it did so. He didn't make any headway, but such was the power of the newly gained path that he wasn't deterred by his failure. He knew that if he could find a way to progress down that path, it would become exponentially more powerful.

He also continued his study of the runes, both at night when he summoned his hut and while trudging through the swamp. He'd gotten to the point where he didn't even need to look at the runes for [**Leech Strike**] in order to visualize the first couple of layers. There were hundreds more, but it gave him some hope that he could one day understand the entire rune.

Or much more. It seemed a far-off goal, but as far as he could ascertain, runes were the basis of everything. The descriptive text accompanying his new artisan path seemed to support that assertion, as well. So, what were the limits? What else could he do? Would he one day be capable of creating his own skills? Maybe, but he knew that going down that path, even if it was possible, would be incredibly long. He was eager to start the journey, though, so he was more than willing to devote his mind to it.

Besides, his earlier fears about the swamp's denizens hadn't yet proven to be true. After the troll warlord, none of the various animals that had attacked him had seemed terribly challenging.

Except the bugs. Those, he could conclude, unequivocally sucked.

Zeke had grown up in the South, so he was no stranger to mosquitoes. However, this new world's version of the pests were the size of hummingbirds, and he suspected that they could've sucked a level one human dry in a matter of minutes. And while they weren't that much of a threat alone, the things were ubiquitous. Still, they were quick enough that they made for excellent practice targets for his mace work. The only solace he got from the things was when he summoned his hut.

If Zeke's aura was a warning, the hut's aura was downright oppressive to the wildlife. Once he summoned it, the swamp's denizens fled, often without regard for Zeke himself. That gave him peace during the nights. In addition, he also discovered that it had an old-school manual pump that he could use to obtain fresh water. That was lucky because without it, he'd have died of thirst. After all, the swamp's fetid water certainly wasn't safe to drink, even with his high vitality.

In addition to the pump, the hut contained a small sleeping pallet, a couple of chairs, and a long table running along one of the walls. He'd also found that it was equipped with a couple of wooden bowls, which made gathering his drinking water that much easier. Aside from those features, it was entirely empty. But Zeke was thankful for the few amenities it had, especially after spending the better part of two years sleeping on bare rock.

Eventually, after more than a week, Zeke escaped the bog. For two days, the dry patches of land had become more frequent, and the cypress trees began to give way to the more expansive oaks and pine trees of a typical forest. Another week passed, and he left the swamp entirely behind. The forest became thicker and the terrain hillier.

Like a lot of southern boys, Zeke had spent plenty of time out of doors—especially in his youth. However, when it became clear to his father that he had talent as a baseball player, most of that time had disappeared onto the baseball diamond or in batting cages. It was ironic, considering that the game was typically played outdoors, that as he got older, he'd begun to spend more time in indoor batting cages and training facilities than outside. But he'd never forgotten how peaceful nature could be.

In another life, he might've become the kind of guy who enjoyed camping and hunting and that sort of thing. But he'd never really had that chance. So, being confronted with pristine wilderness, Zeke was understandably a little awestruck.

Back in the old world, even if you managed to put yourself in the middle of nowhere, there were still subtle signs of civilization. Whether it was someone's discarded trash washing up on a lakeshore or an airplane passing overhead, humanity was always in the background. But here, in this new world, there was nothing but unadulterated nature. And as Zeke walked, it became easier and easier for him to lose himself in it.

Inevitably, his mind wandered. He forcibly stopped himself from thinking about his abusive father. In fact, he didn't want to think about the old world at all. Instead, he continued to focus on the infinite complexity of the runes. He was so deep into his study that he almost didn't notice the subtly changing landscape as the ruins of manmade structures began to pop up. Even so, when he crested a hill, he would have had to have been completely out of it not to see the ruined city stretching out before him.

Taken aback by the sight, Zeke stood there as he tried to understand the scene before him. It had once been a sizable city, but it had clearly been abandoned for hundreds, if not thousands of years. The forest had long since reclaimed it, with trees sprouting in the middle of what had once been wide avenues between buildings. However, from his vantage point, Zeke could clearly see the city's layout as well as the remains of the stone buildings. But as interesting as the city's form was, it also precipitated a slew of questions in Zeke's mind. This was supposed to be a new world, so how did it have the ruins of a long-abandoned city? Had he misunderstood Oberon? Or had someone come before? The trolls in the dungeon had developed a rudimentary society, so it was entirely possible that some other monsters might have progressed even further.

As he stood there, Zeke wondered if it was smarter to explore the ruins or to simply bypass them and come back later once he'd made contact with the rest of humanity. Both options were viable, and for different reasons. On the one hand, he'd had quite a bit of luck with leaving no stone unturned. He'd explored every nook and cranny of the troll caves, and he'd reaped the benefits. The same kinds of rewards were probably available in this new world, as well. But he wasn't so naive as to think there wouldn't be any dangers associated with such exploration, either. He'd barely survived the caracoa caves, and despite traversing the swamp unchallenged, he still expected a sharp increase in danger—especially in a location like abandoned and ancient ruins. Going down there would be gambling with his life.

But was that any different than what he'd done in the troll caves? Or when he combined the blue-spotted mushrooms with the mana water? It had nearly killed him, but he'd come out of it all the stronger. Maybe that was the lesson the dungeon was supposed to teach. No great reward comes without significant risk. If he wanted power, he'd have to put himself in real danger.

That realization made the decision that much easier. So, without further hesitation, Zeke started forward down the slope and into the abandoned city. All the while, his sense of unease mounted. Pushing that aside, he continued onward into the ruins.

28

RUINS

Zeke stepped through a breach in the crumbling wall, turning sideways as he entered the ruined city. That most of the wall was still standing was a testament to its scale as well as its flawless construction. Zeke was no expert in architecture, but even he could see how perfectly the huge stone blocks fit together. Even the ravages of time couldn't bring the wall down altogether. Instead, the erosion of centuries, coupled with the creeping vines, could only poke holes in the ancient barricade.

Once he'd cleared the breach, Zeke took a moment to get his bearings. He had seen the general layout from above, but being on ground level was something entirely different—especially considering that the ruins were far more expansive than he expected. Distance was difficult to judge, but everything he'd seen suggested that the city had once been quite large, spanning at least a few miles in every direction.

As he slowly pushed through an alley that abutted the wall, Zeke wondered who might have lived in such a huge and impressive city. The ruins were well past the point where rebuilding or repair would be possible, and nature had reclaimed much of the place, so interpreting architecture was all but impossible. Instead, there were only hints of what it once had been, and to Zeke, it looked a lot like the old Greek ruins he'd seen in history class, just on a much larger scale.

Idly, he wondered if humans had been the founders of the city. During his time in the caracoa caves as well as trekking through the swamp, Zeke had seen that the trolls were capable of building a rudimentary society. So, was it such a faraway notion that they might build something as mighty as the city through which he'd begun to walk? More, was anything impossible in the new world? Magic existed. He'd benefited from it already. So did fantasy creatures. So, as far as he could tell, the boundaries of possibility had been stretched so far that they had all but ceased to exist.

Zeke's bare feet slapped against the occasional cobblestone as he explored the ruins. Mostly, there wasn't much to see, but he was still awestruck by the place. What's more, he discovered that he wasn't quite alone when, as he turned the corner, he came face-to-face with one of the strangest-looking creatures he'd ever laid eyes on.

It almost looked human, in a way. But coming in at a little more than four feet tall, it was too small, covered in mottled blue-and-white feathers, and had wings. However, its visage was strikingly similar to what he'd expect of a pretty woman. There was an alien cast to its eyes, though, and its feet ended in wicked talons reminiscent of an eagle's. He used [**Inspection**].

Harpy Screecher—Level 14

True to its name, the thing wasted no time before it let out an ear-splitting screech. Zeke clapped his hands over his ears as the sound threatened to overwhelm him. Luckily, his endurance proved enough that it didn't incapacitate him, so he wasn't taken by surprise when the harpy lashed out with its talons. Still, his reactions weren't quick enough to avoid the damage entirely, and he quickly ended up with a trio of long, ragged gashes along his arm.

The pain woke him up, and a primal rage erupted from within. He summoned Voromir from his spatial tattoo and swung it in a short, quick jab. The harpy was fast, and it easily avoided him, continuing its screeching even as it dodged the blow.

For someone who was used to fighting the lumbering trolls, being confronted by a creature that obviously favored agility was a bit of a shock. And it almost proved Zeke's end when he was forced to throw himself out of the way of the harpy's wickedly sharp claws. He narrowly avoided getting his throat ripped out, but the thing still managed to cut him again.

However, by this point, Zeke's battle instincts had begun to kick in. The harpy had taken him by surprise, then further put him on his back foot by displaying such striking quickness. But Zeke's stats weren't just for show, and he quickly adjusted. He'd spent two years battling the denizens of the caracoa caves, and he refused to let a singular harpy cut his journey short.

Zeke felt the now-familiar energy associated with his martial path course through him. It was like all the skill he'd gained over the past two years coalesced into palpable force, but it wasn't just ability. It was knowledge and timing, too. It was as if every last facet of his ability with the mace had been ratcheted up to a new level, and he used that to regain the momentum of the fight with the harpy.

Gone were the long, sweeping blows he might have aimed at the trolls. Instead, they were replaced by quick, jabbing thrusts and controlled strikes. The harpy was taken by surprise, and though its agility was impressive, it took only one clean hit to send it flying into the nearby wall. And when it did, Zeke was rewarded with the sound of crunching bones. It was fast and deadly, but it obviously couldn't take a hit worth a damn.

Zeke loomed over it, putting the pitiful, wounded thing out of its misery. After, he stood there, panting from the exertion. Swinging that many times in such a short span was enough to wind even him, but his recovery came quickly. However, there was no time to rest because he suspected that the harpy hadn't been alone within these ruins. And that screech, while a potent offensive weapon that would've incapacitated many of its enemies, probably served the additional purpose of summoning its sisters. The trolls had often used that same strategy, and Zeke had been forced to learn the benefits of a rapid tactical retreat.

He quickly threw the harpy into his spatial tattoo—maybe it had something valuable on it—and hurried away, using the maze of ruins to hide his withdrawal to safety. After fifteen minutes, Zeke felt certain that if anything was chasing him, it would've either lost track or already reached him, so he settled down to wait for a sign that his fight with the harpy hadn't aroused any response from the other wildlife.

A few screeches in the distance told Zeke that there were plenty of other harpies in the ruins, and for a moment, he wondered if he should simply leave the place behind. After all, given the state of the ruined city, it wasn't likely he would find anything that would make his immediate survival any easier.

But there was also a sense of adventure that tugged at him to keep going with his exploration. He'd barely even seen the outskirts, and there was definitely a part of him that wanted to keep going, to see what secrets the city might hold.

Eventually, the decision came down to a single fact. He was closing in on level ten, and the experience from killing the harpy had made a noticeable difference in the density of his core. It wasn't exact, but he thought he was getting very close to gaining a level. And with that would come another skill—and one he hoped would prove more useful than [**Heart of the Berserker**], which was so situational that he often forgot to even use it.

The problem with the skill wasn't its usefulness. It would help in just about any battle. However, it also came with significant downsides. Not only did it steadily whittle away at his endurance, but upon deactivation, it caused a period of weakness commensurate with the duration of the skill. Zeke had been in near-constant battle throughout his time in the troll caves, so even a short bout of weakness could've proven deadly. And with danger around every corner, he'd decided to use it only when absolutely necessary. The issue was that it was difficult to judge when that actually was.

More than once, Zeke had chastised himself for not using it against Makazith, the troll warlord. But he knew that he'd barely survived the thing's wicked axes; any decrease in his endurance would've likely led him straight into a second death. So, he'd put the skill on the back burner, relegating it to a study tool for his artisan path. One day, perhaps he could mitigate some of the weaknesses of the skill, but for now, it occupied a very niche space in his tool kit.

After a couple more minutes, Zeke continued his exploration, though much more carefully. He wasn't terribly adept at stealth, but he wasn't completely incompetent, either. As he slowly made his way toward the center of the ruined city, Zeke encountered a few more harpies, killing each of them with relative ease. So long as they didn't ambush him, he easily overpowered the birdlike creatures.

The corpses joined the first one in his spatial tattoo; every instinct he had suggested that they might be valuable in some way. Also, he intuitively knew that time moved differently in the space, slowing to a crawl that approached a standstill. It would take years for the corpses to even begin to deteriorate in there. In any case, he didn't want to leave a trail of harpy corpses to lead their kin straight to him.

As he walked, Zeke studied his surroundings, and it wasn't long before he concluded that the city had once been truly impressive, and not just in its size. The closer he came to the center, the more intact the buildings were—and each one was bigger and more ornate than the last. Certainly, none of them were habitable, but hints at their former glory were evident. In addition, there were dry fountains at the intersections of many of the roads, each one studded with well-worn statues of vaguely humanoid shape. Details were impossible to determine, but Zeke thought it was possible that they depicted humans. Or something close to them, at least.

However, as impressive as the city must have once been, Zeke's search proved fruitless. There were no hidden treasure caches. Nor were there any long-abandoned armories. He did find a rusty old dagger while rummaging through one of the more intact buildings, but beyond that, there was nothing. Perhaps it had already been picked clean. Or maybe the treasures simply hadn't survived whatever calamity had befallen the city.

For most of that day, Zeke explored, gradually making his way toward the center of the nameless city. Even though he didn't find any treasure, Zeke didn't regret his decision to explore the place. Each harpy kill had pushed him closer to his next level, which was valuable in and of itself. But even more valuable was the sense of wonder that he felt as he trekked through the ruins. That had been mostly missing in the caves. Thankfully, he hadn't lost the ability to marvel at his surroundings altogether.

As the sun dipped closer to the horizon, Zeke began looking for somewhere to summon his hut. Most of the alleys were too narrow, so he'd have to set up in the middle of one of the streets. He was a bit hesitant, though. Sure, the hut's aura warded away most wildlife, but would it work on semi-sapient creatures like the harpies?

Suddenly, a cacophony of shrieks filled the air. Zeke dropped into a crouch and looked around, but he didn't see a single harpy. A bestial roar cut through the shrieks, and for a brief moment, the harpies went silent. However, it wasn't long before they started up again, and if anything, their calls were even more fervent than before—all coming from somewhere close by.

Looking toward where the sounds emanated, Zeke was torn. He desperately wanted to investigate. But judging by the discordant screeches echoing through the ruined city, there were dozens of the harpies in that direction. Maybe as many as a hundred. And that wasn't even considering what made that roar.

On cue, it erupted again. More desperate this time, but no less powerful.

In the end, Zeke knew there really wasn't a choice here. He would be kicking himself for weeks if he didn't at least try to get a peek. That didn't mean he had to fight or anything. He just wanted a look. So, he started to creep toward what had increasingly begun to sound like a battle between the harpies and whatever monster they'd decided to fight.

29

BETWEEN TWO PATHS

Talia's foot cut through the air like a knife, propelled by her investment in agility. However, just before it connected, her opponent, Master Silas, raised his arm to block. When Talia's foot finally made contact, it was like she'd kicked a brick wall. She heard, more than felt, her bones break, but she didn't let it slow her down. Instead, she activated her skill [**Circle of Mending**] as she hopped back on one foot. In seconds, her bones began to knit back together, but she felt a precipitous drop in her shallow pool of mana.

"Speed is strength," Silas said, and Talia grimaced. The short sentence had become something of a mantra from the old man, and she had long since grown tired of hearing it. However, that didn't mean it wasn't true. "And your endurance is still too low."

Skipping backward, Talia resumed her fighting stance, her face contorting into a scowl as she glared at the head combat instructor of the Temple of the Sun Goddess's martial division, a group that was known as the Radiant Guard. They were small in number, but the division counted many of Beacon's most powerful fighters among its ranks. And Silas was responsible for training all of them.

The man himself didn't appear to be anything special. He was average height, with a middling build, the only notable thing about his appearance being his long, wispy white beard. But he was a true elite who'd achieved the pinnacle decades before, and that meant far more than anyone's physique. Reaching level twenty-five was difficult enough that most people would never do so. Not only did it require an amount of experience that would make the Sun Goddess herself blanch, but it was also impossible for anyone who hadn't evolved their race. The means to do so were rare and extremely expensive, so few had the opportunity to clear that bottleneck at level fifteen.

"I can't put many points into endurance," she spat. "You know that."

"Excuses are irrelevant," Silas said. "Only results matter."

Talia didn't waste any more time with useless talk. Instead, she launched herself at the unassuming man in a flurry of acrobatic kicks and punches. None came close to hitting him, save for the few times he chose to block rather than simply avoid her attacks. And by the time her assault petered out, she had a few more broken bones—not from anything Silas did, but rather due to the force of her own blows. Finally, when both of her feet were broken, she sank to the woven training mat, her breath coming in ragged gasps. Even her [**Circle of Mending**] had limits of how much damage it could heal, and even if it didn't, she had already run dry of mana. It would be hours before she could use the skill again.

"Do you know why you continue to fail?" Silas asked, looming over her. Despite his impeccable control of his aura, Talia could feel his power enveloping her.

Already, Talia could feel the tears forming at the corners of her eyes. Not from the pain—she could handle that much and had done so throughout her training. Rather, the tears were born of frustration. She could not abide failure, even if she knew it wasn't really her fault.

"I'm too weak," she said, the words coming out as a disgusted hiss.

"That is true," the man agreed. "But weakness is only part of the story. The reason you fail is because you are trying to walk two paths. You cannot be everything at once. You must choose, lest you become mediocre at both."

With that, Master Silas extended his hand. Frustrated, Talia took it, and he helped her to her feet. The bones were still weakened, but she could at least stand with only minimal pain.

"Can you talk to her?" Talia asked. It wasn't the first time she'd made the request, and she knew what the answer was going to be.

"I have," Silas said. "She was not swayed."

Talia ground her teeth together as she looked around the training courtyard. It was at least a hundred yards across, as well as twice as wide, and everywhere she looked, she saw people being trained in various forms of combat. The crack of practice weapons coupled with pained grunts and the slap of flesh against flesh filled the air. There were even periodic screams of agony, usually when someone's training went awry and they were injured. Healers dotted the edges of the courtyard, ready to respond when necessary.

Talia grimaced, remembering all the times she had been forced into such duty. [**Circle of Mending**] was a powerful skill, after all.

Healing was a great calling. She knew it was. But her heart had never been in it. Instead, she had always dreamed of being the type of powerful frontline warrior who could stand toe to toe with any monster foolish enough to cross her. And she would've done just that if it weren't for her mother's insistence that she learn the healing arts.

"May I be dismissed?" she asked. "My mother is waiting."

With a nod of assent, Silas said, "You may."

Talia didn't fail to note the sadness in the man's voice. It was understandable, considering that he had been training her for combat since she had turned eight years old. He knew how talented she could be if only her mother would allow her to walk her preferred path. But even Silas, for all his strength and the prestige of his station, didn't have the power to speak against Lady Constance, the Sun Goddess's Chosen and the Shining Light of Beacon.

Talia crossed the courtyard, nodding to her acquaintances along the way. Having grown up in Beacon, she knew almost everyone who called the Temple their home. However, her status as Lady Constance's daughter meant that her upbringing had been a lonely one. The few times she'd tried to make friends, it had become clear that everyone was apprehensive in her company, walking on eggshells lest they offend the most powerful woman in their world.

Even Silas was wary of pushing her too far.

Eventually, she found her way to the Temple's entrance—a set of massive, carved doors that weighed hundreds of pounds. She hardly looked at the intricate carvings that depicted her haloed mother vanquishing an army of foes. The last thing she needed was to be reminded of just how inviolable Lady Constance was.

The Temple of the Sun Goddess was the founding institution upon which Beacon's society had been built, and as such, it wore its wealth like a badge of honor. As Talia strode through the expansive hallways with their marble floors and luxurious furnishings, she couldn't stop her grimace from deepening. A true warrior didn't need wealth like that. She only needed an enemy to fight. Anything else was overkill.

Certainly, her mother had always tried to impress upon her the importance of displays of power, but Talia had let those lessons flow past her. The Temple of the Sun Goddess, and by extension Beacon, wasn't powerful because of gold or marble or fine carpets. It was because of Constance. It was because of the Radiant Guard. No one dared rise up against them because they were simply too strong. It would be a death sentence to oppose the Radiant Guard.

Eventually, Talia wound her way through the maze of corridors to her suite of rooms. She would've been happy with a simple bedroom, but impressions were important. She pushed inside, hardly even noticing the Radiant Guard following her. She couldn't remember his name, but as she recalled, he was quite a swordsman. Handsome, too. Not that he'd ever look at her like that. Nobody did. Another curse of being Lady Constance's daughter was that her romantic possibilities were extremely limited.

With a huff of frustration, Talia slammed the door hard enough that she knew it came close to cracking. That made her feel a little better, at least. A few more points in strength, and she'd get there. Of course, her mother wouldn't like that, which was the whole problem. Sighing, she opened her status screen.

Name	Talia Nightingale
Class	N/A
Level	12
Race	Human (G)
Alignment	Isphodel
Achievements	Progenitor, Bane of Goblins I, The Brink of Death
Strength	41
Agility	69
Dexterity	44

Endurance	23
Vitality	23
Intelligence	64
Wisdom	64
Unassigned Attribute Points	0

To put it bluntly, her stats were a complete mess. According to Master Silas, the only path to true strength was specialization, and while she'd tried to focus where she could, she had been forced to allocate her points into things she knew wouldn't really help her achieve her goals. The problem was that her mother had all but forced her to take support skills.

[**Circle of Mending**] was an extremely powerful area healing ability with a great mana-to-healing ratio. She didn't know precisely what it was, but all the Temple of the Sun Goddess's scholars agreed that it was one of the most potent healing abilities one could easily obtain. By itself, that wouldn't be so bad—she could've been a paladin like Abdul Rumas, who specialized in martial combat while providing powerful utility skills. But then came her level five and ten skills, which further cemented her path as a specialized healer.

[**Meditation**] was useful. Talia couldn't deny that it greatly decreased her recovery time. Even with her relatively low wisdom, so long as she had a little downtime, she could regenerate her mana at an impressive rate. But taking it had kept her from obtaining a combat-focused skill like Master Silas's [**Eagle Strike**]. In one of her training missions, she had seen the seemingly innocuous attack completely obliterate a level twenty goblin's torso, which had left her in awe of the man. That was the kind of power she wanted, but instead, she was left with the useful but ultimately disappointing [**Meditation**].

But even then, Talia had held out hope that her mother would allow her to obtain some way to defend herself at level ten. She was sorely disappointed because she'd been forced to take [**Purify**]. Again, according to all the scholars, it was a necessary part of any healer's skill list, and even Talia had to admit that spending her time curing disease among the populace had been rewarding. It had given her a true appreciation for how the normal citizens of Beacon lived.

It wasn't real power, though, which was what she craved more than anything else. Not like Silas wielded. And certainly not the sort that her mother enjoyed. Everyone said that her father had been a powerful healer, that he'd been all but invincible and capable of self-healing that could outstrip even the most powerful attacks. But he'd died only a few years after Talia was born, so that was just proof that it wasn't a viable path to true power, wasn't it?

Her issues didn't end with her skills, though. Even with the wrong skills, she could've allocated her stats in such a way that would allow her to at least hold her own. However, in order to be minimally effective at her given role, Talia had been forced to spend the bulk of her points in intelligence and wisdom. Even then, her mana pool was shallow, and without [**Meditation**], it took her forever to regenerate even that relatively small amount.

It brought to mind Silas's words. She knew she couldn't walk two paths, regardless of how hard she worked. She was too weak to be a real combatant, and her lacking staying power meant that she couldn't really be a focused healer, either. One or the other would have to win out.

Typically, healers focused on intelligence and wisdom first, every other level splitting off five points into endurance. By comparison, Talia was half as effective as other healers, and she could only make even that paltry claim because of [**Meditation**]. She was even worse as a fighter. Something would soon have to give if she was ever going to gain any degree of real power, as opposed to hanging on to her mother's coattails.

These issues swirled through Talia's mind as she cleaned herself up and got dressed for her daily meeting with her mother. Lady Constance was a rigid woman who didn't accept half measures, especially from her daughter, so Talia took quite a bit of time to make herself presentable. Once she was finished, she looked into the expensive mirror on the wall of her dressing room.

The girl that looked back at her looked every bit as young as Talia's seventeen years of age would suggest. Clad in tight-fitting leather pants and a billowy blouse, with well-polished, high boots, she certainly cut a unique figure. Like her mother, she had no use for the traditional trappings of femininity; she outright refused to wear any dresses or skirts. The only concessions she'd made to societal expectations was her long black hair, which she kept in a single, tight braid that fell down her back.

Even so, she was satisfied with her appearance, and she knew she was reasonably attractive.

"A lot of good that does me," she muttered at the thought. She couldn't even remember the last time she'd enjoyed the company of a boy her own age. Instead, most of her time was spent with the healing masters or Master Silas.

Satisfied with her efforts, Talia checked the mana-driven clock in the corner of the room. It was time to go see her mother.

Without any further stalling, Talia quickly fled the room, ignoring the Radiant Guard who was her shadow for the day. Had his gaze lingered a little? Maybe. But that didn't mean he liked her or anything, right? As if it mattered.

Talia's traversal through the palace-like temple was long but uneventful, and eventually, she found her way to the administration wing that housed her mother's offices. The Temple of the Sun Goddess was a huge organization, with clergy that numbered in the tens of thousands. Organizing that many people, even when they all had the same goals, was a nightmare, and it required an equally nightmarish bureaucracy. Talia shuddered at the thought of interacting with those sorts of people each day; how her mother managed to stay sane, she'd never know.

Despite being one of the most recognizable figures in the Temple, Talia was stopped at multiple checkpoints, each of which was manned by Radiant Guards. At each one, a specialized mage would cast a series of skills intended to pierce through illusions or detect any sort of subterfuge. Talia bore their attention with as much dignity as she could, but by the fourth, she was well and truly frustrated. She hid her impatience, though, enduring it with outward placidity.

Half an hour after she'd entered the administration wing, Talia found her way to her mother's offices. Or the Sun Throne, as it was known among the clergy. A Radiant Guard let her inside.

Idly, Talia wondered what outsiders who met with Lady Constance thought upon entering such a gaudily named place. Because, while the moniker may have suggested something impressive, the reality was an austere office, populated only by Constance's desk; a plain, straight-backed chair; and a painting of their patron, the Sun Goddess, hanging on the back wall.

The painting itself was an immaculate piece of art depicting a beautiful, white-robed woman who seemed to be extending her glowing hand to whomever regarded the painting. For Talia's part, despite the painting's artistic merits, she'd always found the thing extraordinarily creepy. Not only did its eyes seem to follow her wherever she went, but the hand was constantly shifting its perspective so that it always looked like it was coming right at her. She suppressed a shudder as she focused on her mother.

Constance had always claimed that decorating her office in finery was pointless in the face of a depiction of her chosen goddess. To a degree, that was true. The painting was overwhelming. But the real reason Constance didn't bother with such things was because she dominated every room in which she stood. Her aura billowed off of her in waves, visible even to the naked eye, and presenting itself as rays of unsullied light. Against that, what was gold? What was finery? Nothing else could compare.

"Good afternoon, Mother," Talia said, bowing at the waist.

"Daughter," Lady Constance said, nodding slightly. Then, to her attendants that Talia had trouble even noticing amid the light, she said, "You may leave. I wish to speak with my daughter alone."

The three women and one man, all dressed in identical white robes trimmed in gold, scurried from the room. Even after the doors shut behind them, silence stretched between Talia and her mother.

Finally, Constance's aura dimmed to nothing, and she practically fell into the chair. Immediately, Talia saw the strain behind her mother's eyes as the older woman massaged her temples.

"I have a mission for you," she said. "Have you ever heard of the Micayne Estate?"

Talia had. "They say it's haunted," she said. "The original owners dabbled in forbidden magic, and—"

"Abraham Micayne was a fool to claim it," Constance said, shaking her head. Micayne had been one of Constance's original party, a group of legends that included Lady Constance and Talia's father, Jeremiah, as well as Micayne and his wife. Rounding out the group had been Abdul Rumas and Master Silas himself. The woman leaned back with a sigh. "I haven't seen him in more than a decade. Sometimes..."

"Are you okay?" Talia asked.

"The same old problems. Regrets of a long life," Lady Constance admitted. "Nothing for you to worry over."

"But—"

"It's nothing," the older woman said, cutting Talia off. "The mission is simple. You and a team will head to the Micayne Estate, ascertain

Abraham's fate, and if possible, bring him home. However, if you deem the attempt too dangerous, you are to retreat and relay your findings to the Radiant Guard."

Talia nodded, but in her mind, she knew she would never retreat. She might not be as strong as some of the others, but she would not be a coward. Already, Talia was imagining her heroic return, even as Constance gave her the details of her team. To her disappointment, it would be comprised of almost two dozen people, including a full complement of warriors, two other healers, and the legendary paladin Abdul Rumas. It was like her mother didn't trust her to fill an actual role, and she had overcompensated by saddling her with a veritable army of babysitters.

Finally, once Constance finished, she said, "How is your training going?"

"Master Silas—"

"Not that training," she said dismissively. "Your real training."

Talia ground her teeth together in frustration. It didn't matter how hard she worked with Master Silas; her mother considered it only a distraction akin to a hobby. But the time she spent with the master healers? That was what was important—at least to Constance. To Talia, it was one more brick in the ever-growing wall that was her dissatisfaction.

But this mission—it was the first time she'd be going on a mostly unchaperoned adventure. She'd fought before, but always, there'd been someone like Master Silas there to make sure she didn't end up dead like so many other adventurers. Abdul Rumas was powerful—a veritable legend—but he wouldn't fill that kind of role in the party. Hopefully, he'd treat her just like any of the group's other members. If so, she'd have only her contemporaries as backup. And while that meant she'd lose her safety net, it also meant that she would have a chance to prove herself.

And that was all Talia really wanted—to prove her strength.

30

MAMA BEAR

Zeke crouched behind a ruined and crumbling wall, hoping to remain unseen. It was a tall order, considering that there were at least a hundred harpies swooping around the expansive square. Most were little different from the ones he'd already fought, but scattered throughout the crowd of monstrous, avian humanoids were a few that were bigger, stronger, and higher-level. The harpies weren't the subject of his interest, though. Instead, his gaze was focused on the giant creature that seemed to be guarding a mostly intact building.

The bear wasn't much bigger than a typical grizzly, but it radiated a palpable sense of power that Zeke could feel even a hundred yards away. Despite its obvious strength, it was also fighting a losing battle against the flock of harpies. Every couple of seconds, one would swoop in and rake its claws across its thick hide, sending a spray of blood flying against the building's walls. One or two such wounds were easily ignored, but it was obvious that the battle had been raging for quite some time because the bear's pelt was matted with congealed and drying blood.

But the bear remained steadfast, completely unwilling to move from its position in front of the door. It also gave as good as it got, often paying back the harpies with a powerful swipe of its own. But there were hundreds of attackers, and against such a numerous foe, it did little good.

For a solid ten minutes, Zeke watched, transfixed by the battle playing out before him. There was a big part of his mind that wanted to anthropomorphize the monsters, assigning roles like good guy and bad guy. And given its status as the obvious underdog, the bear was definitely playing the part of hero in Zeke's mind. Certainly, he knew that neither fit those designations—they were beasts, after all—but that didn't stop his thoughts from running along with the notion.

Idly, he wondered if he should help, but he quickly discarded the idea. If he went down there, mace swinging, both the harpies and the bear would probably turn on him. And even with as capable as he'd become, Zeke had no illusions about surviving something like that.

Slowly but surely, the harpies wore the bear down. Its swings became less frequent, its movements more lethargic. But it didn't give up. It didn't try to run away. Nor did it attempt to take the battle to its enemies.

Because it was guarding something.

Was it some kind of treasure, perhaps?

Despite spending two years in the troll caves and another few weeks traversing the wilderness, Zeke didn't really know how the new world worked. Was it like a game, where he'd have to fight some sort of boss in order to find treasure? Or was it more organic than that? Perhaps the bear was just what it appeared to be—an unlucky animal that had run afoul of the wrong sort of monsters.

But Zeke couldn't escape the notion that he was missing something important. So, he resolved to stick around until he figured out just what was tugging on his mind. After all, he was far from the fighting, and if circumstances demanded it, he could escape with little difficulty. The harpies were dangerous monsters, but they weren't the most intelligent of creatures, regardless of their partially humanoid appearance.

Finally, after a few more minutes, Zeke found what he sought when the bear shifted and he caught sight of another, much smaller pile of fur. Was it a mate, perhaps? A fallen comrade? Zeke couldn't tell, but the discovery further cemented his inclination to side with the giant bear.

Then, in a sudden rush, a pair of the bigger, more dangerous harpies cut through the air with lightning speed. Their wicked talons flashed, and the bear roared in pain and defiance as the pair of harpies cut into something vital. Suddenly, blood gushed out of the bear's side, pooling on the remnants of a cobbled street. Heroically, the bear remained standing, but it looked like it was on its last leg.

Perhaps it was because Zeke had been on the receiving end of such punishment. After all, he'd been forced to fight an entire city's worth of trolls. Or maybe it was a sense of fair play that objected to the harpies dominating the bear via sheer numbers. Or it could have been that, after having a few run-ins with the harpies himself, Zeke very clearly remembered the feeling of those sharp talons. Whatever the case, Zeke soon found himself moving.

He didn't think about how stupid it was. Nor did he hesitate. Instead, Zeke summoned his mace, Voromir, from his tattoo and swiftly closed the hundred-yard gap between him and the closest harpy. It never even knew Zeke was there before its brains were splattered all over the cobbles. But Zeke wasn't done. So long as he had the element of surprise, he would kill as many of the harpies as he could.

Quickly, he mowed through another handful of the hideous creatures before the frenzied flock of harpies began to take note. Zeke activated **[Leech Strike]**, then continued his slaughter. Four harpies. Then ten. Then twenty. He was a whirlwind of blunt force trauma as he steadily destroyed the lesser harpies.

And it felt good.

Not just because he could finally let loose and go on a mass rampage. That played a bigger part in his enjoyment than he wanted to acknowledge; he'd become very well acquainted with death and carnage during his time in the caves, and Zeke could admit, at least to himself, that he enjoyed the feelings that came with slaughtering his foes. However, his enjoyment was twofold, owing at least as much to the steady stream of experience gathering in his core. He could feel it filling up, bit by bit, and soon, he knew he would reach level ten. And finally, after building up the battle between the heroic bear and the devious harpies in his mind, Zeke felt a certain satisfaction, like he was on the side of justice.

It was silly. He knew that. But at the end of the day, he'd chosen his side, and he felt in the bottom of his heart that he was right.

Finally, he broke through a clump of harpies to find himself standing face-to-face with the bear. And it was worse off than he'd expected.

Though they'd been hidden by its thick fur and considerable distance, Zeke could now see the jagged grooves that had been carved into its flesh. Barely a single inch of the bear was without matted blood, and Zeke could see that it was favoring its front left paw. In addition, flecks of red-tinted foam coated its snout, like it had been coughing up blood.

But looking past that, Zeke could see the fire in the bear's eyes. It wasn't fighting for its own survival. Instead, it battled for something far more important. And now that Zeke was close enough, he could see precisely what drove the bear to such lengths.

Behind it, lying on its side, was a tiny bear cub. It was no bigger than a small dog. Maybe twenty pounds, if that. And though Zeke could see the thing's chest moving with its labored breaths, it was grievously wounded, its own pool of blood big enough to mingle with its mother's. Just past that ball of bloody fur were three more cubs, though none of them still breathed.

Fire erupted in Zeke's side as an enterprising harpy took advantage of his brief pause to rake its talons across his ribs. He quickly spun around, his mace arcing out to destroy the monster. When it connected, Zeke was rewarded with the sound of multiple broken bones and an explosion of feathers. He must've ruptured some of its internal organs because he immediately gained another stream of experience as it succumbed to death.

Zeke's arrival attracted the attention of the rest of the harpies, and many of them diverted their efforts in his direction. He gritted his teeth as the effect of [**Leech Strike**] did its work and began to heal the wound along his ribs as he defended himself.

Though Zeke preferred the more aggressive tactic of taking the fight to his enemies, he'd been forced onto his back foot enough that the shift in strategy happened completely naturally, and soon, he found himself backed against the stone wall of the building and fighting shoulder to shoulder with the bear. He knew it was dangerous. The creature was a powerful monster. But Zeke had seen a glimmer of intelligence in the thing's eyes, and he trusted that it would see his help for what it was.

Besides, Zeke hadn't come across anything that could kill him yet. Sure, if he stood still and let them do it, the harpies could probably manage. But so long as he remained capable of defending himself, Zeke felt confident that he could at least survive long enough to run away. The bear was clearly more powerful than the harpies, but Zeke was certain that it wasn't as strong as the troll warlord had been. So, Zeke decided to take a chance and trust the bear to recognize the situation.

Luckily, it did just that, and over the next few minutes, the pair of them slaughtered one harpy after the next. The smaller ones, called harpy screechers, were little more than cannon fodder, and generally, it took only one swing from Voromir or a swipe from the bear's claw to kill them. At best, if the thing was especially quick and managed to dodge most of the blow, it took two. However, the bigger ones, called harpy matriarchs, were a few levels higher and exponentially more powerful.

Alone, even they weren't much of a threat. The only problem was that they were never, ever alone.

A matriarch swooped in, its talons aiming at Zeke's face. He shifted to his left, swinging his mace. Before he could complete the attack, though, a pair of harpy screechers dove from above. There was no time to dodge, so Zeke had no choice but to eat the attacks. The swooping matriarch cackled with glee. Or maybe it was just a birdcall. But it certainly sounded like mocking laughter.

Zeke narrowed his eyes.

He needed to be smarter. But more than that, he knew he'd have to make some sacrifices.

So, when the next matriarch tried the same move, Zeke let it come. Its talons ripped into his shoulder, tearing a good chunk of muscle out before it flapped its wings and shot away. Predictably, a trio of screechers came in a split second later, thinking he would be distracted. Zeke was waiting for them, though. Ignoring the not-insignificant pain in his shoulder, Zeke sent his mace singing through the air. One down. Then two. The third tried to abort its dive, but it was too late. An overhand swing of Zeke's mace sent it crashing bonelessly to the ground.

Since gaining [**Leech Strike**], Zeke had discovered a few things about how it worked. First was that the amount of vitality it stole was based on how much damage he did. So, the harder he swung, the more it healed him. And Zeke could swing very, very hard. The second thing he'd learned was that when he did so, the steady stream of mana that kept the ability active spiked. Theoretically, if he hit hard enough and often enough, he could exhaust his mana completely. However, because of his extremely high stats and the relatively small cost of the skill, Zeke never even came close to that. So, effectively, so long as he could keep fighting, he was functionally invincible.

Or that's what he thought, at least. The troll warlord had certainly pushed him to his limit. But that was because, with a single blow, it could've obliterated a good portion of Zeke's body—not dissimilar to what Zeke was doing to the harpies. But with foes like the birdlike humanoids that relied on speed and agility? He was uniquely suited for fighting them.

But that didn't mean it didn't hurt. Zeke wasn't sure if it was just that he hadn't been wounded much during his trek through the swamp, or if there was something about those sharp claws that made it hurt more, but regardless of what caused it, it was agonizing. Still, Zeke was well schooled in ignoring pain, and with an effort of will, he shunted it off to an isolated corner of his mind.

On and on, Zeke fought a seemingly endless stream of harpies. He killed screechers. He dispatched matriarchs. But still, they came. Eventually, Zeke slipped into that well-worn battle trance where nothing existed but him, his weapon, and his enemies. There were no fancy tactics. No ingenious plans. He simply swung when appropriate, dodged when he could, and took the attacks he could handle. Soon, he was covered in just as much blood as his animal compatriot, though a quick glance told him that it didn't have healing capabilities on par with his.

If Zeke had shown up earlier, perhaps the bear could have made a go of it. But by the time he had arrived to lend his aid, it had taken too many hits. It had accumulated too many wounds. The result was that it could defend itself from only about a quarter of the attacks, which only made the wounds pile up even more quickly.

Zeke was about to do something drastic when a deafening screech filled the air. Strangely, the gathered harpies screamed in response, furiously beating their wings as they backed away. No more attacks came. Zeke stood there, his breath coming in gulps. He glanced toward the bear, whose limbs were trembling. Its eyes were barely open, and the pool of blood beneath it had grown even wider.

"Hang in there," Zeke muttered, his voice hoarse from disuse. The bear was clearly not encouraged, and it threw its head back with an arrogant snort that sent blood-tinged foam flying through the air.

The screech came again, this time from much closer. Zeke looked up to see a huge shape streaking down from the sky. He had only a brief second to use his identification skill on the creature.

Harpy Queen—Level 20

"Shit," he spat.

And then the thing was on top of them, its foot-long claws digging into the bear's thick hide. Its wingspan was at least twenty feet, and its body was nearly the size of a full-grown human. More, instead of the shapeless, birdlike torso of its subjects, the queen had a feminine form covered in thick, gray feathers.

As Zeke sprang into motion, he caught a glimpse of the creature's eyes. Its face was almost entirely human, but its eyes were wholly alien, and they sparkled with unrepentant menace. This was a cruel creature, Zeke had no doubt. And he had no qualms about ending it.

Unfortunately, his ability couldn't quite match up with his aspirations because he soon found himself sailing across the square, bowling over harpies in his path. His shoulder popped out of joint, and he picked up a handful of broken ribs, as well. The thing wasn't just fast. It was incredibly strong, too. Not quite on the level of the warlord, but it made up for it in sheer velocity.

Zeke was up in an instant, carving his way through the flock of harpies. His wounds healed rapidly as his fury coupled with his martial path to lend weight to his blows. His bear companion roared its defiance and pain, but Zeke could see that it was losing the battle. The harpy queen was simply too fast, and it was strong enough to make quick work of the bear's hide. However, the bear wasn't without power, and it managed to land a couple of shots of its own. The most damaging of which was a vicious swipe to the queen's delicate wing. It crumpled, its hollow bones cracking audibly as it fell from the air. But even bound to the ground, the thing was wickedly fast, and it clearly had plenty of experience fighting on foot. The bear reared onto its hind legs, roaring its fury.

Just before Zeke made it back, his heart seized in his chest as he saw the harpy's talon flash toward the bear's neck. Fur, meat, and a gout of blood flew through the air, and the bear's roars became a pitiful gurgle. Even as its blood flowed out in what felt like gallons, it made a valiant effort to hold its ground. But it didn't have the strength, and it ended up stumbling drunkenly to the ground.

The harpy queen tilted its head to the sky and cackled in apparent glee. Zeke's mace, powered by every ounce of his strength, took it at the base of the skull. The queen was strong and fast, but it wasn't very durable. So, the result was predictable.

The lower half of the queen's skull, along with a sizable portion of its spine, were shattered, and it dropped in an instant. Zeke wasted no time swinging his mace again. And again. Three times. Four. He kept swinging until the thing's entire head was reduced to mush. Then, gulping air, he wheeled around and roared at the remaining harpies. In the back of his mind, he realized that he'd gained his much-sought-after level, but he ignored it.

Zeke would never know if they fled because the remaining harpies had just seen their queen killed, or if it was because of his monstrous countenance. But it took them only a second before the air was filled with flapping wings as the monsters took to the skies.

He stood there for a long moment, his shoulders heaving with every breath. Then, he turned back to the bear who'd so valiantly fought beside him. It was already dead.

He howled in grief and rage.

Zeke had no idea why the bear's death hit him so hard. Maybe it was because he'd finally found something he didn't want to kill and hadn't tried to kill him in return. Or perhaps he'd gotten too caught up in the narrative he'd written in his head. It might have even been a simple refusal to accept his failure. He'd never been good at losing, after all.

Either way, seeing the dead bear lying before him, Zeke felt an unparalleled sense of loss. If only he hadn't sat back and watched for so long, he could have made a difference. He could've saved the damned thing.

He didn't know if he was more angry, sad, or both, but he definitely felt some combination of the two. And he'd have probably stood there for even longer if he didn't hear a soft mewling coming from within the ruined building.

The cub!

Zeke quickly abandoned the bear's body and found the cub within. It was even smaller than he'd first thought, and it was just about as pitiful as anything he'd ever seen. A series of wicked lacerations trailed along its side, deep enough that Zeke could see the white of the creature's ribs.

His heart ached for the animal, but what could he do? Zeke wasn't a healer. Perhaps he could clean it, but would that make any difference? He had no bandages. No needle and thread. Even if he did, he didn't know how to sew a wound shut. And what about the blood the cub had already lost?

Zeke slammed his hand on the ground in frustration. He couldn't save the animal's mother, so what made him think he could save the cub? He was just a killer, like the troll warlord had implied. Even the monsters recognized him for what he was.

If only [**Leech Strike**] healed others, all he'd have to do would be to find a few monsters, and the bear cub would be fine.

Wait . . .

He'd gotten to level ten, hadn't he? Perhaps there was another skill available that would help him. Quickly, Zeke opened the appropriate submenu, and sure enough, he found what he was looking for:

[Mark of Companionship] (G)—A hero's greatest strength comes from his allies. Place a rune on your companions, and they will share a portion of your benefits. Upgradable.

Though there were a few other attractive options, Zeke didn't hesitate to choose [**Mark of Companionship**]. It wasn't just for the bear cub, either, though that was the immediate benefit. Instead, he was thinking about the eventuality of encountering other people. It was one thing to lose his briefly allied bear companion. It was something else entirely to lose a human comrade. And with the power of his [**Leech Strike**], he thought he could make quite a difference in keeping other people alive.

But for now, he would put the rune on the bear cub and go find a few more harpies to kill. However, when he tried to do so, Zeke got a very frustrating alert.

Warning: You cannot use beneficial skills on non-sapient creatures.

As soon as the mark—which was just another complicated rune—contacted the bear cub, it had dissipated into nothingness. Zeke frowned. Well, that just wasn't going to work at all. Using his artisan path, Zeke summoned the image of the rune in his mind. It was even more complex than the familiar [**Leech Strike**], but he could see some similarities. Through study and the innate understanding of runes granted by his artisan path, Zeke had also determined what a few of the symbols did. So, it didn't take him long to find the symbol that kept him from using the skill on the cub. But finding it was the easy part, wasn't it? What was he supposed to do now?

Another pitiful whine pierced through his concentration. He didn't have time! The creature was dying, and if he didn't do something soon, he'd be too late. Again. Just like he had been with the cub's mother.

It didn't take Zeke long to make up his mind to forge ahead. Sure, he didn't really know what he was doing. Nor did he think it would work. But he had to do something. Otherwise, he'd never be able to live with himself. So, he closed his eyes and felt the offending symbol.

Like all runes, it was constructed of pure mana. So, wouldn't it be easy to simply destroy it? Then, he could do what he needed to do, right? It wasn't so different than when he'd unraveled the curses. In fact, it might even be easier because he didn't have to destroy the entire rune. Just a tiny piece.

So, without any further hesitation, Zeke cast the mark, using his not-inconsiderable willpower to hold it in place just above the bear cub's skin. Then, he went to work on the appropriate symbol, unraveling it thread by thread. Contrary to what he expected, though, it was exponentially more difficult than dissipating one of the troll curses. The curses were like houses of cards—a single gust, and they'd come crashing down. The rune associated with [**Mark of Companionship**], however, was like a brick wall, and the only way to get the desired result was to chip away at the appropriate spot. On top of that, the more he chipped away, the more difficult it was to hold the thing in place.

But Zeke persisted, the simple refusal to surrender perched in his mind.

Eventually, Zeke managed to dislodge the last bit of the symbol, then with a shove, pushed it into the bear cub. Zeke held his breath as it settled into place.

And nothing happened.

Then, suddenly, a sharp spike of agony went through his entire mind. He screamed in mingled pain and terror, but it didn't matter. He had obviously made a huge mistake, and now he had to pay the price.

31

SOUL BOND

For a split second, Zeke was certain he was dying. After everything he'd gone through, he had finally gone too far. How could he have been so stupid as to think that he knew what he was doing? Runes weren't just incredibly complex; they were intricate, multifaceted whorls of pure power, each bit dependent on the others. Simply burning one glyph out of the design was more likely to see the whole thing collapse than to create the desired result. And through the sharp, stabbing pain in his mind, Zeke could see that was precisely what was happening.

Without that one symbol, the entirety of the rune flexed and vibrated like it wanted to unravel into motes of useless stray mana. And if that happened, Zeke could intuit that it wouldn't turn out well for him. There would be a significant backlash, and one that threatened his very survival.

In a lot of ways, it wasn't so different from the curses with which he'd been forced to become so intimately familiar, really. The scale was inflated, but the mechanics were much the same. And when he'd unraveled those curses, he'd been forced to endure an incredible blanket of mental strain that smothered his willpower. Trying to alter the rune for **[Mark of Companionship]** was similar in that respect, though the pressure was far more overwhelming—not least because it was accompanied by both physical pain and significant mental anguish.

The physical pain was located just behind his eyes, and it felt like someone repeatedly jabbing an ice pick into his brain. That, by itself, was agonizing enough that it precluded any ability to think, much less concentrate on something so delicate as keeping the rune for **[Mark of**

Companionship] from dissipating. On top of that was a psychological torture he'd never experienced.

One second, he was trying to deal with the purely physical portion of the backlash, and the next, he was inundated by a deluge of memories, all from the perspective of the dying bear cub. They were blurry and indistinct, but in that moment, Zeke understood the creature lying before him in way he couldn't really explain. He knew its history. He knew its emotions. He knew its identity in an incredibly intimate way. For that split second, Zeke was the cub who'd just seen its mother and siblings massacred by the vicious harpies. He felt the monsters' ripping claws as they tore through his undeveloped body. He experienced the cub's confusion, then sorrow when he saw his mother finally breathe her last breath. And finally, he felt the cub's fear when he saw the strange, two-legged creature bending over it.

Zeke let out a pained howl of pure emotion, and he very nearly succumbed to that flood of memories and emotions and let himself be washed away. If that happened, he would die. Even underneath all the pain, he knew that as surely as he'd ever known anything else. Perhaps his body would keep going, but any semblance of humanity would be gone, never to return.

And Zeke couldn't let that happen. He'd come too far, and he'd already suffered too much—falling here was not something he could accept. So, he summoned every last ounce of willpower he possessed and pushed against that deluge of emotions.

Kneeling beside the bear cub, he was dimly aware of his own body. His every muscle flexed, and his fingernails dug into his palms. Tears flowed down his dirty cheeks, mingling with harpy blood and dirt as he fought for his very humanity.

By that point, Zeke was well versed in fighting for his life. He'd been doing just that for more than two years, and, by necessity, he'd become an expert on survival. However, there was a marked difference between fighting a troll and wrestling with something as ephemeral as another creature's intrusive identity. But there was a very important commonality—they both required significant willpower. A simple refusal to give in that, ever since he'd woken up at the bottom of those troll caves, Zeke had epitomized.

Leveraging every bit of that stubborn refusal to lose, Zeke fought against the tide of the bear's identity, lashing out with everything he had.

It did little, other than to exhaust his mental faculties. After all, you can't fight the ocean, can you? You can only plant your feet and endure.

So, seeing how ineffectual his wild attacks were, Zeke adjusted his strategy. He wouldn't be a warrior. He would be a rock; sure, the bear's identity would wear him down, perhaps even to the smallest piece. But so long as something—even a tiny grain of sand—remained, he would persevere.

Slowly, bit by bit, the pressure lessened, and the tide began to wane. Suddenly, Zeke could feel bits of his own identity receding alongside the bear cub's. He grasped at them, but they were too small, and they were moving far too quickly for him to recapture. So, he had no choice but to watch as little pieces of his mind latched on to the cub's identity. In addition, a steady stream of his mana suffused that tide, taking with it some indefinable part of Zeke's soul.

Finally, the flow petered out, and the pain faded, leaving a panting Zeke kneeling beside the wounded bear. And as soon as that last drop of mana and the two mingled identities dissipated, an achievement notification flashed before Zeke's eyes.

Beastmaster—You have created a Soul Bond with another creature. +3 to all stats.

A second later, another flashed.

Savant—Create a unique rune without the benefit of an artisan class. +5 Strength, Agility, Dexterity, Endurance, and Vitality. +10 Intelligence. +15 Wisdom. +5% Wisdom.

Zeke stared at the pair of achievements in confusion. The second wasn't that surprising, if he thought about it in any depth. After all, he had set out to change the rune resulting from the activation of [**Mark of Companionship**], so it stood to reason that he'd created something new. However, the first really shocked him.

Only a couple of seconds after Zeke had read the notifications, a mass of information flooded his mind. Some of it was associated with the bear cub. He could read the creature's mood, and he could tell how it was injured. On top of that, he thought that, with a little bit of focus, he could even communicate with the animal. He didn't think he could hold detailed conversations with it, but basic commands seemed well within the purview of the Soul Bond. Whether that was due to the nature of the bond itself, or if it was because of the infantile nature of the beast, Zeke couldn't be sure.

On top of that, Zeke could intuit something of how the bond worked. The skill it had been based upon, [**Mark of Companionship**], allowed the recipient of the mark to share experience and benefit from Zeke's skills, and it seemed that that had been unchanged. However, whereas [**Mark of Companionship**] was a temporary skill that required a constant stream of mana, the Soul Bond was permanent. Basically, Soul Bond worked like a beefed-up, enduring version of the skill. On top of that, it was the solution to the problem at hand. If he concentrated, he could funnel the vitality that came from the skill [**Leech Strike**] into the bear, healing its wounds. Zeke wasn't certain how he knew how everything worked, but he chalked it up to the Framework giving him the ability to use the tools he'd earned.

It wasn't precisely what Zeke had wanted to accomplish. In fact, it so far exceeded his expectations that he hadn't even known such a thing as a Soul Bond was possible. But that didn't mean he wasn't happy with how it had worked out. Despite the pain and the fact that he'd very nearly had his identity washed away, he now had the ability to save the bear cub.

But he would have to hurry because in the time that had passed since he initiated the Soul Bond, the bear cub's condition had continued to worsen. So, he scooped the animal into his arms, gathered his mace, and rose to his feet. And it was agonizing. His muscles, stiff from constant contraction, protested every movement. But he could deal with pain—especially when he knew that his bear companion was dealing with so much worse.

Zeke wasn't sure exactly how the Soul Bond worked, but he suspected that if he let the creature die, there would be consequences. On top of that, the pair were now connected in a way Zeke couldn't fathom or adequately describe. It was like their existences had mingled and their souls had twined around each other. Their bond was inextricable, and Zeke equated the bear cub's survival with his own. If the cub were to succumb, he would probably survive, but there was a part of him that would perish right alongside the creature. More than mere self-service, though, there was a deep empathetic connection between them that necessitated Zeke's help. It was past not wanting to see it die. Zeke needed for the animal to live.

So, with that in mind, Zeke activated [Leech Strike] and set out to hunt harpies. Part of it was simple necessity. They were the most pervasive monsters in the area, and there were plenty of them around that Zeke could use his skill to heal his bound companion. But there was another part born of hate emanating from the half-conscious bear in his arms. The cub had seen the harpies steadily rip its mother to shreds, and it desperately wanted revenge for the heinous act.

Maybe Zeke did, too. After all, even before initiating the Soul Bond, he had felt a connection with the cub's mother. They'd fought side by side as allies. And Zeke had felt a kinship with the proud animal. So, his own desires mingled with the muddled impressions he felt from the cub, and in that respect, they were of one mind.

Even though the sun had begun to set, Zeke wasted no time, striding past the scattered corpses of the harpies he and the bear cub's mother had already slain. Instead, he followed in the direction he'd seen them all flee, hoping that he could find their nests. For while healing the cub was his primary goal, he also wanted to eradicate the horrible creatures that had caused so much grief.

As he stalked through the ruins, Zeke wasn't unaware of his hypocrisy. After all, he had far more blood on his hands than the harpies did. But even before creating the Soul Bond, he had chosen his side.

Suddenly, a telltale screech assaulted his ears, announcing the arrival of a pair of harpy screechers. For someone with less endurance, the aural attack might have been debilitating, but for Zeke, who had become acclimated to the attack, it was only an annoyance. His mace, having adjusted its weight for his one-handed grip, sang as it swept toward the harpies. The first screecher never even knew what hit it as the mace ripped through its torso, sending a spray of rib fragments, gore, and intestines flying through air. The rest of its body soon followed, the momentum of the ferocious attack sending it smashing into a ruined wall. To its credit, the half-standing wall only shuddered, a testament to the quality of its original construction. The harpy wasn't so lucky, and the sound of its bones shattering all at once joined its fellow's cry.

Immediately, Zeke felt the vitality of [Leech Strike] flow through him, and he breathed a sigh of relief when a bit of it siphoned off toward the bear cub. It wasn't enough to heal his newly bound companion, but it was enough to at least stave off death. More than that, it confirmed his ability to save the creature—a discovery that lessened the dreadful weight of responsibility that had settled across his shoulders.

That was all Zeke needed to spur him forward, and he quickly dispatched the other screecher with practiced ease.

Over the next hour, as dusk settled into night, Zeke stalked through the ruins, killing any harpy he could find. Each of the slain monsters injected a bit of vitality into the bear cub, and with every passing minute, it healed a little. Even so, its wounds had been dire, and it would take far more to ensure its survival. So, he pushed on, driven as much by his need to heal his new companion as by the bloodlust born of his desire for vengeance against the hateful and hated harpies.

By midnight, Zeke was forced to admit that the density of the harpies was growing with every step. He'd lost count of how many he had killed, but he knew he'd eclipsed the century mark, and by quite a bit. But his bloodlust still hadn't been sated. Perhaps it never would be.

To Zeke, killing had come surprisingly easy. Even back in the cave system, he hadn't been bothered by reaping the lives of so many trolls. In fact, he hadn't felt much at all. They were monsters, sure, but they were also at least nominally intelligent creatures. The same could be said for the harpies. However, Zeke felt no pity for them. No empathy.

Perhaps some part of him had died in those caves, so long ago. Or maybe he was so tuned in to his own survival that he hadn't had the luxury of unraveling such moral quandaries. Either way, he spared no thought for the fact that he'd already committed one genocide within the cave systems, and he was well on his way to committing another against the harpies.

After all, they were the enemy. And he didn't have the time nor the inclination to empathize with his enemies. So, Zeke didn't rest until, just before dawn, he found precisely what he'd been looking for.

He crouched beside a mostly intact building, studying the scene laid out in front of him. The harpies had clearly lived in the ruined city for quite some time, evidenced by the fact that they'd built hundreds of nests in the square in front of him. The square itself was a little bigger than a football field, with an enormous, dry fountain in the center. The statues in the middle of the fountain were so eroded that Zeke could only discern that the subjects were humanoid in shape; all other details had fallen to the ravages of time. Other smaller fountains dotted the square, giving Zeke a vague impression of just how impressive it must have been, once upon a time.

The remnants of tall buildings, looking as if they'd been knocked down by artillery fire rather than simple erosion, lined the square. And in those buildings, Zeke saw hundreds, if not thousands, of harpies. Most were the comparatively harmless screechers, but there were quite a few matriarchs there, as well. In addition, Zeke saw a few even larger figures that could've given the queen a run for her money.

But there were also smaller, less humanoid creatures fluttering around that Zeke quickly identified as juvenile harpies. He was reminded of his earliest days within the troll cave, when he'd been forced to kill the troll larvae. And while he wasn't eager to revisit his infant-killing past, he knew that these smaller creatures wouldn't hesitate to attack him. After all, they were monsters. That was what they did.

Besides, he still had vengeance to seek.

So, Zeke pushed himself back to his feet and strode forward, entirely willing to do what was necessary.

32

TUA'TA'ALAR

Abby wove through the forest, dodging between the trees as she wrung every last bit of stamina from her body. It wouldn't be enough, though. Three times since she'd escaped from Julio and his cronies, she had very nearly been caught. And she knew precisely what would happen if she let up even a little bit.

The previous couple of weeks had been absolute hell. Not only had she been chased for more than a hundred miles, but she'd also been forced to go without even a hint of rest. And even though her body had been reforged by her relatively high level and the increased stats that came with it, she was running on empty. Soon, her endurance would give out, and she'd be forced to make a last stand.

During her flight, Abby had had plenty of time to revisit her many mistakes. The first was partnering with Julio and his men in the first place. From the moment she'd accepted that invitation, her days had been numbered. In retrospect, it was obvious that Julio would betray her. It was who the man was. And the worst part was that she knew it, but she had gone along anyway, thinking that she could handle whatever came, then turn the tables on the man. That had been a mistake, and one for which Vladimir had paid the ultimate price.

Abby could still see the shock on her friend's face before he'd been exploded by Julio's skill. She still didn't know what the skill was, but it had been deadly. Vladimir hadn't concentrated on endurance, but he'd had enough durability to withstand most normal attacks. It had meant nothing against Julio's skill, though. By contrast, Abby's own endurance had been enough to mitigate the worst of the skill, but she could feel the curse regenerating. She was safe, for now, but if Julio caught up, she knew it would only be a matter of time before he could control her once again. Or worse—trigger the curse and kill her. She'd endured the previous explosion, but that had been caused by the rune losing its fidelity. If Julio triggered it after it regenerated, things would be much worse.

That was why she had chosen her current course, hoping that she could lose her pursuers in the Myrewood Forest, which was home to plenty of monsters that could prove a danger, even to Julio. She knew it was a risk; those same creatures were even more of a threat to her. She had spent most of the past few years working as a scout, so despite the fact that she lacked any real skills associated with the role, she was capable of avoiding any undue trouble. So long as she didn't run across anything too powerful, at least. Either way, she was willing to take her chances with the monsters if it meant losing Julio and his band of unsavory characters.

Her pursuers were determined, their pursuit dogged, and they'd continued to follow her with little difficulty. Even the few times she'd managed to ambush them, she'd slowed them down only enough to maintain her lead. Clearly, someone among the group was an actual scout who possessed some variant of tracking—more evidence that her inclusion in the group had been a setup all along.

Over the next few hours, the terrain continued to slope steadily upward, giving her a hint at her general location. So, when she burst out of the forest and looked down on the valley that contained the ruins of Tua'Ta'alar, she wasn't really surprised. However, just because she'd expected it didn't mean she was happy to see the ruined city that had once been home to a civilization of elves. That had been more than two thousand years ago, and any trace of the enigmatic race had long since disappeared. Only the crumbling remnants of their city persisted, and even that had been overwhelmed by a tribe of dangerous and cunning harpies.

Even though she knew she didn't have much time, Abby took a moment to think. Standing there and gazing out over the sprawling ruins of Tua'Ta'alar, she considered her options. First, she could circle around the edges of the ruins and hope to lose her pursuers before fleeing back toward Beacon, where she hoped she would be safe. Doubtless, Julio had thought of that already. And if it came down to her word versus his, she knew precisely how that would go. In Beacon—and more importantly, among her guildmates in the Champions of Light—power trumped all. And Julio was undeniably more powerful, both individually and regarding his influence within the guild.

Her other option was to wage a guerilla war against the group. During her flight, she'd already wounded a few of her pursuers, and she couldn't deny how satisfying that had felt. However, not only did they outnumber her, but even discounting Julio's considerable strength, their power was on par with hers. Winning out against that kind of force would be more than merely difficult. And as for Julio himself? Unless she caught him completely unaware, Abby had almost no chance of taking him out. The gap was simply too wide.

Which led her to her final option. Lead them into the ruined city and hope that she could somehow use the harpies' presence to her advantage. It was easy to imagine a scenario where she deftly slipped past the vicious avian monsters while Julio and his crew were forced to battle it out. They were powerful, but the ruins of Tua'Ta'alar were avoided for a reason. Part of it was because the city had been picked clean of anything of value, but it was mostly because of the harpies. Individually, they weren't overwhelmingly powerful, but there were thousands of the monsters in the city—some of which were truly dangerous, even to warriors in their high teens. If Abby could somehow thread the needle and avoid drawing the harpies' ire, there was a good chance that she could lead her pursuers into a mass of monsters that even Julio couldn't handle.

But that was assuming she could avoid the monsters' attention while staying ahead of Julio's crew, which might just prove more difficult than she expected. However, Abby didn't think she had much choice in the matter. Going through the ruins seemed like the only viable option. And at the end of the day, she was confident in her ability to escape the harpies. So, choosing to go into Tua'Ta'alar wasn't necessarily the end of the line. She could always change course if things got out of hand.

So, with that settled, Abby unslung her bow and started her descent into the ruined city. She didn't take her time, but she didn't rush, either. Caution marked her every step, lest she run into something she couldn't handle. But even after almost ten minutes of trekking through the once-mighty elven city, she hadn't encountered a single harpy. It was unnerving; every story she had ever heard about the city made it clear just how dangerous the place was. So, why hadn't she seen a single monster?

After another ten minutes, she got her first answer in the form of a clump of corpses. The creatures looked like they'd been overwhelmed by an avalanche. Broken bones jutted through their tough skin to sprout amid their blood-soaked feathers, and that was for the most intact bodies. Others seemed like they'd simply exploded.

Had some intrepid group decided to raid the place for experience? That strategy wouldn't be without benefit. There were so many of the harpies that an enterprising group of adventurers could effectively gather a good deal of experience in a short amount of time. However, doing so would come with significant risks, as well. Only the most well-rounded of groups, complete with the rare healer who was willing to venture out into the world of monster hunting, could hope to survive such a plan. But if they did, the rewards could prove monstrous.

Not that Abby cared much about experience at the moment. Even if she hadn't spent the previous two weeks running for her life, she was level capped at fifteen until she found a way to evolve at least one half of her race. Which was why she'd chosen to participate in the ill-fated mission in the first place. The Fruit of Nascent Zeal that would've been her reward was her ticket to pass the level fifteen bottleneck, and she was willing to take any number of risks to get one.

Despite her haste, Abby wouldn't pass up the opportunity for a little loot, though. So, she bent down, and with her camp knife, she carved out the monsters' beast cores, tossing them into her pack. They weren't terribly dense, but they were still valuable enough that she couldn't in good conscience leave them. Why the monsters' killers hadn't done the same, Abby couldn't know. Perhaps they'd bitten off more than they could chew, and they simply didn't have time for harvesting the cores.

She pushed that mystery aside and glanced at the still-rising sun. It was only a couple of hours past dawn, which meant that the harpies would be at their most active. Hopefully, she could make use of it.

Once she'd stowed the cores away in her enchanted satchel, Abby continued along her path, weaving in and out of various alleys in an effort to stay hidden. She needn't have bothered because there didn't seem to be a single living thing in her way. There were plenty of corpses, though. She counted more than a hundred of them before she stopped bothering; eventually, she was forced to pass up the loot, too. If she tarried too long, Julio and his men would catch up. So, leaving all that wealth behind, she pushed deeper into the ruined city.

The place really did live up to its reputation. Even though many of the buildings had succumbed to the ravages of time, what was left was still impressive. And the city was enormous, stretching for miles in each direction. At one point, it must've housed more than a million of the legendary elves.

Abby had grown up in New York, one of the greatest cities in the old world. And while Tua'Ta'alar wasn't quite that city's equal in terms of sheer scale, it wasn't that far off, either. And where it fell short of that mark in size, it more than made up for in character. Everywhere she looked, she saw one more wonder. Delicate statues, ravaged by wind and rain. Frescoes, faded by the sun. Fountains, crumbling under their own weight. Buildings whose majesty could rival anything built by human hands, mostly fallen and all but forgotten.

If she hadn't been running for her life, Abby would've stared in awe. Not many people got to see such sights, and even through her stress and fatigue, she felt lucky to bear witness to the elves' achievements.

For more than two hours, Abby made her way through the ruined elven city, and not once was she attacked by its new rulers. However, she did continue to see plenty of corpses. There were enough that Abby began to worry that perhaps she wasn't following the trail of a human adventuring party. Perhaps some demon had wandered up from the Lake of Flames. If that were the case . . .

Abby shook her head, unwilling to dwell on that possibility. The Lake of Flames was nearly seven hundred miles to the southeast. If a demon had come so far, someone would've noticed. The entirety of Beacon would have long since mobilized to see to the threat, and that wasn't even considering the reaction of Sanctuary or the handful of way stations along that path. Even Lady Constance herself would have likely responded to such a threat.

Abby pushed on, both through the city and from that line of thinking.

Finally, Abby found herself nearing the great square at the center of the city. According to legend, the square had once been the site of an expansive bazaar where the elves sold their goods from temporary stalls. When humans had first been reborn into the new world, the elves had welcomed them with open arms, and for a while, the two races had lived in harmony. However, due to some schism between their respective leaders, they had gone to war with each other. And after a few decades of near-constant battle, humans had come out on top. It took a further hundred years for the elves to be exterminated by the ever-growing population of humans. And now, two millennia later, the once-proud race had gone extinct.

Abby couldn't help but wonder what had caused the war. Though she was obviously happy that humanity had been victorious, she also regretted that it had been necessary in the first place.

Regardless, all thoughts of elves and mostly forgotten wars fled when she finally found herself looking out across the square. Hundreds, perhaps even thousands, of harpies lay dead or dying. Shrill screeches cut through the air, and even from a considerable distance, Abby felt like someone was driving spikes into her skull. She shoved the pain to the back of her mind as she tried to make sense of what she saw.

Because at the center of that mass of corpses was a solitary figure, brutally swinging some sort of primal club at the attacking harpies. At the moment, he was facing off against a few of the larger, higher-level monsters, but judging by the similarly sized corpses at his feet, they wouldn't be the first.

Where were his allies? Had he been abandoned? Or was he the last one alive?

Even from so far away, Abby heard the sound of his club impacting the nearest harpy. The blow ripped through the monster's wing to collide with its torso with such power that Abby's senses screamed danger in her mind. The creature collapsed atop the mounting pile of corpses, and the man turned his attention to the next monster foolish enough to attack him.

Abby gaped. She had never seen anyone strike with such overwhelming strength. And that was swinging with only one hand. In his other arm, he cradled some unidentifiable mass of fur.

The man himself looked just as bestial as his bone club. He was tall—perhaps an inch or two over six feet—and well muscled. However, that muscle wasn't like what she'd seen on the men who spent all their time training. Instead, he was lean. Deadly. His entire body was covered in gore, as well, which served to accentuate that impression. Finally, Abby couldn't help but blush a little when she realized he was basically naked, save for a few strips of stained cloth that might've once been his pants. All in all, he looked more like a prototypical caveman than an adventurer.

How long had he been out here, to arrive at such a sorry state?

But regardless of how he looked, the warrior had yet to reach the end of his endurance. Far from it, judging by how easily he dispatched the harpies before him. Finally, Abby used her inspection skill, hoping to identify him.

Ezekiel Blackwood—Level 10

Level ten?! Abby's jaw dropped even further. How could a level ten be so powerful? She was five levels higher than him, and it had taken her only a couple of seconds to determine that she wouldn't last long in a direct confrontation with the man. Perhaps if she managed to surprise him with a few arrows before she knew he was there . . .

No. She wouldn't preemptively attack someone like that. For one, though he certainly looked the part of the brute, he'd done nothing to warrant her ire. And for another, if she failed in the ambush, she'd make another powerful enemy.

But wasn't the opposite true? If she helped him, perhaps he'd help her, as well. Abby wasn't certain if the man could win out against someone like Julio, but he could perhaps tip the scales in her favor. Besides, the mysterious stranger had single-handedly dismantled her plan to have the harpies run interference. So, what choice did she really have?

Without pondering it any further, Abby summoned an arrow and loosed it at one of the harpies. Before it connected, three more were in the air, each propelled by her skill's manipulation of the wind. The first punched through an unlucky harpy's chest, felling it with a single blow. However, the next two managed to only wound her targets. But that was okay. She had plenty more where that came from.

And so, she let loose a barrage of arrows, hoping that the mysterious man would notice her help and feel obligated to return the favor.

33

AN AUSPICIOUS MEETING

Zeke knew she was there, watching and waiting. Still, he was a little surprised when the mysterious woman suddenly began firing arrows at the harpies. In his arms, the bear cub squirmed; even now, it wasn't entirely healed. However, it had recovered enough to regain consciousness, and it used its regained health to attempt an escape from Zeke's clutches. It didn't want to run away, though. From the Soul Bond, Zeke could tell that the ball of fur and half-formed claws trusted him even more than it had trusted its own mother. But it was still an adolescent, and as such, it was curious about its surroundings as well as the waves of monsters. Zeke wasn't so cavalier that he would let his newfound companion loose, though. It was too dangerous, even considering that the bear cub had gained three levels since Zeke had begun his slaughter.

That was one thing that took him by real surprise. He and the bear shared experience, and while the cub received only a trickle compared to Zeke's raging river, it had begun at a much lower level. And as such, the pool of experience required to gain a level was much shallower. Even as Zeke crushed another harpy screecher, he wondered how the beast's stat allocation worked. He could feel the cub growing more powerful, so it was clearly gaining stats. Zeke simply didn't know if the bear was picking the appropriate ones or not. For all he knew, it was all predetermined.

The archer's first arrow punched through a harpy's heart, and the monster fell a split second later, dead before it hit the ground. It was an impressive shot, though Zeke felt confident in his ability to mitigate it, should the archer target him. A moment later, another pair of arrows hit a pair of harpies, but the wounds weren't fatal. It didn't seem to matter, though, because in only a second or two, the air was full of the silver projectiles. Some killed the targets outright, and others merely wounded; however, the volume was so prolific that the effect impressed him. And combined with Zeke's own efforts, it wasn't long before the harpies realized that they were fighting a losing battle. Almost as one, the remaining creatures turned and fled without so much as a backward glance, leaving Zeke alone with the archer.

He stared at her across the square, hoping she wasn't hostile. His instincts said she wasn't—after all, she had helped him kill the harpies—but he wasn't quite willing to implicitly trust his intuition, not when it came to another person. People, unlike monsters, were complicated, and their motivations weren't always clear. For a long moment, they faced each other, trying to take each other's measure. That gave Zeke plenty of time to study her appearance.

From a size perspective, she wasn't anything special. Average, if Zeke could trust his eyes. Slim, and dressed in a mostly browns and greens, she wore leather armor over her torso, sturdy boots, and leather pants. At her hip was a wicked-looking hatchet, and she still held her bow. There was no quiver, so Zeke had no idea where the dozens of arrows had come from.

After a handful of seconds, the mysterious woman broke the standoff and stepped toward him. As she drew closer, the analytical part of Zeke's mind gave way to more practical concerns. Suddenly, he was very aware that he was wearing little more than a loincloth, and it didn't take him long to see that the blonde archer was quite attractive, with high cheekbones, luminous, blue eyes, and a delicate bow of a mouth.

Finally, when she was only a few yards away, she said, "You killed all of these yourself, didn't you?"

"I . . . yeah," he croaked. "Why?"

"Who are you? Where did you come from?" she demanded. "And what's that in your arms?"

Suddenly, the bear cub growled. It wasn't an overt threat—more that the animal wanted to make itself known.

"This . . . it's complicated," Zeke said. So many questions flowed through his mind. He wanted to know who she was. He wanted to know where they were. He wanted to know about what society might exist in the new world. But he suppressed his curiosity, focusing on the most important query. "What do you want?"

It was a valid question. After all, the woman had clearly waited to help, like she'd been debating whether or not it was worth it. Once she saw that he didn't actually need the help, she had started shooting. That implied that she wanted something from him.

She narrowed her eyes, then said, "Fine. We'll skip the pleasantries, then. I'm in trouble. There's a group of men who have been hunting me for the past two weeks. If you can help me—"

"Why?" he asked, interrupting.

"I can make it worth your while," she said smoothly. "I've got a missive for—"

Again, he interrupted, saying, "No—why are they hunting you?"

"Because..."

The woman trailed off, then sighed. For a moment, Zeke wondered if she was actually going to answer. Then, just as he was about to prompt her further, she started talking. She told him about the missive, mentioning places and things that meant nothing to him. However, he understood enough to recognize how despicable of a character this Julio was.

"... And if I can get away, you and I could go to Nightweb Ravine, kill the drachnids, and collect the reward back in Beacon. I'll split it with you."

The moment the archer had explained the situation, Zeke had already decided to help. However, he wasn't averse to getting a reward, even if he didn't quite understand what it was for. His experiences in the caves had taught him not to turn his nose up at anything. Still, he was curious, so he asked, "These fruits—what are they for?"

She blinked in confusion. "What? You don't know?" she asked. "I thought... I thought everyone knew about the Fruits of Nascent Zeal. They're grown on the slopes of—"

"I don't care where they're grown," he said. "What do they do?"

"Rude," she muttered under her breath, but with Zeke's improved senses, he heard it clearly. Perhaps he should stop interrupting. However, two years alone had scraped most of his social graces clean. Then, looking extremely proud of herself, she explained, "They're to evolve your race. One fruit is enough to improve your body by an entire grade."

"Huh," Zeke said, scratching his chin.

That clearly wasn't the reaction the woman had expected. "I don't know where you came from, but I don't think you understand how unique of an opportunity this is," she said. "There aren't that many ways to evolve your race, and it's necessary to get past the bottleneck."

"That . . . won't be a problem," Zeke said. "But even if I'm not that interested in these fruits, I'll help you. Where are these—"

"Well, well, well," came a new voice. Zeke looked up to see a tall, slim man standing only twenty yards away. He was flanked by a handful of other men who looked like nothing so much as disreputable bandits. "What do we have here? Cheating on me, Abby?" The man clutched at his chest. "I'm hurt. Truly, I am wounded."

"Go to hell, Julio," the archer spat.

Zeke glanced at his new ally, asking, "This the guy?"

She nodded, saying, "He's dangerous, though. He's level nineteen, and—"

Julio's laugh cut her off, and Zeke heard Abby mutter about "lack of manners" and "interruptions." But anything else was lost when the tall man said, "You came to this poor idiot for help? Didn't you learn your lesson with the big Russian? Fine. If you want to lose another ally, I'll certainly oblige."

Julio gestured, and a mass of rainbow-colored mana smashed into Zeke's chest. Then, with a wide grin, the man snapped his fingers. A split second later, it felt like every cell in Zeke's body had erupted into agony. However, it wasn't nearly on the level of what he'd felt when he'd combined the blue-spotted mushrooms and the mana water. Or the pain he'd been forced to endure while unraveling the curses cast by the troll shamans. Or any number of other instances where he'd been subjected to unrelenting pain. By comparison, it was little more than a twinge.

Zeke didn't say anything. Instead, he spat out a mouthful of blood, then set the bear cub down. Mentally, he commanded it to stay there. Finally, after straightening back to his full height, he turned to Abby and asked, "You want me to kill him?"

"P-please," she said.

Julio clearly hadn't expected his attack to be so ineffectual, and surprise was etched across his face. He pulled his sword, saying, "Now, listen here—"

Zeke didn't let him finish before he charged. With a roar, he hefted his mace, and in an instant, he'd closed the ground. In that time, Julio had yanked his single-edged blade from the scabbard at his waist. He slapped it against his metal bracer, and a wave of weaponized sound slammed into Zeke like a crashing wave.

He grunted. It wasn't much different than the harpies' screeches. Maybe a little stronger, but not so potent that it could stop his charge. After all, he'd spent the past couple of days being inundated by the harpies' aural attacks, and while they still hurt, he'd grown accustomed to them.

To Julio's credit, he managed to raise his sword to block Zeke's rapidly descending mace. It was just enough to shift the blow from Julio's head to his left shoulder, which shattered beneath the attack. But Julio still possessed stats commensurate with his level, which a quick [**Inspection**] had put at level nineteen, and while he obviously hadn't invested much into endurance, the man had still fought his way to his current power. He rolled with the attack, lessening some of the force, and then hopped back.

"Attack!" he bellowed, and his men reacted accordingly. Before Zeke knew what was happening, the thugs had closed in on him. They attacked with a variety of skills, including one man whose spear was wreathed in flames, and for a moment, Zeke found himself on his back foot.

However, Zeke hadn't spent the past two years idly strolling through his new life. He'd had to fight every step of the way, normally against superior numbers. So, being surrounded by bloodthirsty enemies felt like nothing so much as coming home. Using his impressive constitution, Zeke dodged and blocked all but one of the attacks. He wasn't quick enough to evade them all, though, and he took a shallow cut along his ribs from a dagger-wielding villain. Instantly, it began to burn like someone had poured acid on an open wound.

"It's poison!" came Abby's shout from behind. Then, an arrow smashed into the man's eye, killing him instantly. Truly, the woman's arrows packed quite a punch.

Zeke activated [**Leech Strike**] to counteract the poison, then went on the offensive. The bandits weren't the most skilled opponents Zeke had ever faced, but after fighting nearly mindless monsters for so long, it was a bit of a shock when they displayed something more than animalistic cunning. Still, there was a significant difference in stats that no amount of strategy could overcome, and that was saying nothing of Zeke's well-honed battle instincts. Soon, the men were lying on the ground, dead or dying.

Julio looked on with horror, his sword held in a loose, one-handed grip. His collarbone had been crushed, and he was in obvious pain. However, the man's shock had overwhelmed the agony of his shattered shoulder.

"W-who are you?" he muttered.

Zeke didn't bother answering. Instead, he shot toward the man with murderous intent. Julio attempted to run, but he got only a couple of feet before an arrow slammed into his upper back. Then another sprouted from his kidney. And another glanced off his skull, sending him stumbling. By then, Zeke had closed the ground between them, and with finality, swung his mace in a baseball swing. The familiar motion was powered by every ounce of Zeke's considerable might; in front of that, Julio's meager endurance couldn't stand, and it caved in the man's entire torso.

Still, Julio wasn't dead. Mortally wounded, perhaps, but in a world where such injuries could heal incredibly quickly, nothing was certain. Zeke stood over the man, wondering what he should do. Certainly, he'd become a killer, and by necessity, he had made peace with that fact. But that was with monsters. Killing another human being, even one as vile as Julio, was something else altogether—especially when it was done in cold blood.

Luckily, Zeke didn't have to think about it much because a mere instant later, Abby was beside him.

"Abby, please—"

The woman didn't hesitate before she brought her foot down with a vicious stomp, right on the man's neck. It didn't kill him outright, but it didn't matter because Abby kept stomping. Over and over, all the while screaming, "That's for Vlad, you piece of shit!"

Finally, after a full thirty seconds, everything above Julio's shoulders had been reduced to mush. Zeke just shook his head, then turned around to see that his bear companion hadn't remained idle. Instead, utilizing its sharp claws, it had already dispatched the wounded members of Julio's band of miscreants.

Zeke glanced back at Abby, who still stood over Julio, her chest heaving. Finally, she seemed to come back to herself, and she looked up, saying, "He . . . he killed someone important to me. And he used his power to take advantage of . . . girls . . . back in Beacon. He deserved it."

"I'm sure he did," Zeke said, kneeling beside one of the thugs. He shooed the bear cub away.

"What are you doing?" Abby asked.

"I don't know if you noticed, but . . . I'm kind of . . . well, I need some clothes," he said, suddenly very aware of his near nudity. "This guy's close to my size."

"Gross," she muttered, but even as Zeke started undressing the corpse, Abby began to pick through the bandits' equipment. She took their weapons, Julio's bracers, and a couple of rings the man had worn on his fingers. Finally, once they'd finished, she said, "Do you want any of this?"

Zeke shrugged, "Any of it useful?"

"Not really," was her response. "There are a few odds and ends that might make life a little more convenient, but nothing combat oriented. They weren't that successful. Maybe Julio had some better stuff, but I'm beginning to think that most of his reputation was for show."

"He did seem pretty weak," Zeke acknowledged, still a little surprised at how little difficulty he'd had with a man almost twice his level.

"Right," Abby said, her voice betraying her exhaustion. "What about the beast cores?"

"The what?" Zeke asked.

"Beast cores," she repeated. "You know, all the harpies. Some of these are evolved, too. And even with the lesser cores, there are so many that this is still worth a fortune."

Zeke's eyes lit up, and he said, "Show me."

Over the next couple of hours, Abby showed Zeke how to harvest the beast cores. Even though it was gory work to retrieve the cores from within the creatures' rib cages, it wasn't difficult. However, it was time consuming, and before they'd even finished half of them, the sun had begun to set.

"We should make camp somewhere," Abby said. "There are a lot of nocturnal monsters around here, but I have a skill that can make things easier."

Zeke snorted, saying, "I've got it covered."

Then, with a gesture, he summoned his hut. Doing so crushed a few harpy corpses, but otherwise, there was plenty of room in the square.

"W-what is that?"

"It's . . . a skill," Zeke said, unwilling to elaborate further. He and Abby had become allies, of a sort, but that didn't mean he trusted her. It was better to be cautious. "It keeps monsters away."

To that, Abby just laughed. Then, she said, "Makes my skill seem ridiculously underpowered, I guess. But whatever. This just makes things easier."

Then, she went into the hut. It only took her a moment before she said, "Wait—you've got fresh water in here, too? Jesus . . ."

Zeke could only grin. Perhaps his rewards had been even more unique than he originally thought.

34

TRUST

Zeke leaned against the wall of his hut, his fingers snaking their way through the bear cub's soft fur. Using the hut's water pump, he'd cleaned the cub's coat as best he could, but it was still matted in places. However, his rampage through the harpy population had accomplished his goal; the bear was entirely healed. For a couple of hours after Zeke had summoned the hut, the bear had even been frisky, and he'd spent a while just playing with the animal—much to Abby's amusement.

"What's his name?" the archer asked. She was nearby, sorting through the various pieces of equipment they had looted. There were piles of leather armor, a variety of weapons, and a few packs. She'd also set aside Julio's pile of jewelry and other accessories, which had proven to be mostly useless. Most hadn't even been constructed with real jewels; they had been part of the man's costume.

"Huh?" Zeke asked, taken by surprise by her sudden question. She'd been almost entirely silent for quite some time. Still, it took him only a second for his mind to catch up to the question. "Oh. I haven't named him yet. I just . . . well, we just got together yesterday."

Abby shook her head, saying, "I still don't get how you did it. Most monsters . . . it's just that they're not really tamable. And you've got that thing acting like a puppy after only a day? How is that possible?"

For a moment, Zeke didn't answer. While he very much wanted to trust Abby—after all, she was the first human being he had seen in more than two years—he couldn't help but be wary. Something told him that in this new world, giving out too much personal information could get a person killed.

"It's a skill," he said. "Just a one-time thing. Me and my new little buddy are stuck together now."

"Oh," she said. "Then you should definitely give him a name. Something fierce. Like Fang. Or Claw. Something like—"

"Pudge," Zeke said. The moment the idea of giving the bear a name popped into his head, he knew precisely what it would be.

"W-what?" Abby asked. "Isn't that . . . I mean, he's not even fat . . ."

"Not a baseball fan, I guess," Zeke said, raising his eyebrow.

"Not . . . um . . . particularly" was Abby's response. "Does that make a difference?"

"Well, Pudge Rodríguez was the best catcher I've ever seen play," Zeke stated. In fact, considering that Zeke had played that position, he had been his hero growing up. "It wasn't even close, either. Defensively, offensively—he was great."

"This guy's name was actually Pudge?" she asked.

"Nickname," Zeke answered. "His real name was Iván, but everyone called him Pudge."

Abby shook her head, muttering something about "men and their stupid sports," but she didn't further criticize his choice. However, the next moment, a notification flicked across his eyes.

Would you like to rename your Soul-Bound Companion "Pudge"? Y/N

As soon as Zeke selected the affirmative option, the newly renamed Pudge stirred, raising his head to regard his companion. Pudge's eyes flashed for a moment, then he settled back down.

"Well, I guess it's official, then," Zeke said, inspecting his companion.

Pudge—Level 4

"So," Abby said after she'd finally sorted everything out. By that point, night had fallen completely. "What's your deal? How are you so strong? And why do you have so many weird skills when you're only level ten?"

"Eleven, now," Zeke said. At some point during his massacre of the harpies, Zeke had gained another level. Or maybe it was during the fight with Julio and his flunkies; he couldn't be sure because it had all sort of devolved into a haze for him. For his last two levels, Zeke had continued to pile points into strength, but given that it had risen past two hundred, he had begun to consider allocating them into a different stat. Perhaps vitality or endurance. Either way, he'd figure it out when he got to level twelve; from what he could tell, though, that might take a while. There had been quite an increase in the amount of experience required for level eleven, and it felt like it would take half again as much to get to twelve.

Abby rolled her eyes. "I could really grow to hate you," she deadpanned. "It took me almost a year to go from ten to eleven. How long did it take you?"

"Um . . . a day?" he said. "Or two, maybe. I don't know. It all started to blend together after a while. There were a lot of harpies."

"So? Not going to tell me how you did it?" she persisted.

Zeke sighed, then looked down at Pudge. The bear was still napping away contentedly in his lap. Would it be such a bad thing to trust her? Though he hadn't really needed her help, she'd had no way of knowing that. As far as she knew, he'd been in mortal danger, and she had hesitated for only a few seconds before deciding to help. Sure, she had an ulterior motive, but that didn't negate her choice.

Trust female. Smells good.

Zeke flinched as the words sprang into his mind, seemingly from nowhere. However, he didn't need Pudge's sudden stare to tell him where the thought came from. Until that point, he'd gotten only vague impressions from the bear, but was it so surprising that they could communicate via thoughts? After everything Zeke had seen since being reborn, that he shared a telepathic link with a bear wasn't even that shocking.

What was surprising, though, was that he trusted the bear's judgment. Zeke couldn't quite understand why that would be so, but he did, implicitly. If Pudge trusted the blonde woman, then he would, too.

"Okay, so I've spent the past two years in my beginning dungeon," Zeke said. "I had a few lucky fights, and I had some opportunities that I think probably aren't normal. Like, for instance, I evolved my race when I was only level three. I almost died doing it, but . . . well, I got an achievement for it. And I guess everything just sort of flowed from that. And when I finally killed everything in the dungeon, I got more achievements. Some quest rewards, too. Like my mace. Or this hut. I even got this weird spatial storage thing that's tied to the—"

"Wait—you've got spatial storage?" Abby asked. "Where is it?"

Zeke pulled a tattered strip of linen that had once been a shirt—and had since performed admirably as a makeshift bandage—aside, revealing the tattoo on the upper part of his chest. "Right here," he said. "It's not that huge. Only about a thousand square feet, as far as I can tell. But it's really helpful."

Abby just stared at him, her face blank. Finally, after a few awkward seconds, she said, "I . . . I don't know what to say. Two years? Spatial storage? And you've already evolved your race? Do you have any idea how rare that is?"

"Not really," Zeke said. "I've only been out of the dungeon for a couple of weeks."

"Okay, okay," said Abby, holding her hands out in front of her. "Let's just address the racial evolution. I've been here for seven years now, and I haven't evolved even a part of my race yet. There just aren't a lot of ways to do it, and those that are available are pretty closely controlled by the heads of the guilds. Or the church. Or the Temple. Either way, it takes years of hard work and a lot of luck just to put yourself in a position to get access to the natural treasures you need for an evolution."

"Really?" Zeke said, suddenly wishing he'd brought more of the mushrooms out of the caves. Not knowing that they were valuable, he'd devoured his stock already.

"And then there's your dungeon . . ."

"What about it?" Zeke asked.

She sighed. "It sounds like it was a lot more elaborate than what people normally get," she said. "For instance, mine was just a valley. I only had to kill a few bugbears before I got out. It took two days, and I got out within sight of Beacon. That you were all the way out here . . ."

Zeke didn't respond. He'd suspected that his experiences within the troll caves were abnormal, but he'd had no idea just how strange his circumstances had been. For so long, he'd been so entirely focused on survival that he never even considered how odd the difficulty was. He'd only managed to survive because of a few lucky opportunities. If one of a dozen things would've gone even slightly differently, he would never have escaped those horrible caves. So, it didn't stand to reason that everyone would have it so hard. If it was just as difficult for everyone, there would be only a few survivors.

"What about the bear?" she asked.

"Oh," Zeke said, self-consciously running his fingers through his companion's soft fur. "That actually is a skill. Kind of. I have this skill called [**Mark of Companionship**] that lets me share experience and benefits with other people. So, when I saw that Pudge was dying, I sort of altered the rune associated with the skill and—"

"Wait, what?" Abby interrupted. "You altered the rune? That's not possible."

"It's possible," he said. "Not easy, but possible. It's not so different from unraveling a curse. You just have to—"

"Unraveling a curse?" she interrupted again. "What the hell are you talking about? You can't just unravel a curse. You have to have a special skill, and anyone who does belongs to the Church of Purity. They charge an arm and a leg just to cleanse basic curses."

Zeke shrugged. "I don't have a skill," he said. "But I do have an artisan path that helps me. Not that I had it when I was unraveling curses in the dungeon. I suspect it would be a lot easier now. Would probably still hurt, though."

Abby just stared ahead in disbelief. She very clearly didn't understand how any of what Zeke had described was possible. Briefly, he considered trying to explain things more fully, but before he could do so, she said, "Can you unravel a curse that Julio put on me?"

Zeke shrugged. "Maybe?" he said. "I've never tried on anyone else. But it shouldn't be that difficult, I guess. Do you want me to try?"

For a second, hesitation filled the air, but then Abby nodded, saying, "Do it. But if you kill me, I'll . . . I'll haunt you for the rest of your life."

Zeke chuckled, then said, "Fair enough."

Then, he gently shifted Pudge off of his lap, eliciting an annoyed snort from the bear. He ignored it, rising to his feet and crossing the small hut. Once he was next to Abby, he knelt beside her and asked, "Where is it?"

She indicated her left side, just below her ribs. In that exact spot, Abby's armor had been rent, looking like it had exploded from the inside. Below that was a half-healed wound. Vaguely, Zeke could feel the malevolent rune, pulsing just beneath the surface of her skin. It was weak—far weaker than the curses cast by the troll shamans—but he could feel the energy within the rune slowly building upon itself. If left untreated, it would return to full strength within a few weeks. And while Zeke had no idea what it was supposed to do, he knew it couldn't be good. Otherwise, it wouldn't be a curse.

He placed his hand on Abby's side. She flinched, but only slightly. Still, that slight tremble was enough to make Zeke incredibly uncomfortable. He wasn't a complete novice when it came to the opposite sex, but two years alone had certainly dulled his social skills. He said, "Sorry. Should've warned you. I'm going in. Try to stay quiet."

Out of the corner of his eye, Zeke saw that she was biting her lower lip. He forcibly ignored the woman's anxious expression. Instead, he focused on the task at hand. Slowly, he extended his awareness into Abby's body, quickly latching on to the ominously pulsing curse rune. Then, with a thin thread of his mana, he started unraveling it.

Abby hissed in pain, the muscles in her stomach clenching. However, that was expected. He knew precisely how agonizing it was to feel a curse unraveling inside you. So, he pushed past the thought and bent his willpower to his task. Gradually, he managed to wrap his mana around the weakest point before beginning the process of loosening the tightly woven bonds of foreign mana. Thread by thread, then symbol by symbol, he unmade the malevolent rune until, finally, it was nothing more than a mass of disorganized threads of mana.

"Okay, so this is going to hurt," Zeke said, looking up into Abby's pain-filled eyes. After almost an hour of constant pain, a sheen of perspiration clung to her forehead, and her eyes had become red-rimmed and bloodshot. Still, she nodded, telling him to get it over with. He complied, and with agonizing slowness, dragged the foreign mana out of her body. It took another half hour, but eventually, he got it all, letting it dissipate into the air. When he'd finally finished, he let out a long sigh, saying, "There. It's done."

Abby groaned, leaning back against the stone wall of the hut. "God, you weren't kidding about how much that would hurt, were you?" she muttered, tilting her head toward the thatched ceiling. "But it's gone now. So, thank you. I wasn't looking forward to trying to get back to Beacon before it regained its power."

"What would the curse do?" Zeke asked.

"I'm not sure," she admitted. "When Julio was alive, he used it to subvert people's free will. It only worked a little on me, but . . . I have no idea what it would do now that he's gone."

"Glad he's dead, then," Zeke said. He hadn't felt guilty about killing the men, per se, but it did help that they were bad people. "What now?"

Abby arched an eyebrow at him, saying, "Well, don't take this the wrong way, but you might want to . . . ah . . . put on some normal clothes. I know you probably aren't too keen on wearing a dead man's clothes, but . . . well . . ."

Suddenly, Zeke was once again very aware of just how little coverage his shredded rags really gave him. He had originally planned to get dressed sooner, but a host of distractions had sidetracked him. Now, he wanted nothing more than to put on some clothes.

"Most of these have sizing enchantments," she said, indicating the pile of armor and clothing she'd been sorting. "So, just pick something that suits you, and I'll . . . ah . . . well, I'll make a fire outside."

"Thanks," Zeke said. Then, he started rummaging through the pile, hoping he could find something appropriate.

35

PARTNERSHIP

Zeke tugged on the uncomfortable leather armor. After spending the better part of two years with nothing but a few strips of linen cloth for a shirt, the piece felt incredibly restrictive, though it fit almost perfectly. The resizing enchantments did their job well, but that didn't make it any more comfortable. He could ignore that, though; after all, he'd spent hour after hour wearing a chest protector while catching. He could handle some leather armor.

It had actually taken Zeke quite some time to find something he liked. While he didn't care about fashion, there were certain pieces that just didn't feel right. So, he'd rummaged through that pile of armor until he found the best options—a segmented leather cuirass with attached pauldrons that made it look like some sort of insectile T-shirt. Beneath that was a lightly padded gambeson and a long-sleeved black shirt that seemed to have been made from cotton.

On his forearms were a pair of matching bracers, and he'd chosen a pair of leather pants that had armored plates on his thighs. He had also picked a pair of leather greaves to protect his shins. And finally, for his feet, he'd chosen a pair of heavy boots. All in all, Zeke felt like a Renaissance fair cosplayer, but when he'd tested the armor, he'd found that it was surprisingly durable. And given the danger they faced in the wild, any extra protection would be helpful. He suspected that he wouldn't always be able to rely on his high endurance and ridiculous vitality; eventually, he'd run up on something that could truly hurt him. And he needed to be prepared for that eventuality.

"Looks good," Abby said, looking up from where she'd been picking at her fingernails with a sharp dagger. "It even matches. Now, we just need to get you a haircut, and you'll actually start looking presentable." She wrinkled her nose. "Well, after a proper bath, maybe."

Zeke sighed. "Still kind of disappointed that the armor doesn't add any stats," he complained.

"Doesn't work like that," she said.

"I know, I know. You told me," Zeke responded, raising his hands in surrender. She had already explained it to him, and the last thing he wanted was another expository lecture. Still, while choosing the armor, Zeke had taken the time to study the runes embedded within them. To his surprise, they were actually somewhat simple—at least compared to the runes associated with skills or curses. In terms of complexity, if the armor enchantments were puddles, then the skill runes were vast seas. He still didn't completely understand them, of course. Instead, he had only a vague sense of what they were supposed to do.

The first enchantment was the one he already knew about—the resizing enchant. It was a useful function, and one for which Zeke was incredibly grateful. After all, none of the bandits had really been of a perfect size with him. The closest was Julio himself, from whom Zeke had gotten most of his gear, but even he'd been much narrower across the shoulders. So, the gear possessing the ability to shrink or grow appropriately was an incredible boon for Zeke's overall comfort.

The second enchantment the items uniformly possessed to varying degrees was a strengthening rune. As far as Zeke could tell, it simply injected different amounts of mana into the pieces, fortifying them so that they could withstand more punishment. The truly interesting part was that these enchantments actually drew power from his own pool of mana. It was a minuscule, barely noticeable amount, but it was there all the same. But what made it noteworthy was that the rune consisted of various repeaters that multiplied and reinforced that stream of mana so there was enough energy to fuel the desired result. Without those repeaters—which were a series of symbols that looked like mirror images of one another—the mana drain would eventually become untenable, making the armor effectively worthless.

"What are you looking at?" asked Abby, interrupting Zeke's thoughts. "You've been staring at that thing for over an hour."

"Oh," he said, a little embarrassed that he'd zoned out so completely. In his defense, though, he'd spent quite some time alone, and in that time, he'd been forced to make do with nothing but his own company. So, he'd gotten into the habit of filling his downtime, usually while he recovered from various wounds, by studying runes. "Sorry. Just looking at the runes on this armor."

"You understand them?" she asked. "I've never developed the knack, you know? They've always just looked like nonsense to me."

Zeke shrugged. "I wouldn't say I understand them," he admitted. "More like I can recognize pieces, here and there. Kind of like how when you first start learning a new language and you hear a native speaker. Every now and then, you can hear a word you recognize, but there's no way you can really tell what they're saying."

Abby glanced toward the door to the hut. It was still quite dark, but a new day would soon dawn. There were still plenty of beast cores to harvest, but it wouldn't be long before they had to make some decisions about their temporary partnership.

"Do you want to come with me?" Abby asked, almost as if she could read his mind. "I still intend to do what I set out to do and cull the drachnids. I think I could maybe do it alone. It'll take me a long time, but . . . I feel confident in my abilities. But it'd be a lot easier if I had you along."

Zeke's initial instinct was to accept the invitation. Ever since he'd conquered the beginning dungeon, he had been a bit listless. Certainly, he hadn't stopped moving. However, without a concrete goal like he'd had in the troll-infested caverns, he was somewhat aimless. Even though he'd accomplished a good deal, gaining two levels and forging the bond with Pudge, Zeke knew that his good fortune was just that—luck. If he didn't gain some direction, he'd doubtless wander into a situation he couldn't handle.

But Abby had been in the new world—which she referred to as the Radiant Isles—for years. So, she knew the ins and outs of the world. Already, she'd proved an invaluable source of information, and Zeke knew they'd only scratched the surface. He was suddenly very aware of just how much he didn't know about his new home. And though he was strong—incredibly so, judging by Abby's reactions—he held no illusions about being the strongest thing out there. The simple fact was that he needed help.

However, he barely knew Abby. And in a world fraught with danger, what he didn't know could certainly kill him. It wasn't difficult to imagine a situation where she stabbed him in the back at the worst possible moment. And given the covetous way she'd looked at his mace and the veritable mound of beast cores they'd already harvested, she had plenty of reasons to turn on him.

Pudge let out a loud snort from where he was curled in the corner. He didn't say anything via their mental connection, but his intentions were plain. After all, he'd already made his stance clear. He wanted to trust the archer. And though Zeke didn't want to get into the habit of taking advice from a bear cub, he found himself in agreement. For one very simple but incredibly powerful reason: he was lonely.

Not in a romantic sense. Though Abby was quite pretty, he refused to let that color his opinions. Much. But more than simple attraction between opposite sexes, there was a need for human companionship. So, regardless of the pros or cons of trusting Abby, he decided his course because he didn't want to be alone again.

"I think that would be for the best," he said, his throat raw. Was he really getting choked up at just the prospect of being alone? "How far is it?"

"A few weeks," Abby answered. "Maybe a month. We weren't that far from Nightweb Ravine before Julio . . . did what he did, but I went in the opposite direction, hoping that they'd get tired of chasing me and turn back to the mission."

"You okay?" Zeke asked.

She shook her head, but for a few seconds, she didn't respond. In that time, Pudge decided to waddle over to her and put his head in her lap. Immediately, her hand found a spot just behind his ear. A feeling of contentment radiated from the Soul Bond, telling Zeke just how much Pudge enjoyed the contact. More, Abby visibly relaxed.

"I had a dog back in the old world," she said, scratching Pudge's ear. "A Jack Russell terrier named Jack, of all things. Yeah—I know. Not the most imaginative name in the world, but I loved that little dog. Never shut up. Sometimes, I wonder what happened to him . . . you know, after I died."

"How did it happen?" Zeke asked. Only a second later, he realized that he'd made a serious faux pas. Abby looked at him like he'd just asked the most personal question in the world, and given that they barely knew each other, it had obviously taken her by surprise. "Sorry. I guess it's not polite to ask?"

"No," Abby said. "I mean, it's fine, I guess. I'm not ashamed or anything. I was in a car accident."

"Oh," Zeke said, somewhat disappointed. He'd expected something a little more interesting.

"Well, I told you mine," she said. "Your turn to tell me yours."

Zeke took a deep breath, then looked away. "I died while having surgery," he said. "My brother needed a kidney . . . and . . . well, I guess something went wrong. Oberon told me Tommy survived and lived a long life, though, so I guess that's good."

Abby stared at him like he'd just said the sky was green. After a few moments, she said, "What? Who's Oberon?"

Zeke narrowed his eyes. "Little guy, looked a bit like Peter Dinklage," Zeke explained. "He told me all about what was going on? You might have gotten a different guy, but you know what I mean, right?"

Abby shook her head, saying, "I have absolutely no idea what you're talking about. Nobody told me anything about what was going on. After I chose my skills and allocated my stats, I just got dropped into that bugbear valley. I wasn't even sure it was real until I went into Beacon."

"R-really?" he said. "That doesn't make—"

"You're one of the Chosen," Abby stated.

"What?"

"The Chosen," she repeated. "It makes sense. It doesn't happen often, from what I understand. Like, almost never, honestly. I thought it was a myth to make Lady Constance seem more important. But now . . . it's the only thing that makes sense. You met with one of the gods."

"Oberon is a god?" Zeke said, his voice barely more than a whisper. "But . . . he didn't seem like . . . you know . . . what the hell am I supposed to do with that information?"

Abby shrugged. "That's kind of up to you," she answered. "But don't tell too many people in Beacon about it. If it gets back to Lady Constance, she might have you killed. The Sun Goddess doesn't tolerate anyone encroaching on her territory."

Zeke let that statement hang in the air for a while. In fact, neither he nor Abby said another word until the sun had already risen. Instead, Zeke thought about the implications of the conversation. Sure, Oberon could've been a god, but something told Zeke that that wasn't the case.

The dwarf was obviously powerful, but Zeke wasn't quite ready to deify him yet. And besides, it didn't make much difference, did it? Maybe one day it would, but for now, he needed to focus on survival.

So, when the sun rose, Zeke and Abby set about harvesting the remaining beast cores. It took them most of the day, but by the time they were done, there was a significant pile of the marble-sized chunks of condensed mana. Idly, Zeke wondered if his own core resembled something like that, but despite not having any real evidence either way, his intuition told him that people were different.

The pair spent that next night either playing with Pudge, who acted more like a dog than he had any right to, or sleeping in their respective corners. Neither needed much rest, given their enhanced constitutions, but some sleep was necessary, if only to reset their bodies. So, when they set out for Nightweb Ravine, they were in as good a shape as they possibly could be.

36

REASONS AND MOTIVATIONS

Abby crouched next to Zeke, a conjured arrow already nocked as they watched Pudge charge the kapwan for what felt like the hundredth time. The bear cub already bore a dozen wounds in various states of mending, where the frog-like humanoid had managed to land strikes. Pudge had just been thrown, judo style, by the kapwan, but he'd come out of the brush completely unshaken to resume his series of attacks.

"Just say the word," she muttered, hating the scene before her. In the few days since she'd met Zeke and his pet bear, she'd grown quite attached to the furry creature. The bear—not Zeke, she reminded herself. Cutting her eyes in the man's direction, she couldn't help but think that the descriptor could've described her new ally, as well, considering the state of his wild hair and unkempt beard.

"He's fine," Zeke said, his voice low. His eyes never wavered from his companion. However, Abby had noticed the slight grimace every time Pudge took a wound. She didn't understand their bond, but she suspected that, at some level, Zeke felt the cub's injuries. He bore the strain without complaint, though, insisting that the bear needed the practice.

"He's only level six," she whispered. "That kapwan is twice his level. It's unreasonable to—"

"I said he's fine," Zeke hissed. "He's got this. He's almost got it figured it out."

Abby was about to ask what, precisely, the bear was supposed to be figuring out when a diffuse red cloud erupted from the bear's paws. Beside her, Zeke pumped his fist, whispering, "Yes!"

Pudge hit the kapwan—a primitive, four-foot-tall mixture of frog, goblin, and human, with mottled green skin, a short spear, and a hide buckler—in a flying tackle that sent the kapwan tumbling to the muddy turf. Pudge's sharp claws raked out, gouging into the creature's rubbery skin, and to Abby's shock, she saw the wounds on the cub's side begin to close a bit with every strike. More, the claws bit deeper than they ever had before, and soon, the long-limbed amphibian slithered out from under the bear and tried to scramble toward the nearby lake. But Pudge, reveling in his newfound power, wasn't about to let it reach the safety of the water, and he pounced on the kapwan's back. He didn't weigh much yet, but there was significant force behind the attack. His claws bit deep into the kapwan's spine, crushing the thing's vertebrae and severing the nerves within. Immediately, the frog-like humanoid went limp from the waist down, its powerful legs completely unresponsive. Still, with a low-pitched bellow of anguish, it didn't give up in its quest to reach safety. It dragged itself forward, digging handholds into the soft mud.

With a roar, Pudge bit down on the kapwan's neck, silencing it forever. The thing died only a foot away from the water. Then, because he didn't quite understand that the kapwan had died, Pudge worried the thing a few times, shaking it back and forth and slinging bright-green blood all over the lakeshore. The motion reminded Abby of when, back in her old life, her dog would play with its rope toy. Just with more blood and loss of life. That impression grew even stronger when Pudge dragged the kapwan to where she and Zeke were waiting, almost as if he was presenting them with his trophy.

"Good boy," Zeke said, grinning as if he hadn't just watched his pet kill a near-sapient creature. That was the thing about her new comrade. He showed absolutely no hesitation when it came to killing, and he didn't appear to empathize with any of his victims. Sure, he didn't go out of his way to kill anything that didn't attack him first, but that didn't make his lack of feeling any less creepy.

And then there was the day they had come upon that troll village.

Abby shivered at the memory. Zeke hadn't hesitated, charging into the midsize village without a word. Pudge had gone right with him, too, forcing Abby to participate in what turned out to be an unmitigated slaughter. Despite the fact that most of the trolls had out-leveled him, Zeke had been a whirlwind of destruction, felling a blue-skinned troll with nearly every swing of that primitive mace of his. The few wounds he and Pudge managed to score healed in seconds, driven by that overpowered skill of his.

But the real surprise had been Pudge. Abby didn't really know how their bond worked, but there was clearly some sort of emotional leakage between the pair. If she hadn't been convinced of that before the troll village, she would've been afterward because Pudge had gone on a rampage that, in terms of intensity, if not effectiveness, rivaled that of his companion. The bear cub had killed a couple of trolls by himself, which given his level was a testament to how recklessly he'd thrown himself at the monsters.

For her part, Abby had shot a few trolls herself—more so that Zeke would know that she'd helped than because her aid was needed. It wasn't that she had a soft spot for the monsters, either. She didn't. Rather, Abby was used to avoiding trouble when she could, and for most people, a troll village posed the kind of threat that wasn't easily overcome. For Zeke and his bear cub, though, it took them only about an hour to completely massacre the village's population down to the last troll. In the end, they'd killed almost a hundred of the monsters.

Afterward, Zeke, who was covered in blood but unhurt, had only said, "I hate trolls."

That had been the day after they'd left the ruined city of Tua'Ta'alar behind. Since then, four days had passed, and though Abby hadn't seen a similar rampage in that time, she still couldn't forget the sheer unthinking savagery of his attack.

"Why?" she finally asked, watching Pudge drop his prize and cock his head sideways.

"I told you," Zeke answered. "Pudge needs to learn to activate the skill on his own. He can't just rely on me to heal him with the splash effect of my own attacks."

"No," Abby said. "I'm not talking about that. Though I still think you're pushing him too hard, that's not . . . I was asking about the other thing. The thing with the trolls."

Zeke stood, and suddenly, Abby felt very small. Even if she hadn't known that his stats far outstripped hers, she probably would've felt at least a little intimidated based on size alone. The man was built like an NFL linebacker, with wide, heavily muscled shoulders; thick limbs; and a narrow waist. He carried that size like he knew how to use it, too, moving with the sort of grace usually reserved for apex predators—an effect that was only enhanced by his wild, unkempt hair and bushy, untrimmed beard.

Or perhaps it was the aura of violence and animalistic savagery that clung to him. It was ephemeral and amorphous, but it was there, permeating his very surroundings. Abby had even seen a few lower-level monsters slinking away, terrified to disturb the predator in their midst. Even Julio, with all his levels, hadn't prompted that kind of reaction.

Zeke ran his hand through his hair, saying, "Ah, that. I . . . I'm sorry. I lost control. It won't happen again."

Abby stood. "Do you want to talk about it?" she asked, her old life bubbling to the surface. Back then, she'd fancied herself a mental health professional. Certainly, even before she had died, it had been years since she'd actually worked in the field, but the training was still there, buried beneath a mountain of denial, regret, and forced forgetfulness. She didn't want to even think about the person she had been back then, much less utilize those skills. But the same traits that had led her to major in psychology drove her to put her hand on Zeke's chest. He flinched slightly. Clearly, he hadn't been touched by another human being in quite some time. "It might help."

For a few seconds, Zeke didn't answer. Instead, he kept his steely, green-eyed gaze trained on the nearby Lake Rathekar. The waters were choppy, and every now and again, a huge fin would cut through to the surface, evidence that the monsters that permeated their world weren't confined to the land. Beneath those waves were hydras, water goblins, and, if rumors were true, a few huge serpents—each one of a level with which Abby would be hard-pressed to survive an encounter, much less come out on top.

Finally, after almost thirty seconds, Zeke shifted his eyes to the ground, saying, "It wasn't the fact that they tried to kill me, you know. I mean, it is. From the very moment I came into this world, I was being attacked by trolls. First, it was the larvae—I called them croco-rats because they looked like a mixture of crocodiles and rats—but then it was the adults. They're vermin. But that's not what gets me . . . so . . . so angry."

Abby saw his fists trembling with rage. "What is it, then?" she ventured.

"I gave you the short version of my time in the caves," he said, glancing in her direction. "But I left something out. A few months in, I came across this cavern. Inside, I saw all these troll larvae. Hundreds of them.

But in the center of this huge cave, there was a giant sluglike creature. Like, the size of a school bus big. It was the grossest thing I ever saw. The trolls' Brood Mother. I don't know if it was the only one, but it might've been. The second I walked into that cave, everything attacked me, and I killed it. That's where I got my mace. It was an extra quest."

So, the mace was a quest reward? Judging by its appearance, Abby had simply assumed that Zeke had looted it from something he'd killed. With its bone shaft and rough metal studs, it certainly looked like something a troll would wield. However, its being a quest reward meant that it was far more than it appeared to be. Those sorts of weapons were incredibly rare, and every one Abby had ever heard about was extremely powerful.

The more Abby learned of her new companion, the warier of him she became. He was just too strong, and in the grand scheme of things, he was just getting started. What would he be in a year? In two? If his claims of already having an evolved race were to be believed, he wouldn't even hit the bottleneck, which meant that the only thing standing between him and real power was his willingness to slaughter monsters. And given what she had seen so far, that didn't seem like it would be a problem.

"I found this door," he said. "First real door I had seen in the whole cave system. So, thinking it was important, maybe that it led to some kind of treasure, I went inside. There were guards inside. I killed them, expecting that where there were guards, there had to be something good. I was riding high off of getting my mace, so . . . I guess it never even occurred to me just to leave it alone. I wish I would have."

He turned away from her, his shoulders hunched. But Abby didn't put two and two together until he spoke again, his voice raw with emotion. "Bodies," he said. "Hundreds of human bodies, hung up like sides of beef. Severed arms and legs. Heads. Men. Women. Children."

Zeke turned his head back to her, and she saw the tears cutting through the light dusting of dirt on his cheeks. In that moment, he looked so much younger. So much more human than ever before. "It was a larder," he said. "A meat locker. They were food."

Abby's hand clapped over her mouth. "Oh god," she breathed.

"After that," he went on. "I . . . I killed them all. Before, I'd skip troll villages if I thought I could. Part of it was self-preservation. But part of it was this . . . I don't know . . . unwillingness to kill them if I didn't have to. They were sentient. They had lives. Villages. They were primitive, but they weren't much different than people. After seeing that . . . after seeing those . . . bodies, I lost all sentimentality. I didn't care if they were sentient. I just wanted them dead. So, that's what I did. I say I was down there for two years, but it might have been a lot longer. Time . . . time was funny down there. Hard to track. And I lost myself for a long time."

For the first time in her life, Abby had no idea how to help someone. She had been trained as a therapist, but in the face of this kind of raw trauma, her training seemed so weak and minuscule. Instead, she responded as one human to another, saying, "I-I'm sorry. You . . . you should never have had to deal with something like that. But I think . . . I think you did the right thing."

Abby wasn't sure she actually believed that. In fact, she felt certain that she would've made another choice. However, she hadn't been there. She hadn't seen those bodies. So, she had no right to judge him for doing what he thought was right, for giving in to the rage and letting it drive him to genocide.

Zeke barked a harsh laugh. "Something tells me that's only the tip of the iceberg," he said, his tone scratchy and raw. He sniffed, wiping his cheeks. "This is only the beginning. I know you weren't asking about Pudge just now, but in a way, you were. I'm teaching him to take care of himself because this is a harsh world, Abby. I think you recognize that. And it's only going to get worse."

Abby tightened her grip on her bow, remembering the people she'd lost. She'd escaped her own watered-down version of a beginning dungeon seven years before, and in that time, she'd seen a host of friends and companions die. Vladimir was only the latest to succumb to the whims of their new world, and she suspected that he wouldn't be the last. Danger lurked around every corner, and if she wasn't careful, she would share their fate. Abby knew that. She'd accepted it long ago. But at some point, she had forgotten it. She'd grown confident and complacent, sure of her own superiority.

That was just in her own little world, though. She'd put herself into a bubble where she was strong. And Zeke had come along, shattering her preconceptions about what strength really was, bursting that bubble with his mere presence. That's what made her so uncomfortable around him. He didn't fit into her world. In fact, he nullified everything she thought she knew.

"Do you think they were real?" he asked, filling the silence. "The trolls in the dungeon, I mean. That's what I can't stop wondering. When I got out of the caves, I turned around, and there was nothing there. So, do you think it was . . . I don't know . . . do you think they were just props in somebody's sick game? Or do you think they were a real people, once?"

"I . . . I don't know," Abby admitted. She'd never even heard of a beginning dungeon like the one Zeke had experienced, so she had no notion of how such places worked.

He sighed. "It felt real enough" was his response. Kneeling, he reached out to scratch Pudge's ear. "Come on. I think we should get moving before the smell of blood attracts something more dangerous than a frog goblin."

37

NIGHTWEB RAVINE

After his emotional outburst, Zeke knew that things had changed. When he had begun to recount his experiences in the troll caves, he hadn't intended to pour his heart out. However, for more than two years, he'd been balanced on a razor's edge. On one side was a transformation into a true monster, little more than an unfeeling, unthinking machine bent on killing anything in his path. On the other was a complete breakdown motivated by constant violence and the overwhelming drive to survive. And even though he'd left the caves behind for the relatively low stakes of the real world, he still carried with him the emotional consequences of his actions. If he hadn't let those emotions loose, he'd have continued his descent into madness.

Even so, Zeke was surprised at the tears he'd shed. From an early age, he'd always been taught that crying was a sign of weakness. More times than he could count, he'd wept tears of frustration when he didn't perform up to his or his father's standards. And the moment he began to sob, his father would launch into a tirade denigrating his manliness. It didn't matter that asking a seven-year-old to act like a man was patently ridiculous; what mattered was that he didn't "cry like a little bitch." Under that kind of pressure, it didn't take Zeke long to leave his tears far behind. So, the fact that those tears had finally been freed during his conversation with Abby was more than a little shocking. It had helped, though. He certainly wasn't entirely past the trauma he'd experienced in those caves, but he'd taken the first steps. And that was what was important.

Zeke felt a hand alight on his shoulder, but he didn't need to look up from where he crouched to know it was Abby. His own hand rested on Pudge's back, idly massaging the bear's fur.

"What do you see?" she asked, her voice low.

"Monsters," he muttered.

And that was certainly the case. They knelt at the head of a ravine that, according to Abby, went on for miles before dipping underground. During the spring, the dry riverbed would flood with snowmelt from the nearby mountains, but for now, it was entirely dry. More, gossamer webs stretched from one side to the other, high enough that when the floods did come, they would be untouched. Here and there were birds and various rodents who'd been unlucky enough to be caught.

There were only three drachnids visible, but Zeke's instincts told him that there were hundreds more in the ravine that was their home. According to Abby, farther into the canyon, there were shallow caves that pockmarked the sides of the ravine; that's where the monsters slept and kept their larger prey.

And monsters they were. Abby had made that abundantly clear. They were an invasive, territorial species that had moved into the ravine only a year or two ago, and since that point, they'd made a habit of attacking anything that dared cross their ephemeral borders. Normally, that wouldn't be such a bad thing, but one of the major trade routes between Beacon and Sanctuary, the two largest human cities on the main island, crossed into the drachnids' supposed territory. So, the creatures had made a habit of attacking the trade caravans that ran between the two cities. That was the reason for the mission to annihilate or cripple the population of murderous beasts.

In terms of appearance, the drachnids were, for lack of a better descriptor, spider people. It was like if centaurs had consisted of arachnids instead of horses, crossed with humans. Of course, it wasn't as simple as merging a human torso onto the thorax of a spider. Whatever evolutionary path the monsters had taken had clearly been corrupted by both its progenitors. The humanlike torsos were covered in what looked like thick, armored chitin in various colors. The material gave off an iridescent sheen, much like when a thin coating of oil lay on top of a puddle of water. Only their heads were mostly human, with the chitin giving way to maggoty white skin. From his vantage quite some distance away,

Zeke couldn't see much more than that, but what he could discern was troubling enough.

"What are the terms of the mission again?" Zeke asked, never taking his eyes from the creatures. He thought that he and Abby were hidden, both by distance and the thick brush, but he'd been wrong about such things before. And he wanted as much warning as he could get if the things decided to charge.

Abby answered, "Kill the queen or five hundred drachnids. Proof will be required. . . . ah . . . well, we were going to collect teeth."

"Do we get double credit if we kill both?" Zeke asked.

Abby shook her head, saying, "Doesn't work like that. It's not a Framework quest. We're just here to solve a problem. Killing the queen would probably make this hive relocate. You know, to join another hive somewhere else, hopefully where they won't cause too much trouble for us. And five hundred is a crippling loss that will curtail their efforts for years. Maybe as much as a decade. More if there's a follow-up to kill the queen later, which is possible. I think that's what Julio was gunning for. You know, two missions, two rewards. We would kill the number necessary for this mission, then get one to kill the queen after we've turned the other one in."

Zeke frowned. From a purely logical standpoint, it made perfect sense to play it like that. But something about it sat wrong with him. What if they were wrong? What if five hundred wasn't the crippling blow they expected it to be? In that case, the attacks against the trade caravans would continue, and more lives would be lost. So, Zeke debated with himself, with one side grasping at extra rewards he knew he might need, and the other side clinging to the sanctity of human life. In the end, it was the latter that won out.

"What if we just kill everything?" he asked. "Clean the whole ravine out."

"T-that . . . that's suicide," she said. "There's a whole society in there. Tens of thousands of these creatures. Maybe more."

"But you said five hundred would be a crippling blow," Zeke pointed out.

At that, Abby sighed. "Not all of them are warriors," she said. "Think of them like those trolls you fought. Plenty are noncombatants. I've heard that some hives even trade with humans. They make this silk that's just . . . never mind. That's not important. What is important is that five hundred is just the estimate of what it would take to hobble their raiding parties. It won't really put a dent in their overall force, but it would be enough to keep them from attacking our caravans for a while. Besides, nothing says they can't send another party in here if it's not enough."

Zeke grunted at the subtle reminder that he'd killed so many trolls that had likely posed no real threat to him. Certainly, they wouldn't have hesitated to attack—and they had fought with every ounce of ferocity they could muster—but could he really blame them? He had been a dangerous invader. An interloper who clearly didn't belong. And even before he'd clashed with a single adult troll, he'd already slain dozens of their larvae and juveniles. Did it matter that they'd attacked him first? To Zeke, maybe. But to the trolls? Probably not.

Not that it made much difference, of course. He couldn't change the past. Nor could he avoid the simple reality that these drachnids were dangerous, and they'd been attacking humans without provocation. If left to themselves, they could become a real problem.

He sighed, running his hand through his hair. He'd tried to bathe at the lake, even using some rough soap that Abby had spirited away in her pack, but he still hadn't gotten completely clean. And besides, two weeks had passed since then. Two weeks of trekking through the forest, killing various monsters, and trying to make do with the water from the pump in his hut. The only solace was that he'd found a freshly fallen tree, a portion of which he'd hollowed out into some semblance of a bowl large enough to mimic a sink. That made things a little easier, but he still wasn't anywhere close to clean.

In the caves, he hadn't cared much about hygiene. Sure, he'd tried to wash off in the various underground rivers and streams he found, but that had just been an effort to rid himself of the foul-smelling troll blood. Or to avoid his various cuts and lacerations being infected. He wasn't sure if, with his increased vitality, infection was even possible, but he didn't think it was smart to take that chance.

But now that Abby was there, cleanliness had become more of a priority. Zeke didn't have a lot of experience with women. He'd had girlfriends in the past, but because of his age and his dedication to his development as a baseball player, they'd been shallow affairs that were as much for show as they were due to any genuine feelings between him and the girls in question. At the time, he never would've admitted as much, but two years of introspection and near-death experiences had aged him beyond his years and given him plenty of perspective on the matter.

And then Abby had come along and shattered that perspective. In the few weeks since they'd met, Zeke had developed a crush on the slender blonde. It wasn't overwhelming, but it wasn't uncommon for him to find himself sitting in his corner of the hut, absently tracing his skills' runes with his senses while imagining a future where the pair of them got together and lived happily ever after. It was silly and immature—after all, he suspected that, despite her appearance, she was quite a bit older than him—but that didn't stop his mind from running away with the notion.

Part of it was the fact that she was quite attractive. Built like a model, with long, lithe limbs, she had the kind of face that would've been completely at home on the cover of a magazine. High cheekbones, penetrative blue eyes, and a dainty nose that could only be called cute definitely assisted Zeke's imagination to the point where he often had to stop himself from staring.

But it was also the way she moved—all limber grace and well-worn confidence. Like a deadly dancer who knew precisely who and what she was. Her no-nonsense attitude and willingness to throw herself into danger helped, as well, engendering respect. More than once, she'd shown just how quickly she could spring into action, killing the monsters that populated the forest with an ease that impressed even Zeke.

Altogether, it added up to an awkward situation where Zeke often found himself worrying as much about how she saw him as anything else. And that was a dangerous thing in a new world where everything seemed hell-bent on killing them. So, he tried to suppress those burgeoning feelings as best he could, though he wasn't even remotely convinced of his own success.

"What was the plan?" he asked. "Before, I mean."

Abby shrugged, saying, "I'm not exactly sure. Julio wasn't really the sharing kind of guy, you know? But from what I understood, we were going to skirt the edges of the ravine, killing the drachnids from above. I guess once we'd thinned them out, someone was going to go down there and get the teeth. But that's not from Julio. In fact, it's worse than second-hand information. Vlad was more of a people person than me, so most of the information came from his conversations with Julio's men."

"And any idea what they do?" Zeke asked, trying to get a handle on what to expect. "Like, are they poisonous? Do they shoot webs like Spider-Man? Or what?"

Abby raised an eyebrow at the pop culture reference, but she didn't comment. Instead, she answered, "Some are poisonous, but it's not what you think. They don't have to bite you. They throw these globs of poison that paralyze their victims. Then, once you can't move, they wrap you up in webs and take you back to their caves."

"Doesn't sound too bad," Zeke muttered.

"Maybe for somebody like you with whatever ridiculous endurance and vitality you have," she said. "But for me, it'll put me down after only a couple of minutes. Even Julio was wary. And that's not even the extent of their abilities. That carapace is like living armor. And they're supposed to be really quick, too."

"And the queen?" was Zeke's next question.

Abby shrugged. "Depends," she said. "I did some reading before we left, and from what I can tell, each queen is different. Some use magic. Others are physical warriors. It's kind of like with people, I guess. They all have unique skills. And they're huge. Like, a thorax the size of a Volkswagen."

Zeke's brows furrowed as he considered the problem. Killing the requisite number of mundane drachnids was exponentially easier than killing the queen. For one, their abilities were predictable, while the queen would be a complete mystery until she opened up on them. On top of that, simply getting to the queen would probably put them close to satisfying the numerical option. So, almost any way he looked at it, it made no sense to go after the big, bad queen.

But that choice just didn't sit right with him. He'd never been the type to leave a job half done, and leaving the queen alive would be just that. Besides, while Abby said that there wasn't a Framework quest, he had a little experience in that arena. And any time he'd gone above and beyond the minimum requirements, he'd been rewarded by the Framework. It was like it wanted them to risk their lives and reach for greatness rather than simply get by, which was an attitude Zeke could certainly get behind. That made the decision easy in his mind.

However, he couldn't make the choice for Abby, so after laying out his reasons, he said, "So, I want to do both. Kill the drachnids and their queen."

"I already told you—that's stupid," she said, shaking her head. Her high ponytail swayed back and forth. "We only have to do one to get the reward from the guild."

"But what about the Framework?" Zeke asked. "I think we might get rewarded with a quest if we go the extra mile."

She rolled her eyes. "But we'll be dead long before we get that chance," Abby said. "This mission, it was supposed to be completed by an entire team. Julio might've been an asshole, but his group wasn't a joke. They'd been working together for years. Same with Vlad and me. And you want to go the extra mile with just the two of us? That's suicidal, even as strong as you are."

Zeke answered, "For one, there are three of us. Pudge is already level seven. And he'll probably get a few more levels before we hit the queen. Two, I think you're selling yourself short. I've already done something like this, and it was a couple of levels ago. I'm stronger now. And I have you and Pudge. We can do this."

"But—"

Zeke went on, "It's going to hurt, though. I can guarantee that. And we might die. But do you really want to go through this new life being afraid to take a chance? I have plans, Abby. Plans past these islands. Or minicontinent. Whatever it is. I have it on good authority that this is just the beginning—like an extended tutorial or something. And from what you've told me, most of the people here, they're failing. Miserably. I don't want to be one of them, and I don't think you do, either."

By the time he finished, Zeke's heart was pounding out of his chest. It wasn't that he was socially inept. He wasn't. In fact, his father had always expected him to be the leader of any team he played on, and often, he was expected to talk to the team and get them riled up for their games. So, he was used to that kind of thing. However, with that, he'd always felt like something of an imposter. Like he was just playing the role his father wanted him to play. But talking to Abby, he meant every word he'd said, and in a way he had never really experienced before. The result was that his adrenaline was already pumping in expectation of the fight to come.

More important than his own reaction was Abby's, though. He could see her tense muscles, the way her jaw flexed with determination. She wanted it as much as he did; she just hadn't had the same opportunities he'd been given.

"Fine," she said, bending down to pet the cub. "But if anything happens to Pudge, I'll put an arrow in your eye."

Zeke laughed. Abby didn't.

"I won't let anything happen to him," he muttered, realizing that she wasn't really joking. The pair had developed quite a bond in the couple of weeks the group had been together. In some ways, they were even closer than Zeke and his own Soul-Bound Companion. Not that he minded. Abby's attention always made Pudge happy, even if the bear still struggled to articulate his feelings. "But there's something we need to do before we get started. And don't freak out because I think this is going to feel really weird."

"What are you—"

Zeke didn't wait. Instead, he reached out, gripped her shoulder, and formed the unaltered [**Mark of Companionship**]. It was temporary, but the skill would allow the two of them not only to share experience, but also would give her access to a watered-down version of [**Leech Strike**]. It didn't let him funnel vitality to her like he had with Pudge, but it would still be a great help.

Once he'd formed the rune, he let it sink in to her body, where it latched on to her mana channels. They were a little more intricate than his, but his were a lot thicker. In any case, the moment it connected, it became part of her system. It was clearly temporary, but it would last quite a while, as far as he could tell. And with an effort of will, he could easily renew it, too. The only downside was that it cost a steady trickle of mana to maintain the rune's cohesion. The initial cost was pretty extensive, as well.

"Oh . . . oh!" she breathed, her body going rigid. It only lasted a couple of seconds before she relaxed. However, her breathing had quickened, and Zeke could feel that the pace of her mana flow had increased to compensate for the addition of the new rune. "W-what was that?"

"It's called [**Mark of Companionship**]," he said. "It temporarily lets us share experience as well as gives you access to [**Leech Strike**], which is my vitality-stealing skill. I think. I've never used the mark before. But that's what the text said. I can . . . remove it, though. If you don't want it."

Abby shook her head, saying, "No. Leave it. But you really need to . . . you know . . . ask before you do something like that."

Zeke nodded, but he didn't respond. Perhaps his social skills weren't as strong as he thought.

"Are you ready, then?" Abby asked, looking up at the sky. It was midday, so they had plenty of time to assault the ravine.

Shaking his head, Zeke said, "No. Let's do it in the morning. We can go back to that clearing we passed a couple miles back, and I can summon the hut. That skill . . . it actually took a lot of my mana. I need some time to recover it."

Abby nodded once, then said, "Let's go, then. The longer we stay here, the better chance we'll be spotted."

So, the three of them began the short walk back to the clearing, where they would prepare for the next day's assault.

38

ASSAULT ON NIGHTWEB RAVINE

Zeke launched himself at the pair of drachnids, instinctively adopting a zigzag pattern when they began to hurl shards of bone-like carapace at him. The spikes were jagged to the point of serration, with wickedly sharp tips that tore into the rock walls of the ravine like they were made of paper.

"You didn't say anything about them shooting spikes at us!" he yelled.

"They're probably poisoned, too!" came Abby's shouted reply. Then, in a more even tone, she added, "So, try not to get hit."

Zeke didn't have time to growl his intended response, which would've included some variation of him sarcastically saying just how helpful that advice was. As if he intended to let himself be hit. But just as the thought crossed his mind, pain erupted in Zeke's thigh when one of the spikes clipped him, slicing through the thick leather of his armored pants with ease. The wound was shallow—barely noticeable, if Zeke was being honest—but with it came fiery agony followed by the cold numbness of a paralyzing poison. He stumbled, missing a step, but it took only the barest of seconds before his high vitality overwhelmed the toxin, restoring his body to what passed for his new normalcy.

He swore, narrowly dodging a handful of spikes as he continued to close ground. When he reached his target—the leftmost drachnid—he was stunned to see that they were far less humanoid than he'd initially thought. Not only did they have the traits he'd observed the day before, but he also noted a host of differences that he hadn't seen. For one, he couldn't help but notice the spikes jutting from their forearms, especially when every swing of their arms sent at least a pair of those sharp, four-inch projectiles careening toward him. In a macabre way, they reminded Zeke of the razor-like fins on the sides of Batman's gauntlets, except they were detachable and organic.

In addition to those spikes, the drachnid's resemblance to a human was further subverted by the sharp slivers of carapace slicing through otherwise-unmarred skin. The most prominent of these were the ones at the apex of each cheekbone, but they were also present on the creature's brow, jawline, and along a prominent ridge running the length of its forehead.

Finally, there were the eyes, which were probably the most alien part of an already insane-looking creature. Multifaceted like a gemstone, they represented every color of the rainbow, each facet reflecting a different wavelength of color. Taken alone, those eyes would've been beautiful, almost mesmerizing. However, due to the fact that they were attached to a monster that was, at that very moment, intent on killing him, Zeke didn't let his own eyes linger long on the phenomenon.

His mace, Voromir, whistled as it cut through the air in an overhand swing, and just before he was about to make contact, an arrow tore into the drachnid's unprotected throat. It didn't penetrate too deeply, though—a testament to the drachnid's durability. Over the couple of weeks since they'd begun traveling together, Zeke had seen Abby's arrows, propelled and guided by her control of the wind, punch through plenty of tough hides.

Voromir came soon after the arrow, crashing into the drachnid with monstrous force. At the last moment, the creature shifted slightly, which threw off Zeke's aim by just enough that he didn't hit his intended target. Instead, the head of the mace dug into the drachnid's shoulder, collapsing it with a sickening crunch. But despite the obvious pain, the monster retained enough presence of mind to lash out with its claws, raking them across Zeke's chest.

By reflex, Zeke recoiled as the claws bit deep into his flesh. Part of his reaction came from the sheer pain. The burning, which after only a moment became freezing numbness, coupled with the more mundane agony of the wounds themselves. It was a chorus of anguish, the likes of which he had never felt before. It wasn't the volume of the pain, but rather the novelty of it that prompted the reaction.

Zeke shoved his feelings deep down, squaring his shoulders to finish the job he'd started. He needn't have worried because Abby had used the short delay to pepper the monster with a half dozen arrows, firing them with a rapidity reminiscent of a machine gun. Her hands were a blur as she summoned and loosed her silvery arrows in an impressive display that stunned Zeke, who'd begun to develop a deep sense of superiority. Abby dispelled that with her show of expert archery. No single arrow did the job, but Abby kept shooting until the damage finally passed the threshold where the monster couldn't remain standing any longer. As it collapsed, Pudge pounced, raking his claws across the monster's face and neck until they were little more than fleshy, bloody ribbons.

During this time, the remaining drachnid hadn't been idle, though. Nor had Zeke forgotten it. They'd simply made the choice to focus their fire when possible. That plan turned out to be a mistake because the drachnid, eschewing its ineffective spikes, scuttled forward like a cockroach to rake its claws at Abby. She reacted well, but she didn't have Zeke's agility. And judging by the deep gashes it inflicted upon her stomach, nor did she have anywhere close to his endurance. But to her credit, she didn't cry out. Nor did she retreat. Instead, Abby dropped her bow, drawing her hatchet at the same time. Then, dodging past the drachnid's next attack, she swung the small axe at the creature's thorax in a backhanded blow. It bit deep, spewing rubbery flesh coated in some milky substance with the consistency of syrup. The drachnid tried to react, but surprise and pain mingled to slow it down just enough to let Abby pass.

Zeke felt the weaker version of his skill [**Leech Strike**] activate, stealing vitality from the drachnid and knitting Abby's wounds together. It had been something of a surprise when the [**Mark of Companionship**] had allowed for that, making it a far stronger skill than he'd originally anticipated. Even so, it wasn't nearly as strong as his own version, but she'd put everything she had behind that strike. And as such, the proportional healing was strong enough to keep her guts from spilling out. That was enough because Zeke had already closed the gap.

He swung his mace in a baseball swing. Powered by his considerable strength, guided by his equally impressive dexterity, and driven by decades of practice, his swing did precisely what it was intended to do. When it collided with the hard carapace of the drachnid's torso, it met with only token resistance before the natural armor cracked, then shattered. The monster let out a horrible, high-pitched scream of mingled terror, pain, and disbelief as Zeke's mace continued on its unerring path, biting into the monster's flesh. It didn't stop there, though. The mace tore through the flesh and was quickly met by the drachnid's squishy organs, which practically disintegrated under the blow. The mace didn't even begin to slow its momentum until the monster's spine was destroyed, its every organ liquified, but there was enough force leftover for Voromir to erupt from the other side, completely bisecting the creature with the sheer momentum of his blow.

As a commensurate amount of vitality, yanked from the drachnid via his skill, mended the cuts in his chest and nullified the poison coursing through his blood, Zeke followed up with another thundering strike to the fallen creature's head. Its life ended with a gurgle, but both sides of its body, though unconnected, continued to twitch.

"You are so overpowered," Abby muttered, appearing at his shoulder. She quickly pushed past him and bent down, retrieving her knife from a sheath at her belt. However, instead of digging into the drachnid's chest and retrieving its beast core, like he'd expected, she instead went for the monster's eyes.

"What are you doing?" he asked, kneeling beside her.

"Drachnid eyes are valuable," she said. "People make jewelry out of them because they're really good channels for mana. I once saw a piece that was enchanted to enhance fire skills by almost twenty percent. Or that's what the guy told me, at least. He might've just been bragging, though. You know how adventurers are."

"Not really," he said, though given Abby's appearance, he could easily imagine a man trying to show off his wealth in order to get her attention. It probably wasn't that different from the old world, where guys would buy fancy cars or expensive clothes in an effort to impress women.

"Well, every time you get a few of us together, everyone's trying to show off," she said. "Bragging about what they've killed, what kinds of missions they've completed—it's kind of juvenile, to be honest. But when almost everyone gets stuck at the same level, your reputation's all you've really got."

"Yeah, I guess I see that," Zeke muttered. Then, turning back to see that Pudge was still attacking a very dead drachnid, he said, "I'll get the other one."

As he strode toward the corpse, Abby added, "Don't forget the incisors! Should be a pair for each drachnid."

Zeke grumbled a little as he bent down to the unsavory task of yanking the creature's teeth out, then retrieving the valuable portions of its body. For a second, he wondered about the morality of harvesting the creatures in such a callous way. However, he'd only managed to dig a single faceted eye out of its socket before an alert flashed across his vision.

Congratulations! You have managed to alter the nature of your bond with the Crimson Tower. Merely touch a monster's corpse, and you will be given an option to retrieve all valuable materials and store them in your spatial storage.

"Seriously?" he breathed. Then, while touching the drachnid's corpse, he harvested it with a thought. Instantly, its eyes, teeth, and the tips of its spiderlike appendages disappeared. Casting his perception into his spatial storage, Zeke was shocked to see that it had grown more expansive. More, in addition to the small pile of possessions he typically stored within the space, there was a neatly arranged stack of items in the corner. He recognized the eyes, the beast core, and the claws. There was also a pair of fleshy and deflated bladders joining the other harvested pieces.

"What?" asked Abby, having heard the tone of his disbelief.

Zeke stood, wiping his bloody hands on his leather armor; it didn't really help, but it was a reflexive action. "Umm . . . I think looting just got a whole lot easier," he said. Then, he proceeded to tell Abby about his new ability. While he did so, he demonstrated the ability on the corpse she had begun to harvest.

"You're just a walking cheat, aren't you?" she said, shaking her head as she looked at the now-looted corpse. "I've never heard about a skill evolving like that. Usually, if people want to evolve a skill, they have to use one of their skill choices on it."

"It's not a skill, though," he said. But was that even true? Sure, it didn't show up in the skill submenu, but it certainly acted like a skill. Did the fact that he hadn't chosen it like his other skills really matter? "And wait—you can evolve skills?"

"Yeah," she said. "You can only do it after you hit level fifteen, though. There are two schools of thought there. Some people think you should choose different skills and become more versatile. Others believe you should just focus on your bread-and-butter skill, making it as powerful as you can. Not that most people ever get the chance to level past fifteen, of course. The materials that can spark a racial evolution are too rare for that."

"But not for us," Zeke said, nodding along.

"Hopefully," Abby said, pushing past him. He could tell that she was still skeptical about whether they could accomplish their goal or not. However, she'd been pushed into a corner, and she didn't have a choice in the matter. If she wanted to keep progressing, she had to take some chances.

Zeke hurried to catch up. "How big is this place, anyway?" he asked.

"You ever visit the Grand Canyon back in the old world?" was her response. Zeke said that he hadn't, and she continued, "Well, this is about half that size."

"Oh," he said, glancing up at the webs draped across the top of the ravine. Here, it was only forty yards wide, but according to Abby, the space between the sides would reach a width of at least a mile. And that wasn't even considering the various offshoots of smaller, shallower ravines. Finally grasping the enormity of their task, he said, "I guess we've got our work cut out for us, huh?"

Abby laughed, the sound hearty and robust—not the soft, feminine giggle Zeke was used to. "Tried to tell you," she said. "The problem was never whether or not we'd have enough targets. It was a question of whether we could kill five hundred of them without drawing the ire of the rest of the hive. Imagine ten thousand of these things all coming at you at once. Individually, they probably wouldn't be that strong to someone like you, but . . ."

She let the implication hang in the air. When an individual warrior had the power of a superhero, numbers didn't mean as much as they once might have. However, they still mattered. Even Zeke, with his massive advantage in stats, could still be overwhelmed. Certainly, he'd fought his way to the top of that spiraling cavern in the troll caves, wading his way through a thousand trolls to fight the warlord. But that had been a special circumstance. Not only had most of them been much weaker than the two drachnids they'd just faced, if only because they didn't use any real abilities while the drachnids had poison on their side, but the ramp had been narrow enough that the numerical advantage hadn't really counted for as much as it should have. Once the ravine widened, though, that wouldn't be the case.

That didn't mean Zeke wanted to back down, however. So long as they were careful, they could avoid being overwhelmed. And besides, he wasn't alone now. He had Abby. And Pudge.

Hopefully, that would make all the difference he needed. So, without further thought on the matter, he hurried to follow Abby deeper into Nightweb Ravine.

39

USELESS

Talia leaped over the ambulatory corpse, twisting in the air to land on the other side. Immediately, her foot lashed out in a roundhouse kick, destroying the half-rotted creature's skull before it even had the chance to turn around. She followed it up with a quick punch, caving in the horrible monster's chest. When she pulled back, her hand was coated in disgusting black ichor that tingled as it attempted to burn through her skin.

"Girl!" came a nearby voice. Talia had no issues standing up to the zombies that infested the Farindale Forest, but the moment she heard that voice, she couldn't help but flinch. It had dogged her through every step of the journey, and she wanted nothing more than to turn around and take her frustrations out on its owner. Not that it would do any good, of course. The man would take her apart without breaking a sweat. But that didn't stop her from imagining it. "Back with the group!"

Talia spun to cast a glare at the rest of her party. The man in the lead was built like a bear, with broad shoulders, a torso like a barrel, and thick, powerful legs. His imposing size was enhanced only by the gleaming, bulky armor he wore. Most adventurers eschewed plate mail, instead trusting to lighter armor and their own endurance to deal with most attacks. But Abdul Rumas, the leader of the expedition, wasn't like most adventurers—a fact that he'd proved time and time again when he'd single-handedly subdued threats that would've normally taken entire parties to overcome.

In addition to the bulky armor, Rumas also wielded a kite shield as well as what normally appeared to be a utilitarian sword. However, right now, the sword glowed with holy light—a trademark of the powerful Paladins of the Sun Goddess. A legend within the temple, he was well-known for his prowess against the undead. In fact, in Talia's personal opinion, the man was extremely overqualified for the mission they had been given, and she suspected that his inclusion was her mother's way of giving her a babysitter. Lady Constance wasn't above using one of her powerful friends to ensure her daughter's safety.

Talia quickly retreated past the party's frontline fighters to reluctantly join the healers, archers, and other casters, all the while chastising herself for letting the tide of battle sweep her away. Though she was far more powerful than any individual zombie, the creatures were so numerous that even Abdul bore the risk of being overwhelmed.

But it wouldn't have been an issue if she'd been included in the frontline fighters. Instead, Abdul—likely at Lady Constance's insistence—had grouped her with the fragile casters where she could do little good. Her lone healing skill, [**Circle of Mending**], radiated out from her body, healing the people around her. It was a powerful ability, but it also had a glaring downside. In order to get the most out of it, she had to be in the thick of the fighting, putting herself at risk. And Abdul was not going to allow that. So, she'd spent most of the journey feeling incredibly useless.

"Cure!" Abdul called out, pointing at one of the frontline warriors who'd just been bitten by a zombie.

Eager to do something other than stand around, Talia sprang forward, the rune associated with her skill [**Purify**] already activating. Mana flooded the rune, so when she touched the man—she thought his name was Johan, though she couldn't be sure—she released the skill and flooded him with cleansing fire. Blue flames rushed across the man's body, but they didn't hurt him. In fact, it was quite the opposite; the flames quickly flowed from where Talia had touched him on the shoulder, across his torso, and to his left arm, where they flared brighter and hotter. In an instant, they disappeared, and with them, the disease of a zombie's bite dissolved, as well.

The disease itself wasn't all that powerful. It simply robbed an infected person of a few stats and crippled their regeneration. However, what really hurt was that it remained active until it was cleansed. Or until it crossed some nebulous threshold and the infected person started turning into a zombie. That wouldn't happen for days—or sometimes weeks—but without someone with the right skill, getting diseased by a zombie was a death sentence. Or an undeath sentence, maybe. Either way, it wasn't something anyone wanted to experience.

That, as much as Lady Constance's desire for her to remain safe, was why Talia wasn't supposed to join the front lines. After all, the party's other two healers didn't have the requisite skill to cure the disease. Instead, they'd specialized in direct healing. And while Talia knew she was an integral part of the expedition, that didn't make her feel any less useless.

Over the next couple of hours, they endured the horde of zombies, felling hundreds of the creatures. From time to time, Talia would be tasked with curing someone's disease. Or she'd spring forward and heal the group of frontline warriors with [**Circle of Mending**]. She knew she was just as responsible for the party's success as anyone—maybe even more so, considering she was the only one who could cure the disease that came with the zombies' bites. But casting a skill here and there wasn't nearly as satisfying as crushing a zombie's skull with a well-placed kick or a thunderous punch.

Talia had rarely been allowed to truly let loose. She'd always had minders. Guards. People to tell her to hang back and let the real warriors do their work. But she lived for those rare occasions when she lost herself in the heat of a real battle. Dancing between her foes, her fists and feet lashing out like bolts of lightning, narrowly avoiding her enemies' attacks—that was what she craved. That was who she desperately wanted to be.

But that wasn't who she was.

No matter how much she trained, no matter how hard she worked, she would never be a real warrior. She was just a healer, and a weak one at that. Life would've been so much easier if she could just make herself accept her role, like her mother so clearly wanted. She'd wasted a few stats, but she could right the ship if she followed her mother's advice going forward.

Finally, Abdul took down the last of the zombies. The entire group stood there, panting from the exertion. Black ichor covered everyone, but they were whole and, if necessary, they could've kept fighting for another few hours. Maybe longer, given Abdul's high level and effectiveness against the undead. Luckily, that wouldn't be necessary.

Abdul glanced around the ruins, his great chest still heaving beneath his sturdy breastplate. He'd single-handedly accounted for more than half of their kills, and he looked it. His normally gleaming armor was so covered in the black ichor that it was now a matte black that reflected almost no light. Not that there was much illumination within the Farindale Forest. Between the forest's thick canopy and the ever-present mist that clung to the entire area, even at midday, the place was dark and foreboding—a fitting home for the undead.

"Ten minutes," he said. "Then we forge ahead until we find an appropriate place to make camp. For now, Dev and Felicia, you are on watch. The rest of you, rest. We dare not linger here long."

Though she was contrary by nature, Talia couldn't argue with the paladin's orders. However, she could make a quick round to ensure that no one needed her help. She hated being relegated to the back lines, but that didn't mean she would shirk her duties as a healer. Luckily, though, none of the fifteen-strong party was infected with disease, and only a few needed healing. She gathered them around her, then used [**Circle of Mending**] before settling down to [**Meditate**]. The skill settled into her core, churning the mana to increase her regeneration, so by the time Abdul announced their departure, she was close to full capacity.

The next couple of hours found the group warily stalking through the eerily silent forest, careful not to draw too much attention. They could deal with a horde of zombies, but the closer they got to the Micayne Estate, the more dangerous it would become. Why the insane Abraham Micayne had made his home in the middle of a zombie-infested forest, Talia had no idea. Perhaps the grounds were powerfully enchanted to keep out even the worst undead. Otherwise, the man couldn't have survived, regardless of how powerful he was.

So, why hadn't he responded to Lady Constance's summons? Had he finally been overrun? And if so, what was strong enough to threaten an elite like Abraham Micayne? Those questions had haunted Talia throughout their arduous journey, but no answers had been forthcoming. Likely, they wouldn't discover the truth of the matter until they finally reached their destination. Even then, it was unlikely they'd get the entire story.

Abdul called a halt when they reached an abandoned hovel atop a hill. The building had crumbled to mostly nothing, its thatched roof rotted and all but one of its walls fallen. The one holdout precariously clung to its structure, though it looked as if single strong gust would fell the rough stone wall. Either way, the spot hadn't been chosen for the thin protection the hovel might provide. Instead, it had been chosen because of its location atop the shallow hill, which would offer the scouts better sight lines in the event that they were attacked.

Immediately, the bulky and bearded paladin began a circuitous route along the base of the hill, circling it completely before he repeated the action, only ten feet farther in. Then another circle. And another. The entire time, Abdul's face held an expression of intense concentration. His heavy brows furrowed, and his mouth compressed into a thin line, buried amid his thick beard. Finally, the man reached the center of the camp, having circled it nearly twenty times. Once there, he planted himself inside the hut, where he stood for close to half an hour. He didn't move a single muscle. He didn't blink. He simply stood like a statue, his eyes focused on something only he could see and his head tilted toward the sky.

Finally, Talia felt an incredible amount of mana gathering. Some of it came from Abdul, gushing out of him like a torrential river. But it was nothing compared to the turbulent sea of energy overlaying the hill. Talia felt like she'd been submerged in a pit of lava, the wild mana sloughing at the very edges of her soul.

Then, all of it rushed inward. Even her mana, tightly packed inside her core as it was, leaked out, joining the stampede. Other, less aware members of the party gasped as they were sucked dry, as their mana was stripped from them. It hurt. Even Talia, who'd expected it, and thus, had marshalled her willpower against it, keenly felt the agony of the theft. But for those who hadn't, it was exponentially more excruciating. Luckily, it was only a second before Abdul gathered all that mana—whether it was the ambient energy of the area, his own mana, or that of the rest of the expedition—and channeled it through his own pathways. It shot back out, guided by his will into the giant rune he'd drawn around the hill. It drank the mana eagerly, and after a handful of seconds, everything died down.

Abdul finally sank to his knees, his breath coming in shallow spasms. He bent over, resting his palms against the ground. Talia watched with keen eyes. It wasn't every day she got to see someone cast [**Consecration**], which made the entire hill repellent to the undead. With that in play, they could rest in peace.

The skill was likely the most complicated ability Talia had ever heard of. Not only did it require the user to draw the requisite rune upon the ground, but it was also incredibly mana hungry, to the point that it often required more than a single person could generate. Sometimes, less skilled paladins would link with other casters, siphoning mana from them. But true masters like Abdul could bleed the mana from their surroundings. Her mother, Lady Constance, could power the skill on her own. Such was the might of one of the rare Chosen.

It took Abdul about thirty minutes to regain strength enough to stand. He was still wan, his complexion pale, but the big man powered through it. In the meantime, everyone else had set about making camp. Tents were raised, fires started, and meals begun. For her part, Talia had her own tent, which had been enchanted to erect itself, so she used the time to gather herself. So, when the paladin found her, she was sitting cross-legged in front of her tent, meditating before the small fire she'd started. No one had dared erect their own tents within fifteen feet of hers. That was the cost of being the daughter of the most powerful woman on the Radiant Isles.

His armor creaking, Abdul sat next to her, propping his forearms on his knees. For a while, the man remained silent, content to stare at the flames as he continued to recover his strength. Finally, he sighed, saying, "You can't keep doing this, Talia."

Talia ground her teeth together in frustration. "I know," she muttered. "But Dev would've gone down if I hadn't—"

"It's not your job," the big man growled. He wasn't nearly as taciturn as his looks might indicate, but he still wasn't the most personable man in the world. He turned, pointing an armored finger at her as he added, "You are a healer. You heal. You don't rush into a horde of zombies like you're a superhero."

The last word served to highlight the difference between her and most other people. She wasn't the only person to have been born in the Radiant Isles, but they were certainly the minority. Almost everyone else came from that other place. They'd lived and died and been reborn. And while Talia had heard enough stories about Earth—mostly from her mother and various teachers—the old world was still a very mysterious place to her. It also further exacerbated the realities of her station, adding her uncommon origins to the distance created by her being the daughter of the most powerful woman on the island. Perhaps the world.

"I know," she sighed. "I just wanted to help."

The man reached out, gripping her shoulder. She almost flinched away, so unused to human contact was she. However, with an effort of will, she remained still, if very tense. Abdul had to notice, but thankfully, he didn't remark on the tension he felt.

"Help by doing your job," he said. "None of us would've made it through that without your cures. And if something happened to you . . ."

"My mother would kill you all," Talia spat. She wasn't certain if she believed that, but her mother's temper was legendary. When Talia's father had been slain, the woman had gone on a rampage that left half the island in flames. Or so she'd been told.

Abdul laughed, the sound a deep, basso rumbling that probably would've been better served as the portent of an earthquake. "Probably, yeah," he said. "But I'm not worried about Constance. I'm worried about the people under my command. Without you, they all die. Slow, horrible deaths, too. Remember that the next time you're tempted to leap into the fray."

With that, the paladin rose to his feet and went on his way, stopping at the next tent to converse with Johan. Abdul did that every night, taking the time to speak to everyone in the party. And while Talia knew from her own education in leadership that it was a simple command tactic designed to simultaneously make everyone feel included and engender loyalty, she didn't begrudge the paladin's efforts.

If only his assurances had worked to dispel the feelings of uselessness that had become her constant companions. Sighing, Talia shook her head. Eventually, she would have to make a choice. Would she embrace her given role as a healer? Or would she defy her mother and pursue a life of action, as she truly desired?

40

A GRUESOME TASK

Zeke's fingers tightened around the haft of his mace, the worn leather of the grip squeaking from the pressure. As he glared into the cave, his face remained impassive, betraying nothing of his rage.

Abby's fingers settled onto his arm, and she asked, "Are you okay?"

"I'm fine," he grunted, his eyes never wavering from the cocooned bodies within the dark cave. Hundreds of wrapped bundles of spider silk hung from the ceiling, their size evidence enough of what they were. Zeke couldn't see to the back of the cave, but he suspected that it went on for quite some distance.

"Should we . . . should we cut them loose?" Abby asked. Though her voice was little more than a whisper, it sounded like a shout in Zeke's ears.

Zeke shook his head, saying, "I . . . I don't know. What would we do with them? I can't fit that many in my spatial storage, and I can't dig through rock. Can't burn them, either. A fire would attract the rest of the drachnids. Maybe when this is all done . . ."

He let the sentence trail off into nothing. The cave full of bodies was a clear parallel of what he'd seen in the troll caverns, and there was a part of him that wanted to react the same way he had before. A rampage would certainly make him feel a little better in the short term. Or at least give him something on which to focus so he didn't have to think about the fate of all the innocent people who had ended up in those cocoons. However, he knew from experience that, in the long term, it wouldn't do much good. Massacring the troll population hadn't. In fact, the unthinking rampage had very nearly killed him, and more than once. Besides, he'd always intended to kill the drachnids. He just couldn't let the emotions sweep him into doing something stupid. So, he restrained his rage, forcing it aside so he could look at things as logically as possible.

But with those silk-wrapped bodies looming over him, it was difficult. Very, very difficult.

It would've been different if the creatures were unthinking monsters. But according to Abby, other tribes of drachnids managed to coexist with humans, even trading with them on occasion. So, it wasn't some animalistic instinct that propelled them to raid those caravans. They were the actions of sapient, albeit primitive, creatures.

Finally, Zeke strode forward into the darkness, touching each bundled corpse along the way. With a thought, he looted every one of them, stripping them of valuables as well as the silk that had been used to bind them. Naked, desiccated corpses fell to the ground, thudding with a finality that echoed in Zeke's mind. It wasn't dignified, and he got nothing aside from a few personalized mementos in the way of loot, but it was necessary, if not for practical reasons, then for his sanity. He couldn't just leave them behind. He had to do something, even if it was a useless gesture.

As he moved from corpse to corpse, Zeke said, "We'll put them in a pile, then burn them on the way out. Once we've finished the drachnids."

Abby didn't verbalize a response. Instead, as Zeke looted the corpses, she set about the arduous task of gathering and stacking the bodies. Meanwhile, the normally rambunctious and playful Pudge was subdued, his shoulders drooping as he followed along behind Zeke.

Memory. Mother. Loss.

The interjection cut through Zeke's determination, not because of the thought itself. Rather, it was the emotion that came with it. The sense of loss that came from Pudge was nearly overwhelming, and it once again reminded Zeke that his companion was only a child, little more than an infant, that had lost his only family. In the face of that, Zeke considered himself a poor substitute.

Pausing in his gruesome task, Zeke knelt down to ruffle the bear cub's fur. "It's okay, buddy," he whispered. "I'm here for you."

Pudge. Here. Too.

As the thought brushed against him, Zeke felt an outpouring of unconditional loyalty and love. And though he knew part of it was due to the Soul Bond, he also knew that the bear had cast him as a surrogate mother figure. Or protector. The emotions were strange and tangled, and Zeke was in no position to try to unwind them. But he was thankful for the bear cub's support.

"Thanks, buddy," he muttered, pulling the bear cub closer. Then, he stood and continued through the cave. His first inclination was to try to divorce himself from the gruesome task, to retreat within his own mind and let the numbness take over. It would've been easier, certainly. But he thought he owed it to these people, nameless strangers though they were, to at least acknowledge them, to grieve their losses, and to push ahead.

Once he'd finished looting, he'd counted more than four hundred bodies. And though there was little tangible evidence, he was certain that plenty more had already been consumed by the drachnids. Task completed, he began gathering the drained corpses by putting them into his spatial storage. It wasn't big enough to hold them all, but it was better than trying to carry them by hand.

It took them about an hour to gather the corpses into a neat pile near the front of the cave. Half-rotted and drained of all their fluid, they took up far less space than Zeke would've expected, but the pile of stacked corpses was still intimidatingly large. He, Abby, and Pudge stood there, staring at them for a long moment, just taking in the results of their labor. Through the Soul Bond, Zeke could sense his own feelings echoed in Pudge's emotions—longing, sadness, and loss.

"Do you want to make camp?" asked Abby, her voice soft. "Or do you want to keep going?"

Zeke glanced outside the cave, noting that there was still plenty of daylight left. They'd been hunting drachnids within the ravine for almost a week, and in that time, they'd killed more than two hundred of the spider-human hybrids. Most had come in pairs, but on two occasions, they'd been forced into a pitched battle with more than a dozen of the creatures. Those had been much more difficult than Zeke cared to admit, primarily due to the drachnids' poison. He could easily handle a handful of the poisoned spikes they shot, but any more and they'd begin to affect him. Numbness would come first, then a sluggishness to his movements, and finally, full paralysis. Only a few days before, he'd been reduced to a mostly immobile pincushion, and it was due only to Abby's rapid-fire bow shots that they had managed to survive.

"I think we should move on for a couple of hours," he said. "I don't want to camp near here."

Abby pointedly didn't disagree, and the pair, along with Pudge, quickly left the cave. Outside, the ravine was nearly a mile wide, and in that space were giant pillars of rock that jutted toward the sky. In addition to the drachnids, Nightweb Ravine was also home to a species of spiders about the size of Zeke's hand; they were fuzzy analogues of tarantulas, though unlike their earthbound counterparts, they were incredibly venomous, traveled in packs of a hundred or more, and moved with ridiculous speed. In only a few seconds, they could swarm their unlucky prey and inject them with a potent necrotic poison that, without powerful vitality and endurance to combat it, could rot a creature alive.

For Zeke, a swarm of nightweb spiders was merely painful, but for Abby, whose constitution wasn't nearly as robust, the spiders could prove deadly. Curiously, Pudge wasn't affected at all by the venom, and he quite enjoyed playing with the deadly swarms of spiders.

There were other, less numerous creatures that made their homes within the ravine—six-foot-long lizards that looked a lot like Komodo dragons, a species of snake that was so well camouflaged that it was largely invisible until it struck, and whirling rock dervishes that mostly kept to themselves, to name a few—but the drachnids and the nightweb spiders had driven all but the hardiest competition away.

As they made their way up the ravine, Zeke and Abby ambushed a pair of drachnids, quickly dispatching them with practiced ease. So long as there weren't more than a few of them, the monsters stood no chance. And even if Zeke and Abby were grossly outnumbered, they'd proven that they could come out on top—though, the cost in pain and recovery time was usually significant.

Once they'd hiked for almost two hours, they decided that they'd gotten far enough away from the corpses that they could make camp. So, as Zeke summoned the hut, and Abby went scouting to make sure that they weren't near one of the caves where the drachnids made their homes.

As Zeke looked at the hut, he shook his head, marveling at the changes. Its footprint had grown by about three feet, as far as he could tell, and the thatched roof had been replaced by crude wooden shingles. In addition, the stone from which the walls had been constructed had morphed from simple gray rock to something much lighter. It was almost white, with subtle pink veins running through it.

But more importantly, it had come with in-person access to his spatial storage.

He stepped into the hut and quickly found the trapdoor in the center of the single room. Opening it, he climbed down the ladder and saw the physical representation of his spatial storage. The cellar was of a size with the rest of the hut, which meant that the storage had grown right alongside it. Still, the evidence of their efforts in Nightweb Ravine was evident from the piles of loot inside.

In one corner, there were beast cores—small, marble-sized chunks of jagged rock that flickered with untapped power. In another, there were the drachnid eyes, which appeared to be faceted gemstones that reflected a rainbow of colors. Beside the eyes was a pile of drachnid fangs, the proof of their efforts. On the other side of the room were various pieces of equipment. Most were old and rotted—useless, as far as Zeke was concerned, but Abby claimed that skilled artisans could make use of them. And that meant that they weren't worthless. Then there was the small pile of mementos—personalized treasures and keepsakes that were all that was left of the drachnids' victims. And finally, there were the miscellaneous pieces of monsters. Piles of spider legs, a few snakeskins, a handful of scorpion pincers, and a wide variety of other pieces were all arranged into their own neat piles. Thankfully, his looting skill automatically sorted everything; otherwise, he'd have had to do it by hand—a task that seemed not only tedious but incredibly time-consuming.

After inspecting everything, Zeke climbed the ladder back to the ground floor of the hut and found that Abby had returned. She raised an eyebrow, saying, "Like a dragon with his hoard."

"What?" Zeke asked, confused.

"Dragons," she said. "You know, they're famous for coveting their hoards? Haven't you ever heard of Smaug?"

Zeke shrugged. The name sounded familiar, but he couldn't place it. So, he said, "No. Is that a dragon in this world or something?"

Abby laughed, and Zeke felt his cheeks redden in embarrassment. "You seriously never read *The Hobbit*?" she asked. "Or *The Lord of the Rings*?"

He shook his head, saying, "I never really had the chance to read. I was too busy."

She quirked a half smile, saying, "With what?"

Zeke wanted nothing more than to leave his old life in the past. It didn't matter now. None of it did. Even before he'd died, he'd tried to move forward. Unsuccessfully, sure, but he had recognized that dwelling in the past was a bad idea. Of course, spending two years with no company but his own had pulled a lot of that back to the surface.

"Baseball," he said. "I was... I don't know... I was good. Like, getting drafted good. And baseball's not like a lot of sports, you know? It's not just about athletic ability. A great athlete could step onto a football field and be pretty good, even if he was completely new to it. But baseball? You can't cut corners. The only way to be good is practice. Hours and hours of practice. So, that's what I did instead of reading books. Or watching movies. I practiced."

He went on, almost as if, once he'd begun, he couldn't keep it down. He told Abby about his schedule, where he'd get up, go to school, and as soon as he got out, he'd head down to a hitting lesson. Then a catching lesson. A workout. Every single day, he'd work on baseball until well into the night. Then, when he got home, he'd do what homework he could and go to bed, only to repeat it the next day.

"That sounds exhausting," Abby said. "My cousin was like that. She was a figure skater. But she didn't even go to school. Instead, she had a tutor. The rest of the time, she was practicing. That would've driven me crazy. I've never met anyone so driven, though. She almost made it to the Olympics, so I guess it was worth it."

Zeke shrugged. "It wasn't really that bad, honestly," he said. And it hadn't been. He had always loved baseball, and even more, he loved the results he got. There was something to be said for seeing the tangible results of all your hard work. But what he left unsaid was the way his father had treated him. The yelling. The screaming. The insults. The occasional beatings. The overwhelming feeling that, regardless of how well he did, it would never be enough. The certainty that his father only cared inasmuch as he could live vicariously through him. "I never really knew anything else, so you get used to it."

Abby shook her head. "I guess," she said, pulling some rations from her seemingly bottomless satchel. It was just dried meat and some sort of hard bread, but it was filling enough. She tossed him a couple of pieces, saying, "How long do you want to stay down here?"

"Until the job's done," Zeke answered, tearing a chunk of dried meat with his teeth. "I want to kill the queen, at least. And as many of these monsters as we can. Like I said before, I think there might be a quest if we do it."

Abby sighed. She clearly didn't have his bloodlust, but she couldn't keep the anticipation from affecting her expression. After all, Zeke's way had clearly netted results so far, and she obviously wanted to reap some of those same rewards.

"Fine," she said. "But we're going to have to think about food pretty soon. My rations won't last forever."

Zeke nodded, saying, "We'll figure something out. I think those snakes are edible. Maybe we can find more of those. And I bet the scorpion pincers aren't much different from lobster claws. We should be fine, so long as you're not a squeamish eater."

Abby made a gagging noise.

Zeke tossed a piece of dried meat to Pudge, saying, "You should've seen the sorts of things I ate in the troll caves. Mostly these blue mushrooms that I'm pretty sure were kind of poisonous, but there were also these wall-crawling octopus-monkey things. Their tentacles kind of tasted like fish. But slimier."

"Octopus-monkey . . . things?" asked Abby.

"Like chimps, but instead of legs, they have tentacles," he said. "The tentacles had these hooks they used to latch on to walls, so they'd drop down on you without any warning. Oh, and they were mildly poisonous, too. God, I hated those things. Believe me, you've never been as scared as when you wake up to a bunch of tentacles wrapping around your face . . ."

"I think . . . I think I'll take your word for it," she said. "But I'm not eating spiders. Or drachnids. I just want to make that abundantly clear."

Zeke shrugged. "You'd be surprised what you'd eat if you're hungry enough," he said. "Plus, those octopus things gave a pretty good boost to regeneration. Not as good as the flying fish, but . . . well, when your guts are spilling out, you take what you can get. Anyway, those lizards and snakes are decently high-level. I bet they're good for that kind of thing. So, keep an eye out when you're scouting. Might just save our lives."

And with that, Zeke leaned against the wall, closing his eyes. However, as he tried to sleep, all he saw was a pile of desiccated corpses.

41

SWARMED

Abby collapsed beside Zeke, who was so covered in gore that he looked like he'd been turned inside out. Between ragged breaths, she said, "That could have gone a lot better."

Heedless of the blood and accumulated viscera all around him, Zeke lay back in exhaustion. Then, he laughed, a necessary release of tension after fighting drachnids for close to seven hours straight. Nearby, Pudge rolled in a particularly nasty pile of severed legs, dislodged chitin, and, of course, plenty of drachnid blood. The bear cub had no idea just how grotesque his display was, which only served to enhance the absurdity of the scene.

The day had actually started out fairly well, with Abby and Zeke slowly picking off small groups of drachnids as they made their way through Nightweb Ravine. However, disaster had struck when they made the mistake of chasing a deserter into one of the caves dotting the ravine's outer walls. They'd managed to kill the monster, but not before it raised an alarm with the hundreds of drachnids within. They weren't all combatants, but even the civilian versions of drachnids were still deadly monsters.

"It wouldn't have been so bad if they hadn't gotten reinforcements," Zeke said. His armor had been ruined, just like Abby's, and if it hadn't been for his [**Leech Strike**] and the [**Mark of Companionship**] that let him share the skill, they'd have both been dead a dozen times over. "How many do you think we got?"

"Plenty," she said.

"Not all of them, though," Zeke muttered, all mirth disappearing from his tone. It reminded Abby that beneath his gruff yet mostly affable exterior, there was a deep, throbbing potential for hatred. When they weren't in battle, Zeke reminded her of a Labrador, all likable naivete and optimism. However, the moment he summoned his mace, he became an insatiable and unstoppable hellhound. And that had been before they'd found the bodies. After, he had been infected with a need for vengeance that had transformed him into something altogether more terrifying.

Part of the intimidation was due to the fact that he didn't seem to care about getting hurt. He didn't even seem to acknowledge that throwing himself at hundreds of monsters might result in his own death. And from experience, Abby knew that, despite his ability to heal from wounds that would kill other men, his injuries still hurt. In their minor war against the drachnids, Abby hadn't taken quite as many hits as Zeke, but she'd experienced her fair share of injuries. And though she'd healed via the borrowed [**Leech Strike**], she hadn't been able to escape the agony of having her body torn apart, piece by piece.

Zeke seemed to sneer at the pain, though, refusing to even acknowledge it, aside from a grimace or an errant grunt. Instead, he always waded forward, swinging that terrible club, heedless of the damage he took. That, more than anything else, marked him as unique. Of all his impressive attributes or his interesting skills, his ability to take a hit and keep moving forward was the most impressive and frightening of them all.

"You did something new at the end there," she said. "A different skill. You got faster."

"Stronger, too," he said, sitting up. He ran his hand through his hair—or at least he tried to. His hair, matted by blood, didn't seem to cooperate, though. "It's a skill called [**Heart of the Berserker**]. It gives me a boost to my physical stats, but the longer it goes on, the more vulnerable I get. And when I stop using it, there's a period of weakness."

"You've never used it before," she said.

He shrugged. "I forget sometimes," he said.

Abby just shook her head. It sounded like an extremely powerful ability, especially when she had seen how much stronger and faster he got under its influence. Even with the downsides, it was the sort of ability that most adventurers would build their entire fighting style around. But for Zeke, it was an afterthought, an oft-forgotten and rarely needed tool.

"Do you think the mark will let me use it, too?" she asked.

Again, Zeke shrugged his muscular shoulders. "No idea," he said. "Maybe? I'm kind of new at this grouping up thing. But I know Pudge can use it. Even when I tell him not to."

Abby frowned as she remembered the bear cub's sudden surge of strength. For a couple of minutes, Pudge had held his own right beside his Soul-Bound Companion. It had been quite a sight to see the cub dismembering drachnids five or six times his size. But then he'd started taking injuries. Swipes that normally wouldn't have pierced Pudge's thick hide had ripped him to shreds. Zeke didn't say so, but Abby was experienced enough to know that Pudge had very nearly died. It was only toward the end of the battle, when he could attack injured drachnids and utilize [**Leech Strike**] that he had begun to heal.

"He's just a baby," she said, looking at the cub. He'd grown a little in the weeks since Abby had met Zeke in Tua'Ta'alar, from the size of a mid-size dog to almost four feet long. She had no idea of Pudge's age, but she suspected that his growth was unusually fast. In a year, he'd probably reach adulthood.

"More like a stubborn teenager," Zeke mumbled. His jaw flexed as he stared at the bear cub still rolling in the blood of its enemies. "It got close there for a little while. Really close."

"Yeah," she said, reaching out to grip his shoulder. Since being reborn into the new world, Abby hadn't really had many friends. There were plenty of acquaintances and allies—in that respect, she was popular enough. Most of the other adventurers in Beacon knew her by reputation, if not by sight. However, she hadn't allowed herself to get close to anyone in a while. Even her relationship with Vladimir hadn't been a true friendship. There was loyalty there, but he'd been her subordinate. But Zeke was different. With him, she'd felt a nearly immediate kinship. "We got through it, though. It probably won't be the first time we come close to dying, right? Otherwise, we'll never progress."

Zeke nodded, and for a few seconds, neither of them moved. Instead, surrounded by the corpses of their enemies, they merely sat, lost in thought. Finally, Zeke's face split into a grin as he said, "Speaking of progression—I finally leveled to twelve."

Abby shook her head, saying, "Your leveling speed is ridiculous." Then, she looked around, "Or maybe not. Honestly, killing this many monsters should've gotten you even more experience."

"It's [**Mark of Companionship**]," Zeke reasoned. "I'm sharing experience with both you and Pudge. On top of that, the skill that lets me summon the house costs a portion of my experience, too."

"It's probably your constitution, as well," Abby said. "Some of the Temple's scholars say that the higher your stats, the more experience it takes for you to level. It's one of the reasons that higher levels require exponentially more energy to advance."

And given what Abby had seen, Zeke was blessed with stats that were expansive enough for someone five levels his senior. Maybe more, considering she had no notion of how high his intelligence, wisdom, or vitality really were. For the first two, she'd never seen him utilize any mana-hungry skills, so she couldn't judge their values. And with vitality, [**Leech Strike**] sort of skewed everything; she had no clue where its effects ended and where Zeke's vitality began. However, she had seen enough of his strength, agility, dexterity, and endurance to know that they were within the upper tier of anything she'd ever seen, even among the masters within her guild, the Champions of Light.

And he was only level twelve.

A shudder went up Abby's spine as she considered how powerful the man might become as he continued to pile on levels. It wasn't outside the realm of possibility that he could eventually even challenge legends like the paladin Abdul Rumas or Lady Constance herself.

"You've mentioned this Temple before," Zeke said. "And you've talked about your guild. But you've never really explained how any of that works. I mean, is Beacon run by this Temple? Or does the guild run things?"

"Sort of," Abby said. "The Temple is nominally neutral. There's a bureaucracy in Beacon. An elected council, too. They run the city on a day-to-day basis. But when the Temple of the Sun Goddess wants something, they get it because they have all the real power, and the people trust them. Then there's the Church of Purity. They're mostly neutral, but nobody wants to offend them because they've got all the healers. They're not interested in power, though. Think of them like a charity organization combined with a hospital."

"And your guild?" Zeke asked, standing. He bent down to touch a drachnid corpse, looting anything useful. Immediately, its eyes disappeared along with the claws that remained intact. The drachnid's incisors followed suit before he moved to the next one. Abby stood and followed, though she couldn't assist in the looting.

"The Champions of Light," she said. "Third most powerful guild in Beacon, after the Sun Worshippers and Night's Bane."

"What's with all the names? Everything's to do with the sun or light," he said, continuing his looting spree. Abby was more than a little jealous of that ability. Harvesting monsters properly was an acquired skill, and one that very few people managed to obtain. Even then, it was a messy, time-consuming, and tedious process. Zeke's ability, by comparison was quick, easy, and clean. Most adventurers would kill for something with half that utility.

"It's Lady Constance's influence," Abby explained. "She's the leader of the Temple of the Sun Goddess. The Goddess's own Chosen One, and the strongest person around. Rumor is that she actually founded Beacon, though that would put her at around five hundred years old. I'm not sure I believe that, but I do know she's extremely strong. When her husband died about ten years ago, she unleashed a wave of flame that destroyed an entire forest and anything unlucky enough to live there. It was before my time, but where the forest used to be is still a wasteland of ash. It even spawns weak fire elementals now."

"And the guilds chose their names to curry favor," Zeke reasoned. "But they don't have any official connection to the Temple, right?"

"Right," Abby said.

"Sounds stupid," he said. "Just because someone's powerful doesn't mean they know how to rule. I mean, just because someone can hit home runs doesn't mean they can coach, you know?"

Abby shook her head. The baseball analogies were getting more infrequent, and she knew from experience that, eventually, he'd leave them behind. Even though she'd been in the new world for less than a decade, her old life had faded into something of a blur. She could still remember things if she focused hard enough, and some wounds would probably never fully leave. But the old world was like a dream to her. More ephemeral than real. It happened to everyone, so long as they survived long enough, and it would surely happen to Zeke, as well—especially considering how young he'd been when he died the first time.

Shrugging, she said, "I don't make the rules. That's just how it is."

For a while, neither of them spoke. Instead, Zeke continued to loot the hundreds of monsters, and Abby contented herself to simply follow along, keeping an eye on their surroundings so that they wouldn't be ambushed. They had made quite a ruckus, after all. It would've been naive to think that they'd gone unnoticed. Pudge followed along, his head hanging low; clearly, Zeke had mentally admonished the bear cub for his recklessness, and he'd responded by pouting.

Finally, after a couple more hours, when the sun had begun to set, they finished the arduous task of looting the carcasses of the monsters. Then, they pushed forward along the ravine until they were a mile or so from the remains. Once they had put a reasonable amount of distance between themselves and the site of the battle, Zeke summoned his hut.

Not for the first time, Abby marveled at the ability. In a lot of ways, it was even more impressive than Zeke's skills or his constitution. Not only did it function similarly to her [**Makeshift Camp**] skill, acting as a monster repellent, but it also seemed possessed of the ability to evolve. Since the first time she had seen it, it had grown larger and sturdier. The hut, which could better be called a cottage now, had traded out its straw roof for wooden shingles and replaced its mundane gray stone with something that looked far more exotic. Pale white, with red veins, the stone that comprised the cottage's walls seemed to radiate a certain power that Abby could only barely sense, much less understand.

By rote, Abby gathered some wood from inside the cottage and quickly made a fire, infusing it with [**Makeshift Camp**]. There was some overlap between the skill and the cottage, but over the past couple of weeks, the two had twined together into a synergistic aura that was more than the sum of its parts. Within that cottage, their potential for recovery would skyrocket, wounds would regenerate at unheard-of speeds, and no monster would come within a hundred yards of the place.

As always, Zeke descended into the cellar that was the physical manifestation of his spatial storage. He did it every time they made camp, almost as if he didn't quite trust his own ability.

Abby ignored it, instead focusing on cleaning off the blood and gore from that day's battle. It wasn't exactly one of Beacon's bathhouses, but at least she could get reasonably clean. It took her almost thirty minutes to finish the awkward bath, but Zeke didn't make an appearance until well after she'd pulled a fresh set of clothes from her enchanted satchel and redressed. When he finally emerged from the cellar, she was scrubbing her armor clean. That day's clothes were hanging nearby, already as clean as they were going to get.

Zeke slapped a slab of meat on the rough-hewn table; she thought it was from the tail of the enormous lizard they'd killed early in the day, but

Abby's stomach wasn't strong enough to ponder the meat's origins too deeply. She could eat it, and so long as she didn't think about it much, it almost tasted like chicken. But that didn't mean she had to like it.

"You mind?" he asked. "I want to get cleaned up, too."

Abby rolled her eyes at Zeke's preference for privacy. Perhaps that was why he disappeared each time he summoned his cottage—to give her privacy so she could bathe in peace. Thoughtful, if unnecessary. She wasn't exactly an exhibitionist, but spending years in the field, fighting and camping alongside men and women alike, had rid her of many of her hang-ups about nudity. Still, Abby couldn't help but feel thankful for his consideration, as misguided as it may be. She'd be remiss if she didn't return the favor.

So, Abby grabbed the meat, then went outside to do the cooking. As she skewered the slab of flesh and set it to roasting over the flames, Abby considered that maybe that was his plan all along; perhaps he just didn't want to cook.

The rest of the night went much the same as the previous few weeks, with them sharing small talk or playing with Pudge, who'd whined the entire time Zeke had spent cleaning his fur. Then, they went to sleep, hoping that the next day would prove a little easier. Or at least that was Abby's hope. As for Zeke, she wouldn't have put it past him to want a tougher challenge.

42

THE DRACHNID HORDE

Zeke lay on his stomach, his head barely peeking over the slight rise, as he studied the scene laid out before him. Without looking away, he whispered, "How many do you think there are?"

"I stopped counting at three hundred," Abby said, lying prone beside him. "That was maybe half of them. Conservatively. There might be as many as a thousand."

"Damn it," Zeke muttered, backing away. They really were lucky that the veritable army of drachnids had gathered in a depression. It made it far easier to scout, then retreat a couple of miles back to where he'd left the cottage summoned. An itch at the back of Zeke's mind told him that if he went much farther, it would de-summon on its own.

The pair of adventurers remained silent as they quickly traversed the uneven ground of the ravine, and even though neither got into a hurry, Pudge still had to push himself to keep up. It was good for him, though. He needed the exercise. More, he needed to know his limits; if he didn't, he would put himself into a situation he couldn't handle. And Zeke wasn't so certain that he'd always be able to jump in and save the stubborn cub.

When they finally reached the cottage, Abby didn't waste any time before she used her **[Makeshift Camp]** skill, which synergized with the cottage's aura to keep monsters well away. In the meantime, Zeke retrieved some snake filets he'd stored in the cellar, and before long, they were sharing an unappetizing meal that tasted like a blend of fish and chicken, and not in a good way.

"I would kill for a freaking hamburger right now," he muttered. "There was this place back home called Stan's Super Burger. I didn't really appreciate how good they were back then. And the milkshakes . . . God. I'd jump in the middle of that drachnid horde if it meant I could have one of their banana shakes again."

Abby snickered. "You act like that's not precisely what you're going to do anyway," she said.

"What's that supposed to mean?" he asked.

"That you have two speeds," Abby said. "You're either preparing to risk your life against unreasonable odds, or you're wading into a sea of monsters. That's pretty much your thing, as far as I can tell."

Zeke frowned. He knew Abby didn't mean anything by her statement. In fact, there was a playful tone to her voice. However, it was still mildly offensive because it painted him as a dumb, battle-mongering brute. Which, if he thought about it, might have actually been kind of true. Still—he didn't appreciate her pointing it out.

"I fight when I have to," he said, tearing a piece of snake off a stick that served as a skewer. He popped it into his mouth, adding, "I'm just trying to survive."

Abby rolled her eyes. "Oh, please," she said. "Don't even try that crap. You and I both know that you're doing more than trying to survive. You're addicted to this. The fight, the leveling, everything. That's not a horrible thing, though. In fact, you're in pretty good company because I'm the same way. It's gotten easier over the past couple of years when I've been stuck at fifteen, but I still feel it—that need to improve, to fight, to win. It's why I'm out here in the first place. It's why I didn't leave you behind when you decided to march into Nightweb Ravine with nothing but me and a bear cub as backup. But you know what's really funny? I think you'd have done this even if you were completely, utterly alone."

To punctuate her statement, she bit into a particularly charred hunk of snake. He knew just how horrible it tasted, but Abby kept her expression neutral as she chewed. Finally, she swallowed. "Well, that was all sorts of terrible," she muttered. Then, she grinned in spite of herself.

"What?" Zeke asked.

"Just thinking," she said, her voice suddenly wistful. "I had alligator once. You know, in the old world. My . . . my husband and I, we went down to Louisiana to visit some of his family, and they insisted I try it.

I can almost convince myself that this snake kind of tastes like that did. You know, if the restaurant had cooked it for way too long and hadn't used any spices."

"You were married?" was Zeke's next question.

Abby nodded. "Didn't end well," she said. Then, obviously wanting to change the subject, she asked, "What are you planning to do when we get to Beacon?"

Zeke had certainly given it a lot of thought, but the reality was that he didn't know enough about this new world to make any lasting decisions. The only thing he really knew was that he wanted to keep progressing. He hadn't asked outright, but Abby—and by extension, the rest of this new world—seemed to have no idea that there was anything past level twenty-five. To them, that was the end of the road. The pinnacle of power. Zeke knew differently, though. Oberon had told him that he would get a class at level twenty-five, which implied that whatever else the Radiant Isles were, they were only the beginning of the journey.

More than that, Zeke knew that there was a war going on between the forces of light and darkness—a war Oberon expected him to help fight. Before, when he had been in that mysterious white room, Zeke had dismissed that as a possibility. He wasn't a warrior, back then. But now? He'd been fighting for more than two years, and though he didn't want to admit it, Abby was right. He'd grown to crave the action. That moment of triumph when his enemies had fallen before him. That flood of experience. The sudden influx of power when he gained a level. It was intoxicating.

"I don't know," he said. "Can I join your guild?"

"I'm sure they'd take you," she said. "If that's what you want. It's not my choice, though. And even if they want you, you'll have to pass a trial of some sort before they let you in."

"What kind of trial?" Zeke asked.

Abby shrugged, then took another bite of the horrible snake meat. After swallowing, she said, "With me, it was a tournament. Top five got in. But I've seen them assign other tasks. It should be well within your capability to complete, though."

"Is there any reason I wouldn't want to do it?" he asked.

"Lots of reasons," Abby answered. "Maybe you want to go solo. Some adventurers do that, and a lot of them are reasonably successful. They work like subcontractors for the various guilds. The rewards aren't as good, but you can pick and choose from all the guilds' missions. Plus, you don't have to deal with anyone telling you what to do."

Zeke nodded, but Abby went on, gesturing with her own skewer as she spoke. "You could also join a different guild," she said. "The Champions of Light are one of the best, but the Ruby Warriors are just as good. And there are a couple of others that are better in almost every respect. They have a bigger rosters and a higher average level. There are also some other guilds that specialize in certain areas. Like the Holy Crusade, who focus on undead threats. Or Maurice's Minions—terrible name, by the way—who hunt down rogue adventurers. There are almost a dozen others, all with their own sales pitches."

Zeke didn't know much, but he knew he'd never become anyone's minion, even if it was just a meaningless name. He was also a little surprised to find that there were undead, so he asked, "There are undead here? Like vampires and zombies?"

"Mmhmm," Abby murmured. "Specters, banshees, and draugrs, too. And a hundred other kinds of unliving creatures with varying degrees of sentience. There are even some people who have taken skills to control them, to certain degrees. Needless to say, all the guilds hunt them down. I did a mission about a year ago to fight an undead horde that a lich had raised. That's why I took [**Cure Disease**] as my level fifteen skill. As much as I hated not getting something more universally useful, it let me save a few lives when our Priest of Purity got jumped by this undead demon-dog thing. Otherwise, we'd have all turned to zombies."

Zeke nodded along as she told the story; apparently, zombies and other select undead carried a disease that was transmitted via their bites. Like in the movies, this disease turned the zombies' victims into undead themselves. But it wasn't a death sentence. Anyone with a disease-curing skill could get rid of it, so long as they caught it before the transformation into undead truly began. However, those skills weren't available to everyone, so anyone who had them was a hot commodity when it came to any mission that dealt with the undead.

He shook his head, dispelling these thoughts. None of that was important right now. Instead, he focused on the problem at hand—specifically, the horde of drachnids a couple of miles away.

"We're sure the queen's in that direction, right?" Zeke asked.

"Complete change of subject, huh?" was Abby's response. "Sure. I mean, I guess? I don't know any more about this place than you do at this point. When we took the mission, our intention was to pick them off at the edges, not charge straight through the middle of the canyon and murder every drachnid we saw. We never even considered going after the queen herself."

"Why not?" he asked.

"Other than the obvious?" she said, arching one delicate eyebrow. "Our estimates were way off when it came to their numbers, but we knew we'd have to go through a lot of monsters to get to her. And even if we came out the other side, the queen's probably level twenty-five. Probably even an elite."

"Uh . . . what?" Zeke asked.

"An elite," she repeated. "Like, a boss monster. You played video games, right? Think of the queen as the big bad at the end of a level."

"And they're harder, I guess," Zeke said. Abby nodded, confirming that they were, indeed, more difficult to kill, but Zeke cast his mind back to his previous encounters. Had the warlord been an elite? What about the harpy queen? So, he asked, "Is there any indication when you're dealing with an elite?"

"You've got an inspection skill, right?" she asked. He nodded. "Well, there will be an *E* beside its name. I've heard there are other, higher designations, but I've never seen any of them." She shook her head. "I've never even seen an elite, if I'm honest. Not a live one, at least. So, I'm just as much in the dark as you are."

"That's great," Zeke muttered.

"You know, it's not too late to turn back," Abby reminded him. "We've already killed enough drachnids to satisfy the mission. We don't have to—"

"And what about all those people they killed?" Zeke asked, remembering the desiccated bodies they'd found wrapped in spider silk. In addition to that first cave, they'd discovered four more along the way, each larger than the last. "You know as well as I do that we've barely made a dent in them. They'll keep raiding caravans and killing people unless we do something."

Abby turned away. In the time since they'd gotten back the cottage, the sun had begun to dip below the lip of the ravine. There was still some daylight left, but with the orientation of the canyon, the shadows made it seem like night came a lot more quickly than it really did. As a result, it was already getting dark. The light from the campfire flickered across the woman's face, throwing her distinctive features into shadowy contrast as she lost herself in thought. Zeke couldn't help but stare; he had grown used to her beauty, but every now and then, it still hit him like a sledgehammer.

Finally, she said, "You're right. We have to do this. We could go back to Beacon and gather more adventurers, but that would take too long. How many caravans could they hit in that time? How many people would die while we played it safe?"

"Too many," Zeke said.

Abby nodded, "On that, we agree. So, what's the plan?"

"Uh..."

"Don't tell me you just want to rush them," she said. Seeing his expression, she hung her head. "That's it, huh? Just run in there, club swinging while I shoot them from that ridge?"

"I'm open to suggestions," Zeke said, looking sheepish. "And it's a mace."

"Whatever. You're really bad at this, you know," Abby teased.

Zeke shrugged, saying, "It's worked so far. Why change?"

Abby sighed, then said, "Okay—so, here's what we're going to do. We don't have a lot of options, what with there only being two of us—"

Pudge snorted.

"Okay, two and a half," she said. "But we can still be smart about this. You don't happen to have any ranged skills, do you?"

Zeke almost said he didn't, but then he remembered his tactics in the fungal forest where he'd first fought the troll shamans. There, he'd used his superhuman strength to launch lethal rocks at the monsters. And given the rocky nature of the canyon, Zeke had no reason to think that he couldn't do the same here.

"I have a pretty mean throwing arm," he said. She narrowed her eyes, and he said, "Baseball, remember? And I'm pretty strong, now. I bet I can chuck a rock hard enough to at least knock the drachnids senseless. Maybe even kill them."

Abby said, "I suppose that's a start."

Then, she started laying out her very simple plan. Zeke felt a distinct sense of relief that he didn't have to shoulder that burden. He wasn't stupid. He could grasp strategy well enough. However, Abby had the benefit of seven years of experience under her belt. More, where Zeke's plans always hinged upon his ridiculous constitution, Abby knew how to play it safe. And given the sheer magnitude of the threat arrayed against them, that was a necessity if they wanted to survive.

"Well, I think that's the best we can do, given the tools at our disposal," Abby said. "If only we had a holocaust cloak..."

"Or a wheelbarrow," Zeke said, grinning as he caught the reference.

"Wait—you know *The Princess Bride*?" she asked, obviously surprised.

"It was my mom's favorite movie," he said. "I've probably seen it a hundred times."

Abby returned his grin with a smile of her own, saying, "I knew I liked you. All that monster killing and traveling together aside, I don't think I could've trusted any man who wasn't a *Princess Bride* fan."

The two spent the next few minutes talking about the classic film, quoting their favorite lines. After a while, with the ghost of a smile still spread across his face, Zeke said, "It's hard to believe I'll never watch a movie again. I mean, movies and stuff were never a huge part of my life or anything, but... I don't know. It's still going to take some getting used to. I've been dead for over two years, but my time in the troll caves was... I don't know—the days, they kind of blended together, I guess. It didn't feel like two years. It might've even been a lot longer. I don't know."

"You're still grieving the life you lost," Abby said. "It happens. Some people never adjust completely."

"Did you?" Zeke asked, absently scratching a spot on Pudge's neck. The bear had found his place at Zeke's feet, a position from which he pleaded for scratches.

Abby rubbed the back of her neck, saying, "I don't know. Mostly? A lot of it just fades away. Like, I remember the important stuff, but the details feel like a dream."

"Honestly, I hope it's like that for me," Zeke said. "Most of it I don't want to remember. I just want to start fresh and live this life on my terms."

And he meant it, too. Back on Earth, his entire life had been lived according to someone else's whims. Specifically, his father had controlled everything about him, had molded him into whatever it was he had become. But now he was free. Now, he could be his own man. He could forge his own path, heedless of what anyone else wanted. It was a comforting notion, even if it was more than a little terrifying.

But the first step was to deal with the drachnids in the morning.

"Let's get some sleep," he said, standing and stretching. "Big day tomorrow."

Abby looked up, her face bathed in firelight as she said, "As you wish."

The pair shared a laugh, but even as Zeke found his way into the cottage and to the corner where he usually slept, he couldn't quite escape the meaning of those three words in the movie. Obviously, he didn't think Abby loved him. They barely knew each other. And from what she'd said, despite looking like she was of a similar age to him, he guessed that Abby was old enough to be his mother. So, there was no way she was flirting with him, was there? No—she was just being a good adventuring partner. A friend.

Rationally, he knew these things. But that didn't stop him from dwelling on it until unconsciousness overtook him.

43

ATTACK ON THE DRACHNIDS

"What are you doing?" asked Abby, cutting through Zeke's concentration. She leaned against the wall of the cottage, her forearms on her knees. Pudge lay beside her, his paws draped over her hip. For Zeke's part, he sat near the center of the cottage, a pile of discarded rocks beside him.

He looked up from the rock in his hand, saying, "Experimenting."

"It looks a lot like you're just staring at rocks," said the woman. It was nearly morning, and neither of them had gotten much sleep that night. Unlike Zeke, Abby hadn't even really tried, instead trusting her constitution to keep her alert. That was one of the many benefits of the new world; sleep wasn't nearly as necessary as it had been before. They needed a little—Abby more than Zeke, due to the differences in their stats—but in a pinch, they could push through that necessity with few repercussions.

Zeke said, "I'm putting runes on the rocks. If they work like they're supposed to, they'll explode when they hit something with a decent amount of force."

Abby eyed the pile of rocks beside Zeke; he had hundreds more in his spatial storage. Once they had a plan for dealing with the drachnids, they'd had nothing left to do except get ready. So, they'd spent most of the previous day preparing the intended battleground; after, he had spent an hour or so gathering rocks, with which he'd been toying all night.

"Wait, what?" she asked. "What kind of runes? You're a crafter?"

Zeke shrugged. "Sort of? You know I have an artisan path for runes," he answered. "It gives me some understanding of what different runes do. One of the guys who were hunting you had some interesting arrows on him. They were kind of weak, but there were these runes etched onto the arrowheads that when they hit, they caused this wave of . . . force."

"Concussion arrows," Abby said. She'd seen them before, but even though archery was her primary focus, she'd always discounted them. They were weak, only really useful against lower-level enemies.

"If that's what they're called," he went on. "I beefed up the rune a little, but it still wasn't very strong. Maybe it would stun a drachnid for a second, but it was still too weak."

"Yeah," Abby said. "That's the problem with trick arrows like that. They're an interesting concept, but they're not all that useful."

"Right," Zeke said, discarding his rock into the pile. "That's exactly what I thought. Until I found Julio's sword. Did you know it had the ability to catch fire?"

Abby rolled her eyes. "A party trick," she said. "He'd use it to impress women. He'd go into a bar and wave around his flaming sword, and inevitably, there'd be some naive girl who thought he was something special. By the time she'd realize he was a creep, it was too late. Or at least that's what I heard."

"Right," Zeke said, obviously uncomfortable with the subject. He was incredibly innocent at times, especially when the subject of women came up. Not that Abby blamed him; when she was his age, she hadn't been terribly confident around men, either. It was one of the reasons she'd ended up with her husband. In any case, Julio's antics had been mostly benign, if it wasn't for the fact that, on those occasions when he didn't manage to pick up some idiot girl, he would resort to other, less savory methods of satisfying his urges. Even when his victims survived—and that was rare enough, according to rumor—they were broken women. But Julio had been a powerful member of the guild, and as such, he'd been untouchable.

Until Zeke came along.

"Anyway, I decided to combine the two runes," Zeke said, drawing Abby away from her thoughts. "I also enhanced the glyph that governs mana capacity. It's kind of cobbled together, and it won't last more than a day or two before it becomes too unstable. I think the problem is that rocks just aren't good for this kind of thing, but it could just be my inexperience, I guess."

Abby eyed the pile of rocks. There were probably a hundred or so fist-sized stones there. "You're saying that that entire pile is . . . what? Magic grenades or something?" she asked.

"Something like that," he said. "But they're safe for now. You have to power them up before they'll work."

"But there aren't any markings on them," she said, fighting the urge to inspect the rocks more closely. If what Zeke claimed was true, then he'd just done something that nobody else could do. Well, that wasn't necessarily true. She'd heard about an alchemist in Salvation who specialized in magical bombs, but even if he was real and not just some story, all his skills probably revolved around it. For Zeke, though, it was almost an afterthought.

"Not really necessary," he said. "For temporary items like this? An external rune would be overkill. Besides, I don't really have any tools for that kind of thing."

Abby just shook her head. She'd known that he had some understanding of runes, but it seemed that his knowledge extended much deeper than she expected. It shouldn't have been all that surprising, given that he'd already demonstrated the ability to unravel a curse. Also, she knew from experience how much help a martial path could give an adventurer. Her own archery path hadn't just given her attacks more power; it had been a veritable injection of knowledge that had fine-tuned her entire approach to archery. Apparently, an artisan path was no different, albeit with a noncombat focus.

But then again, Zeke had already incorporated his knowledge of runes into combat, hadn't he? Abby wasn't certain, but he'd hinted that he could unravel curses while fighting. Without a skill, that was completely unheard-of, and it made her wonder how many truths that she had so far taken for granted weren't as ironclad as she'd been led to believe.

"So, they explode?" she asked, pushing those esoteric thoughts to the side. They were hours away from assaulting the drachnids, and she couldn't afford the distraction.

"I haven't tested them yet, but I think so," he said. "If I'd had another couple of days, I would've gone back a few miles and done some test runs. But I have a feeling we need to get this done as soon as possible, or we're going to get overrun."

That much was probably true. They'd been in their current location for only two days, and already, the drachnids had swarmed almost a half mile closer. It was as if they were reproducing at a rapid pace so they could replace the drachnids they'd already lost. Which was ridiculous. More likely, there was a warren of caves near the end of the canyon where the majority of the monsters lived.

"You're probably right," she agreed.

As dawn continued to creep closer, Zeke continued creating his runic rocks while Abby began her mental preparations. If the need arose, she could be combat ready in an instant. However, when time permitted, she liked to put herself in the right frame of mind for wholesale slaughter. It was a combination of focus and putting distance between her active mind and whatever part of her felt empathy for all living creatures. The drachnids were monsters who had murdered hundreds of people. She had seen the evidence. But that didn't mean she would enjoy killing them. At best, she would feel a sense of accomplishment for the success of the mission. At worst, she would dwell on thoughts of the sort of world where it was necessary to slaughter an entire community of sentient creatures.

Not that Abby would let it affect her. She was well past that. Any hesitation to do what was necessary had been scoured clean the moment she'd seen a monster kill an ally or butcher an innocent bystander. She had lost too many people. But she could never enjoy killing, even if she acknowledged its necessity. Even if she liked the rewards.

Finally, the sun rose. Pudge roused himself. And Zeke announced, "It's time. Are you ready?"

Abby nodded, gathering her bow. She stood, stretching sore muscles before saying, "Let's do it."

Zeke quickly sent the pile of rocks to his spatial storage before the trio—man, woman, and bear—exited the cottage. Abby smothered her fire, ending her [**Makeshift Camp**] skill, while Zeke dismissed the cottage. She would never get used to that, regardless of how many times she saw the small house poof into thin air. It was one more casual display of strength that Abby still hadn't grown accustomed to.

After making sure the campsite was clear, she, Zeke, and his companion began the mile-and-a-half-long walk to where they would begin their assault. The plan was simplicity in itself. At first, they would focus on ranged attacks, with Zeke taking the brunt of the attention. Once the drachnids swarmed, he would wade in and do his thing while she peppered them with arrows. In short, it was the same plan that they'd used countless times before, except that Zeke would begin the fight by throwing his runic rocks as opposed to simply charging in like some crazed berserker.

Besides, they'd spent the previous day preparing the intended battleground so that she could fire from a raised position, and Zeke could fight without getting overrun from all sides. It wasn't much—neither of them were combat engineers, after all—but Abby hoped it would be enough to make the difference they needed.

Abby wished they'd have had more options. If they'd had more people, they could've set up a real plan of attack. But they were just two adventurers, and thus, their options were limited. Three, if she counted Pudge, which she didn't. The bear cub was powerful for his level, but he was still only level seven. He couldn't take a single drachnid on his own, much less survive within a horde of the monsters. He wasn't useless—often, he finished off the monsters Zeke left maimed—but he wasn't self-sufficient yet, either. That was only a matter of time, though. Abby suspected that, eventually, the bear cub would grow to be just as powerful as any adventurer.

Eventually, they made their way to the rise where she would be positioned. The small man-made hill sloped down into a basin within the canyon. Along the downward slope were low walls they'd built with the intention of slowing the drachnids down. In the center of the basin was a huge pillar of rock, probably thirty feet wide and at least a hundred feet tall. It was covered in webs and pockmarked with tiny holes; Abby could see the small, furry forms of spiders scurrying along its facade.

"Do you wonder why all the drachnids are gathered up like this?" asked Zeke. "They've been like this for two days. Probably longer."

"I think they're massing for a strike," she said. "There's a pretty sizable mining village about forty miles away. San'gin, I think it's called. Maybe they're tired of hitting caravans."

It was a horrifying prospect, and it only cemented Abby's resolve. If there was one thing about her new life that she had no doubts about, it was her resolution to protect people who couldn't protect themselves. Certainly, there was a part of her that looked down on those people who refused to fight, but the rational part of her brain told her that not everyone was built for the life of an adventurer. The vast majority of people wanted only to live their lives in safety and comfort. Just because Abby could never be happy like that—she'd tasted that kind of life before, and it hadn't worked out well—didn't mean that nobody could.

"Then that's it, then," Zeke said. "We can't call this off now, even if we wanted to."

If they had nothing else in common, she and Zeke shared a need to do what was right, to protect those who couldn't protect themselves. And failing that, to avenge them. It was one of the reasons they were so comfortable together.

"Alright—I'm getting into position," he said. "Keep Pudge safe."

Then, he took off at a jog, careful to remain concealed from the horde of drachnids as he cut across the canyon floor. The plan, as simple as it was, required them to attack from different directions. If everything went the way they hoped, the majority of the monsters would swarm Zeke, who was tailor-made to survive that kind of situation. Meanwhile, she would rain arrows down upon them from afar. Pudge would remain with her because Zeke didn't think he could guarantee his companion's safety. Abby suspected that he'd convinced the bear to stay with her by asking the cub to protect her.

Idly, Abby reached down and scratched Pudge's neck, just where he seemed to like it. Otherwise, she remained still, watching the horde for any indication that she had been discovered.

None came. For long minutes, she watched diligently until, at last, Zeke began his assault.

The first explosion was powerful enough that Abby felt the vibrations, even hundreds of yards away. Zeke had lobbed the rock right into the middle of the horde, and where it had hit, a four-foot crater had suddenly appeared. Blood, gore, and pieces of drachnid geysered into the sky before raining down on the army of monsters. Only a second later, another rock sailed into their midst, exploding with impressive fervor. The effect was almost like a grenade had gone off, except instead of sending out deadly shards of metal that rode the concussive force of the blast, the rock was vaporized by the explosive combination of runes Zeke had etched upon them. More rocks fell among the monsters, each one taking a drachnid or two with it.

Instantly, Abby saw the issue with the rocks. They were effective, so long as they hit a monster directly. However, if Zeke's aim was even a little off, the blast radius was too small to truly injure the creatures. Luckily,

Zeke's claims of baseball prowess hadn't been mere boasts, and his skill quickly became apparent.

The only problem was that there were so damned many of the monsters that even firing the rocks as quickly as he could, his efforts made little difference. Soon, the monsters homed in on his location, and all at once, they surged toward him.

That was Abby's cue.

She rose, smoothly summoning a silvery arrow and firing. Her aim, guided by the instinctive understanding of archery granted by her martial path, her [**Gust of Wind**] skill, and more than seven years of experience, was unerring. Each conjured arrow slammed into a vital spot, felling a drachnid. With her concentrated fire along with Zeke's bombardment, the drachnids died in droves.

But it wasn't enough.

Soon, Zeke's bombardment petered out, and Abby knew that the drachnids had finally reached him. They'd paid a terrible price—dozens of the monsters lay dead, their pieces scattered across the basin. But there were so many that the horde seemed unfazed.

A contingent of drachnids broke free, angling in her direction. Abby smoothly shifted her focus, peppering them with arrows as they climbed toward her, skittering over the low walls she and Zeke had constructed. The walls served their purpose, slowing the creatures down, but she could fire only so quickly, and the charging monsters could cover ground in a hurry. Moments later, they were upon her.

Abby darted to the side, firing arrows as quickly as she could pull her bowstring. It was an impressive display of skill that she could hit anything at all, but her aim still suffered. Standing still, she had no trouble hitting vital spots, but those shots became far less fatal if they were even an inch off. The result was that the charging drachnids became pincushions for her conjured arrows, but they were merely wounded.

Luckily, that's where Pudge came in.

For all that both Abby and Zeke worried about the bear cub's safety, when push came to shove, he could become a vicious little killer. However, given his size, he fought more like an enraged badger than a traditional bear. His claws were razor-sharp, and they cut through the drachnids' thick, armor-like chitin with ease. And when he launched himself at their relatively unprotected faces, his viselike jaws went to work. The drachnids gave as good as they got, but Pudge had [**Leech Strike**] active, and he quickly healed from whatever wounds he took. If she'd had time to think, Abby would've once again mused at how overpowered that skill really was.

Meanwhile, Abby continued firing, one arrow after another, until, finally, the first monster reached her. It swiped at her with its talon-like fingers, narrowly missing her stomach. If it had connected, it would've disemboweled her, right then and there. And the last thing she wanted was to try to fight with her intestines hanging out. She'd been there before, and she never wanted to revisit that situation again.

Slipping her bow over her shoulder, Abby drew her hatchet. She didn't have any skills pertaining to the weapon. Nor did she have a path. But she did have skill and superhuman attributes. So, when the monsters closed within melee range, she went to work.

Abby excelled in agility and dexterity, but because the power of her primary skill, [**Gust of Wind**], was based on intelligence and used mana, she'd been forced to make some hard choices when it came to the allocation of stats. So, she had eschewed strength in favor of more intelligence and wisdom. That meant that, when it came to melee, she had adopted an acrobatic fighting style that utilized her greatest assets. It required immense skill and concentration, but it had been effective enough to see her through. She wasn't Zeke, but she could more than hold her own.

Ducking another attack, she swung the small hand axe in a horizontal slash. It ripped into the carapace that covered most of the drachnid's torso, but it didn't get deep enough to do any damage. However, the next three strikes, all in quick succession, reduced the hard chitin to a pulpy, bloody mess. And the fifth strike disemboweled the creature.

It screamed in pain, trying to bring its own claws into the battle. But it was too slow, its natural weapons finding only air. Abby leaped, using her momentum to add force to an overhand blow that quickly found the drachnid's forehead. It split open like a melon, the monster dying in an instant.

Abby was already moving, though. There were more drachnids bearing down on her, and she couldn't stop for even a second.

44

SLAUGHTER

"This was a big mistake," Zeke muttered as he stared down the horde of drachnids coming at him like a tidal wave of insectile legs, shiny black chitin, and murder. He hurled another of his runic rocks, and it collided with the lead drachnid's face, vaporizing half its torso along with the thing's grotesque head. It fell, only to be trampled by its fellow monsters.

Despite killing his target, Zeke swore in frustration. The rocks were powerful, but they weren't nearly as effective as he'd expected. If only he'd had a little more time to work on the runes, he felt confident that he could've increased the radius of destruction, but as it was, each rock was normally worth only a single kill. Maybe two, if a pair of drachnids were practically on top of each other. In short, it was far from the backbreaking barrage he'd hoped to achieve. Still, the rocks showed some promise; they were at least better than throwing unmodified stones, as he had in the troll caves. Zeke had a feeling that if he tried to repeat that underpowered technique against the drachnids, the rocks would do little to no damage. Even so, he wished his new creations had been a little more effective at thinning out the horde of monsters.

Through his bond with Pudge, he knew that Abby had engaged the enemy, as well, but when the bear cub got excited—and fighting monsters definitely did that—Pudge was a less-than-reliable source of information. What few impressions Zeke managed to fish out of the cub's thoughts were laced with so much battle rage that they were largely useless. Of course, the mere fact that anything came through was enough to let Zeke know that, for now, they were alive. That would have to be enough.

Zeke continued his bombardment, and with each throw, a drachnid fell. Not for the first time, he found himself marveling at the fact that his arm actually worked. Before he'd died, when his elbow had still been held together with titanium pins, throwing anything at all would've been a study in anguish and disappointment. More, it would've been grossly ineffective. But now? He was lobbing rocks more than two hundred yards, and he didn't even feel strained. In fact, he was more limited by the sight lines than his throwing ability.

But the wave of drachnids kept pushing forward, heedless of the fall of their brethren. Zeke had always known it would come down to a melee of close-quarter slaughter. No matter how effective his runic rocks were, he had only so many. Even now, his stock was running low. However, he'd positioned himself as well as he could at the mouth of a small cave—more of a crack in the canyon wall, really—so that he could be assaulted by only a couple of the horrible monsters at a time. Zeke and Abby had also built the area up, piling midsize rocks in order to further narrow the gap. So, when the drachnids finally crashed into him, he would be capable of holding his ground without being overwhelmed by sheer numbers.

Throwing one last rock that exploded only ten feet away, Zeke summoned his mace from his spatial storage. Even as his fingers wrapped around the worn leather grip, he felt a sense of overwhelming comfort. No matter what else happened in this crazy new world, this was something familiar. In fact, as he swung his bone-hafted mace in a two-handed grip, it felt like he was coming home.

The studded head crashed into an unlucky drachnid with enough force that its entire body was thrown aside. Even over the strange, insectile clicking that passed for speech among the drachnids, Zeke heard a sickening crack as the monster's neck snapped from the whiplash. Experience washed over him, but he couldn't enjoy it because an instant later, the rest of the drachnids were upon him.

Zeke's fighting style had both improved and devolved in the time since he'd found his way free of the troll caves. From a purely technical standpoint, he knew he'd made plenty of sacrifices. The sweeping strikes he employed against the drachnids would be next to useless against a better-trained foe. But for all their cunning, the spiderlike humanoids weren't overly skilled. In fact, despite their appearance, they fought more like beasts than sentient creatures. From an anthropological standpoint, the drachnids might have been on the cusp of creating a real society, but in terms of fighting style, they were woefully lacking.

That didn't mean that they weren't dangerous. Far from it. It was a similar danger to what Zeke might expect when fighting a horde of beasts, as opposed to an army of sapient creatures. However, what they lacked in refinement, they more than made up for in sheer ferocity and numbers.

Which was why Zeke had subtly changed his style. He didn't bother with feints. Nor did he use the quick, jabbing thrusts he had developed to deal with the more sophisticated troll warriors. Instead, he used long, loping strikes that, if they connected, could put a drachnid out of commission with a single hit. This had the unfortunate side effect of leaving him open to attack, which was why, only a minute into his battle, Zeke's leather armor was already shredded, and he was bleeding from what felt like a hundred wounds along his torso.

It hurt.

No, it went beyond pain and into the realm of torture, and in a way that would've had the old Zeke curled up in a weeping ball of agony. But the new Zeke took the pain as the simple price of doing business. He wasn't built to leap around like some kung fu master. He could have done it, sure. His agility and dexterity were incredibly high, just like the rest of his stats. Despite that advantage in stats, though, when he tried to employ a more acrobatic fighting style, he felt awkward and uncoordinated. Besides, this was a battle of attrition. He had plenty of energy right now, but he'd also barely made a dent in the drachnids' numbers. So, he'd made the decision to eschew the conventional wisdom that told him to avoid any and all attacks, instead letting his endurance, vitality, and the effects of [**Leech Strike**] see him through.

He didn't just stand still, though. Instead, it was a balancing act. Take the hits he could handle while avoiding the ones he couldn't. There were far more of the former than the latter, but every now and then, one of those drachnids would aim particularly well. Such was the case when one drachnid—a huge creature that was at least a head taller than any of the rest—swept an attack at Zeke. He leaned back, the thing's daggerlike claws narrowly missing the opportunity to rip his throat out. Zeke knew he could heal from most injuries, but he wasn't willing to test his limits by letting something like that connect.

His mace arced out, thudding into the big drachnid's chitinous natural armor. A spiderweb of cracks flowed from the impact, but it didn't shatter. Zeke mentally activated his **[Inspection]** skill, and he was soon rewarded by the creature's information flashing before his eyes.

Drachnid Alpha—Level 23

"Huh," Zeke muttered. "That's new."

Indeed, the rest of the monsters had been labeled as a mixture of drachnid drones, warriors, scouts, and burrowers. The drones usually were between levels fifteen and seventeen, with the warriors and scouts being a couple of levels higher. The burrowers had a much greater range, but none of them had been higher than level twenty. Strangely, though, the burrowers went down far more easily than any of the others, prompting Abby to label them as experience piñatas.

The new arrival was clearly on another level, though. At level twenty-three, its power was theoretically on the same tier as the troll warlord. But as he avoided another brutally powerful attack, returning fire with a sweeping strike of his own, Zeke couldn't help but feel a little disappointed. The second attack further compromised the chitin's integrity, and the third shattered it completely. The monster screeched in pain, but Zeke gave it no quarter. Four attacks later, it joined the growing pile of dead monsters at his feet.

Idly, as he continued to hold his ground against the surging drachnids, Zeke wondered if the ease with which he'd dispatched the alpha was due to its own shortcomings or if he'd just grown that much more powerful. He couldn't be sure, but he suspected it was his growing strength that had made things so much easier. After all, he'd gained a few levels since the fight with the troll warlord that had given him so much trouble. He'd also gotten a few achievements that had further enhanced his overall potency. Most of his stats had doubled since then, and the effect was a truly intoxicating level of power that let him punch far above his weight class.

How much more powerful would he get?

It was a worthwhile question to ask, especially considering that Abby's presence had given him some context into how unique he really was. Not only did he have advantages like his title as the Steward of the Crimson Tower, and all the perks that came with it, but he was also capable of fighting monsters twice his level and winning. More, when compared to Abby, despite being a couple of levels lower than her, he was in an entirely different category. Certainly, she was capable—incredibly so. And she had her strengths, especially when it came to dealing great damage from afar. But in terms of raw power, she might as well have been a child next to his inflated stats.

Zeke continued to fight, and gradually, he began to whittle down the horde of drachnids. Every now and then, he'd gain enough of a reprieve to loot the corpses before him; without that, there would have been a wall of dead arachnid bodies. Looting them with a touch and a mental command had reduced the corpses to piles of goo and dismembered body parts that, in turn, dissipated into nothingness after only a few minutes.

He fought mechanically, his every swing felling a drachnid. They were so close together that he couldn't miss, even if he tried. But on he fought, even as the weight of his actions pressed against his endurance. His muscles burned with the exertion. His chest heaved. And his mind became a muddled quagmire of disparate thoughts. For a while, he lost himself to it. Drachnid after drachnid fell before him, but he hardly noticed. One of the monsters was much like the last. Even the scattered alphas weren't enough to draw him out of it. They fell, the same as the rest, even if it took marginally more effort.

Zeke had felt himself descend into that exhaustion-induced state of mind before. In the troll caves, when he'd been climbing the spiraling ramp before he fought the troll warlord was the first time, but it had been repeated in the harpy-infested and ruined city of Tua'Ta'alar.

But even when he was in the old world, he'd had the ability to divorce his mind from whatever was happening around him. At first, it'd been a necessary tool to combat his father's constant abuse, both verbal and physical, but it had quickly infected his rigorous training, as well. It was always so easy to just space out while he worked himself to exhaustion. However, he'd quickly learned that it was a dangerous habit to get into. Real training required concentration, especially when it came to something like baseball, where even a minute degradation of technique could be the difference between a roaring success and abject failure. So, Zeke had been forced to learn when to turn his mind on and off, an ability that had come in handy while fighting hordes of semi-dangerous monsters—a great strategy right up until Zeke found himself sailing across the canyon and crashing into one of the stone pillars that dotted the ravine.

Zeke screamed as he felt his collarbone break, even as the chunks of rock dislodged by the impact rained down him. However, he didn't have time to think before a drachnid was on top of him, ripping into his belly. Pain turned to agony, and he lashed out, kicking the creature away. It was sheer luck that let him connect, and the thing went flying into the vastly reduced horde of drachnids that hadn't moved a muscle since the new arrival had attacked.

Thankfully, [**Leech Strike**] had been running when he'd kicked, and he felt a rush of vitality begin to stitch his collarbone back together. As the life energy did its work, Zeke picked himself up and quickly found his opponent, who was climbing back to its feet. A quick use of [**Inspection**] told him what he was facing.

Bara Kar, the Drachnid Champion—Level 25 (E)

Zeke didn't need to read the creature's name to know it was unique. Even if the force of its blow hadn't been enough to cement that in his mind, Zeke could see that this monster was a different breed altogether. For one, where the other drachnids looked like arachnid versions of centaurs, with spiderlike lower halves and mostly humanoid torsos, this creature was bipedal. On top of that, it was much smaller than its brethren—or maybe subordinates, given its level. In fact, it wasn't much bigger than Abby. It was also covered in segmented, chitinous carapace from the neck down. The ridges on its face were sharper and more pronounced than the other drachnids', too. In short, it looked like an entirely different, far more dangerous species.

But size didn't really correlate to strength, as far as Zeke could tell. And besides, he'd felt the thing's attack. More than that, he could barely even perceive its actions, it had moved so quickly. One second, he'd been mechanically mowing through the more mundane monsters, and the next, there was a flash of black claws. Then, he was sailing across the canyon.

Zeke rolled his shoulder as he glared at his opponent. Had the drachnids planned it? Had they intended to lull him into a false sense of superiority? Sacrificing so many just to make him drop his guard seemed pointlessly cruel. Or had he finally done enough damage to warrant a response from their big hitter? Zeke had no way of knowing.

The other drachnids backed away from the champion, Bara Kar, further confusing Zeke. Only a quarter of them remained, but when combined with the champion, they could've easily overwhelmed him. Such was the difference its obvious power could make.

With one hand, the champion banged against its carapace with enough force that Zeke could hear it even fifty yards away. Then, it let out a screech, followed by a series of clicks. Zeke didn't understand the creature's language, but he got the meaning well enough.

Zeke retrieved Voromir from where it had fallen when he'd collided with the rock pillar. Then, he flexed his shoulder again, testing it. Good enough.

With a roar, he accepted the champion's challenge.

45

SHATTERED

Zeke darted forward, his mace held high, and with each step, clouds of dust and gravel erupted into the air. The drachnid champion didn't move, instead remaining rooted in place, its long limbs vibrating with unspent need.

Zeke didn't care to even notice. He was riding high off nearly two years of unmitigated success. Certainly, he'd experienced his fair share of failures, but in the end, he'd always managed to come out on top. Whether it was trolls, harpies, or drachnids, they'd all ended up falling before him. So, despite the elite monster being a new classification of threat, he was understandably confident that he could win.

His confidence was woefully misplaced.

The mace sliced through the air in an overhand swing that Zeke meant to crush the champion, but at the last instant, the monster swayed to the side, slapping the deadly weapon with the flat of its palm. Voromir crashed into the ground, stones cracking from the impact. Unbalanced, Zeke could scarcely react when the champion lashed out, its claws digging furrows in his side. They stopped only when they hit his ribs.

The creature wasn't finished, though. Twice more, its hands blurred, and when Zeke finally managed to disengage, his torso had been sliced to ribbons. What's worse, he hadn't managed to hit the monster, so [**Leech Strike**] remained impotent and unused. He gritted his teeth, his fingers tightening around the worn leather of Voromir's grip.

For a long moment, the pair of combatants stared at each other. The champion's face was impassive, though there was a glimmer of hatred in its multifaceted eyes. It wasn't just protecting its people. It wanted revenge. The same desire was reflected in Zeke's own expression; he would never forget the cocooned bodies he'd found, the people he hadn't saved. More, the bodies he hadn't found, but he knew had to exist, haunted his thoughts.

It was an irrational line of thought. He knew he wasn't responsible for these people. They'd been strangers, most dying before he'd even made it out of the troll caves. Judging by the state of decay, some might've even been killed before he'd been reborn into this new world. Their deaths were a tragedy, certainly, but they had nothing to do with him.

But reason was one thing, and it had its place. However, that kind of thinking went out the window after spending entire days stacking corpses, after seeing the desiccated and bloodless bodies of men, women, and children who'd been treated as nothing more than food.

That same reason might have told him that the drachnids couldn't be blamed, that they were little more than animals who were merely acting according to their nature. But Zeke had seen plenty of evidence that that wasn't true. For one, there was a nearby forest full of animals that could've sustained the drachnids, but they had gone out of their way to raid the caravans and hunt human beings. Maybe it was easier. Perhaps it was part of their nature. But if that was the case, it only meant that they were a threat that needed to be put down.

And then there was the fact that they were at least semi-sapient. They'd created a crude sort of society, which spoke of self-awareness and intelligence that exceeded that of mere animals. So, shouldn't they be held accountable for their actions? Shouldn't they be treated just like a murderous band of bandits?

But putting aside all the moral justifications, Zeke was confronted with one simple fact. He wanted to win. That his first attack had been so summarily defeated—almost as if it was an afterthought—was a source of burning frustration and unremittent anger. But he'd been fighting for his life on a daily basis for the better part of two and a half years, so he didn't let his frustration overwhelm him. Nor would he make the same mistake twice. So, he stood there, mace at the ready, and let his impressive vitality as well as the last dregs of life energy he'd stolen via [**Leech Strike**] go to work on his wounds. It didn't close the surgical gashes—not completely—but it did stem the bleeding, which would have to be enough.

The champion, its claws dripping Zeke's blood, cocked its head to the side as it watched him. Its movements were twitchy, and every second or so, a whistling click would escape from between its blackened lips. Now that he was closer, Zeke got a better look at the creature's pale, maggoty white skin and the purple-black shimmers of its carapace. Thoroughly disgusted by the monster, Zeke wanted to look away, but he didn't dare so much as a blink. The thing was fast enough to take advantage of even that minute of a distraction.

The face-off lasted for almost thirty seconds, and all the while, the other drachnids surrounded them. Zeke had hoped that Abby would be able to help, but there was no way she'd get through so many of the monsters in time to lend any aid. No—he was on his own.

But then again, he was used to it.

Suddenly, the champion blurred forward, its claws singing through the air. Zeke reacted on instinct, ducking under the first attack and leaping away from another, but the elite monster kept coming, a whirlwind of black claws. Zeke tried to fight back. He tried to give as good as he got. And he managed to land a couple of strikes, but they were weak and ineffectual. Even so, they were enough to keep him on his feet as [**Leech Strike**] tended to his wounds with an influx of stolen vital energy.

The problem was that Zeke's proficiency with his mace was that of a brute, using his stats to overwhelm anyone in his way. On a purely statistical basis, he could very nearly keep up with the champion. Certainly, the thing was faster, but as the fight went on, Zeke realized that the champion's speed wasn't that much greater than his own. However, it knew precisely how to use its speed to its advantage. Where Zeke's idea of technique was just to swing his mace faster or harder, the champion was well versed in feints, blocks, and parries. It moved with brutal efficiency, making Zeke pay for his every mistake.

In short, the champion was a better fighter than him, and though that was nothing new, it was the first time one of his opponents had the stats to take advantage of the huge gap in fighting proficiency.

So, after every exchange, Zeke picked up at least one more wound until, after a few minutes, his leather armor had been completely shredded, and his body wasn't much better off. The majority of the lacerations were shallow, but there were a few that had done real damage. It would've been worse if the champion chose to press the fight, but when Zeke disengaged—always a tricky proposition—it let him retreat, though it never allowed the distance between them to grow more than a few dozen feet.

"You're toying with me," Zeke muttered, clutching his side after one such retreat. The other drachnids shifted, allowing him to back away. "You like playing with your food."

It didn't respond, aside from a few rapid clicks that echoed through the canyon, but then again, it didn't need to. Zeke could see the malice in the thing's alien eyes. The cruelty. His own anger burned ever hotter.

But fury couldn't win this fight. Nor could brute strength. He had to think. He had to make a plan. The issue was that Zeke didn't really have any other assets to bring to bear. Abby and Pudge couldn't make a difference; they were halfway across the canyon, and there was the remnant of the army of drachnids between them. Besides, they were dealing with their own problems, as evidenced by the steady stream of experience he'd been getting the whole time.

Aside from his physical gifts, what did Zeke really have? He didn't want to use [**Heart of the Berserker**]; it was a last-ditch kind of skill that would leave him weakened after it ran its course. So, even if it made the difference against the champion—and he wasn't sure it would—he'd still have to deal with the rest of the drachnids while coping with the penalties that came with the skill's use. That didn't bode well for his survival.

He still had a few runic rocks in his spatial storage, but even if he managed to hit the incredibly quick champion, he questioned whether or not it would do much good. Its armor-like carapace was hard; even the few hits he'd managed to land hadn't done more than a superficial degree of damage. So, the rocks weren't good for anything more than a distraction.

As he considered his options, Zeke attacked once again. It didn't end any better than his previous attempts, but he was afraid that if he left it for too long, the elite monster would decide to bring the fight to him. Zeke wasn't sure he could survive that, and even if he did, it wouldn't be for long. So, he went through the motions, his mind searching for something—anything—to give him an advantage.

Zeke hopped back, narrowly avoiding a claw aimed at his throat. It had connected, but only barely, tracing a red line across his neck. Behind him, he could feel the rock pillar he'd been knocked into earlier in the fight. It wasn't solid rock; like all the other pillars in the canyon, it was honeycombed with holes that housed the ravine's native spiders. Zeke put some distance between himself and the column of rock; the last thing he needed was to be swarmed by the smaller spiders. Such a distraction would get him killed.

Predictably, the champion maintained the same degree of distance, eventually stopping next to the column. That's when Zeke attacked, a plan suddenly blossoming in his mind. After a furious exchange of blows, during which Zeke actually managed to hit the champion a couple of times, he retreated again. The champion remained in place, waiting.

It was almost too easy.

Zeke's hand was a blur as he peppered the area with his runic rocks. The first one took the champion in the chest, but predictably, it didn't do much good. As far as Zeke could tell, it didn't even stun the creature. So, when he kept throwing them, it just looked at him, cocking its head in curiosity—especially when the majority of them missed.

Seventeen stones, seventeen explosions—and nothing happened. Zeke cocked his arm back, then let loose with his last one. If it didn't work, he would have to run. He knew he couldn't beat the champion. Not with the way things were. He had to change the playing field, and if he failed, his only chance of survival lay in retreat—and Zeke was less than optimistic about his chances if he turned tail and ran. Surely, the champion was fast enough to chase him down.

Besides, the idea of running away didn't sit right with him. He would do it if necessary, but that didn't mean he had to like it.

That last stone hit the column, and for a long second, nothing happened. Then, finally, with an earsplitting crack, everything changed.

The column beside the champion shattered under its own weight, falling directly onto the elite monster. It was so surprised that it didn't move, even with tons of rock falling toward it. Zeke sprang back as the hundred-foot pillar of rock crumbled atop the champion. Even so, he caught a couple of strays himself, and they nearly knocked him senseless. Still, he maintained enough consciousness to get clear of the fallen pillar.

Once, Zeke had seen a building demolition on television. Some stadium that had been replaced was being turned into a parking lot for its successor, so it had had to go. The huge arena had been brought down with strategically placed explosives that, when they were detonated, weakened the structure to the point where it fell in on itself. When it did, it had thrown up a cloud of dust that blanketed the area for almost a mile in every direction. The collapse of the pillar was like that, just on a smaller scale.

Dust and debris filled the air, giving Zeke the opportunity to quickly kill a few stray drachnids and heal himself via [**Leech Strike**] before descending upon the pile of rocks and what he hoped was a buried champion.

Zeke picked his way through the debris, homing in on where he thought he'd last seen the monster. Climbing over the rocks, he quickly found his quarry, half buried under a pile of man-size boulders. Only its torso was exposed, and it looked like nothing so much as a trapped wild animal.

Its claws scraped against the rock, digging deep grooves but doing little good. With enough time, maybe it could work its way free. But judging by all the blood and its shattered carapace, Zeke didn't think it had a shot at survival. For a few long moments, he watched the thing's desperate attempts—and there was a part of him that felt a cruel satisfaction at the creature's suffering.

It made Zeke sick, that feeling. He didn't have an issue with killing, especially when it came to survival. If something attacked him, he would fight. And he would win. Usually, that meant killing. He'd come to terms with that. The same attitude extended to the protection of innocents. But feeling satisfaction at another creature's pain and suffering? That was wrong, and he wanted nothing more than to excise that dark, shadowy part of his soul that felt it. It was a part of him, though, and the best he could do was to push it aside.

Doing just that, Zeke stepped forward, raised his mace, and went to work on easing the monster's obvious suffering. It took seven full-strength strikes to the champion's head before the monster succumbed, and a flood of experience flowed into Zeke. Doing so made one simple fact clear—he'd never stood a chance against the champion in a straight-up fight. Without the trick with the pillar, he'd have been soundly defeated. He would've ended up in one of those cocoons as food for the other drachnids.

It was a sobering thought, and it shattered the aura of invincibility he'd been cultivating since leaving the troll cave. But that just meant he needed to get stronger. Faster. He needed to be better, or else he wouldn't survive. So, after bending down and looting the champion, he took only a moment to watch its corpse deflate as its valuable bits suddenly disappeared into his spatial storage before hefting his mace and getting back to the extermination of the drachnids.

46

INTO THE MAW

Zeke was on his last leg. Literally. His fight with the drachnid champion had torn his right thigh to shreds; strips of meaty muscle hung from it like bloody ribbons of flesh. Normally, that wouldn't be much of an issue, considering his rapid rate of regeneration, especially when the healing was aided by the influx of vitality that came with [**Leech Strike**]. However, there was something pressing against his regeneration, blocking the majority of his ability to heal. Some had trickled between the gaps—enough to stanch the bleeding, at least—but the flesh stubbornly refused to knit back together.

Poison, probably. He'd felt the tingling numbness a few times during the fight, but he'd been so focused that he'd summarily ignored it. Now, though, he could think of little else, especially considering that he was facing a veritable army of drachnids who were howling—or screeching, really—for his head.

"Guess they didn't like me killing their champion," he mused, his voice little more than an inaudible mutter amid the screeches and clicks that characterized the drachnids' speech.

Zeke considered the loot he'd gotten from the champion. In addition to the typical smattering of carapace, faceted eyes, and teeth he usually got from the drachnids, he had also received an Intact Poison Gland, Carapace of the Drachnid Champion, and Claws of the Spider Lord. It was a good haul, as far as he could tell, though he couldn't spare the attention to examine any of it more closely because all at once, the army of drachnids surged forward.

If Zeke's fighting style had depended on movement, he would've died right there. However, because he was used to simply planting his feet and meeting strength with strength, he managed to hold his own, despite the fact that he couldn't put any weight on his wounded leg. His mace was a blur as he blocked, parried, and struck back against the tide of arachnids, the strength of his mighty blows enough to crack their thick, armor-like carapaces, destroy their ridged faces, or detach their insectile limbs.

But like with the champion, he didn't come out unscathed. Slowly, his lack of mobility began to show itself, and he accumulated a host of shallow wounds. Alone, they weren't enough to slow Zeke down. But after ten? Fifteen? Even twenty? Anyone would feel that effect.

The only saving grace was that his [**Leech Strike**] continued to work, though at a near-crippled level. Where before each landed strike flooded him with a veritable tide of vital energy, the poison reduced it to a mere stream. It was unequal to the task of dealing with the totality of his wounds, but it still managed to take the edge off and keep him from succumbing due to blood loss.

Zeke was exhausted, though. Not only had he spent the better part of that morning tirelessly bludgeoning a swarm of bloodthirsty drachnids, leaving hundreds of the creatures dead, but he'd also fought the most difficult opponent he'd ever faced. He had barely escaped his battle with the champion alive, much less unscathed. And now, he was back to fighting the horde of spiderlike humanoids again, with scarcely a break in between. His arms were like lead, and his chest heaved like a bellows.

Until that point, Zeke hadn't realized how much he'd relied on [**Leech Strike**] to see him through. On the surface, it wasn't a very powerful skill. It didn't add much damage to his attacks, and without his massive strength driving it, the amount of vital energy wouldn't have been significant enough to heal more than minor wounds. However, because its healing effect was percentage based, its effects became overpowered to the extent that it didn't merely heal wounds. It also fed him energy enough to stave off exhaustion. But with its effects greatly reduced by the champion's poison, Zeke had begun to see just how much he'd taken his nearly limitless energy for granted.

But still, through exhaustion and pain, he fought on—because there was no alternative. It was either that or be overwhelmed by the monsters. And he hadn't fought for as long as he had to simply give up to some overgrown spiders. So, summoning every ounce of his willpower, he bent himself to the task of extermination.

Every blow felled a drachnid. Whether he faced warriors, drones, scouts, or burrowers, he didn't give an inch. He even killed a smattering of alphas who, after his fighting the champion, didn't really live up to their name. Slowly, he made progress—picking up plenty of injuries along the way. Zeke ignored them, instead splitting his focus between fighting the battle and wrestling with the steady stream of vital energy he siphoned from the drachnids.

It wanted to spread out through his mana channels to equally attend to his many wounds. Zeke wouldn't let it, though. It was like wrestling with a thousand wet noodles, each with a mind of their own, but through an effort of will, he managed to gradually redirect them into a mighty river that led to his ruined thigh.

It met a dam of pure, malevolent energy. The poison, unless Zeke was grossly mistaken. The vital energy battered against it, eroding it bit by bit, but it was a potent barricade, and it wouldn't be pummeled into submission so easily.

Seconds passed into minutes, and minutes passed into more than an hour, and still, Zeke pressed on. Hundreds of drachnids fell before him, but he paid them little heed. His mind was instead occupied by a different battle, one against an ephemeral blockade of hostile energy. He pushed the energy into a more concentrated stream, the resulting density digging into that poisonous dam. It cracked, a tiny, barely noticeable thing that soon spiderwebbed across the entire blockade.

Then it began to crumble.

Bit by bit, it fell apart, but Zeke knew—whether by instinct or via some arcane knowledge he'd picked up during his fight, he couldn't be sure—that if he let up for even a moment, it would rebuild itself. Then, he'd have to start all over again. So, he continued his internal battle, even while he mindlessly waged war against the swarm of drachnids.

Zeke lost track of time. One enemy blended into the next. Whether it was the dam of poisonous energy or the spiderlike monsters, it didn't matter. Zeke knew only the battle, and slowly, he began to win. Even as the monsters thinned, the last vestiges of the poison broke down, dissipating into harmless motes. Suddenly, the trickle of vital energy became an inevitable tide, washing away even that and flooding him with energy and healing.

With every blow, Zeke's wounds healed. His once-ruined leg became whole, the ribbons of flesh clinging together until they became muscle. Over that new, exposed muscle crept new skin, covering it in its protective embrace. Minor wounds across Zeke's body followed suit, closing and healing, bit by bit, blow by blow, until, at last, he stood whole. The process took hours, during which he'd continued his war on the drachnids, but in the end, he stood victorious over both the horde of monsters and the wounds inflicted by the champion.

He stood there, feeling both exhausted and full of vitality, all at the same time. His skin crawled with unspent energy, a jittery feeling not all that dissimilar from what he'd feel if he'd been drinking coffee all day. But as fresh as his body might feel, his mind swam in a sea of fatigue—and for good reason. The battle had been as much mental as physical, and he'd worn himself out on both ends. It was only because of the surge in vitality from [**Leech Strike**] that he'd managed to remain upright.

At some point during his battle, Pudge had joined him. Zeke glanced down to see the bear cub, who had a particularly long insectoid appendage in his mouth. Pudge shook it, looking like nothing so much as a dog with an overlarge toy.

"Gross," came Abby's voice. Zeke turned and saw her picking her way through the piles of dead drachnids. Quite a few had silvery arrows in them, but even the ones Zeke saw were rapidly dissipating into motes of mana that then faded away into nothingness. Abby's attention was on Pudge, who seemed to be enjoying himself quite a bit. "And kind of cute, too. You know, if it wasn't for all the murder and whatnot."

The slim blonde approached, asking, "You okay? You seemed like you were in another world for a while. And you ruined another set of armor, by the way."

Zeke looked down at his shredded leather breastplate. It was barely hanging together, and his pants were in a similar state of disrepair. The only pieces of his gear that remained unaffected—aside from his stalwart mace, Voromir, of course—were his boots. But even they hadn't escaped the battle without damage; his left boot—and his calf, he supposed—had a claw driven clean through it. Zeke bent down and yanked it out. Abby winced at the disgusting squelch that came with it.

"I'm alright," Zeke said. "I got poisoned for a minute, though. I had to deal with that for a while."

"Of course you did," she said, shaking her head, her high ponytail swinging back and forth. "Which one poisoned you, though? I was hit a couple of times, and I didn't notice anything."

That's when Zeke noticed that Abby's armor was a little worse for wear, as well. She had a few long gashes along her midriff, exposing the skin beneath her leather breastplate, as well as a couple on her arms and thighs. She even had a small splash of blood tracing a line along her cheek.

"Are you hurt?" Zeke asked, eyeing the evidence of Abby's wounds.

"I'm good," she said. "That skill of yours is really handy. I don't think I'd have made it without it. Pudge definitely wouldn't have, the little berserker. No sense of self-preservation. Just all attack, all the time."

Vaguely, Zeke recalled feeling Pudge's pain through their bond, but he'd been so focused on dealing with the poison that he hadn't paid it much attention. Luckily, the bear cub was durable and had access to [Leech Strike], otherwise he wouldn't have survived. Zeke didn't even want to think about that, but he couldn't help himself. His bond with the bear cub was more than what one would expect between a person and a pet. They were companions, and Zeke could feel emotions and thoughts through their bond. Their souls were intertwined in a way he couldn't even begin to understand, and his stomach twisted itself into knots when he thought of going on with his life should the cub die.

Abby raised an eyebrow. "So?" she prompted.

"What?" Zeke asked, jerking himself from his contemplation of the Soul Bond.

"What poisoned you?" she asked.

"Oh," Zeke said, turning around. At some point, he'd moved about forty yards away from the fallen pillar. In that space, there were dozens of drachnid corpses, but around the pillar was clear, and the part of the champion's body that hadn't been crushed by the falling rocks was still visible. Zeke pointed, saying, "That."

Abby stared at it, obviously examining with her inspection skill. She gasped, saying, "That . . . t-that was an elite."

Zeke ran his hand through his hair—or at least, he tried to. He got only a few inches before his fingers got tangled up in the blood and gore that had suffused his locks. "Hit like a freaking truck," he said. "Faster than me, too. If it wasn't for that big rock pillar, I doubt I'd have survived."

That much was true, and Zeke knew precisely how lucky he was to have come out of that fight alive. Thinking about how close he'd come to dying, Zeke couldn't help but shiver a bit. But amid that natural fear of mortality was a sense of pride. He'd faced that monster, and he'd won. Sure, he'd cheated a little, but that didn't really matter, did it? No. All that really mattered was that he'd survived while his enemy hadn't.

Abby let out a harsh laugh, saying, "I guess I shouldn't be that surprised at anything you do anymore. Fighting an elite at level thirteen? Sure. Why not? That's totally normal."

Zeke shrugged. "Not like I sought it out," he said. "It kind of just ambushed me."

"That's what I'm saying, though," Abby said, shaking her head in disbelief. "If an elite ambushed me, I wouldn't last more than a second. It would rip me to pieces without even slowing down. But you killed one. You're two levels lower than me, and you beat it. That's so far outside of normal that . . . that . . . I don't even know!"

She ended with a huff.

Zeke had no idea how to respond. In his old life, before he'd died, he had dealt with that kind of thing before. When he was twelve, he was playing on a team with sixteen- and seventeen-year-olds—and excelling, too. People had been gawking at his ability to exceed external expectations all his life. So, it wasn't really all that different when his actual power exceeded what someone might expect from his level. He should've been used to it. But the way Abby looked at him—almost like he was a different species altogether—unnerved him in a way nothing ever had before.

"Whatever," she said. "I don't suppose you saw the queen anywhere, did you? Maybe she's buried under another pile of rock somewhere?"

Zeke managed a grin, saying, "Nope."

"Fine," Abby said. "Then, we've come this far, right? Might as well end this."

Zeke couldn't agree more.

Even though looting the drachnids required only a touch and a mental command, there were enough of them that it still took more than an hour to clear the bodies. After that, Zeke wrangled Pudge away from the puddles of gore, and the three of them made their way back to the basin. Behind the giant pillar at its center was a gaping hole, yawning like the maw of some gargantuan beast.

"Well, that's not ominous at all," Abby muttered. "Was that there before?"

Zeke shrugged. "I have no idea," he said. "Maybe?"

Before, the basin had been flooded with so many drachnids that it was more than possible that the hole had been hidden by the press of arachnid bodies—especially given that they'd been some distance away when they'd scouted the horde. Now, though, there was only a scattering of corpses, most of which had been blown apart by Zeke's runic rocks.

"Don't suppose you have something else up your sleeve, do you?" Abby asked, glancing in his direction. "Maybe a nuclear warhead we can just drop into that hole?"

Zeke answered, "If I had a couple of weeks, I might be able to put something together . . ."

Abby gaped at him, and Zeke laughed. She punched him in the shoulder, saying, "I wouldn't put it past you. Seriously, though—any ideas on how to tackle whatever's in there?"

"Not a clue," he said. "I'm not usually much for plans, honestly."

"You can say that again," said Abby. Pudge snorted in agreement. "Your big plan for dealing with an army of drachnids was to throw some rocks at them."

"But it worked, didn't it?" he said.

"Only because you're a monster," she muttered. Then, she gestured to the gaping hole. "So, I guess you want to just climb down there and pummel the queen into submission, huh?"

Zeke said, "If it ain't broke . . ."

With a huff, Abby said, "Fine. Whatever. But you're going first."

47

THE DRACHNID QUEEN

Peeking over the edge and directly into the yawning maw, all Zeke could see was darkness. He asked, "How far down do you think it is?"

Abby massaged the back of her neck, answering, "Like I know. You have better vision than me. Drop a rock and count. I think it's like two and a half seconds for the first hundred feet. Three and a half for double that. I don't want to do the math if it's deeper than two hundred feet."

"How the hell do you know that?" Zeke asked, eyeing her in disbelief.

Abby didn't want to answer. In fact, she wanted nothing more than to forget everything about her former life. She'd made so many mistakes, both in her personal and professional lives, that she knew she would be better off if she left it all in the past.

"I minored in physics in college," she told the big man. At a few inches under six feet, Abby was a bit above average height, for a woman. Zeke still towered over her, but his size wasn't merely limited to height. Broad shouldered and narrow waisted, he had rippling muscles for days, though he wasn't nearly as bulky as Vladimir had been. And with his armor all ripped to shreds, Abby could see almost everything, which only served to remind her just how lonely she'd been for the past couple of years.

"What?" Zeke asked, noticing her stare, and reminding Abby just how clueless the man really was. Boy, really. He was barely twenty years old, which meant that Abby was old enough to be his mother, even if she had the body of a woman in her midtwenties.

"You really need to get some better armor," she said, dragging her eyes away. "You're half naked again."

At least he looked embarrassed at the reminder. It would've been adorable if he hadn't been covered in drachnid blood.

Zeke flashed a shy grin, saying, "This was the last of the armor we took from Julio and his guys, so I don't really have much of a choice for now." He glanced over the lip of the sinkhole, adding, "Besides, I have a feeling that I'd just ruin another set when we hit the queen, anyway."

"Because you don't know how to dodge," she muttered. Toward the tail end of the fight against the drachnid horde, Abby had seen what passed for Zeke's fighting style. The best that could be said for it was that it was effective, though that effectiveness was more due to the synergy between his ridiculous stats and his primary skill, [**Leech Strike**]. He would parry the odd blow, and he attempted to dodge, but more often than not, he simply took the hits and trusted in his boosted regeneration. The strategy allowed him to deliver some truly devastating blows, but at the cost of taking plenty of damage. It was no wonder he'd struggled with the elite; having his regeneration cut down was one of the only effective strategies against that monstrous man.

"I know how to dodge!" Zeke insisted, sounding slightly offended at her assertion. Then, he looked down at his ragged armor and conceded, "I just . . . I'm just not that good at it, I guess."

"Understatement," Abby muttered. "We could take a couple of days to regroup. I see you got a level."

Zeke nodded, saying, "Already allocated the points, too. But I'm as close to a hundred percent as I'm going to get. Might as well get this thing finished."

Abby didn't respond. Instead, she looked over the lip of the pit. Down there was the queen, and unless Abby missed her guess, it was at least an elite, like the champion Zeke had fought. The thing had very nearly killed him, and if he hadn't cheated the fight by dropping a few tons of rock on top of the monster, it would've ended Zeke's story, right then and there. The young man had all the advantages, with stats that Abby suspected could rival some of the guild's max-level adventurers. And still, he'd very nearly died. So, what business did she have pitting herself against a monster like the queen, who was at least equal to the champion in terms of power?

She hated that question almost as much as she hated that it pointed out her very real deficiency in power. Abby had never considered herself exceptional. Above average for her level, certainly. Maybe even good. But she was still only level fifteen, and she couldn't help but wonder if she could even scratch a boss-tier monster, much less contribute to killing one. She had no illusions about how it would have ended if she'd have been the one to fight the elite-tier champion. Abby knew she would have been ripped into tiny bits in a matter of seconds.

But Abby wanted more.

She hated her own weakness, and if she wanted to do anything about it, she knew she couldn't shy away from deadly challenges. If nothing else, Zeke had taught her that much. Abby had spent far too long skating through her new life. Despite her assertions that she wanted to progress, she had played it safe, only taking on challenges she knew she could overcome. That wasn't enough. Danger begot progress—of that, she was certain. And what was more dangerous than a level fifteen attacking an elite- or even boss-tier monster?

"Fine," she said. "You have a rope in that spatial storage of yours? Or do we need to free-climb?"

"I was kind of hoping you'd have one in your pack," Zeke admitted.

"Nope," she said.

Zeke huffed in annoyance, then stowed his mace away. It simply disappeared from his hand, deposited into the cellar of that summoned cottage of his. A second later, Pudge climbed onto Zeke's back, his sharp claws digging into Zeke's flesh. He winced, but he otherwise didn't acknowledge the wounds.

Masochist, Abby thought, shaking her head.

"You good, buddy?" Zeke said, looking back at his Soul-Bound Companion. That was yet another oddity about Zeke; Abby had heard about skills that let people tame animals and other monsters. However, Zeke didn't have any skills. He'd simply created one on the fly. Pudge let out a grunt of acknowledgment. "Alright then. Here we go."

Then, Zeke started climbing down. The pit's walls were rough, so there were plenty of handholds, and the going was reasonably quick. Meanwhile, Abby retrieved a rope from her pack, secured it to a nearby boulder, then tossed the other end over the edge. The climb down went quickly, and before long, she'd made it to the bottom, barely beating a clearly annoyed Zeke.

"What?" she asked innocently.

"You did have a rope," Zeke growled as Pudge dislodged himself from his back. "Do you have any idea how annoying of a climb that was? And it was closer to two hundred feet."

Abby grinned, shrugging as she patted him on the shoulder. She said, "Don't be like that. Climbing builds character."

For a moment, Zeke seemed fit to burst. Then, it all faded away, and he laughed, shaking his head. "Touché," he said. "Let's go kill a spider queen."

"Drachnid, but yeah," Abby corrected, pulling her bow off her shoulder. With a thought, she summoned an arrow. Beside her, Zeke summoned his bone club from his spatial storage, and Pudge . . . well, Pudge just stood there looking as cute and cuddly as a murderous bear cub still covered in gore could look. Abby gestured down the tunnel that branched off from the pit's floor, saying, "After you."

Zeke took the lead, grumbling, "Why does it always have to be caves?"

The trio stalked forward as silently as they could, and Abby found herself impressed with Zeke's stealth ability. He didn't have a skill for it, but he was light on his feet and made little noise. He was almost as undetectable as Abby, who was entirely silent. Even Pudge, who waddled along behind them, was incredibly quiet.

The tunnel itself was rough-hewn and rugged, but it was clearly unnatural. It had been dug, probably by the woefully inept drachnid burrowers that she'd dubbed experience piñatas. At least they had some use, she mused. Gradually, the slight decline led down into the earth, the air growing more and more stale with every step. It was still breathable, but it tasted wrong. Inert, almost. And there was a hint of something rotten clinging to everything.

"This is probably a huge mistake," she muttered, eliciting yet another grunt from Zeke. He really wasn't the talkative type. Probably for the best, she thought—she wasn't exactly the best conversationalist, even when she wasn't stalking through an underground tunnel that likely housed a monster that could and would probably kill her. "Fun times."

Not for the first time, she wondered what the old Abby would've said about her new life. She probably would've been horrified. But then again, Abby hadn't been the adventurous type back then. In fact, she'd been so danger averse that she'd married a horrible, abusive alcoholic just because he provided financial stability. And eventually, that decision had killed her when, drunken and arguing with her, her husband had lost control and wrapped their car around a telephone pole. Abby had died instantly. She could only hope that her asshole husband had followed suit. Maybe, one day, she could find him in the new world and put an arrow through his eye. That might make things better. Maybe. A little.

While she missed her friends and family, particularly her sister, she still considered her death to be the best thing that had ever happened to her. On Earth, she'd been a former middle school guidance counselor who was rapidly approaching middle age, but here? She had the body of her twenty-year-old self, which would've been enough of an endorsement of her new life, all by itself. But she was also free from her husband, who represented the worst mistake she'd ever made. To top it all off, she was practically a superhero. And she could get stronger. She could control her own fate. All it took was a willingness to face down death, time and time again, and come out on top. She would make that deal every single time.

So, she continued to stalk forward on silent feet, following Zeke toward the monster that might just put an end to it all. She didn't waver, though. She accepted the fear, internalizing it to the point where it became fuel for her determination. Through it all, Zeke remained silent, ever the stoic warrior. It made it easy to forget that he was so young.

Finally, after almost two hours, the tunnel leveled out, and only ten minutes later, it opened up into a vast cavern. Abby's jaw dropped in awe as she beheld the chamber. The ceiling was largely hidden by dark shadows, the only evidence that it existed being the barest twinkling of crystalline stalactites. The cavern floor was similarly awe-inspiring, as it bore a thick carpet of luminous moss, its red glow the only light in the entire cave. Veins of crystals snaked through the walls, reflecting that relatively weak light and bathing the cavern in its illumination.

It would have been one of the most beautiful things Abby had ever seen, if it weren't for the elephant-sized monster in the center of the cavern. Or the hundreds of gooey green eggs dotting its floor. Waist-high and much taller than they were wide, their shells were obviously malleable because Abby could see them distorting under the pressure of whatever they contained. More drachnids, surely. But they weren't what drew her focus. Instead, her eyes locked onto the monster that dominated the room. She didn't even need to inspect it to know it was the queen; even so, reflexes were difficult to stop, and with a slight flicker of thought, she used her inspection skill, [**Keen Eye**].

Ara Kamana, the Drachnid Queen—Level 25 (E)

Abby breathed a sigh of relief. Not a boss-tier monster, at least. Then, she gave herself a mental shake. An elite was plenty to kill her. And this one looked stronger than most.

If the champion had veered more toward the humanoid side of the drachnids, then the queen went in the exact opposite direction. For the most part, it looked like a giant, spindly-legged spider. Its thorax was rust red that became black at its sharpest points. Like its eight legs. Or the scorpion-like tail that hovered over it like a snake. Or the tips of its claws. Abby shuddered.

The queen's torso was vaguely humanoid, though it was probably ten feet from the waist to the top of its head. And it was completely covered in that same rust-red chitin. All but its strikingly human face, which resembled that of a beautiful woman—if said woman had sharklike teeth and eyes like black gemstones.

All in all, the drachnid queen was every bit as frightening as Abby could have anticipated, and if it wasn't for Zeke standing beside her, she might've turned tail and run away. After all, the tunnel from which they'd come wasn't big enough to accommodate the queen. Though she was probably strong enough that that might not matter. If the tunnel wouldn't allow passage, the queen would probably just smash her way through.

"You dare to disturb this holy place?!" screeched the queen, its voice a strange amalgamation of the clicks that characterized the drachnids' communication and human speech. It sent a shiver up Abby's spine, almost like someone was running their fingernails down a chalkboard.

"Yeah," Zeke said, sounding entirely unperturbed. "Sure."

Then, without further hesitation, he darted forward faster than she'd ever seen him move. In barely more than a second, he'd covered the forty yards or so between the tunnel's mouth and the drachnid queen, and when he drew close enough, he leaped high into the air, his mace already swinging for the creature's face.

An instant later, the creature's thick tail rammed into him, sending him rocketing back from whence he'd come. He flew through the air so quickly that when he collided with the wall near the tunnel's mouth, the stone cracked and cascaded around him.

For a moment, Abby felt panic rising within her. Had the thing really just dealt with Zeke so easily? Despite her determination, she knew that without him, she didn't stand a chance. But thankfully, a second or two later, the rocks shifted, and Zeke pulled himself out of the rubble.

He spat blood, then rolled his shoulders before saying, "Yeah, she seems pretty tough. Might've bitten off more than we can chew."

Then, before she could suggest retreat, the big man shot forward once again, and the battle began in earnest.

48

NEVER LEAVE YOUR FEET

As the drachnid queen's scorpion-like tail lashed out, striking him in the shoulder and driving him into the ground, Zeke began to wonder if, in all his battles, he'd learned anything at all. His technique, such as it was, was perfectly serviceable, so long as he could muscle his way into overpowering his enemies. However, the moment he met his match—or worse, an enemy that far outstripped even his Herculean stats—he inevitably found himself tossed around like a rag doll.

He knew he needed to fight smarter. The problem was that he just didn't have the requisite knowledge to get better. His martial path helped a little, enhancing his instincts to a degree that gave him more of an edge, but it was a poor substitute for actual training. At the end of the day, he was still a stupid kid swinging a club, as opposed to a seasoned warrior with a mace.

"You couldn't have expected that to work, right?" called Abby from her position a few dozen feet away. She steadily peppered the queen with her conjured silver arrows, driving the hulking monster back. The arrows didn't sink very deeply into the queen's carapace, and Zeke was certain that they didn't cause much real damage. But Abby's accuracy was uncanny, so she was adept at hitting the creature's softest spots, inflicting pain and frustration with each arrow. It was enough of a distraction that Zeke managed to wrench himself free of the barbed tail. "Never leave your feet. That's, like, Fighting 101."

As the queen retreated before Abby's barrage of arrows, Zeke rolled to his feet, flexing his shoulder. The queen's attack had hit mostly meat, causing little more than a flesh wound. It hurt, but it didn't impede his movement.

"Doesn't feel like it uses poison," he muttered. "So, there's that."

"Joy," Abby said, firing one arrow after another and keeping the queen at bay. "Got any bright ideas that don't involve jumping at her like an idiot?"

"Uh..."

"You're just going to run at her and try to hit her with your caveman club, aren't you?" she asked, cutting her eyes at him.

"It's a mace."

Zeke could practically hear her eyes rolling when she said, "Of course it is."

The problem was that he really didn't have much of an idea how to attack the creature. It was the size of an elephant, and it was stronger and faster than him. Between its tail and its sharp legs, its attacks could come from a variety of different directions. And Zeke knew it had some aces up its sleeve, too. The champion had had its poison; it only stood to reason that the queen would have some sort of unique attack, as well.

"I could go for its legs," he suggested. "You keep the tail occupied, maybe?"

Abby never took her eyes from the creature as she continued firing arrows at it. "Sounds good to me," she said.

Zeke gathered himself, getting ready to dart into battle.

"Don't jump," Abby reminded him.

"I wasn't!"

"Or yell," she said.

"I...I wasn't going to," Zeke lied self-consciously. Even in the middle of a battle against a monster that could very well tear him limb from limb, Zeke still had the presence of mind to be embarrassed when a pretty girl called him out. Letting out a battle roar just seemed natural, didn't it? That didn't make him weird, right?

"Sure you weren't," Abby said, a hint of a smile on her face. "Now, go on. Do your thing."

Zeke shook his head and tightened his grip on his mace. With a roll of his shoulders, he pushed all his distracting thoughts to the back of his mind. Given that he still wasn't quite sure how he saw Abby, it wasn't easy. But two-plus years of nearly constant battle had given Zeke enough mental fortitude to clear that hurdle and focus on the task at hand. After all, there was a monster to kill.

"Alright," he said. "I'm going in."

Protect Abby, he thought at Pudge, who'd been itching to join the fight. Zeke would've loved some extra help, but the bear cub just wasn't ready for something like this. Even if he'd had the levels, which he didn't, he was still little more than an infant. If he could've left Pudge behind altogether, Zeke would have. But there was always the chance that they'd missed some of the drachnids on the surface, so leaving Pudge up there wasn't safe. But then again, Zeke was rapidly beginning to see that nowhere in his new world qualified for that designation. Monsters were everywhere, and given his run-in with Julio and his band of miscreants, he didn't expect civilization to be any better. Different. But still just as dangerous.

The bear cub sent his assent, and Zeke pushed himself forward. Each step thudded heavily against the rocky earth, announcing his charge. He suppressed the urge to let out a roar—when had he gotten into that habit?—as he covered the distance between himself and the monster. When he drew near, the queen tried to spear him with its tail again, but Zeke had learned his lesson.

And with his feet firmly planted on the ground, he could actually dodge. *Maybe Abby's onto something*, he thought.

Pudge returned that thought with one of his own, though his was liberally coated in syrupy smugness. *Pretty lady smart*, the cub sent. Zeke couldn't really disagree with the bear's assertion.

Taking something of a crowhop, Zeke swung his club—no, it was a mace, damn it!—at the monster's spindly, insectile legs. The queen reacted, pulling its leg aside with frightening speed, but Zeke still connected. When Voromir hit, the force sent reverberations down the haft of the weapon and into Zeke's hands.

Once, after a particularly bad tournament where he'd failed to even put a ball in play, Zeke had decided to take his frustrations out on the dugout wall. He'd swung his bat with everything he had, and the resultant collision was enough to chip the wall. However, he did far more damage to himself, the impact and vibration fracturing his glove hand. His father had spent the entire drive home berating him, but the man had waited until they'd reached the confines of their own home before beginning the real punishment. Zeke ended up with more than one injury that day. He'd been ten years old.

Past punishments aside, hitting the monster's leg felt frighteningly similar to hitting that cinder block wall, and if Zeke hadn't been possessed of preternatural durability, he was certain that his hands—and probably his forearms—would've shattered from the impact. As for the drachnid queen's leg, a tiny crack appeared, but the hard chitin remained mostly unscathed.

"This is going to suck," he muttered, already dodging another descending thrust of the monster's tail. It clipped him, opening up a long, shallow wound on his back, but he ignored the fiery pain. Instead, he kept moving, weaving in and out of the monster's legs. It danced around, trying to spear him with the sharp, spear-like tips, but Zeke managed to stay just ahead of the battle. However, he barely had the time or reaction speed to keep from being impaled, much less enough room to do any damage. He managed a few swings, but they were relatively weak and largely ineffectual. Combined with [**Leech Strike**], they were enough to keep his various wounds from affecting him, stemming the bleeding, but far from enough to close them entirely.

It was a stalemate, though. And Zeke suspected that he would succumb to exhaustion long before the drachnid queen lost any of its vigor. Not only did it have levels on him, it was on an entirely superior tier of power. Without Abby constantly peppering the huge drachnid with her arrows, Zeke knew he'd have long since fallen. Even with their combined efforts, the best they could do was to hold their own. Something had to change, and soon.

Of course, that's precisely what happened.

Suddenly, thousands of fuzzy, hand-sized spiders erupted from the eggs scattered throughout the cavern. More of the small spiders rained down from the ceiling where they'd perched unseen. They landed with loud thumps, and for the barest of seconds, they were disoriented. Then, the entire mass of arachnids surged. One wave went for Zeke. The other, for Abby.

There's something altogether primal about a fear of spiders. Whether it's an evolutionary instinct born of a natural aversion to creatures that are usually venomous, or if it's just their appearance or their jerky movements—it's a nearly universal thing among humans. That same fear was present with the drachnids, though it was mitigated somewhat by their humanoid upper halves. But few people can look at a veritable flood of arachnids and not flinch.

Zeke wasn't one of those people.

Logically, he knew they didn't pose as much of a threat as the drachnid queen looming over him. However, as the tide of spiders reached him and began climbing up his legs, he couldn't help but react. Suddenly, he didn't care about the queen's spear-like appendages. For the briefest of instants, his only concern was to fling as many of the eight-legged creatures from his body as possible.

He was only marginally successful.

As one, the monstrous spiders sank their fangs into his flesh, injecting a familiar poison that very nearly froze him in place. Numbness enveloped him, burning through his veins. He didn't even feel it when he was speared by the queen's leg. A dark cloud of unconsciousness began to envelope him, to wrap him in a warm blanket of nothingness. A part of him welcomed it, wanting to give in and give up. But another part, a fire of survival that burned in his very core, wouldn't let him.

And then a thought erupted in his mind. *Fun!*

He had the presence of mind to turn his head just enough to see Pudge pouncing on spiders, swiping them with his claws. Each blow squished a spider, and somewhere in his core, Zeke could feel a steady trickle of experience. More than that, he could read Pudge's emotions; the bear cub was having the time of his life playing with his new toys.

More than that, though, there was a stream of something else wrapped around the flow of experience. Something vital. Before, the altered [**Mark of Companionship**] that had bonded them together had been something of a one-way street. It gave Pudge the ability to use [**Leech Strike**] while also allowing Zeke to funnel vitality to his companion. However, now, the vitality was going the other way. It wasn't much. The bear cub wasn't powerful enough for that. But it was enough to push the worst of the poison back. And once the numbness began to fade away, Zeke took care of the rest, smashing spiders and letting his own [**Leech Strike**] do its job. Before long, he was able to turn the tide, and the flood of spiders abated, leaving him with only the drachnid queen to worry about.

She hadn't been idle, though. With every passing second came another attempt at spearing the warrior beneath her. And through it all, Zeke persisted. The queen's screeches of frustration filled the air; she wasn't accustomed to failure. However, it wasn't enough to simply endure her attacks. Zeke was there to take care of the problem. And to do that, he had to kill the queen, lest she raise another army of drachnids and begin her decimation of the caravans once again. Or worse.

Zeke needed to be stronger. Faster. He needed an edge. And though he was loath to brave the cost, he knew precisely where to get it. With a thought, he set his core to spinning and practically threw mana through his pathways, shoving the energy into the appropriate rune.

[**Heart of the Berserker**] activated, and power surged through him. Rage coursed through his veins as his muscles swelled with unspent potential. He felt like an angry god, and he hungered to put the drachnid queen in her place. She was nothing. A bug. A pitiful monster who dared to challenge her betters. And Zeke would crush her.

Zeke abandoned the plan to slowly cripple the creature. Gods didn't take their enemies apart, one leg at a time. Instead, he would challenge the monster directly like a proper warrior should. So, he pummeled his way through the forest of insectile limbs and leaped atop the monster's carapace. Then, with a mighty roar and an overhand swing, he began to smash its thorax into submission. The first blow, powered by every ounce of strength Zeke could muster, did little, save for send an echoing thud careening around the cavern. The second was little better. But the third rewarded him with a tiny crack. That small success spurred him forward.

Seven strikes later, and the monster was screaming in frustration and agony. Silvery arrows sprouted from its humanlike torso. None went very deep, but they added to the creature's obvious pain. And Abby hadn't let up one bit, instead shooting one conjured projectile after another with the rhythm of a metronome. Zeke's own efforts were even more impressive, digging a huge crater in the monster's back. It tried to buck him off, but with [**Heart of the Berserker**] active, his physical stats were unmatched, so he kept his balance with enviable ease.

But it wasn't enough.

They needed more. And as [**Heart of the Berserker**] wore on, Zeke's situation grew steadily more dire. His endurance dropped, and the spearing strikes from the drachnid's tail bit ever deeper. Great furrows split his flesh and what was left of his leather armor. And despite the might of his descending mace, the influx of vitality from [**Leech Strike**] was quickly becoming overwhelmed.

They were fighting a losing battle. Unless something changed, they would, all three of them, perish. Zeke refused to let that happen. So, doing something he knew he shouldn't do, Zeke leaped from the monster's back. It chose that moment for a tail strike, but unlike before, Zeke had accounted for the blow. Still, it very nearly sent him spinning off his mark.

He dropped his mace. For what he had planned, it would only get in the way. It flew to the other side of the cavern; if his plan didn't work, he'd be disarmed and out of position. He knew it was a gamble, but the alternative wasn't much better. He could last a while, but eventually, the detrimental effects of [**Heart of the Berserker**] would push him past the point of no return. With every thirty seconds, he would lose a little more endurance until the drachnid queen ripped him to shreds. The moment he'd activated the skill, he'd been put on a time limit, and he was quickly careening toward the end.

He almost missed. Despite his monstrous dexterity driving his coordination and balance to preternatural levels, he only barely managed to grab hold of the carapace covering the most vital parts of the queen's humanoid torso. The carapace itself was comprised of a series of panel-like pieces of rust-red chitin that met at her sternum. He dug his fingers into a seam.

The monster clicked and howled as it dug its sharp claws into his back, but it could find no purchase. With his lowered endurance, they raked through him like a molten knife through butter. It was pure agony, but in the depths of his skill-based rage, Zeke barely felt it. He sank deeper, pulling from the skill harder than he'd ever pulled before.

The carapace snapped, exposing the drachnid's chest.

"The heart! Go for the heart!" he bellowed, even as he lost his grip and was thrown free.

Abby didn't need any more prompting. In the space of a couple of seconds, she had three arrows in the air. Because the monster jerked unpredictably, the first arrow missed the mark by a couple of inches, burying itself between the drachnid's exposed ribs. The skin beneath the carapace was far softer than anywhere else, so it sank deep into the queen's torso. The second arrow hit a little closer, but still, it missed the heart. But the third flew true, tearing into the exposed skin with unerring accuracy.

The drachnid screeched its pain and fury, but all Zeke heard was a death knell. He slowly picked himself up, his body still singing with a berserker's violent fury.

"It's already dead," Abby called. "It just doesn't know it yet."

Zeke nodded. "I know," he growled, his voice harsh with unspent rage. Then, he sprinted back into the fray. This time, things were different. With the monster unable to concentrate on anything but its own impending mortality, it was too uncoordinated to score any major blows. For his part, Zeke did little damage, but that wasn't the point. He was hurt, and bad. If he didn't get a little more vitality in him, there was every chance he wouldn't make it five minutes after the queen died. So, even without his mace, he attacked.

He punched. He kicked. He even bit the monster's spindly legs. And slowly, it died, giving tiny bits of life energy each time he landed an attack. It wasn't enough vitality to heal him completely, but it was enough to stave off the worst of it. So, by the time the monster finally gave in to the inevitability of death, he was no longer in danger of bleeding out.

Zeke deactivated [**Heart of the Berserker**], which was a huge mistake. Immediately, weakness overwhelmed him, and he collapsed atop the slain drachnid queen. Before he lost consciousness, he barely managed to raise his head and say, "That was . . . a lot . . . harder than I expected."

And then the darkness that had been creeping around the edges of his vision enveloped him, and he lost consciousness completely.

49

AFTERMATH

Only a minute or so later, Zeke awoke to a cacophony of pain. Predictably, given its name, one of the downsides to using [**Heart of the Berserker**] was that when it was activated, he rapidly lost any sense of self-preservation. With the skill active, there was only one thing on his mind: attack. Other goals were cleansed by the fiery rage that came with it. That, as well as the slow loss of endurance and the period of weakness that came after deactivation, was the biggest reason he hesitated to use it. But when his life was on the line, the significant boost to his stats was worth even the most severe downsides.

"You going to help clean all this up?" came Abby's strained voice. "Or are you going to lie around for the rest of the day?"

Zeke glanced to his right to see that Abby was busy fighting one of a trio of drachnids. A couple more lay dead nearby, evidence that even though the queen had been defeated, the battle had never stopped for her. Luckily, the drachnid she was fighting seemed completely insensate, devoid of any sort of tactical skill. Instead, it attacked like a wild animal, simply throwing itself at Abby. She made quick work of it, hacking it apart with her hatchet before turning her attention to the other two that had lagged a little behind.

Zeke heaved himself to his feet, feeling weaker than he had since being reborn into the new world. It wasn't surprising; he'd kept [**Heart of the Berserker**] running for far longer than he ever had before, and the weakness that followed was proportional to the length of its activation.

He wobbled forward, intent on helping out, but his assistance was unnecessary because only a second later, Pudge came out of the shadows and pounced on a drachnid's back. Immediately, he dug his claws into its hard carapace, raking huge grooves into the chitin. It took him only a few seconds to reach something vital, but he didn't stop until the entire thorax was little more than pulp. Then, he went to work on the humanoid torso, which parted even more easily under his attention. In less than thirty seconds, Pudge had finished killing the drachnid. By that time, Abby had dispatched the other, leaving the cavern eerily silent.

Zeke glanced around at the carnage they'd left in their wake. The queen's body had become a hillock of carapace, flesh, and gore, and it was surrounded by a sea of the smaller spider corpses. Some twitched, barely clinging to life, but the vast majority were still. The cavern had only had a few stalagmites jutting from the ground, but most of those had been smashed to bits by the drachnid queen's rampage. There was nothing left of the malleable eggs that had contained the smaller spiders; even their fleshy shells had dissolved after the spiders had broken through. Zeke hadn't realized it at the time, but his fight with the elite monster had ranged all across the cavern, and her huge form hadn't been kind to the landscape.

Abby broke his reverie, saying, "Well, that sucked."

Zeke looked up to see her slipping her bow over her shoulder. Pudge padded his way to Zeke, then licked some of the gore off his hand. Idly, Zeke knelt and scratched behind the cub's ear. It was Pudge's spot, and the bear leaned into it.

"Are you okay?" Zeke asked Abby. "Any injuries?"

"A few scratches," she said, clutching her side. "Nothing that won't be fine in a couple of days. You?"

"I feel like I got attacked by a pack of rabid honey badgers," he answered, inspecting his body. It was covered in shallow cuts, and there were a handful of deeper lacerations that would take some time to heal. In addition, he felt sure that he had a few broken ribs, a dislocated shoulder, and a few fractures in his arms and legs. Finally, there were the pair of puncture wounds on his upper back where the queen's tail had speared him. Other than that, he felt like one big bruise. Curiously, it wasn't all that dissimilar to how he'd felt after the car wreck that had ended his baseball career. The only difference was that he could already feel his vitality going to work on the injuries. Even if he didn't prop his recovery up with [**Leech Strike**], he felt positive that he'd be back to fighting shape in a week or two. A month, and he would be in pristine condition. With an influx of vitality from [**Leech Strike**], it would probably be only a day. Two, at most.

"You look like it, too," she said. "If you're going to keep fighting like that, you're going to need to get some good armor."

Zeke shrugged. "I seem to be doing okay," he said.

Abby shook her head, saying, "What are you, some kind of masochist? I know you can heal, but it still hurts, right? Besides, there are some pretty good artisans in Beacon. A few of the best ones even have smithing paths."

"And I'm sure they'd just outfit me for free, then," he said. "I don't have any money, remember?"

Abby laughed.

"What?" he said.

"With all of these drachnid eyes, you can probably afford just about anything you want," she said. "And that's not even considering the beast cores. Or whatever you get off the queen. With all that, you're practically a one-percenter."

"Oh," he said, the possibilities opening up to him. He already had Voromir, his mace, and he was more than happy with it. But what else was out there? Magical armor? Accessories with mystical effects? Julio had had a couple of enchanted rings, but they were useless in a fight, so Zeke had ignored them.

"But since we're talking about loot, we need to discuss our arrangement," Abby said, finding a likely rock to sit on. Zeke sat next to her, grateful for the break. It would be hours before he got over the drain of [**Heart of the Berserker**].

"We're not splitting everything fifty-fifty?" he asked.

"I was more concerned with the reward for the mission," Abby answered. "They won't let you collect, since you're not part of the guild."

He glanced her way, saying, "Might've been nice to know that before I risked my life for it."

Abby sighed, saying, "Yeah—I'm sorry about that. I can still give you one of the fruits, but I was hoping—"

"I don't need it," Zeke said.

Abby stared at him, her mouth agape. After a second, she managed to ask, "What?"

"You know I've already evolved my race," he said. "So, unless this gets me to the next, I don't need it. Unless you don't need it . . . I'm still a little unclear on how it works. You said it did half, right? Just your soul. But if you use two, does it work on your body, too?"

"No," Abby said. "One's the limit. Otherwise . . . well, it would be wasted. But . . . I think they'd let me trade the reward. It won't be a one-for-one substitution, but I think . . ."

"What else would make the difference?" Zeke asked. "I have it on good authority that I'm kind of rich now."

Ignoring his poor attempt at levity, Abby glanced toward the queen's corpse, then said, "Probably her core. The beast core from an elite monster is worth a lot." She scrunched up her face, obviously thinking. Then, after about thirty seconds, she said, "Okay—here's what I think's fair. You take everything but the queen's core and the teeth. I'll collect the reward and use it to evolve."

Zeke shook his head, saying, "Half. You get half of everything. And take the rewards, too. You worked for this just like I did." Then, he thought about it for a second before adding, "But I want that carapace I got off the champion. I think somebody could make a breastplate or something out of it."

"Why?"

"Well, you said I needed some armor, and—"

"No, you big idiot," Abby said. "I'm talking about the split. Even if I wasn't taking the rewards for myself, there's no way I deserve that much. You killed the vast majority of these monsters."

"Can't a guy just be generous?"

She glared at him.

"Fine," Zeke said. "I don't want to do all of this by myself, okay? We work pretty well together, and I would like for that to continue until we get out of here."

"What? Out of here? What are you talking about?" she asked.

"Okay, so . . . here's the thing," he said. Then, he launched into a full explanation of what he knew. He told her about Oberon, about the hints that there was something after level twenty-five. And he told her about his intention to clear that hurdle and see whatever was on the other side.

"That's . . . that's a lot," she said.

Zeke shrugged. "It's what Oberon told me," he said. "He said there was a war with demons, and this whole thing is meant to make us all strong enough to fight them. But from everything you've told me, things don't seem to be working the way they're supposed to work. I don't know why, but I think I'm here to figure it out and . . . I don't know . . . unclog the pipes or something."

"Or maybe it was all a hallucination you dreamed up to help you cope," Abby suggested.

"Maybe," he conceded. That thought had certainly crossed his mind more than once. "I was in those caves for a really long time. But I don't feel crazy."

"Says the guy whose idea of battle tactics is jumping at his enemy while screaming," she muttered. "Fine. So, you want to team up?"

"I do," Zeke stated. "Until we get to the end."

Abby thought about it for a second, during which time Pudge thrust his head under her hand and lay his chin on her thigh. Idly, she scratched him in his spot. After a second, she sighed, "Okay. Let's do it, then."

Suddenly, it was like a weight had been lifted from Zeke's chest. Over the course of their partnership, Zeke had begun to trust Abby in a way he'd never really trusted anyone in his life. They'd known each other for only a couple of months, during which they'd had precious few real conversations. He still didn't know her all that well—not in the way he was used to knowing people, at least. He didn't know what kind of movies she liked, aside from one notable exception. He didn't know about her favorite music or books or whether or not she liked sports. In fact, he knew very little about her life before being reborn, save that she was probably twice his age, had been married, and had worked as some kind of mental health professional. Her life since being reborn was less of a mystery, but only just.

However, Zeke felt like he knew her on a deeper, less superfluous level. They'd fought together in a handful of life-and-death struggles, and they had lived together in his cottage for all that time. To him, Abby felt comfortable. Familiar. Trustworthy.

And Pudge liked her, which counted for more than Zeke cared to admit.

He smiled and grimaced as he was suddenly reminded of a few cuts on his face. Wincing at the stinging pain, he said, "Alright. The skill I used at the end has a couple of side effects I'll still be dealing with for the next hour or so. So, it'll be a minute before I'm ready to loot. Then, we can go topside."

Abby shrugged, saying, "Sounds good to me."

After that, Zeke let the weakness wash over him, and he lay back on the rock, closing his eyes. Then, he finally got to the part he'd really been looking forward to. When they'd killed the queen, he had reached level fourteen. More than that, he had gotten another achievement:

Arachnophobia! You have slain a drachnid queen and more than two-thirds of her spawn. +5 to all physical stats.

In addition, he'd completed a hidden quest.

Congratulations! By killing the drachnid queen, you have completed the (Optional) Quest Invasive Species. Reward: Greaves of the Spider Queen

Zeke didn't accept the reward yet. Instead, he moved on to inspecting his gains. It had been a while since he'd really looked at his status. Even when he'd gained his last couple of levels, he hadn't bothered to do more than allocate his stats. He quickly allocated his free fifteen points into endurance, then studied his status screen.

Name	Ezekiel Blackwood
Class	N/A
Level	14
Race	Human (G)
Alignment	Isphodel
Achievements	First Blood, Hasty Evolution, Above and Beyond, Genocide, Overachiever, Completionist, Beastmaster, Savant, Arachnophobia
Martial Path	Blunt Weapons—(Novice—Early)
Artisan Path	Runecraft—(Novice—Early)
Strength	239

Agility	132
Dexterity	158
Endurance	240
Vitality	135
Intelligence	117
Wisdom	148
Unassigned Attribute Points	0

Basic math told him that his combination of achievements and his evolved body gave him a very significant edge on anyone else at his level. Also, given the obvious stat differences between him and Abby—and the ease with which he'd dispatched Julio, who had been level nineteen, he felt sure that he was at least as powerful as someone in their twenties. Maybe more, though Abby had assured him that some of the skills available at those levels more than made up for any stat differences. Altogether, though, he was happy with his progression so far. He still needed to gain more power, but he had a good start.

After about twenty minutes, Abby asked, "Did you complete a quest, too?"

Zeke opened his eyes to see her staring at a white-and-gold chest that had obviously only just appeared before her. Zeke nodded, saying, "Yeah. I was waiting to open it, though."

"And an achievement, too, right?" Abby asked.

"Arachnophobia," he said. "Pretty good one, too. Five to all physical stats."

"Pretty good? That's more stats than you get for an entire level!" she exclaimed. "How many achievements like that do you have?"

"Uh . . . nine?" he said. "They give different stuff, though. My best one is called Completionist, which I got when I got out of my tutorial dungeon. It gave fifteen to all stats."

"No wonder you're so overpowered," she grumbled.

Zeke ignored it. "But the biggest difference is my evolution," he said. "That gives me three to everything per level. So, it's like forty-two extra to all my stats now."

"What? Don't you mean from whatever level you evolved it?" she asked.

Zeke shook his head. "No," he said. "I looked at it when I first got it. It was retroactive."

"That's not . . . I mean . . ."

Zeke pulled up his race, going into the submenu that broke down the two halves. It had an additional line that he was sure hadn't been there before.

Body (G): Determines physical limitations. +3 Strength, Agility, Dexterity, Endurance, and Vitality per level. Retroactive due to early evolution. Upgradable.
Soul (G): Determines spiritual limitations. +3 Intelligence and Wisdom per level. Retroactive due to early evolution. Upgradable.

"It says it was because of an early evolution," Zeke said. "But even if it wasn't, I did it at level three, so it's only like nine extra stats."

"Monster," she muttered.

Zeke shrugged, saying, "It won't be as big of a difference once we get to be higher levels. And I'm sure we can find more achievements to make up the differences." After a second, he said, "Are you going to open that?"

"Oh," Abby said. "Yeah."

Then, she flipped open the lid of the chest, reached in, and pulled out a hatchet. It was a bit bigger than the one she normally used, almost big enough to be called an axe. In addition, it had an ornately carved haft, and the edge of its blade had a green tint.

"It's called a Venomous Hatchet," she said, grinning. "It poisons anything I cut."

"Seems useful," Zeke said, nodding.

"Useful? Do you know how rare this is?" she asked. "Nobody I know has a weapon with an actual effect like this. The most you can find is something with self-repair or self-cleaning."

"My mace does," Zeke said. "It adjusts weight based on my strength. So, as I get stronger, it gets heavier. It even changes based on if I'm using one hand or two, so I'm always hitting with as much momentum as I can handle."

"That's . . . I mean . . ." she trailed off, shaking her head. Finally, she said, "Whatever. I don't know why I'm surprised anymore. Now, open yours."

"Yes, ma'am," Zeke said, accepting his quest reward. Another white-and-gold chest appeared before him.

"Ugh," Abby muttered. "Don't ever call me ma'am again. It makes me feel . . . just don't."

Zeke ignored her, instead opening the chest to reveal a pair of armored boots. He inspected them.

Greaves of the Spider Queen (G)—Armored boots made from the carapace of an elite drachnid. Special functions: Self-Repair (minor), Self-Cleaning (minor), Surefooted—Maintain footing, even in treacherous terrain

"Whoa," Zeke breathed, pulling the greaves from the chest. As soon as he had, the gilded chest disappeared. The greaves themselves were just what the description said they were—a pair of leather boots with rust-red armor running along the top of the foot and the shin. He quickly discarded the old, mostly destroyed boots he'd pilfered from Julio's group of murderers and put on the new greaves. The greaves came up to just below his knee, armoring his entire lower leg. More than that, they fit perfectly and were more comfortable than they had any right to be.

"Nice," Abby said. "I think the Framework is telling you something."

"I think you might be right," Zeke said, hopping from foot to foot to test his new footwear. Even though the rocky ground of the cavern was slippery with gore, he didn't notice the slightest difference in his footing.

After a little more testing, Zeke set about looting the queen and the three drachnids that Abby had killed. The smaller spiders didn't have anything of value, though. When he looted the queen, he got a queen's carapace, a pair of larger-than-normal fangs, and an elite beast core. It was a bit bigger than the marble-sized cores that came from the other drachnids.

"Wait—why didn't the champion drop one of these?" he asked, pulling the elite core from his storage. It was about the size of a softball and quite a bit heavier than the other beast cores he'd looted.

Abby shrugged, saying, "Not all elites have elite cores. It's kind of a crapshoot, really. I don't know why it's like that."

Zeke frowned, feeling shortchanged. They had killed two elites, and so, they should've gotten two cores. It just didn't seem fair. But then again, the new world didn't seem to be any fairer than the one they'd left behind, so maybe it was to be expected.

Finally, after looting everything, the pair made their way back through the tunnel and to the pit where they'd made their original descent. Luckily, the rope remained in place, and they began the arduous process of climbing back to the surface.

50

REST THE DEAD

Zeke heaved the tacky, web-covered corpse onto the pile in the center of the canyon. He hated the webs as much for their stickiness as for what they represented; after all, most of the people who'd been cocooned had been alive to some degree when they'd been wrapped in the hateful webs. Zeke could only hope that most had suffocated before the drachnids had drained them. The alternative just wasn't something he wanted to contemplate.

With a sharp exhale, Abby threw another corpse onto the growing pile. Wiping the sweat from her brow, she said, "You know, we don't have to do this."

"I kind of think we do" was Zeke's response, a sentiment he'd clung to since they'd begun to gather the desiccated corpses into what would soon become a funeral pyre. It had taken days to gather enough wood from the forest that abutted one side of the canyon, a process that had Zeke free-climbing the walls, cutting down the trees with an axe he'd looted from one of Julio's band, then dragging them to the edge before rolling them into the ravine. Even with his ridiculous strength and endurance, it was an awkward, time-consuming process that had taken him far longer than he'd anticipated. He had persevered, though. Something inside of him wouldn't—or couldn't—just leave those people to rot. They deserved better.

After completing the arduous process of building an adequate base for the funeral pyre, Zeke and Abby had set about gathering the corpses. For the first trip, Zeke had merely put the web-wrapped bodies in his spatial storage, but it soon became apparent that they left a smell and residue behind. His entire cottage still smelled like corpse, and it had been airing out for almost a week. So, he'd resolved to simply carry the corpses to the pyre the old-fashioned way. The only solace could be found in the fact that he'd positioned the pyre's base at the mouth of the cave that had the most corpses, reducing the amount of time spent walking back and forth.

"This is going to take weeks if we keep going like this," Abby said. Though she obviously didn't agree with his decision to cremate the corpses—according to her, their time was better spent elsewhere—she hadn't complained much. Nor had she withheld her help, going at it with stoic—or perhaps fatalistic—determination. "We should make a litter or something so we can get more than a few at a time. Otherwise, we're going to be walking back and forth between those other caves for a month."

Zeke stretched his back, saying, "Yeah. You're probably right. I'm just not looking forward to climbing that wall again. And going all the way around the way we came in would take two or three days."

Abby shrugged, saying, "This was your idea."

"I know."

Zeke didn't say anything else. Instead, he began trudging back into the cave to get the final few corpses. Already, the pile had grown out of control. There had been hundreds of victims in this cave alone, evidence that their massacre of the drachnids had been entirely justified.

In the past few days since they'd climbed out of that pit, they had run into only a smattering of the monsters. And those had been entirely crazed, almost as if they'd gone rabid. According to Abby, the three drachnids she'd fought right after the queen had been the same way, lending credence to the idea that they'd shared some sort of necessary mental connection with the queen. Once, Abby had even come across a pair of drachnids that had been fighting each other.

Pushing those thoughts aside, Zeke turned his mind to the problem at hand. Even as he grabbed a pair of corpses, slinging one over either shoulder, he considered his next moves. Abby was right. If they kept going at it like this, it would be a month or two before they made their way back to Beacon. And after so long living in the wilderness, Zeke was more than ready to get back to some semblance of civilization. The cottage was great. It had made his life immeasurably easier. But it had very little to speak for it in regard to comfort. So far, it had been easy to ignore, but with the prospect of something better looming over him, Zeke found it more and more difficult to delay their trek to the city.

Of course, it wasn't just about comfort. Zeke had plans. According to Abby, he was now quite wealthy, and he was more than eager to put that wealth to good use. He had the carapaces he'd looted from the queen and her champion, as well as various other odds and ends he thought might be useful to a skilled artisan. He already had his greaves, and he wanted a set of armor to match. Abby's constant teasing about his penchant for getting torn to shreds, as well as the fact that he'd very nearly died fighting both the champion and the queen, had awakened a need to augment his survivability. And there was no better way to do that than with good equipment.

But the biggest reason Zeke wanted to get back to Beacon as soon as possible was probably the most human of them all. He'd had Abby as a comrade for a couple of months, and though neither of them was terribly personable, the simple human companionship was comfortable in a way Zeke hadn't expected. Even though he wasn't a particularly personable guy, he was a little surprised just how much his solitude within the troll caves had affected him. When he was alone, he thought about little other than his past and basic survival. But the addition of Abby and Pudge in his life had broadened those horizons, making him think about his future. Without them, he would've become little more than an animal scraping by to live another day.

Over the course of the rest of the day, Zeke and Abby finished emptying the cave. Pudge followed them around, pouncing on any of the ubiquitous spiders for which Nightweb Ravine had been named. The bear cub had grown more powerful, reaching level eight, so the spiders posed little threat to him. Their fangs couldn't even pierce his tough hide.

By the time they'd finished off the cave, the sun was beginning to set, so they made their way back to the cottage, which Zeke had left summoned a half mile away from the pyre. Once there, the pair took turns gathering water from the pump so they could achieve some semblance of cleanliness. It was a poor substitute for a shower, but it was still better than most people could expect in such a wild place.

"I don't think I've ever felt so dirty in all my life," Abby said, coming out of the cottage. She shook her head as she sat on a stump Zeke had cut into some semblance of a stool. It wasn't much more than a circular block of wood, but it was better than sitting on the ground. Beside her, Zeke was turning a makeshift spit—one of Abby's contributions—upon which was a huge chunk of snake meat.

"You should've seen me after I first got out of the troll caves," Zeke said. "There were a lot of streams and springs in the caves, but by that point, I hadn't washed the gunk off of me in a few weeks. And I'd just cut through, like, a couple hundred trolls. So, I was pretty bad. Then, I had to make my way through a swamp. So, I guess I was pretty ripe."

"Ugh," Abby said, wrinkling her nose. "I bet even the monsters avoided you."

"Not as much as you'd think," he said, shaking his head with a wry grin. "There was this crocodile that almost got me, too. I bet it was thirty feet long. I thought it was a dinosaur, honestly."

"You know when you say 'honestly' or 'to tell the truth' or any other variant, it makes you sound dishonest," Abby said. Then, as if she had only just realized what she'd said, she clapped her hand over her mouth and muttered, "Shit. Sorry. That was kind of rude."

Zeke shrugged. "A little," he said. "But we're partners now, right? We can afford to be a little rude with each other."

Abby relaxed. "Yeah," she said. "Still, though . . . I'm sorry. It's just that it's kind of a pet peeve of mine. My husband used to say stuff like that all the time, and he was probably the most dishonest person I've ever known."

Zeke didn't really know what to say to that. At the end of the day, he didn't have much life experience from which to draw. Less than most people his age, really. His entire life had been about baseball, so he was less worldly than his age might suggest. So, instead of saying something and putting his foot in his mouth, he just turned the spit, watching the snake steak's juices drip into the fire.

"So," Abby said, breaking the silence. "You're going back up there to gather materials for a litter tomorrow, huh?"

"That's the plan," Zeke said. "If we can move twenty or so bodies at a time, we'll be finished in a week or two at most."

Pudge, who'd been inside the cottage, padded out the front door and planted himself at Zeke's feet. The cub looked back at his companion and chuffed, his annoyance clear. Zeke reached down and scratched behind the bear's ears, eliciting a wave of satisfaction emanating from Pudge's thoughts.

"Is he getting bigger?" asked Abby.

"Yeah," Zeke said. "I think his growth is tied to his levels instead of his actual age. In his head, he's still a cub, though. I don't really know much about how quickly bears are supposed to grow, and even if I did know how it worked on Earth, there's no guarantee it'd be the same here. I'm not even sure what kind of bear he's supposed to be."

"Dire bear," Abby provided. "They're as big as grizzlies when they're full-grown, but they're built a little differently. More heavily muscled."

"How do you know that?" Zeke asked, wishing for the thousandth time that he'd remembered to inspect Pudge's mother. He'd had other things on his mind, though. Like killing a murderous harpy queen.

"There's this priest in Beacon, he's pledged to the Church of Purity," she said. "I don't remember his name, but he's one of the few people in the Church who doesn't specialize in healing. Instead, he's a researcher. From what I understand, he got started down that path so he could categorize the different venoms and poisons. That way, the Church's healers would be better equipped to cure them. Anyway, he unlocked some sort of artisan path that let him identify monsters, and he established the Menagerie."

"Like a zoo?"

"No," Abby explained, shaking her head. "All the monsters are stuffed. He's got hundreds of them on display. There's also a book, but most people don't bother with it because dealing with monsters usually boils down to hitting them harder than they hit you. And the book's expensive, too."

Zeke said, "And you saw a bear like Pudge at this Menagerie?"

Abby nodded. "Yeah," she said. "A full-grown one. The thing was huge, too. Like, twelve feet tall and scary as hell. If I remember it right, they lean toward strength and endurance, with hide that's hard to pierce. Once he gets bigger, Pudge is going to be a pain to deal with, especially with that leech skill of yours."

Zeke ruffled Pudge's fur, saying, "Unkillable monster bear, huh? That suits us just fine, doesn't it, buddy?"

The pair continued their small talk until the snake was done, and after eating, they both turned in for the night. As exhausted from the day's work as they both were, sleep came quickly, and neither woke until the next morning. Not for the first time, Zeke was grateful for the cottage, which allowed them to rest in relative safety. Without it, he wasn't certain he could've slept at all.

After a quick breakfast of leftover snake, Zeke de-summoned the cottage, and they began their trek to the next crypt. Once there, Zeke recalled the cottage and began his climb. The next handful of days passed in relative monotony, broken only by the odd monster attack. By this point, both Abby and Zeke were more than capable of dealing with anything in the area, so they were in little danger as they continued their work.

Finally, a few days after constructing the litter, they'd finished that cave, and they moved to the next. With experience on their side, they quickly finished that cave off and moved on to another. Then another. When it was all finished, they had a pile of almost a thousand corpses, and more than a week had passed. It had been grueling work, but seeing that massive mound of bodies only cemented that it was all worth it.

"Should we say something?" Abby asked, standing beside him. Both she and Zeke had torches they'd made from discarded wood and the surprisingly flammable webbing, which they'd wrapped around one end and set alight. "I feel like we should say something."

Zeke ground his teeth together, frustration furrowing his brows. Over the course of his efforts gathering the bodies, Zeke had come to nurture a simmering anger. More than a thousand people had died, and whoever was in charge of Beacon had only seen fit to send a single group? From the very first attack, there should've been an army descending upon the drachnids. Instead, they'd waited, and people had died.

That wasn't how government was supposed to work. Sure, most governing bodies were infected with differing degrees of corruption, and many had lost their way. But in exchange for power, they were supposed to provide safety and security. Beacon—and whoever ran it—had given neither. Not for the people who'd been killed by the drachnids, at least.

There was so much power in this new world, and from his short experience, it seemed that everyone used it for selfish reasons. Zeke had no doubt that, should they have really wanted to, Beacon's leaders could've dealt with the drachnids shortly after the first attack. But they'd chosen not to. That choice, though it wasn't his own, was like a burr in Zeke's mind.

"These people should never have died," Zeke said, tossing his torch onto the pyre. It quickly caught, and in seconds, the flames spread across the mound, enveloping the desiccated corpses. "I'm sorry that we couldn't have done more."

Abby threw her torch onto the opposite side of the pile, and after only a few seconds, the stench of burning corpses filled the air. Neither Zeke nor Abby looked away. Even Pudge, who only vaguely understood what was going on, sat at Zeke's hip, the cub's own mind dwelling on the death of his mother.

For hours, the trio stood beside the pyre, watching it burn the remains until, finally, Zeke looked away with a sigh. "I guess it's time to move on," he said.

Then, an achievement flashed across his field of vision:

Rest the Dead—You have avenged and put your fellow humans to rest. +15 Wisdom, +5% Wisdom

With a flick of his mind, Zeke pushed the notification away. Achievements were all well and good, but they did nothing to quiet the roars of anger and frustration in his heart. A gasp from nearby told him that Abby had received one, as well, but like him, she had little interest in wallowing in her rewards. Instead, they began their long journey out of the ravine, leaving the burning pyre behind them.

51

LIFE AND DEATH

Talia scuttled backward like a crab, desperate to avoid the enormous scythe slicing down at her. She narrowly succeeded, scrambling back to her feet just in time to dodge a horizontal slash. The monster didn't stop, its stamina seemingly endless as it aimed one devastating attack after another at her. Red blood and green-tinged ichor stained the blade, a warning of just how deadly the encounter was.

Clad in a black robe with a deep hood that covered its rotting visage, the nine-foot-tall monster was a reaper. With that poison-coated blade, it had already slain two members of the party—both healers—and it had been coming at Talia with reckless abandon ever since. For the first time in her life, Talia was glad that she'd deviated from the accepted norm and allocated points into her physical stats. Otherwise, she'd have been defenseless against the undead monster. As it was, she used everything she had to avoid being cut open by the thing's scythe.

If only she'd had some sort of attack skill, she could've done something—anything—other than try to survive the encounter. Springing to the side, she closed with the rest of the party, pulsing **[Circle of Mending]** as soon as they came into range. Shallow wounds healed, invigorating the warriors.

"Help!" she cried, ducking under another scythe. "I can't keep dodging forever!"

One of the warriors—a woman wearing a chain mail coat and wielding a huge axe—turned toward Talia. That was a fatal mistake. One of the zombies that had been attacking the rest of the group saw the opening and, with a swipe of its powerful, talon-like claws, ripped her throat out. Even as blood and pieces of flesh splattered into Talia's face, the woman fell. Talia used [**Circle of Mending**] again, but the damage was too severe. She knew that the moment the zombie had attacked. But she had to try, useless as the attempt may be.

That brief distraction was all the opening the reaper needed, and an instant after the warrior went down, a line of fire cut into her back. She screamed in agony, the poisoned scythe already eating at her flesh. Instinctively, she cast [**Purify**] on herself, halting its progress even as she tumbled to the ground.

Untold hours of practice with Master Silas proved their worth as she turned her fall into a graceful roll, casting [**Purify**] again as she found her feet. Pulsing [**Circle of Mending**], Talia felt the laceration on her back knitting itself back together. One cast wouldn't completely heal her, but it would at least close the gaping wound.

All around her was chaos. The entire party was in disarray. Men and women who'd been whole and confident only hours before were dead and dying as hundreds of zombies, dozens of reapers, and a handful of flesh golems descended upon them. The attack had come without warning, the zombies tearing themselves out of the ground all around the party of adventurers. The two healers and a couple of warriors had been killed before anyone even knew what was happening, and the battle had only gotten worse from there.

Even as Talia put some distance between herself and the reaper, a blindingly white light descended from the sky, burning everything within a seven-foot radius centered around the reaper. The monster, so terrifying only a moment before, melted into nothingness, taking a handful of zombies with it. Talia gaped at the puddle of ichor and melted flesh that had very nearly killed her.

A bone-chilling scream jerked her attention back to the battle. The chaos had deepened, but there were signs that her party members were slowly getting things back under control. A line of warriors was holding the zombies at bay while a pair of scouts peppered the bigger targets with arrow-based skills. Myriad lights erupted into being as the warriors used one skill after another, filling the dusky sky with a rainbow of colors.

And at the center of it all was Abdul, glowing with white light and twice as big as normal. The bearded man's white-enameled plate armor gleamed as he laid waste to zombies and reapers alike. Even as he cut the lesser undead apart, another beam of white light descended from the sky to crash into a flesh golem. Stitched together from a pile of disparate parts, the unholy abomination was twelve feet tall and half as wide—a true monster if ever there was one. The creature faltered, falling to its knees. Its skin boiled, steaming ichor erupting in geysers from its seams. It let out a pitiful wail that shook the crumbling ruins around them.

But it endured.

When Abdul's skill ended, the monster looked like melted wax. Its deathly white skin was stained with green-tinted ichor, and when it rose, it wobbled in place. But rise it did. Talia instinctively inspected it.

Greater Flesh Golem—Level 25 (B)

A boss monster! The other golems were elites, well within Abdul's capabilities. He was the most powerful paladin in the world, after all. But no one fought bosses alone. And given that the rest of the party was either engaged in their own battles, dead, or too low of a level to make a difference, Abdul would get no help. Not unless Talia could get to him. She might be weak and underleveled, but her heal could make all the difference. She hoped. Otherwise, the abomination would kill them all.

Talia sprang into action, darting past the line of warriors. As she went, she activated her [**Circle of Mending**], then, sensing the undead contagion, she used [**Purify**] on a tall, thin man who was barely holding one of the reapers off with his spear. It wasn't strictly necessary—the man wouldn't turn anytime soon. But the disease would slow him as it necrotized his flesh. And given that [**Purify**] cost very little of her mana, she saw no reason not to cast it.

The party was capable, cutting down zombies and reapers with ruthless efficiency. Being elites, the lesser flesh golems were more difficult to bring down, but so long as the group concentrated their skills, it was possible. The real danger came from the half-melted boss closing the gap with Abdul.

The paladin was an avatar of wrath as he cut through the lesser monsters, his shining sword parting undead flesh with ease. His shield, decorated with the golden sun of his goddess, blocked the vast majority of the monsters' attacks, but still, some got through. Claws raked against his armor, finding little purchase even as Abdul continued his workmanlike decimation of their ranks.

Until the Greater Flesh Golem arrived.

It barreled into Abdul's enhanced form, and the paladin raised his shield to intercept the monster's attack. Where it made contact, undead flesh sizzled. The flesh golem shrieked in agony as Abdul leaned into the monster's charge. But as strong as the paladin was, the flesh golem was immense, and its momentum was all but unstoppable. A ton of force crashed into him, buckling his knees and sending him tumbling backward. The flesh golem didn't stop. It wouldn't. Not until its enemy was dead.

It loomed over Abdul, yanking a giant bone spike from its torso. Ichor sprayed all over Abdul's gleaming armor. Stunned, he didn't even react as the spike descended. Talia shouted, but it did little good. The spike, still dripping that disgusting ichor, fell with all the considerable force the monster could muster. It cut through Abdul's armor with ease, exploding into his chest with the sound of rent steel and a fountain of blood.

"No!" Talia screamed, finally coming into range. She pulsed one [**Circle of Mending**] after another, praying that she wasn't too late. Abdul was insanely durable, but he couldn't survive a destroyed heart. No one could. Sensing the already-spreading corruption, she cast [**Purify**], arresting the undead infection.

Then, the golem noticed her.

Talia skidded to a stop, the monster's gaze seizing her muscles. She couldn't move. She didn't breathe. She could barely even think. All she knew was fear, an instinctive knowledge that she was under the eyes of a predator so far above her that her only hope was to go unnoticed. That hope was dashed a second later when the monster took a thundering step toward her.

From somewhere, Talia heard a scream, and it took her a long moment to realize that it came from her own mouth. She pulsed [**Circle of Mending**] again, the skill purely instinctive. Talia hardly even realized she'd used it.

Another step. The flesh golem's melted-wax skin had begun to harden, the once-dripping ichor staining it a mottled black-green on pale white. Its face was brutish, with a heavy brow; jagged, uneven teeth; and beady eyes that bore into her very soul. She screamed again, desperately trying to force herself to move. To run away. To attack. Anything but just standing still like cornered livestock.

She failed, and the monster took another unhurried step forward.

There was basic intelligence in the monster's beady eyes. Cruelty. It chilled Talia to the bone. Its nightmarish mouth gaped open, and even from six or seven feet away, the scent of decay was overwhelming. Talia fell to her knees, unable to withstand the golem's horrific aura any longer.

She was going to die. That much was absolutely clear. With Abdul down, their only hope was to run. It didn't matter if the rest of the warriors dealt with the zombies, reapers, and lesser golems. None could stand before the boss.

Especially Talia.

Never before had she felt so useless. She couldn't even stand before the reaper, much less a monster two tiers its superior.

The golem cocked back its spikelike weapon. Dripping ichor and blood, and with Abdul's flesh still clinging to its imperfections, it loomed over her. Talia stared at it, hoping only that it would be quick.

The spike descended, Talia's impending death stretching each second to its limits. She desperately hammered her willpower against the monster's oppressive aura, but it was like banging her fists against a brick wall. Even if she managed to do some damage, the integrity of the wall would remain unchanged. Such was the fortitude of the golem's willpower. Talia was helpless before it.

Still, she managed to hold her head high as she awaited her death.

It never came.

When the spike was only inches away, a white-and-gold shield crashed into it, followed by a blazing sword that detached the monster's arm altogether. Suddenly, the weight of the monster's aura sloughed off of Talia's soul, and she fell back, shoved away by an armored figure.

Abdul's breastplate was destroyed, but beneath was unmarred flesh. He bellowed his rage as he battled the golem, his sword cutting deep furrows into its ichor-stained flesh. The monster hammered into him with a fist the size of Talia's torso, but Abdul's constitution bore the punishment with surprising ease.

"[**Faithful Fortitude**]," she muttered, realizing that Abdul was burning his highest-level skill. Her mother, Lady Constance, had once described it to her, explaining that Abdul could channel his faith in the Sun Goddess into near invulnerability. It was a short-term ability—no human being, regardless of how high of a level, could withstand the power of the Sun Goddess for long—but it was extraordinarily powerful. In addition, the skill would leave Abdul weakened and unable to fight when it expired. It was a skill of desperation, and one that could only be cast on the rarest occasions. Anything else, and Abdul would be ruined by the sheer power of it.

And he'd used it to save her life.

With its attacks rendered ineffective, the fearsome monster stood little chance against Abdul, who slowly whittled the thing down to a pile of severed parts, some of which were still writhing on the ground. It wailed the entire time, sending chills of terror up and down Talia's spine.

After Abdul finally decapitated the monster, he turned to Talia and croaked, "Don't you have a job to do, girl? Go. Heal them!"

Talia suddenly jerked back to awareness. There was still a battle going on, and as she had watched Abdul slowly dismantle the flesh golem, she had neglected her duties. Chastised, Talia turned back to the line of warriors, and she was horrified by what she saw. Four warriors—three men and one woman—all lay on the ground, sporting a wide variety of wounds. Armor had been rent asunder, blood stained the ground, and pitiful cries of agony filled the air. Talia sprinted back into position, casting [**Circle of Mending**] as often as she could, interweaving [**Purify**] where necessary.

Abdul, still under the protection of [**Faithful Fortitude**], went through the remaining army of undead like a scythe, mowing the monsters down with mechanical ease. They surged toward the paladin, trying to overwhelm him with sheer numbers, but the horde of unliving were far from up to the task.

Soon, with Abdul cutting through their ranks, the tide of the battle turned. But even with the advantage, there were still so many of them that it took hours to finish the attacking monsters off. By the time they killed the last one—a particularly stubborn reaper—Talia had used every ounce of her mana.

She slumped to the ground, exhausted.

"Up, girl," Abdul said, suddenly looming over her. He'd lost his buffs, shrinking back down to his normal size. More, the aura of invincibility that had come with [**Faithful Fortitude**] had faded, replaced by ashen, gray skin; sunken eyes; and a vulnerability that felt out of place on the stalwart paladin. Still, he hooked one gauntleted hand under her arm, dragging her to her feet. "The monsters are still about. We must secure a campsite, lest we be overrun."

The exhausted party followed the paladin from the scene of so much carnage. A pair of warriors gathered their dead, slinging one over each shoulder before trudging after their comrades. It was a tactical move as much as an emotional one, necessary because any dead body left in the area would no doubt turn into a zombie. No one wanted that.

For an hour, they marched along, their shuffling steps bearing them away from the scene of the battle. Talia hardly noticed the ruins around them. Though she knew the area had once been the site of a city larger even than Beacon, it had been destroyed and abandoned for as long as anyone could remember, its former citizens forming an army of undead that thankfully never left the area. If they weren't tied so firmly to the place, the rest of the island would've been long since overrun.

Not for the first time, Talia wondered why Abraham Micayne, once a powerful member of Lady Constance's original adventuring party, had chosen to make his home on the other side of the undead zone. After the tragic death of his wife more than a decade before, he had chosen solitude, though no one knew why. It was only one of the mysteries they'd been tasked with solving. However, it was clear that Talia hadn't been given all the information on their mission. It galled her that she hadn't gained her mother's trust, but there was little she could do, save earn it.

Finally, the group found their way to an abandoned cathedral to some nameless deity. The place was mostly intact, and its architecture was so different from the style she associated with either the Church of Purity or the shrines to the Sun Goddess that she scarcely believed they served the same purpose. Where the Churches of Purity were airy buildings comprised of swooping arches and graceful towers, this building was all sharp lines and pointy, spikelike towers. But it had sturdy walls, which was all that really mattered.

As the group set up inside the cathedral, Abdul circled the building as he cast [**Consecration**]. Without it, they'd be vulnerable to another attack—and this time, they wouldn't survive. It took him far longer than any other time he'd used the skill, likely due to his exhaustion. But eventually, he managed to empower the ritual and shuffle back inside. Once he'd made it, he stumbled, unconscious before he even hit the ground.

Despite her own fatigue, Talia was on him in an instant, casting [**Circle of Mending**]. His eyes fluttered open, and he said, "Don't waste your mana on me, girl. I'm fine. Just a bit . . . tired. Get a camp set up. We're going to have to stay here for a few days while I recover."

With that, he passed out again, and the rest of the party went to work on setting up the camp, burning the bodies of their comrades, and, most of all, resting up for the final push into the Micayne Estate.

52

A NECESSARY DISCUSSION

Zeke pushed through the brush, following Abby through the forest. It was slow going due to the thick vegetation, and curiously, it reminded Zeke of home. Having grown up in the Deep South, he was well used to foliage so thick it almost resembled a jungle. The heat, which had spiked soon after they'd left Nightweb Ravine, didn't help matters, and sweat poured down both of their faces. It was nothing compared to Pudge's misery, though. The bear's thick coat was meant for colder climates, and so, the oppressive heat and humidity was doubly bad for him.

"So," Zeke said as Abby hacked her way through a particularly dense bit of foliage. "What's with the weather here?"

"What?" she asked, a little winded from her exertions. They'd been going like this for most of the day, and even her enhanced stamina was lagging. Zeke had offered to take some of the load, but her only response was to grumble that she was the scout of the group.

"The weather," he said. "The climate, I guess. I've maybe covered a few hundred miles since I've been here. Probably a lot less than that. And I've seen a swamp, a ravine that looked like it came straight out of New Mexico, a regular forest, and now this nightmare that looks like the backwoods of Alabama. The temperature has ranged from just above freezing to right now, where it feels tropical. What gives?"

"Oh, that," she said. "Everything here's kind of exaggerated. We've got an entire world's worth of biomes in a space that's a little bigger than Alaska. Some of the other islands are bigger, they say. But nobody ever goes to them."

"Other islands?"

"Right," she said, shaking her head before hacking at a thick vine that looked suspiciously like kudzu. "Sorry. It's easy to forget how new you are here."

"That's me," he said, a little annoyed by her tone. It wasn't his fault that he didn't know anything about the new world. "All shiny and new."

Zeke could hear the roll in Abby's eyes when she said, "Oh, don't be like that. Nothing wrong with ignorance. It's stupidity you can't cure. Like jumping at a monster twice your size while yelling like an idiot."

"For the last time, I didn't—"

"Anyway," Abby said, interrupting his self-righteous defense of his fighting style, such as it was. "There are hundreds, maybe thousands of other islands in this new world. Some are a lot bigger than our archipelago, which is a collection of islands called the Radiant Isles. Others are smaller."

"Have you been to any?"

"Nobody ever goes to the other islands," she explained, hopping over a downed and rotting tree. "Too many sea monsters. Like, kraken and such. I've heard there's even an ancient leviathan roaming around out there. So, our boats don't stray too far from shore, and even that's kind of a risk. It's one of the reasons we use caravans rather than ships."

"If nobody ever goes to the other islands, how do we know they exist?" Zeke asked, following in Abby's footsteps. He noticed a snake coiled beneath a log, but it was only level three, so it didn't disturb him. A huffing Pudge followed behind, misery coursing through their bond.

"There's some sort of communications array in Beacon," Abby said. "Lady Constance is the only one that can use it, but enough people have seen it in action that it's common knowledge."

"Oh," he said.

Abby went on, "The islands, as far as we can tell, are based on the region where you died. It's why most of the people here are American. Or used to be. Sometimes, it's hard to tell because the Framework translates languages."

"So, that's why I could understand that troll," he muttered, thinking back to his fight with the troll warlord, where the monster had accused him of being a baby killer. Which was accurate, after a fashion. Zeke had slain hundreds of troll larvae, even going so far as to destroy their Brood Mother. However, he certainly didn't feel bad about it. They were monsters, and they would have killed him if he hadn't gotten to them first.

"You talked to a troll?" she said, glancing back at him. He told her the story, to which she responded, "Gross. I hate trolls."

"You and me both," he agreed. "So, these other islands have people from other countries?"

"Mostly," Abby explained. "There's some overlap, I think. Just like there are two or three collections of islands for Americans. It doesn't really matter, though. It's not like any of us are ever going to see them. Thousands of miles of monster-infested water between us and all."

That made perfect sense to Zeke, who had no interest at all in braving the kraken-infested seas. On top of that, he knew the true nature of this world. It was nothing more than a pit stop along the way to something bigger. So, he wasn't afflicted with the need to adventure out into the world and explore. He would stay as long as it took him to grow powerful enough to take the next step, and that was it. But he didn't want to do it alone.

As they made their way through the dense jungle, the pair talked about the nature of the world. However, neither really spoke about their past lives. When Zeke asked about the lack, Abby informed him that it was kind of rude. Most people saw the new world as a second chance to do things better, and so there was a certain stigma associated with talking about their lives on Earth. Not that Zeke minded overmuch. When he'd died on that operating table, he'd been a broken young man, a failure with a painful past. He had little interest in revisiting that emotional state, even in memory. If he could manage to forget it altogether, he would have done so without a second's hesitation.

Finally, as the sun began to set, they came upon a small pasture that was just big enough for the cottage. When they came into the clearing, Abby said, "We should camp here for the night. Bastion is only half a day away, but I don't think it's smart to go through the jungle at night."

"Agreed," Zeke said. One thing he'd discovered was that the nocturnal predators were far more dangerous and higher-level than their diurnal counterparts. Neither he nor Abby wanted to chance being ambushed by something that could actually hurt them. So, he summoned the cottage, which had grown a bit sturdier, if not actually bigger. The tiles on the roof had become clay as opposed to wood, too. But that wasn't the biggest change.

"We have a bathroom now!" Abby exclaimed, peeking into a small room she had discovered at the back of the cottage. "And . . . is that a shower? An actual shower?!"

Indeed, it was. The form was primitive, with the floor made of wooden slats where the water could drain. Using the shower required a simple process where they pumped water into a container, then pulled a chain so the gathered water could be released in a steady stream that could last up to a few minutes. But to people who'd been limited to washing in streams or taking birdbaths at the cottage's other pump, it was a godsend.

Abby wasted no time before she went into the bathroom to make use of their new luxury, leaving Zeke to the tedious process of making camp. He had plenty of firewood in the cellar, so making the fire wasn't difficult, and it wasn't long before he'd pulled some snake meat from his spatial storage and had it on their makeshift spit.

When Abby got out of the shower, seeming refreshed, Zeke followed suit, finding that Abby had even left a rough brick of soap behind. The water was incredibly cold, like it'd come from some mountain spring, but he didn't care. After sloughing weeks of grime from his body, he found himself relaxing more than he had in months. Tension he hadn't even known he'd been carrying on his shoulders fell away, draining between the slats with the filthy water.

Once he was suitably clean, Zeke pumped another container full of water before setting himself to the arduous process of cleaning his clothing. The soap was a poor substitute for detergent, but he made do. Still, everything he owned bore the signs of his battles, sporting numerous rips and tears where he'd been bitten, clawed, and impaled. But by the time he was finished, it was at least passably clean.

After putting on the pair of thick, woolen pants he'd looted from one of Julio's thugs, he left the bathroom and hung his clothing over one of the chairs to dry. Hopefully, they'd be okay by morning, but even if they were a little damp, they'd be a sight better than before.

Finally, Zeke dragged his familiar stump out of the cottage and set it before the fire. He sat with a tired sigh, saying, "That really hit the spot. I had no idea how dirty I was. And we really need to get some chairs."

Pudge sat on the other side of the fire, sitting up like he thought he was a human being. Zeke had set aside some of the raw snake for him, and he was busy tearing into it with considerable enthusiasm.

"No kidding," Abby said, turning the spit. "I'm also getting really tired of snake, by the way."

Zeke shrugged. "I actually kind of like it," he admitted. They had other stores of meat, mostly harvested from the creatures they'd killed in the ravine, but his favorite was the snake. It tasted like a gamey combination of chicken and, curiously, freshwater trout—two of his favorites. Abby did not share his tastes. Still, he wished he could fry it. "So, I've been meaning to ask you something."

"Yeah?" she asked. "What's up?"

"I've told you about Oberon," he said. "About what this place is supposed to be. I don't know if you believe me, but since we're partners now, I think I should probably tell you that I don't plan to stay here any longer than absolutely necessary. I'm going to move on as soon as I can. If I can, I want to fix whatever's wrong with the system, but my primary objective is to take the next step."

"Move on to this next mythical plane, right?" she said. "Do you have any idea how you're supposed to do that?"

"Nope" was his simple response. "But I figure it can't be that hard to figure it out. Judging by how long it took me to get to fourteen, it's going to take a long time for me to reach level twenty-five. And I can't move on before then. So, the way I figure it, I'll have plenty of time to find the way out."

"Okay?" Abby said. "Why are you telling me this? So long as I get to level, I don't really care how we do it. And like you said before, we make a pretty good team."

"I want you to come with me," Zeke said.

For a second, Abby stared at him. Then, suddenly, she chuckled, her blonde ponytail bobbing. "You don't even know where you're going," she stated, shaking her head. "Until you do, there's absolutely no way I'm going to just blindly follow."

Zeke narrowed his eyes in annoyance, but Abby went on. "Listen—I know you're convinced what you saw is real. I'm open to that as a possibility, and if it turns out to be true, you can bet your ass I'll be right there with you. But I'm going to need a lot more than what could've very well been a hallucination."

For a few seconds, Zeke glared at Abby. Hadn't he proven himself trustworthy? He'd bent over backwards for her. He had saved her life. And when they got to Beacon, she was going to evolve her race—all because he'd chosen to help her. And now she was questioning his story? Maybe even his sanity? It was galling.

However, it took only a couple of seconds for that anger to fade. He had taken everything on faith, but what if he had been hallucinating? What if Oberon was just a figment of his imagination? Or worse, if he'd lied? Maybe he was some sort of trickster god who got his jollies by stringing ignorant humans along. In this world, anything was possible.

But Zeke felt sure none of that was the case. He couldn't quite place why he felt the way he did, but he was all but certain that Oberon had been telling the truth. There was another layer to this world, and Zeke was determined to find a way to take the steps necessary to reach it.

"Fine," he said at last. "Reserve judgment. But when the time comes, I hope you choose to go with me."

Abby visibly relaxed. "Me, too," she said, her voice soft. "For what it's worth, I hope you're right."

And with that, the pair of adventurers went silent, finished their meal, and retired for the night. Zeke's mind whirled with the possibilities before him; soon, he'd rejoin civilization, and he couldn't help but wonder what he might find.

53

BASTION

By the time they passed the tree line and broke through the oppressive jungle, Zeke was tired, sore, and drenched in sweat. "Leather armor definitely wasn't made for the jungle," he muttered, adjusting the offending leather breastplate. The extra layer was bad enough in the sweltering heat, but the added humidity—and the sweat that came with it—made the leather gear chafe like crazy.

Abby, who'd been leading the way, snorted, saying, "Quit whining."

"Whatever," he spat, irritated at her lack of compassion. Behind him, Pudge was equally miserable. Bears were not tropical beasts, after all, and his thick pelt was working against him. Zeke could feel the cub's irritability shining through their bond like a bonfire. "How the hell are you so comfortable in this heat?"

She glanced back at him with a smirk, saying, "A girl's got to have her secrets, right?"

"Come on!"

Rolling her eyes, she stowed the hatchet she'd used to hack their path through the thick jungle. Then, she pulled a ring from one of her fingers and handed it back to Zeke. "Inspect that," she said.

Zeke took the ring, which was an unadorned silver circlet. As simple as it seemed, he let out a gasp when he used his [Inspection] skill. Text flashed before his eyes, describing the item's effects.

Minor Ring of Climate Control (H)—A simple magic ring created by a novice jeweler. Effect: Keeps the wearer's body within a

comfortable temperature range. Warning: Does not work in extreme climates.

Zeke stared at it for a long moment before saying, "That's just cheating."

Abby laughed as he handed it back, then said, "They're not that expensive. A lot of successful adventurers have them, but this one I got from Julio."

Zeke didn't respond right away. Instead, he glanced at the satchel on Abby's back. It wasn't any bigger than a typical backpack, and aside from being made of leather, it followed the same general design of an Earth backpack. However, the space inside was almost three times bigger than the exterior would suggest—the result of a spatial manipulation enchantment.

"In fact, there are hundreds of creature comforts you might want to look into getting when we get to Beacon. From retracting ropes to the climate-control rings, they can make your life a lot easier—so long as you've got the money."

Zeke's eyes narrowed. Ever since he'd been awarded his mace, Voromir, he'd spent countless hours studying the underlying runes that gave the weapon its characteristic enchantments. Not only was it insanely durable, but it also adjusted its weight according to his strength. So, whether he was using one hand or two, it always felt the same, even when his strength had skyrocketed due to his levels and achievements. However, because he'd gotten so much stronger, the actual weight of the weapon had grown exponentially, giving his attacks that much extra momentum and power.

On the surface, it seemed like it would be a straightforward enchantment, but the underlying runes that drove it were anything but simple. It was comprised of thousands of interlocking, three-dimensional runes that were in turn covered in exponentially more glyphs and symbols. Some repeated, but others came out of nowhere, breaking up the pattern. And even as complicated as that was, he felt like there was a layer there he couldn't even see, much less understand.

By comparison, the curses thrown at him by the trolls were like a child's first attempts at drawing the alphabet. His runic rock grenades were even more primitive, barely even qualifying to be put in the same category—the result of fumbling in the dark more than actual skill. His artisan's path helped, but it wasn't a skeleton key for understanding. In order to unlock his potential—which he thought might be high, given how far he'd gotten without any help—he would need a teacher. Or failing that, more examples to study.

He shook his head, knowing that he was probably getting ahead of himself. So far, Zeke had only had himself on which to rely—or Abby, to an extent. But to find some random stranger who might teach him more about runes and how they related to enchantments? That seemed like a tall order, especially considering that the artisans who held those secrets likely relied on them to make a living. Sharing their knowledge with a stranger would be akin to cutting themselves off at the knees, financially speaking.

But it wasn't all doom and gloom. Perhaps Abby's guild could help. That seemed like the sort of thing such an organization would do. He only needed to join—something he'd decided was probably in his best interests, anyway. They had resources to make him stronger, which was his ultimate goal. And with how Abby had reacted to him, Zeke thought he might make for a decent candidate.

Abby's voice cut through his reverie as she said, "We should see Bastion just up ahead when we crest this hill."

"Thank god," Zeke said under his breath as they climbed the grassy slope. The heat was still as oppressive as ever, but without the dense foliage to break the wind, it didn't seem quite as bad.

A couple of minutes later, their path led them to the apex of the hill, revealing a wide, shallow, and idyllic valley. A road paved with actual stones ran along its entire length, stretching all the way to the horizon, and planted in the center of the valley was a fort.

"That's Bastion," Abby said, her hands on her hips as she caught her breath. They'd been walking nonstop for hours, and she obviously felt the strain. Even Zeke was tired, though most of his discomfort was due to the heat, sweat, and chafing.

Zeke stopped beside his partner, studying the fort and the walled town that surrounded it. It wasn't huge—maybe a mile across, at most—but it seemed busy enough, with caravans of wagons snaking their way in and out of the gates. The walls themselves were gray stone, the same as the medieval-style castle at its center, but most of the buildings within had been constructed of wood.

"It's a way station," Abby explained. "You'll see a few of these along the road that runs between Beacon and Salvation."

"What's with the names?" Zeke asked.

Abby shrugged, saying, "I guess when people first started being reborn into this world, they were thankful for a safe place to live. Back then, everything was wilder and a lot more dangerous. It still gets bad when you get away from civilization, which is the reason these way stations exist, but monsters hardly ever attack cities or towns anymore."

It made sense. If Zeke's sense of scale was even close to accurate, it would mean that it would take weeks—perhaps even months—for a caravan to travel from Beacon to Salvation. So, it seemed perfectly reasonable that safe places would spring up along the road so those traders could minimize their risks and have a place to resupply. They'd still have to sleep in the wilderness along the way, but a night or two of safety could make all the difference.

When Zeke commented just that, Abby said, "Plus it means there's always help close by. Every way station is run by a capable warrior. Most have a few dozen adventurers they can call upon in an emergency."

"Didn't seem to help those people when they were attacked by the drachnids," Zeke mumbled. "I guess whoever leads Bastion couldn't be bothered to save hundreds of people."

"She could only do so much," Abby said, shaking her head. "She's only one person. That's why the guild got contracted."

Zeke shrugged, saying, "Only one person. That would hold a little more weight if we hadn't dealt with the problem with just the two of us."

Pudge chuffed indignantly.

"Fine, three of us," Zeke amended, which seemed to mollify the bear cub. "And I get it, okay? We were probably stupid to even try it, and we were lucky to survive. But I'm level fourteen. You're fifteen. There had to be some higher-leveled people who could've taken care of it."

"But why would they?" Abby asked. "You need to understand something about this world. People don't just help. Not out of the goodness of their hearts, at least. Those higher levels you're talking about? Do you have any idea what it would take to get them to roll out of bed? Not a drachnid nest, I can tell you that."

"Why? That was a level twenty-five elite," Zeke said. "That should be worth it."

Abby shrugged. "Maybe," she said. "But nobody knew the queen or that champion had evolved. And even if they had, they still might not have bothered because the risk outweighed the potential reward. Not everybody has your ridiculous constitution or that broken skill that keeps you alive. I would've died a dozen times over if it wasn't for you giving me the watered-down version of [**Leech Strike**] through the [**Mark of Companionship**]. The bear, too. And if you hadn't had the skill?" She shook her head again as she continued, "Look—I get it. I know your every instinct tells you to help people. But not everybody thinks like you."

"You helped," Zeke pointed out. Abby could've just taken the fangs she needed to prove that she'd accomplished her mission and run back to Beacon to collect her reward. But she hadn't. She had stayed, and she'd fought something she had no business fighting, same as Zeke.

"Like us, then," she said. "My point is that even higher levels can get swarmed. They can be overwhelmed. They can do a lot of really impressive things, but if they get caught by the wrong thing at the wrong time, they will die."

"It all still seems selfish" was Zeke's response. "Cowardly. And it's counterproductive."

"I don't disagree," Abby said. Selfishness and cowardice aside, she'd seen the benefits of putting everything on the line. By doing so, she'd picked up a pair of achievements and an impressive weapon. "But before we hit civilization, you need to understand just how abnormal your situation really is. Your stats are ridiculous, your primary skill is overpowered, and your weapon is . . . well, it's crude but extremely effective. You can go toe to toe with a level twenty-five elite, which is something most people don't even try without a significant amount of backup. On top of that, you've got your cottage, your spatial storage, and that looting ability."

"You make it sound more impressive than it is," Zeke said.

"If anything, I'm underselling it," she argued. "I've been invited on missions just because of my [**Makeshift Camp**] skill, and it's not nearly as powerful as your cottage. And that's probably the least of your abilities."

Zeke sighed. "Okay, so I'm superspecial," he said. "So? Why are you making a big deal out of it?"

"Because I want you to understand that your perspective is skewed," Abby stated. "You think people should just throw themselves at threats like those drachnids because you did it, and you came out on top, right? Well, most people would've been torn to bits before they made it halfway through that ravine. Heck, I'm pretty sure that even if Julio hadn't turned on me, that group wouldn't have been able to do more than just skirt along the edges and pick off a monster here and there until we had enough fangs. And Julio was level nineteen."

"He was also a dick."

"He was," Abby agreed.

"And did you just say *heck*?" he asked.

She gave him a withering glare, then said, "Anyway. I'm just saying that you shouldn't judge people too harshly for not doing what you can do."

"I can't excuse people for leaving other people to die."

"Okay. Just keep it to yourself, then," she said, compromising. "And when we get into Bastion, don't go running your mouth about what you can do. We've got to be careful with this. Otherwise, we're going to attract a lot of attention."

"And?"

"And you're going to end up getting stabbed in your sleep," Abby said. "Not everyone here's a saint. Most people are selfish assholes, actually. If they weren't when they got here, this world, it has a way of twisting people around. Everything's about survival of the fittest. And with the amount of wealth you've got hidden away in your cottage's cellar . . . it could change someone's life."

"Fine," Zeke said. "What do you suggest, then?"

"We go in, stay under the radar, and try to unload a few things so we can get you the essentials," she said. "And some new clothes, maybe. Yours are a little . . ."

"Ripped to shreds?"

"Something like that," Abby said, giving him a small smile. "And I'd like to eat something other than lizard or snake. I've been through here a few times, and I know a good inn."

"What about Pudge? He going to cause any issues?" Zeke asked.

"Probably not," she said. "People with taming skills aren't exactly unheard of. It's not like whatever you've got going with Pudge, but it's close enough that people will assume you just have one of those skills. And he's not too big yet. So, I don't know. We could just put a leash on him . . ."

Pudge snorted at that suggestion.

Zeke grinned. "I've got to follow all these rules, so you do, too, buddy," he said, bending down to scratch behind the bear's ears. "No leashes unless absolutely necessary, though. I promise."

With that, the three set off down the hill toward Bastion.

ABOUT THE AUTHOR

Nicholas Searcy is the author of Death: Genesis, a fantasy series originally released on Royal Road. He enjoys writing, reading, spending time with family, sports, and, of course, a good cup of coffee.

www.ingramcontent.com/pod-product-compliance
Ingram Content Group UK Ltd.
Pitfield, Milton Keynes, MK11 3LW, UK
UKHW041304180426
11947UKWH00009B/681